A Tip of the Cap

A Tip of the Cap

Rebecca Connolly

Phase Publishing, LLC
Seattle

Phase Publishing, LLC first paperback edition
February 2019

ISBN 978-1-943048-74-8
Library of Congress Control Number 2019931039
Cataloging-in-Publication Data on file.

Acknowledgements

For Colin Firth, who will always be handsome, charming, eloquent, witty, and perfectly dashing. My first celebrity crush, my first historical fictional boyfriend, and the only man on the planet who could ask to play any of my characters and I would consider it a genius idea.

And to Ritz Crackers, possibly my one true love. Pair you with peanut butter and a Diet Coke, and we're the happiest family ever.

Want to hear about future releases and upcoming events for Rebecca Connolly?

Sign up for the monthly Wit and Whimsy at:

www.rebeccaconnolly.com

Chapter One
London, 1825

*T*here were very few things over which Malcolm Colerain, Earl of Montgomery, did not have control.

He was fortunate enough to have the sort of calm, collected persona that enabled him to see with clarity and act accordingly no matter the situation or the distraction surrounding him. He exerted authority and control out of pure instinct, and, more often than not, all things would proceed according to his will. He'd quite gotten used to getting his way and prided himself on not being high-handed about it.

Finding himself a wife was something over which he ought to have had all the control in the world, and yet it had been a year of consciously attempting to do so without any success at all.

Granted, he'd not applied to any woman for her hand in marriage. So, it would follow that he would not have obtained a wife by now.

Honestly, he'd not really courted any women during that time. So, it would have been highly irregular and improper to offer a proposal.

In truth, he'd not really spoken to any women of marriageable age or situation about the possibility of courtship. So, he could not have expected to begin a proper courtship without establishing that conversation.

If he were to be absolutely, perfectly, painfully frank, he would also be forced to admit that he had not been paying that much attention to who the women were who might have been of marriageable age or situation in the last year. Which would make conversation, courtship, the acceptance of an offer, and finally marriage itself, all rather difficult.

So, really, all he had done was think about it. And he did control that... Most of the time.

It wasn't so much that he couldn't control the fact that he hadn't found a wife, it was that he didn't want to find a wife. He wanted the one he used to have, but he couldn't control that, and he needed a wife now.

It ought to have been as simple as setting his mind to the task of finding a suitable woman to care for his four children and run his estate in his absence. He required a capable woman of sense and judgment who could manage affairs without needing his counsel. She must also be a woman of taste and quality who would carry well the respect, authority, and duty incumbent upon the next Lady Montgomery.

And above all else, she would be a woman with whom he would never fall in love. He'd done that once. It was the most painful experience of his life, and he had no desire to repeat it.

Malcolm's criteria had been set from the very beginning. The problem was that he didn't know of any women who fit those expectations, and as none of them would be Caroline, he really didn't see the point in trying.

Caroline...

He still could not breathe if he thought about her for more than half of a second. The pain of losing the love of his life was something he had not recovered from, though it had been more than two years. Every day felt as painful as the first, and for a man accustomed to such self-control, it was too much.

Throwing himself into his work had helped, which might have sounded odd to anybody else, since he was a relatively wealthy earl. What sort of work could he possibly be engaged in other than the management of his estate, lands, and tenants? The world would have been shocked that the staid and respectable Earl of Montgomery was one of England's covert operatives and had been for many years. He had seen more skirmishes than many military men and had been party to more preventative measures where the Crown was at stake than anyone would dare comprehend. He would never speak of it, but because of his efforts and those of his fellow spies, the King still sat on his throne, and Parliament still functioned as it ever did.

Caroline had known of his work, though the more sensitive details and dangers had been kept secret, and she had fully supported him. She had never complained about his absences, sometimes for weeks at a time, and had never made him feel guilty for having to devote so much of his time and energies to their efforts. She never once seemed to be anything but exceptionally proud of him, though he knew she must have felt the weight and burden of managing without him. How she must have worried. Endured. Suffered.

But she never spoke of it. Truly, she had been his most perfect companion.

So, it ought not to have been any sort of surprise that he could not find another wife. Caroline had been a proverbial saint, aside from her wicked wit and occasional moments of distress when the children became too much for her patience. But while the wit had been a near constant, the distress had been very rare.

Their children had been her delight, and his as well. They still were, but he felt the loss of his wife so keenly every time he looked at them. He knew they still pined for her, having always preferred their mother to him. Knowing that he could never fill the void left by her death was more than he could endure.

Malcolm's devotion to his work in London steeped him in guilt over leaving his children so often at Knightsgate to the care of nannies and servants. It had begun to gnaw at his soul, and it was this that reminded him of the need for a wife. Not for himself, but for his children, to have someone to properly manage them.

She would never replace their mother, of course, but a maternal influence was needed in their lives. Particularly for his daughters, who were growing up too quickly for his preference. They needed him to find a wife, no matter how he bristled at the idea, and so, a wife he would find. The sooner, the better, for there was much that needed to be done.

"You're going to be late."

Malcolm shook himself out of his bleak reverie and blinked up at one of his superiors, the one they called Weaver. As one of the

Shopkeepers, he belonged among the select group of men who oversaw all the covert operations in all departments of England. Malcolm had known this man for years, since Weaver's days of being an operative himself. Back then, he'd been known as Fox, and he had been among the best of them. Now, despite his more secret work in the administration of covert operatives, he was a diplomat for the world to see, and in those more publicly observed circles, he was simply Lord Rothchild.

To Malcolm, however, and particularly since this was a social call at his London residence, he was Fritz.

The still-handsome man leaned against the doorjamb of his study with a sort of irreverent elegance that most men could practice their entire lives and never master. He smirked knowingly at Malcolm, the crispness of his cravat almost distracting against the dark blue coat he wore. He was the very picture of a perfectly cordial diplomat, aside from the hint of mischief that was always present in his eyes.

Malcolm shook his head. "I will not. I know exactly how long it takes me to go by coach from here to Mrs. Granger's residence, and I have plenty of time."

Fritz snorted and pushed into the room, clamping a hand on Malcolm's shoulder. "You need to go, and you need to go now. Stop dawdling."

"I never dawdle," Malcolm informed him, turning back to finish the end of his current report.

It had been several months since he and his men in the London League had had much of anything to report, but between the four of them, they had made quite a breakthrough recently. It was a most inconvenient time to try to find a wife. But, he supposed, the sooner he found one, the sooner he could devote himself to his work without the sting of guilt overwhelming him.

"Not usually, no," Fritz drawled, gripping his friend's shoulder in an almost painfully tight squeeze, "but I know what is on your mind. I have been restraining Emily's efforts to offer assistance and candidates at the risk of my own happiness and at my own expense. You know how my wife hates it when I oppose her."

Malcolm gripped his quill pen tightly and tried to keep his breathing steady. "I appreciate Lady Rothchild's concern and

4

interest," he managed through gritted teeth.

"You do not," Fritz laughed derisively. "You'd tell her off, if you were less polite. Emily is an interfering busybody with not enough to do. I'll hold her off as long as I can, but she is a most worthy opponent, and my defenses are weakening."

Malcolm glanced up at his friend briefly and cocked an eyebrow. "Weren't you one of the operatives in Paris during the Revolution?"

Fritz shrugged, as he usually did when one of his many accomplishments was mentioned. "Even Robespierre would have fled from my wife in terror, had he met her." He looked over Malcolm's shoulder and grunted. "Mention Rook's leg injury and you're set there. No need to go on; you know Tailor only skims them."

That did not sound like Tailor at all. He was the spymaster of England and had one of the most brilliant minds that Malcolm had ever known. He knew everything about everyone. He would never take their reports lightly, would he?

"Yes, he would," Fritz replied, answering the question that had not been asked aloud. "You think he doesn't already know what happened?"

Malcolm sighed and finished the report based on Fritz's suggestion, then set his quill aside and pushed out of his chair.

"Then why the reports at all?" he asked as he left the room, Fritz following behind.

"Because it's good for you," Fritz said with a laugh, "and, you know, the nonsense about capturing all the detail for future reference."

Malcolm rolled his eyes and nodded at Clifton, his butler, as they exited the house. Fritz's carriage waited for them in front, as Malcolm rarely kept carriages in his London residences anymore, choosing to walk unless it was a social event. He would have preferred to walk today, to be perfectly honest, but as this outing was one that required his most polite behavior, Fritz had offered him a lift in his own carriage.

Along with his wife, it seemed, for the beautiful Lady Rothchild waited within.

"My lady," Malcolm said with a polite dip of his chin as he

situated himself on the opposite seat. "I did not know you would be joining us this afternoon."

She smiled at him in a rather mischievous way. "Nor did my husband, my lord. But I find I am most wild to see Mrs. Granger again. It has been far too long."

Malcolm tilted his head a little, curious at her statement. "Forgive me, but I did not think you were particularly acquainted with her."

Fritz laughed loudly as he entered the carriage and settled in next to his wife.

She rewarded him with a hearty slap across his chest, which was not unusual for them. "I am not, and I feel rather dreadful about it," she told Malcolm, ignoring her husband's muffled chuckling. "As Fritz was invited along, I felt it was my duty to accompany you both."

"Just to see if I can find a wife among her friends?" Malcolm asked, assessing his friend's wife with a cool stare that matched hers.

"Quite," she quipped, her mouth curving a little more.

He grunted softly and turned his attention out the window. "You will be disappointed."

"That's all right. I know many women who would suit."

"How fortunate for you."

"Monty…" Fritz murmured, a hint of warning in his tone.

"Leave him alone, darling," Lady Rothchild soothed. "It's a hard task before him, but Monty and I know where we stand with each other, don't we, my lord?"

Malcolm managed to smile and glanced at her briefly, wishing he did not find her quite as magnificent as she was. "I am ever your humble servant, my lady."

"Oh, thank you for that token display of *noblesse oblige*," Fritz groaned, leaning back against the carriage wall. "She'll be lording it over me for days."

"And if you had any yourself," Lady Rothchild huffed with a turn of her fair head towards her husband, "our sons might actually be impressing their professors at school, and our daughters would have an idea of what to look for in a husband."

"The girls are fourteen at the most!" he protested with a feigned cry, parrying her verbal jabs at him. "We've done away with child marriages for some time now!"

Malcolm let the two of them go on, bickering as they usually did and wished it did not tug at his heart to hear them. They were a fiery couple, but there was an enormous amount of love and passion between them, as well as unyielding loyalty, and everybody knew it. They were the ideal married couple. At one time, Malcolm could have matched them for the title, though he and Caroline had been less popular. He missed everything about his wife, including their quarrels, playacted or not.

He would never find the same comfort and ease, the same love and tenderness with anyone else that he'd had with her. He could never replace her. It seemed a fool's errand to try. So, he was not looking for a replacement wife, just someone who would love his children.

Everything else was secondary.

"Lord Montgomery, it is so good to see you again!"

Malcolm bit back a groan and turned to face Lady Lavinia Herschel, who was thankfully dressed in a respectable, modest ensemble rather than the provocative fashions for which she was becoming notorious. She was a woman who had certain appetites and made no attempt to hide them. Despite being the daughter of an earl, she had inherited none of the nobility in temperament. Her husband was a senior member of Parliament who was as ignorant of her as he was unsuited to her, but they seemed to be satisfied with their polite distance. She was left to her devices and he to his.

This brash woman had been pursuing Malcolm relentlessly from the moment his wife had died, offering to provide solace and comfort in her own way. She would have heard that he was looking for a wife, and she would certainly have something to say on the subject.

"Lady Lavinia," he heard himself say, bowing politely.

She flashed her dark eyes up at him, toying with one of her long curls with a finger. "My lord, I hear you are looking for a wife," she said, emphasizing each word with a flick of her tongue or a graze of her teeth across her lips.

"You know how I feel about gossip," he replied with all politeness. After all, her husband was an important man, and though Lady Lavinia notoriously hated her husband, she found him useful when it came to offenses against her.

"Yes," Lady Lavinia hissed through her teeth, drawing out the sound, and sidling up to him, pressing against his side in a manner that did not suit her present appearance, "and I'd like to give them something else to gossip about…"

He didn't doubt that, but he said nothing, sipping his beverage slowly, keeping his eyes fixed on the others in the room.

"Why did you not tell me you were looking for a wife?" Lady Lavinia whispered.

"Why should I make my private affairs known to the world?" he asked in reply.

"Not to the world. Just to me." She pressed against him again. "Come on, Monty. Leave off the idea of a wife, and you can have me all to yourself. Yours to do with as you please. Anything you please."

Malcolm stiffened and closed his eyes. This was one of her bolder attempts to convince him, and it was just as distasteful as all the rest. She was a handsome woman, he would grant her that, even at her age. But he was not the sort to engage in such behaviors, and despite his many attempts to convince her, she remained undeterred. She seemed almost more determined with his every refusal to wear down his resolve.

"My lady," he tried, sliding out of her reach as much as he could.

"I'd like to be," she murmured suggestively, tilting her face up to him. "Oh, how I'd like to be."

"Monty, there you are," came a sweet voice from his other side. Mrs. Granger, Caroline's cousin and their hostess, seized Malcolm's arm in a surprisingly tight hold. "Come and assist me, will you? Excuse us, Lady Lavinia."

"At your service," Malcolm replied quickly, letting himself be pulled away and feeling the brush of Lady Lavinia's claw-like nails gripping into his arm as he left her.

He exhaled heavily once they were safely away and patted the hand currently tucked into his arm.

"Bless you, Lily."

She looked up at him with a smile, though it was pitying. "I am so sorry, I would never have let her within ten feet of you had I been close enough. I could not believe Granger invited her, but I suppose we cannot offend Mr. Herschel, can we?"

"Unfortunately not." Malcolm shook his head, shuddering a little. "Her attentions are becoming worse."

"Yes, so I heard." She pursed her lips a little, amused. "Does that sort of thing actually work on men?"

He chuckled as she led him out to the terrace where a few others mingled. "I have no idea. You see the impact it has on me."

"Yes, but you and I both know you are a bit peculiar, Monty," she told him, grinning cheekily.

He smiled down at her, struck again by how like Caroline she looked; the same dark shade of eyes and hair, the same easy smile, and the same tendency towards warmth and cheer, as well as an unflappable manner. She was the only member of his late wife's family with which he had any regular correspondence, and she had never made him feel like anything less than a beloved member of her family. She and Granger were their neighbors in Hampshire and took care to see him, and the children, very often, which made her rather a favorite of his children.

And with him as well.

"A bit, yes," he admitted, bringing himself back to the conversation at hand. He looked out on the gardens beyond, where a scattered group of children played merrily. "Whose children did you invite? I thought this was simply an afternoon tea you'd set up with all your eligible friends."

Lily snorted and moved to the railing of the terrace, watching the children fondly. "I would never be so bold as to trap you into a gathering to influence your decision." She cast a small smile up at him for good measure. "I may invite others who would do so, but I, myself, never would."

"Lily…" he warned, giving her a hard look as he joined her.

She patted his hand gently. "Relax, Monty. I, of all people, would never think to rush you in this matter. You know how I adored my cousin, and the thought of replacing her…"

"I am *not* replacing her," he snapped, his tone suddenly harsh.

Lily gripped his hand tightly. "I know, Malcolm."

She never called him by his given name, choosing his preferred nickname of Monty instead, as most of the world did. He looked at her for a long moment, seeing the genuine concern and warmth, as well as a hint of sadness, in her eyes. He relaxed and allowed himself to smile a little.

"So," he said suddenly, looking back to the children, "whose children are these?"

She gestured to a handful of them currently chasing each other on the green and around some flowering bushes, shrieking gleefully. "Those are the three Gerrard sisters as well as the Gerrard boy, the oldest of the Whitlocks, and the oldest of the Bevertons." She indicated another group of much younger children. "The rest of the Whitlock and Beverton children, the little Bray girl, the Gerrard daughter, the other Gerrard's son, and the Sheffield twins."

"You have collected an army of infants," he mused thoughtfully, enjoying the faint nudge against him from Lily's elbow.

"The 'infants'," she retorted with a smile, "are indoors with their mothers. These are no longer considered infants."

Malcolm glanced down at her in amusement. "Why invite children, Lily? It's not exactly fashionable."

Lily shrugged, smiling to herself. "I adore children. You know that; you've seen me at Knightsgate more than you would like, I'll wager, purely so I can see yours."

"You know you are always welcome."

She shook her head fondly as if she did not hear him. "Besides, it did not seem fair to invite the parents without the children when it is so informal. Moreover, they are well tended, you see."

He looked where she indicated and noticed for the first time a young woman acting as a sentry among the children. She alternated between dashing about with the older children and scooping up the younger ones, tickling them until they squealed, and seemed to be perfectly at ease with both sets. She wore a soft smile constantly, her fingers absently plucking at a sprig of flowers in her hand when she was not otherwise engaged.

One of the younger children suddenly came to her with a doll, looking a little put out about something. She sank down to the girl's level, taking the doll in hand and listening with a serious expression to whatever was being said. She looked at the doll with a suddenly exasperated expression and seemed to scold it for some imagined sin. She then returned the wayward plaything to the girl with a prim nod, which was returned. The satisfied child dashed back to her picnic.

"Who is that young woman?" Malcolm asked mildly. "A new maid?"

Lily looked at him in surprise. "Maid? That's my friend, Miss Owens. We were at school together."

Malcolm jerked and turned to face Lily, shocked and a bit aghast. "She's your *friend*? But she's so young, and... well..."

Comprehension dawned, and Lily smiled a little in understanding. "She comes from a very good family, but a poor one. She is the youngest of ten children, if you can believe that. None of them really takes much trouble with her. She has been living with one of her brothers for the last two years, acting as a governess of sorts to their children. But they have decided to hire someone outside of the family, so Beth must make her own way now. She has four hundred a year, but even that is questionable anymore. She may look a little worn in dress and poor in appearance, but she has the kindest heart in the world."

"I thought that belonged to you," he offered with a smile.

Lily nudged him again. "Flattery will get you everywhere, Monty, but you know how it unsettles me."

"If your husband were not such a great dunce, he would flatter you incessantly, and you would grow comfortable with praise." He brought up her hand to kiss it fondly, then turned back to observe Miss Owens. Her fair hair was blowing a little in the spring air, simply pinned at the base of her neck, but a few locks near her temple and ear had escaped with the energy of playing. She was now chasing all the older children, who regarded her with a mixture of bewilderment and adoration as they ran from her.

"Is she of the Owens family from Oxfordshire?" he asked, considering her in a new light.

"She is, yes."

He nodded slowly, the thought turning over in his mind. It was a good family line, quite respectable. But poor fiscal management and too many children had drained their finances, so there was little to offer anyone but their heritage and breeding. It would have made things rather difficult for a youngest daughter, though the sons could find professions enough to support them.

"She will have to find a position if she does not make a match soon," Lily murmured quietly. "I have no doubt she will do very well, but she is not the governess sort, and I fear she will not have an easy time getting a position."

Malcolm recognized that she would be lucky to gain any sort of position at all. With her looks and temperament, no mother would hire her for fear of a husband straying. She could be the most capable woman in the world and have impeccable references, but it would not be enough.

"Does she have any prospects?" he asked before he could stop himself.

Lily shook her head, smiling as the children turned the tables on Miss Owens and began to chase her instead. "None. But she doesn't seem to mind. It is as though nothing negatively affects her. Nothing dark can touch her."

Lily's suddenly morose tone shook him, and he took her hand in his gently. "Lily…"

She shook her head and looked up at him with a brave smile. "I'm fine, Monty. Really."

He didn't believe her for a moment, but it was hardly proper for him to question her answer.

One of the younger children across the lawn suddenly started crying, for some unknown reason, and their attention was drawn there. The little redhead toddled away from the others, tears falling rapidly, her face flushed with her distress.

Miss Owens came over to her at once, crouching down and taking the child's face in her hand. She spoke to her in very soft tones, smiling all the while, and gently smoothed away the tears. Picking up the little girl, she set her firmly on her hip, still talking to her. The girl nodded and rubbed at her eyes, then dimpled in a small smile. Miss Owens bounced the girl a little, making her giggle, and then made a show of whispering to her before chasing after the older children again with the child still in her grasp.

The older children shrieked with mock terror and laughter, scrambling in all directions. This drew the attention and enthusiastic cries of the younger children who left their separate activities. They ran to join in the melee, having no comprehension of what was occurring, but trailing after Miss Owens as ducklings after their mother.

The adults present all laughed at the madness, but no one as merrily as Miss Owens herself, who navigated the entire brood with a brilliant smile and an unbridled energy. She practically danced as she led the chase, and her joy was as warm and infectious as the sun on a fine day. Soon, it became unclear who was chasing and who was being chased. Through it all, she was in the middle of it, gently reprimanding those who were being too rough and drawing in those who could not keep up with the rest.

Beth Owens was extraordinary. There was no other way to describe her.

Malcolm shook his head in disbelief as he witnessed the magic. "Has she met any of these children before?"

That would explain everything, lessen the rarity of this event, and would certainly settle the odd sensations he felt stirring within his chest at the sight of it. Of her. The strange inability to breathe with ease. Or to look anywhere but at her face, at the flush spreading across her skin, at the small dimple that appeared when her smile was too much for her cheeks to contain.

"No," Lily said, her voice faint but filled with a smile of her own. "No, she only just came to London. She's met the children an hour ago. Isn't she wonderful?"

God help him, but she *was* wonderful. She was perfect!

"I'd like to meet her," he said quietly, the words scraping past his lips. "Today, if possible."

There was a soft laugh beside him. "Yes, I thought you might."

Chapter Two

"*B*eth, do you have a moment?"

Beth Owens cracked an eyelid open to peep at one of her oldest friends, upon whose lawn she was currently lying along with three little girls, collecting rays of sunlight with their skin so they might become fairies.

"You will have to ask one of the others, Lily. I am supposed to become a fairy at this moment."

Lily put her hands on her hips and tilted her head. "How does one become a fairy with a flower crown and sunshine?"

"The flowers attract the sunshine," young Lady Helena Chambers rehearsed from her place on the grass at Beth's left. "The sun is fooled and believes that we, too, are flowers. Then our skin collects the sun, and it becomes magic within us!"

"Oh, that explains a great deal," Lily said with a nod. "Can you spare Miss Owens, my sweet fairies-to-be?"

They all chimed in the affirmative, delighted to win a believer in their attempts.

Beth shook her head, smiling to herself. This day had been the most wonderful sort of fun, romping with the children instead of having to mingle with adults. They tended to pity her and find fault with her appearance, or her manner, or anything else about her. These people, to whom she would soon apply for employment unless something miraculous occurred, would not take kindly to a woman of her situation being one of their party.

But she could tend to their children.

She much preferred the children, anyway. They cared not that her dress was five years old and repeatedly mended, or that her hair was not particularly fashionable, as she did not have a maid to help her with it, or that her dowry amounted to the weekly grocer's bills for some of their parents' kitchens. They only wanted her to chase them and scold dolls and make flower crowns and transform into fairies. It was much nicer to be with the children. It was a distraction, she fully admitted, but she did not mind being distracted.

She got to her feet and brushed herself off, trailing after Lily. "What do you need?"

"Someone wants to meet you."

Beth stopped in the act of brushing grass from her skirt and gaped at Lily's back. "I beg your pardon? Someone wants... what?"

Lily glanced over her shoulder with an uncharacteristic smirk. "A gentleman has asked to meet you."

If her jaw could have dropped further, it would have. "A *gentleman?*" she squeaked. "Lily!"

Her friend tossed her head back and laughed, her dark tresses dancing despite their simple style, then turned back, coming to take Beth's hands. "A gentleman saw you playing with the children, and now he desires to be introduced to you. That's all."

Beth swallowed with difficulty, clutching her friend's hands desperately. "He saw me? But, Lily, I look dreadful!"

Lily pulled a strand of grass from Beth's hair and gingerly removed the flower crown, brushing off the young woman's hair with her fingers. "There, now, don't fret yourself. You look lovely. Very natural and easy. And your frock is quite fetching."

"No doubt stained with all sorts of things," Beth muttered, plucking at the faded and almost too-thin gown.

She was wearing two chemises and petticoats to make up for it, given the dress was a pale color and sheerness would have been more obvious. It was good enough to wear for day-to-day activities, but meeting with a gentleman? Hardly.

Lily made a quick pass around her. "Not even a little stain, you fortunate girl. Now, come quickly. The earl won't wait."

"Earl?" Beth gasped. "You never said he was an earl!"

"Didn't I?" Lily pretended to look confused. "Oh dear." She bit back a giggle and gestured for Beth to follow.

Beth stayed precisely where she was, finding no humor in this situation at all. "Why does the earl want to speak with me?" she demanded, putting her hands on her hips.

She heard Lily sigh, then her friend turned to give her an exasperated look. "He didn't tell me, Beth, but he does have four children who lost their mother two years ago. As she was my cousin, he is very dear to me. So, when he asked me to meet you, I told him he could do so. Now, will you please oblige me?"

The thought of four children without a mother struck her, and she bit her lip, considering the idea. He no doubt needed someone to help manage the children, and while she did not particularly wish to go into the governess trade, she knew her options were limited. She would not be a very good governess, as she had not been particularly fond of sitting still through long hours of study.

But, if he had seen her behavior with the children and had been impressed by it, perhaps her lack of skills would be forgiven. She could offer the children friendship and understanding, and she was not entirely hopeless when it came to intelligent matters. It might be just the thing to help her on her way.

An interview with an earl. That was quite a beginning.

She nodded to herself, then smiled at Lily as she approached. "I will oblige you, of course. I hope I might be able to impress the earl."

Lily seemed to be fighting a smile as they moved towards the house. "Yes, so do I. You'll have to forgive Monty, though. He is not particularly verbose."

"Silence does not bother me," Beth said with an easy shrug. "I've got four brothers who don't talk much."

Lily snorted a surprised laugh into her hand, looking at her sideways. "I thought you had seven brothers."

Beth nodded again. "I do. Four are quiet, the oldest speaks incessantly, and the younger two could never get a word in edgewise with everyone else, but they certainly said enough when the others were gone. I learned to quite adore silence by the time I was grown."

"Well, that is convenient," her friend commented as they approached the terrace steps. "But I think you will find him a little more conversational than that, so you need have no fears on that point."

No, Beth thought, just all the other fears that came along with meeting a powerful earl who might have received a less than favorable impression of her. Only those fears.

She straightened her posture and forced herself to be calm as they mounted the stairs. She could interview with this earl and be presentable and proper. She was very good at first impressions; it came from being the youngest in a family of exceptionally well-behaved children. She'd had two additional mothers in the forms of her older sisters, and lessons in etiquette were a daily occurrence.

But this would apparently be the earl's second impression of her, and she must make up for whatever flaws had been evident in the first. She was always making up for her flaws. It was one of her worst faults. According to Lucy, at any rate. How she had fallen so far from proper behavior, her oldest sister had never explained, but Beth had also grown accustomed to never receiving proper answers.

"He wasn't displeased, was he?" Beth whispered in a worried voice as they continued into the house and headed down a hallway, the gilt-framed paintings on the walls drawing her attention every time she passed. "When he asked to meet me, was he disapproving? I know I did not behave properly with the children, but…"

"Beth," Lily overrode, taking her hand and patting it. "He was not displeased. I think he might even have been amused by your antics."

That surprised her, and Beth found herself smiling. "Really?"

"Well, I don't know for certain," Lily replied with a laugh. "He did not tell me every thought in his head where you were concerned. Just calm yourself. It will be all right."

"Calm myself," Beth muttered, shaking her head. "With an earl suddenly wanting to meet me? I think you forget what high circles you move in, Lily."

Lily paused to give her an exasperated look just outside the drawing room. "Elizabeth Owens, would you be calm? If I move in circles so high, then you must permit me to drag you along for the experience. Now, put on your best face and let me introduce you."

Beth ducked her chin a little, her face flaming. "I apologize. Thank you for taking pity on me."

"Pity?" Lily sniffed and shook her head, her dark tresses dancing.

"Friends do not pity. You will be just fine."

Something in her friend's tone brought Beth's defenses back up. "What are you talking about?" she asked slowly, backing away. "You're not... You wouldn't... You'll be with us the entire time, will you not?" The little smile her friend offered made Beth suddenly go cold.

"Of course not," Lily replied. "I am the hostess. I cannot possibly stay in here and abandon the rest of my guests. But have no fear; one of my footmen will be just outside the room if you should need anything."

That was not at all encouraging. "Lily..."

But her impertinent friend had already turned back and pushed open the door into the room. "I am sorry to keep you waiting, Lord Montgomery, but I have brought her at last."

There was no course but to follow her in. Beth patted the side of her head self-consciously, praying there were no more stray flowers or blades of grass. If her hair looked a fright, it was the least she could do to avoid having plants entangled in it. Exhaling slowly, she entered the room with her hands politely clasped before her.

Consequently, she stumbled on the edge of the carpet and barely managed to catch herself before actually falling to the ground. Beth wished she could have perished on the spot, and she hadn't even looked at the man who had risen from the settee.

Perhaps he would not mind if she exited the room and re-entered for a third impression?

"Miss Elizabeth Owens, may I present Lord Montgomery? Lord Montgomery, my great friend, Miss Owens," Lily was saying in her usual friendly tones, officially ending any hopes that Beth had of fleeing. Now she had to stand perfectly straight, smile intelligently, and meet the earl's gaze directly.

As she did so, she was struck by Lord Montgomery's height, by his rather regal air, and by the most perfect features she had ever seen in her entire life. He was smiling at her, sort of, with one side of his mouth slightly curved. His hair reminded her of aged gold, and it curled ever so slightly at the ends. Chiseled jaw, perfectly sculpted cheekbones, a brow that was neither too high nor too low, and eyes that varied somewhere between blue, grey, and green. Quite possibly the most pleasantly-featured man she had ever seen in her life. And he was smiling at her, sort of.

Oh dear.

"Lord Montgomery asked to meet with you, Beth," Lily said, gesturing towards him. "He's a very old friend and a most excellent man."

Lord Montgomery, who had been staring a bit too pointedly back at Beth for her liking, suddenly slid a wry glance to Lily. "Really, Mrs. Granger, I am neither a very old friend nor a most excellent man."

"And I am certainly not a very great friend," Beth inserted hastily, her hands now gripping at her skirt a little. "She exaggerates."

Lord Montgomery looked back at Beth with a hint of amusement. "She is going to give us false ideas of each other before we begin."

"It's because she has a kind heart, and tries to think the best of everybody," Beth murmured.

The earl nodded, that sort-of smile still quirking. "I admire her greatly for such a trait, but one must allow for honesty."

Beth couldn't help it; she had to smile a little, despite trying to stay somber. "I quite agree, my lord."

"Oh, I despair of the both of you," Lily huffed, rolling her eyes. She swept back towards the door. "I'm going back to my guests. You two do as you like. Monty, do behave yourself, won't you?"

"Always," he said in a serious tone, glancing after her even though she did not look back. He returned his gaze to Beth and regarded her for a moment.

It was really rather awkward with Lily gone, simply standing there in silence before each other.

Was she supposed to say something? Her experience with peers of the realm extended only to those in the lower ranks who had sent their daughters to her finishing school, and hardly a one of them had ever had a kind word for poor Miss Elizabeth Owens.

What was the proper etiquette in a situation like this? Did she stay silent? Did she ask questions? Was she supposed to curtsey or stand here meekly, answering "Yes, sir," or "No, sir," to his every question? But he hadn't asked any questions… yet.

"Will you sit, Miss Owens?" Lord Montgomery asked in a respectful voice.

Beth blinked a little. Oh, was that all? That was a simple enough request. Her mouth twitched in an involuntary smile, and she nodded, lowering herself carefully to the divan behind her.

The earl sat opposite her with ease and with grace. *He*, at least, was not nervous. Nor, she supposed, had he reason to be.

"I hope you don't mind that I asked Mrs. Granger to introduce us, Miss Owens," he said, somehow smiling in his tone but not with his mouth.

Beth shook her head quickly. "Not at all, my lord, I am grateful for the opportunity."

He opened his mouth to reply, then closed it, cocking his head in confusion. "Were you, indeed?"

She nodded meekly. "Yes, my lord." She opted not to say more, trying to remember how to be demure and polite when faced with a powerful man who could give her a desperately-needed position.

Impertinence would not be appreciated, nor would rambling. Beth tended to be inclined towards both.

Lord Montgomery propped his elbow on the arm of the sofa, hand positioned in a thoughtful pose against his face. "Tell me about yourself, Miss Owens, if you please."

Beth straightened up, praying her hands would remain gracefully clasped in her lap. "I am from Oxfordshire, my lord, near Abingdon. My godparents sent me to finish at Mrs. Rampton's School in Berkshire where I received an excellent education, giving me all the skills and knowledge that a competent and capable governess ought to possess. I am learned in French, German, and Latin; I have skills in penmanship, arithmetic, as well as prominent literature. I can teach deportment and manners, as well as…"

"Miss Owens," Lord Montgomery interrupted, a deep furrow between his brows, "I don't wish to engage you as a governess."

Beth stared at him for a moment, then sighed heavily and let her shoulders droop a little. "No, of course, you don't."

She was not entirely sure if she were disappointed or relieved, but she suspected it was an odd mixture of both. In truth, she would have to admit that arithmetic made her itch, and her German accent sounded as though she were ill. Her aggrieved headmistress had maintained that Beth's skills in deportment bordered on 'just enough to not be shocking', so she really would have been quite hopeless.

Her reaction seemed to amuse him. "Why would you think that was why I asked Mrs. Granger for an introduction?" he queried, that sort-of smile returning to his face.

She stared at him rather blankly. "Why else would you want to meet with me, my lord?"

"That… is an excellent question," he said slowly, his thumb grazing his jaw absently as his gaze fixed on her.

It was all she could do to not fidget under such a gaze. "Yes, sir?" she prodded, smiling nervously.

His lips quirked with an ironic tilt. "I haven't yet decided, Miss Owens."

Beth smiled in earnest now, laughing at the bizarre twist of their conversation. "Will you tell me when you have?"

Lord Montgomery gave a slow nod. "Most assuredly."

There was something rather warm about his voice just then, and it made her want to blush a little, for no good reason. She laughed again, still a nervous sound, and then she forced herself to be more collected, though it was much nicer to know that she was not about to be considered for a position, and therefore did not have to be so impressive to him.

"Lily told me that you have children, my lord," she offered with a polite clearing of her throat.

His sort-of smile grew just a little as his gaze drifted more distant. "Yes, four of them. Two girls and two boys."

"Four is a very good number," Beth praised, smiling encouragingly. "And with equal numbers, it is always sure to be a fair fight."

He made a noise that almost passed for a laugh. "It usually is, but it does not follow that they fight fairly."

"Fighting fairly is overrated," she quipped, thinking back on her childhood, "or so I've been told."

Lord Montgomery observed her with interest. "I understand that you are from a slightly larger family, Miss Owens."

Beth snorted loudly and pushed back a stray lock of hair.

"Slightly? I am the youngest of ten, my lord, which means that I was the last to be picked for games, the one most likely to annoy my siblings no matter what I was doing, and I suffered a great deal of confusion regarding who my actual parents were."

He smiled in earnest then, and Beth found herself a bit taken aback by it, for it might have been the most glorious sight out of a church that she had ever witnessed.

"And were you a troublesome child, Miss Owens?" he inquired.

"Not intentionally, my lord," she replied with a shrug, praying that he would stop smiling for the sake of her insides. "But I always seemed to be in the way." She offered him a cheeky smile. "Somehow, I became a most convenient nanny once my siblings' children arrived. I was barely more than a child myself, so I was always assured of companions and responsibilities whenever they were about."

"And how often was that?"

"Almost constantly. Why bother moving elsewhere when someone is at hand to tend your children for the very reasonable salary of nothing at all?"

He was still smiling, blast him, and he dropped his hand from his face. "Why, indeed?" he agreed.

Their conversation continued in rather simple terms, discussing her time in London, which had been limited, her taste in literature, which had been so very restricted, and her travel in England, which had never gone as far as the lakes or the coasts. She must have painted a very boring picture of her life for him, but he seemed content enough with her conversation.

Was he perhaps just a lonely man with a limited number of acquaintances in London? It didn't make sense, but why else would he want to meet with her merely to hear about Oxfordshire and Berkshire and witness for himself just how very much she lacked in all things fine?

He said little about himself or his children, but she had the sense that he was a private, reserved man, and that was certainly nothing to find fault in. She was not inclined to rattle on about herself unless prodded, as he was doing. It never took long to tell her life story, considering the unexciting life she had lived thus far.

"Do you play, Miss Owens?" he asked suddenly, a rather random question since they had just been discussing the pleasures of country living. "The pianoforte, I mean. I know very well that you *play* all sorts of things."

Beth made a face, blushing. "Yes, my lord, I heard that you witnessed my antics. I would be embarrassed, but…"

"You shouldn't be," he assured her, "it was a charming sight."

Well, so was he, but she was hardly going to go about saying such things.

"Yes, my lord," she said quickly, praying he had not noticed how her voice faltered. "I do play. Not particularly well, but enough for dancing and songs with the children."

"But what about for yourself?" he pressed, his gaze suddenly intense. "Do you play for your own pleasure?"

Beth sat back a little, considering the question and forgetting to sit with perfect posture. "I hardly know," she admitted without shame. "I've never played for my own pleasure or amusement, only at the behest of others."

His expression was suddenly unreadable, his eyes slightly narrowed as he stared at her.

It had been an easy conversation between them, and she could honestly say she was not particularly nervous or intimidated by him, save by his exceptional good looks, and so she had no qualms about staring just as boldly back.

"What were you planning on doing next?" Lord Montgomery asked softly, his lips barely moving. "With your life, I mean."

She offered a small smile and a sigh. "Well, no doubt Lily told you of my situation. I have limited enough opportunities, so I was going to advertise as governess in a few days. That's why I thought you were interviewing me. My first official position, you know."

If it was possible, his gaze intensified even more, and he dipped his chin into an almost nod. "I see. Miss Owens, would you consider waiting a bit longer before seeking a position as a governess? Just… wait."

"For what, my lord?" she asked, barely managing to breathe for the odd tingling that had suddenly taken over her body, particularly in her fingers, toes, and stomach.

He seemed to hesitate, then he shook his head and rose from his seat. "I will let you know."

For some completely absurd reason, that response made her smile. "You don't know that, either?"

He surprised her by shaking his head and rising. "I don't. It seems there is a lot to consider." He offered her a hand.

"About me?" she asked, taking it and allowing him to help her rise.

Those eyes of his captivated her again as he murmured, "About everything."

Beth held her breath as she stared up at him. "Well, it is probably best you did not want to hire me, my lord. I would make a hash of something as comprehensive as everything."

His sort-of smile returned, and he led her from the room. "I doubt you make a hash of anything, Miss Owens."

Her breathing restored, in a way, she slid him a mischievous glance. "That is because you don't know me, my lord. No one asks in a governess interview, but I am really quite skilled at making a hash of things. Ask my siblings."

"Which ones?"

"All of them."

"I am beginning to wonder if you have any sensible siblings at all."

"Oh, I don't," she replied lightly as they returned to the other guests. "Sense wasn't required in our family. Not a single Owens of sense in Oxfordshire."

"But one in London, I think."

Beth almost rolled her eyes and looked up at the earl again. "What makes you think I have any sense, my lord?"

He returned her look with one that made her want to shiver, whether in delight or unease she couldn't say. "I've just spent a fair amount of time with you, Miss Owens. I am quite good with first impressions, as well as subsequent ones. I know you have plenty of sense, I can see it, and a great many other qualities besides."

Beth bit her lip against the desire to ask what exactly those other qualities were. "Well, I always improve with every impression, my lord."

He sighed a little as he returned her out of doors. "I was afraid of that."

Chapter Three

"*C*ap, are you sure about this?"

"No, not at all."

"Then why are you…?"

"Because I don't have time to be sure about it."

There was a faint snort, and then Rogue sat back against the carriage cushions. "That's the most ridiculous thing I've ever heard."

Malcolm gave his colleague a sour look. "Mind yourself, Rogue. You know what my reasons are."

"Yes, and you know my opinions on the subject." Rogue lifted a thick brow, challenging him again.

It had been the same argument for months. Rogue never understood why Malcolm needed a wife, if he were not going to find pleasure in it. He recommended the hiring of a very pleasant and qualified governess and nanny to fill the children's void. Gent pleaded with him to wait until he found love again, no matter how long it took, as anything less would not be worth having. Rook… Well, Rook was a bit tied up in knots with his own feelings over a certain fair-haired cousin of Gent's wife and didn't know what to make of it, so he couldn't decide what he thought Malcolm should do.

He'd taken a full week after his pleasant interview with Miss Owens to mull things over, and he was all but decided on his course.

But still, he hesitated.

She would be perfect for his children, he was certain, although he questioned her ability to discipline or act in any sort of authoritative manner. She was warm and child-like, but could she be stern? Could she face the harsh reality of his life without bursting into tears at the slightest provocation? He had been on his best behavior with her the other day, and he'd impressed himself with the warmth he'd managed. He was rarely so congenial these days, and Miss Owens, while having impressed him, might have received a false impression of him.

No, he was not sure of much of anything, but certainty was a luxury, and he did not have it.

"I don't know why you have to bother with this now," Rogue muttered, glowering out of the window. "Don't we have quite enough to be getting on with?"

They did, and Rogue certainly did himself, but it couldn't be helped. There was trouble brewing on the docks, and Rogue was their best operative there, what with Trace's death. So, he was working himself to the bone in less than pleasant circumstances, while the rest of them worked the leads he brought in so he could continue as he was. What was worse was the fact that Amelia was at Whitleigh, nearing her confinement, and Rogue was in agony with anxiety for her. But he knew his duty, and he did it, with Amelia's full support.

It didn't make him any more pleasant, but that was Rogue's way.

"I don't know what you're complaining about," Malcolm murmured, feeling a bit of Rogue's irritability seeping into him. "You've just come from tending the flowers, which might as well be a holiday. You're well-rested, no doubt, which is more than the rest of us can say."

Rogue grumbled under his breath, but Malcolm smiled at it.

With the loss of Trace had come a new responsibility for the League, and one entirely different from their usual tasks. Trace had left behind a girl who had loved him, one who could not know the true nature of his death, or his life, for that matter, and who would not find much healing in the aftermath of her beloved's death. Trace had made it very clear to them that Poppy Edgewood was to be cared for after he was gone, and so they took turns making trips up to Cheshire to be sure that all was well with her, physically, financially and otherwise. Secretly, of course. She had no idea they were involved in any way and had never set eyes on a single one of them.

Malcolm rather wished he had taken his turn instead of Rogue. A trip to Cheshire for general reconnaissance and leisurely investigation would have been quite the reprieve from all else in his thoughts.

But no matter. The thing might as well be done now as at any time.

The carriage pulled up to the Marlowe residence, and the two friends entered as unobtrusively as any other guest. They were more familiar with the house, and their hosts, than anyone else in attendance. But on this particular occasion, they were no more than polite acquaintances invited for a dinner party.

Margaret, Lady Marlowe, looked as lovely as ever. Which was not surprising, as she'd fairly blossomed in recent months; first, in her marriage to Gent, and then with the birth of their daughter several months ago. She greeted Fritz and Malcolm with politeness, but without any hint of overt familiarity. Malcolm was quite proud of her. He and the rest of the London League had all wondered how their wives would take to the secrecy that dominated their lives.

Margaret, Lady Marlowe, and Amelia, Lady Wharton, had acclimated even better than their husbands, in some respects. They had become friends, close friends, but rarely met in social circles. Tonight's party might have marked one of those rare occasions, except the danger stalking Rogue prevented Amelia from attending. She remained safely guarded at Whitfield, fuming from afar at the enforced separation from her husband.

Malcolm had often thought that Caroline would have adored both of them, and how much better it would have been for her to have known other women who similarly had to live a double life. She had borne his absences and his secrets with grace and poise, but always alone.

If he married Miss Owens, she would bear the same burden, though he would likely not tell her for some time, if ever. She would need to be strong enough to endure it, and he was even less certain about that.

"Monty," Gent greeted Malcolm with a brusque nod as he came closer. "You're looking tired."

"Marlowe," he replied, taking in his friend's bored and placid appearance with amusement.

It was all anybody knew of Lord Marlowe and the only way that he could move about as freely undercover as Gent. Everybody forgot what Lord Marlowe looked or sounded like, and while he had a peculiar and charming wife, she was all they could recall.

Gent shook him a little, giving him an odd look. "For pity's sake, Monty, it seems as though you could use a lie-down. Why did you bother coming if you were so fatigued?"

Malcolm gave him a hard look, as Gent knew full well why he was so drawn and tired, and what he intended tonight. "Pardon me, Marlowe, it is just the prospect of an evening in your company. I am half asleep already."

Gent grinned so briefly it was impossible to say if he actually had, and steered his associate towards the music room, where the rest of the guests were mingling before dinner.

Malcolm spotted Lily and Miss Owens at once, though Miss Owens was currently engaged in conversation with Lily's sister Rosalind. Lily stood awkwardly by her husband's side. Mr. Granger stared around the room, as solemn as ever, pointedly taking no notice of his wife, while she appeared to be attempting to ignore his neglect.

Theirs was the saddest marriage Malcolm had ever seen. He had never made mention of it to her, for fear of bringing the pain of it to the surface.

He moved in their direction, catching the austere husband's notice first. Granger shook hands with him firmly, expressed pleasantries, and asked after the children. For all the man's faults where Lily was concerned, Malcolm remembered that he really did like the fellow. Granger gestured towards his wife, and Malcolm turned to her with a fond smile, drawing her hand to his lips.

"Monty," Lily said with a small smile that did not reach her eyes. "I didn't know you knew the Marlowes."

He shrugged a little and took a glass from a passing footman. "I know them well enough. I prefer the wife to the husband."

Lily laughed a little, glancing towards the host and hostess as they now entered the room. "Yes, I believe most do. You know that my sister, Rosalind, is a dear friend of Lady Marlowe. She was quite surprised by the match, but the Marlowes are absolutely besotted with each other, according to her, so there is that at least."

Malcolm snorted, sipping his beverage. "A love match in the

aristocracy of England? I highly doubt that."

"You're a cynic."

"This surprises you?"

Lily's fan suddenly rapped his wrist.

"Really, Monty," Granger intoned from his other side, sounding partly pained and partly amused. "Even the peers have hearts, despite what anybody might say about them. We all do. Why shouldn't they be besotted? I wish more marriages were conducted thusly."

That was a bit surprising, especially from him. And really, Malcolm agreed wholeheartedly. But standing between the pair of them, with their mutual misery and his own, was too much to bear.

"Yes, but what does she see in Marlowe?" he asked with a sardonic look. "She already had a fortune, and his title is not that impressive."

"He *is* rather attractive," Lily offered, smiling a little.

"If you like the dark and rugged sort of thing," Granger snorted.

"I *do*," his wife quipped, seeming to forget that her husband was also rather dark and potentially rugged, and quite honestly the more attractive between the two men.

Malcolm sipped his drink and studiously avoided looking at either as the couple stared at each other. He did not want to know what was going on there; he had quite enough to be getting on with.

"Excuse me," Granger said suddenly, striding away to find another drink.

Malcolm exhaled a very silent sigh of relief.

"Just when I thought we might get somewhere," Lily murmured softly beside him.

He winced as he recalled that Lily actually loved her husband, or had once, at least, and might have wished for a different ending to their unusual banter.

"Did you see Miss Owens tonight?" Lily said with forced brightness before he could turn to her. "She looks so lovely in white, and she has nothing so fine of her own. Rosalind lent it to her, and I find it suits Beth better, don't you?"

It certainly did, Malcolm thought as he gazed at the woman in question. She looked perfectly lovely, with an inner light that outshone any set of candles in the room. Rather a change from the easy, earthy woman from before, he decided. Now, she held herself with poise, as elegantly dressed as any other woman present. Nothing at all indicated reduced circumstances or desperation. No one would mistake her for a servant tonight, and if there were any single gentlemen worth their salt, she would not want for company.

Ever so faintly, he felt something tug at the back of his stomach in discomfort, and he found himself frowning. He might not know what he was going to do with her, or what sort of wife she would be, but he did know full well that he didn't want to give anyone else the chance to find out.

What did that say about it?

"Did she mention anything about me?" he asked in a low voice, still staring at Miss Owens.

Lily hummed a soft laugh. "Not really. She asked me some questions about you, purely out of curiosity, but nothing since. Why? Did you want her to say something about you?"

He sniffed and sipped at his drink again. "Never you mind."

A sudden commotion across the room drew everyone's attention. "That's enough! I've bloody well had enough of you, Pratt, now leave off!"

Malcolm winced, knowing that voice all too well, and wishing to heaven that he were anywhere else. Two gentlemen were currently engaged in a bit of a struggle, the darker one seizing the other by his cravat, and the overly-dressed one bearing a smug smirk that was impossible to remove.

Rogue and Rook were having a show for everyone, only it seemed Rogue was not interested in continuing it.

Dammit.

"What's the matter, my lord?" Rook prodded, his tone mocking and painfully loud now that everyone could hear it. "Can't take a little advice? It's no wonder your wife did not accompany you to London; with the way you dress, they'd think she'd come with the parson instead."

Rogue's eyes grew colder, and his grip intensified on the younger, thinner man. "Not another bleeding word, Pratt. I don't like you, and I don't need your addle-pated advice."

"Do you see what he is doing?" Rook called out merrily to the

31

others in the room. "No wonder he doesn't move about in Society; he's not fit to be in it. Unless we're letting mongrel dogs in these days!"

Malcolm was going to kill him and take great joy in it. Couldn't he see that Rogue was not in the right state for his peacock nonsense? Rook was very good at his character, but intentionally provoking his most dangerous colleague publicly like this when the man was genuinely agitated for Amelia's well-being...

It would be a miracle if no one were murdered tonight.

He glanced over at Gent, who was struggling with his public Lord Marlowe face in favor of the same sort of agitation Malcolm was feeling. They needed to act, and quickly, but without barking orders at them or giving anything away. Surely a gentleman could act in the interest of others without knowing the particulars. He saw Kit Gerrard frowning and starting towards the pair of them, and Gent began to move, as well.

"Now, see here, Pratt... Come now, Wharton," Marlowe managed in the blandest voice in the world.

"I will tear you limb from limb," Rogue seethed, lifting Rook off the ground by a fistful of his shirt front, "if you *ever* mention my wife in any way again. Then we will see who is fit, sir!"

Perhaps Malcolm would be strangling Rogue, too. He understood his feelings, but really, to lose control like this...

"All right, that is enough, both of you," interrupted a sweet, warm voice that did not fit the situation.

Malcolm jerked to see Beth walking towards the two men, her head held high, no hint of nerves or fears, and a serene smile on her face. What did she think she was doing?

She approached them and looked up at Rogue with a small smile. "My lord, if you would kindly replace Mr. Pratt so that his feet touch the floor."

That tone... It was the most perfectly given directive ever, firm with a hint of scolding all coated in honey. It was at once a pleasure to hear and impossible to ignore.

But would it work on a man like Rogue?

Impossibly, Rogue glanced down at her, exhaled roughly, and brought Rook back down to his place.

"Thank you," Beth said with a smile and a nod. "Now, if you would remove your hands from his person, I think his cravat may be trying to strangle him with your help."

Malcolm couldn't believe it, but Rook looked ready to laugh, and he was not the only one. Rogue would not take kindly to this sort of set down, but he couldn't exactly find fault with Beth for it.

Rogue growled a little and released Rook roughly, taking a step back. He looked ready to turn away, but Beth suddenly placed a hand on his arm, gripping a little, effectively holding him in place, unless he wished to create more of a scene than he already had.

"Now, you are both fine men," she told them, looking between them with calmness and no hint of amusement, only a cool grace. "You are better behaved than this, I know." She turned a scolding look to Rook, and it surprised Malcolm to see how severe it was. "Mr. Pratt, you must stop offering unsolicited advice where it is not wanted. Lord Wharton looks very dapper this evening and obviously does not have the same appreciation for finery that you do. That is nothing with which to find fault, as hardly anybody else in London does, either." There was a soft titter of laughter around the room at that, and she allowed a small hint of a smile, despite her severe look. "It was unkind of you to provoke him when he was not in the wrong and is not inclined to your witty banter."

Beth turned to the man whose arm she was gripping and gave him the same sort of look. "My lord, I know you are irritated with Mr. Pratt, which I can easily believe, as I think he irritates a great many people."

There was more laughter at this, and even Rogue seemed to be having trouble not smiling.

"But you mustn't attack him so. It is hardly in good taste to behave in such a way before all these guests, and it's a gross insult to our host. What would your wife have to say about that, sir?" She shook her head a little, clucking her tongue. "There is only one proper way to settle this matter. You must each dance with me and forget about the matter entirely."

There was a general murmuring at that, given that it was a slight *faux pas* for her to ask for a dance from either, but more of what Malcolm heard tended towards amusement.

Rogue and Rook stared at her as if she had sprung up from the ground, though they were each amused by it.

"But," Beth said with a finger in the air, looking at them both again, "you must shake hands and part as friends."

The two men glared at each other, and it was quite evident they would rather have swum the Thames than do any such thing.

"Very well," Beth conceded with exasperation, "then you may part as slightly less hostile acquaintances who won't speak to each other anymore this evening unless it is with perfect politeness regarding the complimenting of my person, or our host's graciousness."

Now the laughter in the room was complete, and even Rogue managed a small smile as he shook hands with Rook.

"I believe that is my cue," Lily murmured fondly, moving away from him to the pianoforte. She struck up a lively tune and Rook led Beth to a cleared space. A few other couples joined in, and the fight was all but forgotten as they danced a quadrille.

Malcolm moved about the room, indirectly heading for Gent, who leaned against a wall, watching the whole thing.

"That was close," he muttered with a shake of his head.

Gent nodded. "Idiot. Where does Rook come off, pulling something like that?"

Malcolm shook his head. "Well, Rogue should never have reacted that way." He snorted in disgust. "Which one do you want to talk to?"

"Neither, if you please. Your future wife handled them both so well. I hardly think it needs to be restated tonight."

"She's not my future wife," Malcolm growled.

Gent turned to look at him, his expression one of bland derision. "Isn't she? I should think her performance just now would have solidified your decision. If she can handle those two so perfectly, she can handle anything Archer and Samuel can get up to."

Malcolm was not yet ready to admit it to anyone aloud, but his decision *had* been solidified by Beth's actions. He'd found himself thinking of her as Beth the moment she'd moved, which seemed something of significance. He still had his doubts, but seeing that side of her had struck a chord within him. He was fairly certain that everything else that could possibly arise from his marriage to her would be much easier.

"I know that much," he admitted, taking another glass of wine from a footman. "But…"

"Monty…" Gent looked around, then turned to face him more fully. "That young woman just settled a rather temper-fueled dispute between two very influential men in Society, in a room filled with other influential members of Society. Look around." He gestured faintly, indicating the small selection of Society's best that had been invited here this evening. "See who is in this room. They are going to be talking about her, Monty, and it is going to be about her poise, her efficiency, and how she had everybody half in love with her by the end of it. Lady Whitlock herself couldn't have done a finer job of it. And let me tell you this," he added quietly, leaning closer, "if I were not already a married man and madly in love with my wife, I'd be after Miss Owens myself." He quirked a knowing brow and moved away, looking bored once again.

Malcolm knew he was right, and he knew Gent would never say something like that unless he truly meant it. He was proud of what Beth had done, but he also wished she had not done anything. Whether that was some twisted version of propriety that had been offended or his desire that no one discover her until she was Lady Montgomery, he could not honestly have said. All he knew was that everything was getting more and more confusing, and he was not the sort of man who enjoyed being confused.

The dancing continued. Beth changed partners, and he watched for several minutes, waiting for her to finish her dance with Rogue. When the pair of them moved away from the other couples to an open window, obviously in conversation, he headed in that direction.

He could hear their conversation before either of them saw him.

"Your wife, my lord, seems to be a very strong woman, and if I have any sense of these things, she would be driven mad by you hanging about to wait upon her, though it is your inclination." She spoke with her hands, gesturing, touching, fidgeting with them, all very natural and easy, and more than a little amusing, judging by Rogue's expression.

Malcolm caught Rogue's eye, and he dipped his chin in

acknowledgement, keeping his attention fixed on Beth.

"I like the sound of her," Beth added warmly, "and I do understand your distress. Would you permit me to call upon her? I have a bit of time on my hands, and no real taste for Society, so the country would be a welcome reprieve. Unless you think I would be a bother."

Malcolm barely avoided scoffing at that.

Rogue managed his version of a smile, though Malcolm could tell he would have laughed. "I think Amelia would like that very much. I'd allow it, so long as you send me very detailed reports of her, as she seems to think I don't deserve to know anything at all."

"Well, I can't make any promises," Beth chirped with a laugh.

"Pardon me, Miss Owens," Malcolm interrupted softly.

She turned and beamed at him, which caught him squarely in the heart. "Lord Montgomery!" She curtseyed quickly, and very properly. "I didn't know you were here, what a pleasant surprise!"

"It is a pleasure to see you again," he complimented, wishing he could get the image of an angel out of his head as he looked at her now, with her pure white gown and glistening golden hair. "I wonder if I might possibly have a word with you?"

Her smile turned playful, and she narrowed her eyes. "Have you finally decided what to do with me, then?"

Rogue coughed a little in surprise but raised a questioning brow.

"Yes, I have," Malcolm told them both indirectly, "and I should like to discuss that with you in private."

Beth dipped her chin in a nod. "Of course, my lord." She turned and smiled at Rogue. "If you will excuse me, my lord."

Rogue bowed more perfectly than Malcolm had ever seen him do. "Of course, Miss Owens. Thank you for the dance, for your company, and for keeping me from making more of a fool of myself."

Beth chuckled a little, shaking her head. "Not a fool, my lord. Never that." She curtseyed and nodded at Malcolm when he gestured the way.

Rogue grabbed his superior's arm quickly before he could follow. "I've changed my mind," he hissed. "I approve. Take her and take her now." He released Malcolm and turned away, leaving the earl to stare after him in shock.

Then, Malcolm's sense caught up with him, and he followed Beth to a quiet parlor just off the music room, catching Lily's eye at the pianoforte as they left.

She gave him a knowing smile and an encouraging nod.

Malcolm nearly groaned. Did *everybody* know what he was about? He looked into the room and saw Beth staring fondly at a mediocre piece of art within, perfectly oblivious.

Apparently, there was at least one person who was still ignorant. Unfortunately, that was the one person who ought to know.

And in a few moments, she would.

"Please sit down, Miss Owens."

Chapter Four

$\mathcal{G}$ood heavens, Beth thought breathlessly, how was a sensible woman supposed to think properly with a man staring at her like that? He'd been handsome enough when she'd first met him in his regular, everyday attire. But in the finery of his evening wear? He was so close to perfect, it buckled her knees.

Everything was perfectly fitted, from his bone-colored breeches to the almost gold waistcoat and the midnight blue coat and tails... Even his cravat was perfect, with just the right amount of style and none of the ridiculous. His hair was darker than she recalled but still golden, possibly amber in color. He looked powerful and imposing and virile...

She swallowed with difficulty. Heavens... That was quite enough of that.

She continued to stare at the painting on the wall without really seeing any of it. She had no idea why Lord Montgomery wanted to speak with her privately again, but she was already tempted to say, "Thank you, my lord," which would have been entirely improper.

He cleared his throat politely. "Miss Owens?"

She jerked and realized he'd been trying to speak with her. "Yes, my lord?"

His brow furrowed slightly. "Please, do have a seat."

Beth swallowed and nodded, not at all composed, and moved to sit in one of the gold-leafed chairs in the alcove. She fidgeted with her borrowed dress, praying she would not smudge it. Rosalind had been so kind to lend it to her, and if she stained it...

"Miss Owens."

Beth raised her head, not entirely sure when she had lowered it, and fixed her gaze on the man now standing before her, looking far too serious.

"Yes, my lord?"

"Do you know why I asked to see you again?" he asked, clasping his hands stiffly behind his back.

She shook her head slowly, feeling rather slow and stupid at the moment. "No, my lord."

He looked a little disconcerted. "Would you… would you mind not answering as if you were a girl in the schoolroom? It's making this harder."

Beth managed to smile, and that seemed to put him more at ease. "I apologize, my lord. I shall try to loosen my tongue and be a little more impertinent."

"That would help a great deal, thank you." He smiled, sort of, and then took a few pacing steps, stopping before her again. "Miss Owens, allow me to be perfectly frank with you and not mince words."

Beth gave him a nod, folding her hands together formally. "Excellent, I do not like to have my words minced."

He paused a moment, looking at her curiously, and she clamped her lips together to keep from laughing. Or apologizing.

He cocked his head slightly, and his brow furrowed again. "Miss Owens, I would like to ask for your hand in marriage."

He would… like…

Oh…

It was suddenly impossible to breathe or swallow, but somehow, she found a way to try to do both at the same time, which caused her to choke and sputter, hardly a decorous way to form an answer. Not that he had actually asked.

He had only said he would *like* to ask.

Would this be an inappropriate time to point that out?

"That would…" she managed to gasp, somehow breathing without coughing, "be acceptable. My lord."

Lord Montgomery looked mildly surprised. "Would it? Really?"

Marry him? Instead of becoming a governess? Surely, he was joking.

Beth nodded, and then found herself unable to stop nodding. "Yes, it would. Very acceptable."

"I'll have to get your father's permission," he said abruptly, pacing again.

"He'll give it," she assured him, though his comment was not directed at her.

"And there is no need for haste, so we can simply have the banns read."

"Indeed." She continued to watch him pace, wondering if he was aware of what he had yet to do.

"And I'd have to bring the children down from Knightsgate, but we don't need to…"

"My lord," Beth tried to interject, but he was not fully aware of her anymore.

"But in all fairness, we could not exclude them," he continued, still pacing. "And there would be no need for a honeymoon trip."

"*My lord*," she said again, louder this time.

He frowned more earnestly. "And there is the matter of a ring, but I think that should be a simple enough errand."

Beth sighed and winced at what she was about to do, then simply blurted out, "Monty!"

Lord Montgomery came to a sudden halt and blinked in surprise.

"I apologize for the familiarity, my lord," she began, trying her very best to look submissive, "but you were rambling on, and I feel the need to point out that… well… you haven't *asked* me anything… yet."

He stared at her for a moment, then his mouth curved a little. "I haven't, have I?"

She bit her lip and shook her head.

He turned to face her fully and bowed formally. "Miss Elizabeth Owens, would you do me the honor of consenting to marry me?"

A hot burst of delight lit her heart, but she contained it well and merely offered a prim nod. "Yes, my lord, I will."

"Really?" he asked with mild interest.

"Yes," she replied, nodding once more.

"No hesitation?"

"None whatsoever, my lord."

He made a faint noise that she could not interpret. "I thought it would take a good deal of persuasion for you to agree."

Beth smiled, shrugging a little. "Well, perhaps this is a good sign."

His gaze fixed on her then. "Of what?"

"Our marriage could be a much smoother affair than we think." Marriage. *Her* marriage. To *him*. She could not help smiling at the thought.

"Or, it could be a disaster," he pointed out with a warning look.

Beth shook her head, still smiling. "If you thought that, Lord Montgomery, you would not have asked me."

His expression became thoughtful. "No… No, I would not." Then his face changed, and he became formal once more. "You should not expect a marriage of affection."

With him proposing a week after meeting her? Even she was not that fanciful. "I understand," she promised.

"Does that bother you?" he asked, his tone formal once again. "No."

He did not look remotely convinced. "It would bother most women."

She opted to give him a frank look. "Then perhaps you oughtn't marry one of them."

At last, he rewarded her with another sort-of smile, and she felt her own smile grow. But like the sun darting behind a dark cloud, his smile vanished.

"Stop smiling like that," he ordered. "I've just told you this will not be a marriage of affection."

"I know, my lord," she said, now positively beaming.

His frown deepened. "Miss Owens, I do not love you."

That made her laugh a little. "I would be quite surprised if you did."

The more she confirmed her understanding, the more flustered he seemed to become, which only amused her further.

"Miss Owens…" he began impatiently.

"My lord," she broke in, shaking her head slowly, still smiling her delight, "you once described me as a creature of sense. I do wish you would believe your own words and understand me when I tell you

41

that I am fully aware, and I fully comprehend the nature of this marriage, with no expectations or sentimentality."

Lord Montgomery stared at her for a long moment. "Forgive me, of course I believe you, but you are smiling so. It just…"

Beth took pity on him and laughed. "My lord, you've just told me that not only will I not be forced to become a governess, which I would have done quite dreadfully, but now I will shortly be married to a respectable gentleman with a title. Of whom my dear friend Lily thinks very highly. There is a great deal for me to smile about, even if this is not a love match."

"I never considered that," he murmured absently, sinking down into a chair near her. "I hope you don't consider this a rescue. I'm not trying to be heroic."

"Not at all," she assured him, "even if it does feel a little heroic to me. But you have need of a wife, a countess…" She broke off, eyes wide. "Good gracious, my lord, do you think I could pass as a countess?"

Now he smiled a little. "My dear Miss Owens, you do not need to *pass* as anything. You *will* be a countess."

"Heavens…" she breathed, fanning herself slowly, having not considered that. She was barely a peripheral member of Society, and now she would be expected to be a leader of it?

"After your performance in the music room earlier, do you expect me to believe that you cannot manage the duties of a landowner's wife or navigate the societal seas of London?" He gave her sardonic look and shook his head. "That will be no problem for a lady of your qualities, Miss Owens. You have grace, poise, and charm. All you lack is experience."

"Thank you," Beth replied lamely, plucking at her borrowed gloves. "I think."

He missed her sarcasm and smirked a little. "What else were you going to say?"

Her mind raced backwards to their previous conversation. "Oh!" she recollected, shifting more towards him in her seat. "Lily says you have darling children. It would be a pleasure to be their…"

"They have a mother," he snapped coldly, his eyes flashing as his expression turned thunderous. "You will not be their mother."

Beth was stunned by his outburst and blinked slowly in response. "Of course not," she answered with great care, her heart pounding unsteadily. "I was going to say 'their friend'. That is all I want to be. I do look forward to meeting them and helping them along."

He still looked markedly upset as he stared at her, but she suspected that he was not looking at her so much as through her.

This might all be much harder than she thought.

"I would never try to replace their mother, my lord," Beth told him softly. "No one ever could."

He seemed to come to himself then, though the shadows remained. "You don't need to 'my lord' me anymore. You may call me Monty, as you did before."

"Yes, my lor..." she started, then she caught herself and smiled sheepishly. "Yes, Monty. And if you would be so kind, I should like for you to call me Elizabeth. Or Beth, if you like. I've never gotten used to Miss Owens, so it doesn't really suit."

Monty grunted and got to his feet. "Well, you will have to adjust to being Lady Montgomery soon enough, so we shall see how well that suits."

"Heavens," she muttered, rising without waiting for him to help her. "What if it doesn't?"

He paused and gave her an assessing look. "Then perhaps you will have made a hash of something after all."

Beth snorted into her glove and raised a brow at him.

He returned the look and led her back out into the music room just as dinner was announced. She managed to walk gracefully into the dining room on his arm and found her assigned place.

Beth could barely focus on anything at all during dinner. How could she? She was *betrothed!* She, Elizabeth Anne Owens, was engaged to be married to the Earl of Montgomery! A handsome lord who made her knees shake, had four children who needed a woman's guidance, a country house, influence, wealth... It was rather a lot to take in for one evening. Or for a lifetime, for that matter... but she supposed she would get used to it. She looked across the table, and several seats down, her betrothed sat beside her friend Lily. He glanced up at her at the same time.

Beth couldn't help it. She smiled at him, relieved and delighted and excited. If she were to be perfectly honest, she was already slightly in love with him, despite her earlier words. She couldn't help it; he was handsome, he was kind, he wanted to marry her... It was undoubtedly gratitude and infatuation, but it certainly felt that it could be love if she tried hard enough.

But he didn't need to know that.

Monty watched her for a moment, and then he, too, smiled. Sort of.

Malcolm sat in his London office and fidgeted with his quill pen, scowling at the list of necessary errands that still had to be completed. He hadn't enjoyed planning his wedding the first time around, and he'd been mad for the woman he was marrying then.

This time he was only mad.

Thankfully, Beth was a fairly simple girl who did not want any sort of fanfare, so the details themselves were fewer and not of as much concern to him. The trouble was actually accepting the fact that he would be marrying again.

It felt like the worst sort of betrayal, though he knew full well that it was nothing of the kind. Had Caroline been able to give him any last words, knowing her fate, she would have told him to move on and take care of the children. She had never been one for overt sentimentality, though she had certainly filled his heart with words of love enough for three lifetimes. She would have scolded him soundly for his current feelings, and he often wondered if she were not standing behind him, watching him with her arms folded and a disapproving expression on her face.

More than once, he had looked behind him just to be sure.

He knew he was fortunate to have found Beth, though she was a surprising choice. His men all approved heartily, his friends in Society thought he was after her pretty face, and his children...

Well, he hadn't actually told them yet, which may have been a problem, as the wedding was a week away. But they would be arriving in London tomorrow with Mrs. Franklin, and Beth would meet them a few days after. There was still time to sort that out.

He didn't think it would be much of a problem with them, as they were young and well-behaved. Jane had not mentioned her mother in some months, and Archer had kept the others firmly in line, surprising him for a boy of eight. The youngest two no longer cried for their mother, so he must assume that they had forgotten her.

That pained him to no end, but what could he do? He could barely endure saying her name aloud. Discussing her... Well, it would not be possible for him.

All the better to give them a new face to consider in a maternal sense. But not a mother. Never that.

"Cap, Rook is coming in now." A young clerk interrupted Malcolm's reverie, his face suddenly appearing in the doorway with his spectacles askew and his ginger hair slightly disheveled.

Malcolm peered at the clerk with curiosity. "Did he ruffle your hair again, Pruitt?"

The man rolled his eyes and tried to smooth his hair. "Yes, he did, sir, the dirty blighter. You know he could only be five years older than me at most, but he treats me like a child."

"It's just his way," Malcolm assured him absently, not particularly caring. The clerks, while diligent in their efforts, were certainly not operatives, and he was weary of dealing with them. "Send Rook in, I'll deal with him quickly." The clerk looked as though he doubted it, but he shrugged and disappeared.

Malcolm rose and moved to the sideboard in his office, faintly registering in his mind to be grateful that he was the only one in the building to have just the one desk in his office. The others had two, as there was always the intention to bring more members into the League and then the operatives would double up in offices. Malcolm, as Cap, however, had been senior enough and experienced enough that there was never a concern about that.

He had more space to think, to move, and more privacy to see to his own matters. No one else shared at this point, as there were only four of them, but the added space was truly something he appreciated. When he wished to pace, as he did now, he could do so.

"Were you going to drink that brandy, sir, or just stare at it in passing?"

Malcolm glared at Rook, who sauntered through the door and flopped himself into a chair. "I have quite a lot on my mind, Rook."

Rook snorted and gestured for a glass. "I'd ask if it was about our little friends, but I believe it is more likely to be *your* little friend than anything remotely French."

Malcolm's glare darkened into an all-out glower as he moved back to his desk, propping his feet up on it in an uncharacteristic lapse of propriety.

"That look," Rook laughed, pointing at him, "tells me I am correct. We are, what, a week from the wedding?"

"Yes, just," Malcolm grunted, sipping his brandy slowly. "You are lucky to still be invited, you know, after your performance at Marlowe's."

"Please." Rook snorted and dropped his head back. "You know full well that Rogue and I staged that whole thing, and if I hadn't done it, you might still be waffling about what to do with Beth."

Malcolm pointed a very steady finger at him. "You will refrain from speaking of her in that familiar fashion until either she or I have given you permission to do so. Is that clear? She is Miss Owens for another week, and Lady Montgomery thereafter."

Rook held his hands up in surrender, still keeping his head back. "Yes, my lord. Of course, my lord. So sorry, my lord."

If he were not such a capable operative, Malcolm would have been rather inclined to shoot the impertinent whelp. But alas, he was very good and had the potential to be one of their best.

As it turned out, Rogue and Rook had improvised that rather convincing fight to distract Mr. Herschel, who had never had any particular interests or dealings with the covert operations of his country, but who had suddenly begun asking too many questions.

How he had thought to ask Rogue, of all people, was astonishing. There was no reason for him to think that Lord Wharton cared about politics or would speculate on the unsettled French in their new government. Rogue had signaled to Rook, who had needed no other invitation, and the fight commenced as Malcolm and the others had seen it.

The distraction of their fight worked to interrupt Mr. Herschel's questions, but it was impossible to say what the old fool thought of it. The most bewildering part was knowing that *Herschel* had asked. He had never been a suspect before, but now…

Well, now he had two very small and almost invisible street urchins tailing his every move.

Once the Marlowes' dinner party had concluded, Rogue had gone back to his dockside alias, and Rook and Gent had taken up investigating their new suspect, searching to find confirmation that any of them had been compromised.

As yet, they had no proof of anything. Even so, extra guards had been placed at Rogue's estate, Whitleigh, and Amelia had been made aware of the potential danger. Eagle had removed himself to the estate, as well, to guard his daughter. Amelia had been none too pleased, as she felt her father's presence was rather like a nanny sent to tend her, but nobody had taken her complaints into consideration. There were far more important matters at hand.

So, it was a most inconvenient time to be thinking of a wedding, really.

But once the deed was done, he could deposit Beth at Knightsgate with the children, be assured of their care, and focus on the dangers at hand. There was even a possibility that he could go back into actual fieldwork once Beth was installed as a parent of sorts for his children. He'd not accepted any serious missions in years, certainly never since Caroline's death. Once he was no longer the sole adult responsible for his children's wellbeing, he would again be able to take up that danger. He missed fieldwork far more passionately than he'd ever imagined he would.

Plus, if the faction had infiltrated more of the London Society, they needed to address that, and cut it off before it could spread any further. He could help there when the time came.

"I've lost you, haven't I?"

Malcolm looked up at his comrade, the one he had known the least amount of time, but the only one at hand, and exhaled slowly. Tossing down the quill, he put his head in both hands and admitted, "I don't know what I'm doing."

Rook had the good sense to look surprised. "You? You always know what you're doing. That's why you're Cap."

Cap had been short for Captain, which was a bit obvious, given his military history before he'd inherited. With his authoritative personality and knack for giving commands, he'd earned the name again, this time with the operatives. Very few ever questioned him or his decisions, and even fewer thought they should do so. He didn't mean to assume authority wherever he went, it just sort of happened.

Except in this case.

"I don't this time," Malcolm sighed, rubbing at his brow and tugging at the poor imitation of a cravat he wore. "I don't have a damned clue."

"But you *want* to marry her, right?"

He shrugged, looking away.

"You don't?"

"I don't want to *not* marry her," Malcolm suggested weakly, hiding a wince behind his hands.

That drew a snort from his colleague. "Oh, tell her that, by all means."

"I don't have to tell her anything," Malcolm snapped defensively. "She agreed to the marriage as it is, without any promise or hope of affection."

"You can't know what she hopes for," Rook scoffed, crossing his ankles. "You're a fine catch, and she'd be an idiot not to hope, no matter what she told you. And as I happen to think very highly of Miss Owens, I cannot consider her an idiot. Just marry her and stop worrying."

Malcolm thought to scold Rook, but actually, it was fairly sound advice. "You think so?" he asked with a raised brow.

Rook nodded all too thoughtfully. "And so do you, Cap. Or you never would have thought of marrying her in the first place. Don't over-think, just act."

The day he started taking advice from Rook would be a cold day in hell. Even if he happened to do as he suggested. Malcolm frowned at his colleague, pretending that he did not feel marginally better for Rook's sage words. "Tell me you didn't come here just to advise me on my impending marriage."

"'Course not," Rook said with a dismissive snort. "I have business."

"Good. Start talking."

Chapter Five

The sooner this day could be over and done with, the sooner Malcolm would be able to breathe with ease again. He was not a great fan of weddings in general, but the notion of having to endure another of his own seemed a cruel twist of irony.

Nearly three times today, he had considered the possibility of crying off, wondering if that would destroy his reputation or make any difference to his future or spare his soul… Anything to avoid the discomfort he now felt as he paced the small vestry waiting for his cue to proceed out to the front of the church and await his bride.

He nearly snorted despite his distress. *His bride.* She was going to be beautiful, he had no doubt, and he would probably feel some sort of reaction to that, as he was a man, but he refused to take any pleasure in it.

He could not.

Beth was a fine enough woman, and that opinion had only grown as he had come to know her better in the weeks following their engagement. In the interest of all honesty, he would admit that Beth had dealt with the details of the wedding and preparation for her new role far better than Caroline had done, though he would have had to work hard to find fault in Caroline as she had been then. But she had been young and desired everything to be perfect, including herself.

With the differences in this situation, that was not a problem.

Beth did not care if everything was perfect. She did not seem to care if anything was perfect at all. She had no strong opinions on the decor or fashion, the guests or the breakfast, and still smiled just as blissfully as if Malcolm were violently in love with her. But she was older than Caroline had been and did not seem to be perturbed by any of this, which initially led him to believe that she was either the most naïve person in the world, or truly not concerned about the task before her.

The more he came to know her, the more he realized that she was not naïve at all. She was actually very wise, and possibly even a better choice for a wife than he could have imagined, considering their short acquaintance.

Lily had told him in confidence that Beth had come to her to ask advice on proper decorum and managing the estate. Beth had become a kind of apprentice to Lily's daily life and had even gone so far as to ask Granger about his tenants in the country and the sort of duties Malcolm would have towards his own. She took copious notes, and when she was not engaged in the study of her future responsibilities, she was practicing comportment and refinement with Lily as if she were back in school.

As Malcolm understood it, Lily's governess had trained her in the more feminine arts and styles. Beth had only her schooling, without prior benefit of a governess. It therefore followed that her manners and gentility, while certainly not lacking, were less cultivated than they ought to have been.

He could not help but be impressed with her efforts, and the determination she had to be fully prepared for what awaited her. Any hesitation he'd had on her abilities as his wife and countess was quickly ebbing away. If nothing else, she would succeed out of sheer willpower.

That was not the problem.

Nor was her natural temperament.

She'd met the children a few days before, and that had been the easiest part of all. While Jane had been her usual timid self, and Archer had looked uncertain about the whole affair, Samuel and Greer had had no such reluctance. From the first gentle smile she offered, his youngest children had been taken with her and spent the entire interview telling her everything about themselves and their home at Knightsgate.

Malcolm knew how fond Beth was of children, but he could hardly have expected anyone to have the tolerance to endure the chattering of a boy of four and a girl of three for very long. Yet she had done it, without showing any signs that she would prefer to be anywhere else. She had been just as engaged with them as she had with him at every interview they'd had. Under the influence of undivided attention, the children were not inclined to keep anything private whatsoever.

Just as they were about to tell Beth all about the various hiding places in the forest behind their home, Malcolm called them to a halt. They all giggled incessantly, which painted a questionable picture of his parental authority in the presence of his future wife.

True to what he was learning was her natural form, she'd had to clamp down on her lips to avoid joining in the laughter, her dark eyes dancing as merrily as he'd seen them do at Marlowe's.

Jane had giggled, too, and that had drawn Beth's attention.

Malcolm had watched her in amazement as she approached his daughter, crouching down to her height and speaking softly with her, never pressing her to interact more than she allowed. Jane had given her very few answers, but she had smiled eventually, and that seemed a miracle. His bright and vivacious daughter had disappeared with her mother's death, and only a somber, shy girl remained in her place. She still smiled for him, but rarely anyone else.

If he hadn't already been engaged to marry Beth Owens, he would have proposed again on the spot, just for that moment.

Archer still was not convinced, but he informed Malcolm only last night that he liked her well enough, and he supposed his father might as well marry her. High praise, indeed.

Now, pacing as he was, Malcolm fought the desire to tug at his too-starched cravat, feeling as though it were strangling him. His palms were sweating, his fingers itched, and he would have given half his fortune for a glass of water to soothe his parched throat. His nerves had robbed him of sleep last night, and they were keeping him company now.

He could not sit still, he could not currently recall what their plans were for after the ceremony, and he found himself perspiring even though it was a cool day. He doubted he had been this nervous for his first wedding, but he had been so absorbed with marrying the woman of his dreams that there'd been no room for anything else in his heart or his head.

Now he knew better.

Despite the offers of his colleagues, he waited in this drafty and too formal vestry alone, without a best man or chaperone. He did not need anyone else to be with him for this. No one must know of his anxieties, and no one could relieve them even if they knew. He should have been perfectly comfortable. Beth was an excellent choice as far as connections went, despite her lack of fortune. She would make a wonderful countess, once she got used to it. She was already winning over his children, and it could only improve from there.

The trouble was that, while she had succeeded in so many respects, there was one area in which she utterly failed.

Beth Owens was most certainly not someone that it would be impossible to fall in love with. What was worse was that he could almost see how he *could* love her, were he anyone else.

He was not admitting to feeling anything for her now. He didn't think he would feel anything of significance in the future, either. If he had been wise, he would have chosen someone far less special and far less pleasant to look at. But that person would not have been right for his children, and he had to think of them.

He had to.

Any minute now, the rector would fetch him, and he would enter the chapel, enduring the stares of whomever they had invited. The guest list included his two oldest children, his colleagues, and Beth's idiot parents, who seemed utterly bewildered by their daughter's marriage, as if they had never expected her to marry at all! He could understand their confusion at her marrying an earl, given their situation, but to *never* marry?

It was the most absurd thing anyone could think. Beth was so perfectly the sort of woman one married. It was inconceivable that she was not already married, she was so perfect for the state. She ought to have been married long before this.

But in just a few moments, she would marry him.

He straightened his coat and forced himself to exhale slowly. He *would* marry her. It *was* the right thing to do. And eventually, the pain of this *would* fade.

The door opened, and the rector appeared with a warm smile

that Malcolm could not return. "All right, my lord. It is time."

Beth's wedding day was hardly shaping up to be as she had always dreamed. For one thing, her husband to be was a right sight grander than she had ever imagined. For another, only three members of her family were in attendance, and she was ever so grateful. The rest of her family were completely overwhelming, and there would have been all manner of chaos, a few fights, and no end of criticism from her sisters and sisters-in-law about how she should look, or how one should act once they were married.

Married. She was married. She had a husband now.

But not just any husband: Malcolm Arthur Colerain, Earl of Montgomery. Oh, la! His given name was Malcolm, which she had not known, and she suddenly thought it the grandest name in the world. She could not think of him with any other name now, and her heart warmed more at every thought of it.

The wedding had proceeded without any sort of fuss, which was what she'd wanted. They had not married in the grandest of cathedrals, just Malcolm's usual parish, and the number of guests had been small for the capacity of the church itself. This was to be expected, as she knew almost nobody in London, and her husband was a reserved man with limited friends and no family other than his own.

She had not minded. She had been involved in several large weddings and a couple of small ones, and the smaller ones had always been a more pleasant experience.

It meant more than anything else that Michael, her absolutely favorite brother, had come for her wedding. He hadn't even said a word about her not knowing her husband for very long. He'd given her a brotherly kiss and said, "I trust you know what you are doing," and then stepped over to become acquainted with her husband. Just before the service this morning, he'd officially given her his approval of the match.

Pretentious fool! As if she would have left off marrying just because Michael thought she should. But then, Michael really was no fool. He knew very well that she would have married Malcolm anyway, so it was impossible to say if he truly approved or if he were just telling her so.

Either way, she thought with a sigh as she sat at her wedding breakfast, looking around at those who had come to celebrate, it was a relief to have it all done. Her gown was her own this time, thanks in part to the generous trousseau that Malcolm had given her, and it was of far better quality than anything she had owned before this. But, as Lily reminded her often, she was a countess now, and she must accustom herself to the finery associated with such a position. She had decided that she could adjust to it very well. And with the way Malcolm had looked at her when he'd seen her, she thought the expense was rather worth it. She could get used to her husband looking at her in such a way.

Her husband.

She barely recalled a word of the service, as she had been too aware of the man next to her and of the task before her to hear a word. It was a lucky thing she had been able to recite the proper words at the appropriate time, and that Malcolm had been able to do the same. He had seemed rather distracted, as well. The last three weeks had given her ample time to become more acquainted with him, and the more she knew, the less she felt she truly knew about him.

Her husband was a complicated man, and every time she saw him, it seemed he was a different version of himself. She was never quite certain how he felt about her, as he would be warm on one occasion and formal the next. He would give her his slight sort-of smile, or he would not smile at all. He had never been as warm as he had that first day they had met, but she thought that version might be hiding underneath all the other layers of him.

She had seen how he loved his children, though he was not demonstrative or affectionate with them, and how pleased he had been that they had seemed to get along with her. The path to her husband's heart was undoubtedly through his children and how they fared with her in their lives. He had made it perfectly clear that she was not their mother, and while she understood the situation and a little of what he must be feeling, she could not pretend it did not pain her to have the words spoken aloud.

She sighed a little to herself as she watched her husband across the room. He mingled easily enough with the guests, though he hardly seemed to fit the part of a groom. He seemed so distant, his mind wandering…

Why had he married her if he chose to take so little pleasure in it?

"Elizabeth, you shouldn't frown so on your wedding day," her mother scolded in her soft way. "It's bad luck."

Beth nearly rolled her eyes at that, wishing her mother would not bring any sort of luck, good or bad, into her marriage conversation. She was concerned enough as it was.

She glanced over at her mother, who had come rather simply dressed in the same pale blue gown and spencer jacket she had worn for Ben's marriage two years ago, and it had been faded then. A small smile was fixed on her mother's face, but it was all for show. Neither of her parents had smiled much, seeming to forget that this was supposed to be a celebration for their youngest child.

Her father had dressed as he did for business but seemed more concerned about the state of his moustache than anything else. Her mother, at least, looked the part. Her silvery curls were pinned up nicely, though she stared at the finery in the room with wide eyes and the barest hint of disapproval in her features. It was absolutely ridiculous, but her parents seemed to take no pleasure in Beth's newfound wealth, though their family had certainly had greater income in the past.

"You must also get used to keeping your expression clear at all times," her mother went on, running her gloved finger along the pristine table linens. "You have children now; they will need to see their mother composed and smiling."

"I am not their mother," Beth reminded her in a low voice, pointedly keeping any bite out of her tone.

Her mother looked at her disapprovingly. "You may not have borne the children, Elizabeth, but you are the only mother those little ones will know. You do not have to be *their* mother to be *a* mother." She covered Beth's hand with her own and squeezed gently.

"Remember that when it gets hard."

"You think it will?" she asked, glancing towards her husband, who had not looked her way in some time.

"I know it will." There was a soft grunt of disapproval as her mother shook her head firmly. "Your husband does not love you, Elizabeth."

Beth stiffened and slid her hand out from her mother's grasp, looking rather sternly at her. "Marriages are not just about love, Mother. Monty and I... We have an understanding."

"Yes, but you should have known better," her mother insisted, frowning more severely than Beth had seen her in some time. "If we wanted to sell you off like property, we could have done so."

"Too right," her father added in gruffly. "Let it never be said that Thomas Owens let his children marry for less than love!"

Her mother made a tsking noise that made Beth wish fiercely that Michael had stayed with them at the table instead of being congenial. She could have used him to retort properly.

"I should never have allowed this," her mother moaned weakly. "Really, Elizabeth, what were you thinking?"

Beth ground her teeth together and closed her eyes. "We were thinking about the children."

"All well and good," her mother huffed, "but who is thinking about you?"

"I believe that task is mine now."

Beth almost wept in relief at the sound of Malcolm's voice and turned to look up at him as his hand came to rest on her shoulder.

He smiled coolly at her parents. "I hope you won't mind, Mr. Owens, Mrs. Owens, but I have several people asking to be formally introduced to Lady Montgomery, and I am anxious to give them the pleasure."

The pressure at Beth's shoulder increased, and she smiled up at him as she rose. She gave her parents no chance at all to comment, not that they would have argued with an earl. Even they were not that foolish.

Malcolm placed his hand on the middle of her back and steered her away, staying protectively close. "I know you said there were no creatures of sense in your family, Beth, but good Lord..."

She winced a little, leaning closer. "They don't mean any harm. They're just exhausted by life. Ten children, you know. And I've never had any prospects, so there is no reason for them to presume…"

"You're barely twenty-four," he scolded gently, giving her a stern look. "That's hardly a spinster."

Beth smirked a little and gave a half shrug. "I'm no flower in her first bloom, either. It makes no difference, truly. I am married now, and they cannot argue with that."

His jaw tightened visibly. "I can if they criticize our marriage."

"They wouldn't dare," she promised, taking his free hand as they slowly walked the room. "It is only the sudden nature of the match and the newness of it. They are so intimidated by you that they will never say anything else about it after today. And they will never ask you for anything."

Malcolm grunted once. "That is a point to their credit, I suppose."

Beth squeezed the hand she held. "Think kindly of them. They do love me, despite what you saw."

He sighed and looked at her again, his expression more open than it had been all day. "I believe they love you. I only wish they loved you better."

Be still her newly married heart! That was the most perfect thing anyone had ever said to her. If he wanted to keep her from falling in love with him, he would do well to avoid saying anything of that sort again.

"How are the children?" she asked through a bit of a tight throat. "Did they enjoy the wedding? It must have been so long to them; Samuel and Greer couldn't have been easy for Mrs. Franklin."

"Beth," he chuckled mirthlessly, "you do not need to concern yourself with the children, today of all days. They are perfectly fine, they've been allowed some cake, and are quite pleased with it. Jane was delighted to have been one of your attendants, Archer was bored out of his mind, and Mrs. Franklin said that Samuel and Greer were perfectly behaved. Today, you can think only of yourself, and I do wish you would."

Beth smiled up at him with a quirked brow. "Why should I think of myself today when everybody else is doing so?"

Malcolm shook his head and patted her back gently. "Oh, Lady Montgomery, you are going to be a challenge."

"You are the one who could not decide what to do with me, my lord," she reminded him, grinning cheekily. "It's your own fault for thinking marriage might solve the issue." She sighed and smiled at a few people whom she had met earlier, though their names now escaped her. "Who wished to meet the new Lady Montgomery?"

"I did," he said simply.

He what? She looked up at him in confusion. "You, Monty?"

He shrugged one shoulder. "That was the first time I've seen you appear even remotely distressed, and my feet were moving before I knew what was happening. I'm sure the entire room wants to meet you, but at the moment, I just want to walk with you. I've been entirely too sociable today."

Beth laughed in surprise and delight, the joy of the day rushing back into her soul. "Well, then shall I walk on in silence beside you to save you the trouble?"

"You may talk if you wish, and I will listen," he told her, his tone as calm and unaffected as his manner.

How curious. She thought he would prefer her silence, but if she could comfort and ease her husband by speaking instead? All the better. "And what should I talk about, Monty?" she asked her husband, smiling still.

Malcolm brought her hand to his lips for a too-polite kiss.

"Anything you like, my dear. Anything at all."

Chapter Six

"*L*ady Montgomery."

Beth jerked at the title for at least the third time in as many days, wondering when she would get used to such addresses. "Yes, Mrs. Rawlins?"

The housekeeper smiled with her genuine warmth, her eyes crinkling at the edges. "The children were asking if they might have a reprieve from their lessons, as it is so fine a day outside," she asked in her northern brogue.

"Oh," Beth murmured, setting aside her pen and the notes she had been writing for their wedding guests. "Um..." She bit her lip, not sure what was proper for lessons and activities outside of the usual schedule. It was not entirely her fault, as they had only been at Knightsgate for three days, and none of the warmth she had felt from the children before the wedding seemed to be evident in them now that they were home again.

And her husband had been so rarely seen since coming here, she was not entirely sure she had actually married him, or that she had the authority to make any decisions about his children.

"If I might suggest something, my lady," Mrs. Rawlins offered, clearing her throat slightly.

"Please do," Beth sighed, not bothering to hide her relief as she pushed an invisible strand of hair behind her ear.

The housekeeper stepped forward, clasping her hands before her. "The terrace is easily seen from here and would not allow the children too much freedom. Mrs. Franklin could continue the lessons, and the children would be outside."

Beth bit her lip, considering the possibility. She knew full well what it was like to be a child cooped up in a schoolroom with the sun shining outside, and that was a very special level of misery. But being so new, and unfamiliar with the children and their routine...

"Would the earl approve?" she murmured hesitantly, forgetting to be the cool and confident countess she wished to be.

The housekeeper's eyes softened, and she looked a trifle saddened by the question. "The earl, my lady, has not taken much interest in the activities of his children of late. So long as lessons are accomplished, and the children are well, he is satisfied."

That didn't sound like the Malcolm she had met in London. He had been devoted to the care of his children, taken great care to introduce them to her and mind their manners, and she had seen the pleasure in his eyes when she had managed to get Jane to speak to her. He had married her to help his children, for heaven's sake!

The description did, however, vaguely resemble the man she had been living with here at Knightsgate. The one she saw only at meals, who had given her a tour of the house that was so minimal that she had become lost and turned around at the end of it, and who had suddenly become as silent as his oldest daughter. None of his behavior seemed out of character to any of the staff. It did concern Beth a great deal, but she was new, and apparently had much to learn.

He'd not taken much interest in his own children? That was absolutely uncalled for.

Beth set her jaw and looked up at the housekeeper. "How well does Mrs. Franklin handle the children during lessons?" she asked, drumming her fingers on the back of the chair.

Mrs. Rawlins scoffed without restraint. "That poor woman. She is a nanny, you know, not a governess. She knows enough to get by, I'll grant you, but Master Archer will be needing something more fairly soon, or he will be behind the other boys when he goes to Eton. I would have thought he would have started with a tutor by now, but..."

"Yes," Beth murmured, thinking quickly. If she remembered, his birthday had only just occurred in the last few months, and at eight, he was quickly going to need more specific instructions. "Has Lord Montgomery said nothing about it?"

"Not a word," Mrs. Rawlins sighed. "But it was always the plan for Master Archer to attend Eton like his father. Lady Montgomery… that is, the late countess…"

Beth waved off her discomfort with a gentle smile of encouragement.

"It was what they always talked about," the housekeeper finished softly. "But since her death, it has never been brought up again."

That was more and more the answer she'd been hearing, and that troubled Beth greatly. She understood that the loss of his first wife had upset Malcolm greatly, as it should have, and altered his life in rather permanent ways, but to give up on their dreams? To almost ignore his children? Surely there was a better way.

She may not be able to reach Malcolm this early in their relationship, but she could certainly reach the children.

Beth smiled up at Mrs. Rawlins. "Tell the children and Mrs. Franklin to come to the terrace. We will continue lessons there, and I will join in."

Mrs. Rawlins nearly gaped, her eyes wide, but her lips quirked as if she would smile. "You, my lady?"

"Yes, I." She rose and dropped her shawl in the now-vacated chair, setting her hands on her hips as she turned to face the housekeeper again. "I was almost a governess, you know, before I married his lordship. I may not be skilled enough to be hired as such by an earl, but I most certainly know my way around a schoolroom." She looked out the window, then back with a wink. "Or a terrace, as it were."

Mrs. Rawlins laughed and left the room to relay the message to the children and nanny, and Beth paced her salon slowly, the last week of her life replaying in her mind.

London had been a whirl of events and changes for her, and there had been no time for her to catch her breath. After the wedding, Malcolm had taken her to the family home, introduced her to the staff, and left her to get herself situated, reminding her that they would be leaving for the country in two days.

He had left her alone for the whole day and the entire night.

She hadn't necessarily expected the sensational wedding night that one occasionally hears about, or even the one that one typically

61

hears about, but she had expected... *something.* When it became painfully obvious that her wedding night would be nothing more than the night after her wedding, she had felt herself changed. She had quite a lovely night's sleep, rose the next morning, dressed with the help of a maid for the first time in her entire life, and then become Lady Montgomery for the staff and for the world.

As yet, she had not become that woman for herself, but there was no reason for anyone else to know that. Mrs. Rawlins here at Knightsgate undoubtedly knew it, but she ought to be the only one.

The trip to Knightsgate had been uneventful, as the children and Mrs. Franklin had gone on ahead yet again. Malcolm had opted to ride his horse, giving her the excuse that he preferred the fresh air and activity to the stuffy and cramped quarters of a carriage. Beth hadn't argued the point, not that he would have listened anyway. She'd spent the ride to Knightsgate flitting between sleeping and scheming, wondering how to get her husband to at least behave like a husband.

She hadn't come up with any answers, but there was time. If she worked very hard at it, she might actually have a husband for a week or so before one of them left this world for the next.

There had been a bright moment when they had arrived at their estate when all the staff had come out to greet them. Malcolm had taken her hand and personally introduced her to every staff member, which had taken quite a long time. He had a rather extensive staff, but he had known every single one. He had smiled; he had laughed! His hand had been warm at her back, and he had looked truly pleased to have her as his wife, even a little proud of it.

Once they had entered the house, however, he had changed once more. His distance, while never cold or cruel, was a palpable feeling. All formality and politeness, but no joy or light. If only he were as pleased with his wife in private as he seemed to be for the public.

The house itself was a glorious place, and Beth was coming to adore every nook and cranny. She'd had to find her way for herself, as her husband's tour had not been nearly as impressive as his introductions. But with the comfortable and capable Mrs. Rawlins helping her along, she'd been able to feel more at home than she had anticipated.

It was a far grander house than any place she'd ever imagined herself living, but it also had the look of being a comfortable country cottage. There was nothing cottage-like about it aside from the appearance, but that was beside the point. Knightsgate had been built in the sixteenth century, with all the fine Elizabethan styles that came with the era.

Owing to poor finances over the next two hundred years, there had been no alterations or additions to make it seem grander. Certain parts of the house had been restructured for safety and modernized by necessity, but the overall charm remained perfectly intact.

There were many windows throughout the house, giving way for much natural light, and intricate carvings decorated many of the elegant oak panels and grand mahogany staircases within. There was a lovely gallery that she itched to explore in more depth, which had been added to by several former occupants of the house who bore artistic talent. She would not be so fortunate, as her skills lay in other areas, but she could certainly appreciate them for the masterpieces they were.

The bedrooms were all beautiful and in grand condition, with tapestries and carpets unlike any she had ever seen. There was a perfect balance of light and dark in the décor of the house, nothing seeming too masculine or too feminine, and even her rooms, situated comfortably in the west wing with the rest of the family, were perfect for her tastes. She wondered why her rooms did not adjoin her husband's, as surely would have been customary in their situation, but they were not far from his, so the point was probably moot anyway.

Her favorite part of the estate, above all else, was the grounds, which she had taken to wandering daily. While not as extensive as one might have expected for a house of this size, they seemed rather perfect to her. There were woods and hills and streams, and even a glorious ravine that gave one a spectacular view of the surrounding areas. The gardens were pristine, and the gardener well-compensated for his efforts, as he ought to have been. It was an enclosed garden, which only added to the romanticism, as the crumbling rock of the walls seemed more part of the garden than any sort of boundary.

Truly, Knightsgate was a lovely place, nestled snugly in the beauty of Hampshire, with the same warmth and invitation one could feel from the county's landscape itself. Pity that the warmth it portrayed in timber, trestle, and tone did not touch its thorny master.

But Beth would fix that. She could make things better, she was sure of it. Surely it would not always be like this. She bit her lip suddenly, wondering if that could possibly be true. What could she do?

She heard a noise on the terrace and turned to see the children and Mrs. Franklin settling down to resume their lessons. While Archer and Jane were not smiling, the younger two were delighted with being out of doors.

Well, she could certainly start with some lessons, and see where that got her. And then, perhaps, a few games.

Laughter was not a sound that Lord Montgomery had heard in some time. He recognized that he was partially to blame, as he rarely felt the inclination to laugh or be playful these days. One could hardly expect the children to feel the same exuberance they felt when their mother was alive. Once upon a time, he had been a cheerful and teasing father, the sort to run around with them and make mischief and have his wife scold him as much as the children. Now, he had to be both mother and father to them, and the weight of that burden was too much to bear for play.

He knew it was not the sort of life children should lead. They ought to see their father smile and laugh, and ought to feel permitted to smile and laugh themselves. He'd seen the changes in Jane and Archer, and the guilt he felt for their change unmanned him every time he looked into their somber faces. If it weren't for his youngest two children, who had yet to adopt the more serious mannerisms of their older siblings, they might have been completely without joy or light.

But he heard laughter this morning, and it drew him out of the private refuge of his study to investigate.

Out on the terrace, Mrs. Franklin sat with the children, all of whom were fixed with rapt attention on something he could not see off to one side.

He frowned a little. It was odd to have them outside this time of day, but he didn't mind it. With the weather in England being what it was, one must take advantage of the fine days to properly appreciate them.

He did wonder at Mrs. Franklin sitting *with* the children instead of instructing them. She was not a governess, merely a nanny, but he hadn't had the patience for attempting to hire a governess. Their last one had departed shortly after Caroline's death when the children had been unruly and uncooperative for a time. The governess had been sympathetic, but she'd refused to continue her work under those conditions.

Malcolm could not blame her for that, but he had not known what to do about it, either, so he had left well enough alone and charged Mrs. Franklin, who had the patience of a saint, with the care and education of his children until a better situation could be found.

He moved to the other side of the room to see what they all stared at, and he stopped when it came into view.

Beth was in the middle of a recitation of some kind, looking like the countess she was by appearances, but not at all by her composure. She was fully engaged in what she was saying, using her expressive hands to great effect and gazing at each of the children in turn.

He watched her for a long moment, as captivated as the others. He'd been a poor excuse for a husband since their marriage, albeit a rather typical one by Society's standards. He'd left her to her own devices while going about his own business, choosing to spend as little time with her as possible for his own sake.

Ever since bringing her to Knightsgate, he felt as though he had made a gross error in judgment by marrying her. Not because of her or her situation, but because he might not have been prepared for it. He still considered Beth to be a remarkable woman and an excellent choice for a wife, but he was not ready for a wife. Not yet. It was too soon; it had all happened too fast.

Admiring Beth made him feel guilty, as she was a beautiful woman, and the effects of her appearance seemed like infidelity to him. Thinking constantly about Caroline also made him feel guilty, as he was married to Beth but still yearned for Caroline.

There was nothing but guilt for him here, and it was a suffocating feeling.

He couldn't think of duties or responsibilities regarding his new wife; in fact, he could barely manage to think of Beth as his wife. He had spent the last three days revisiting matters of his estate and seeing the tenants about whom his estate manager had informed him. It was good to see to the details that defined his life at Knightsbridge. The reminder of life as he had once known it gave him focus and purpose, though it did not take his mind away from what he could be doing in London.

He could not be distracted from thoughts of the work they had to do, the dangers they needed to mind, the investigations that were underway to prevent disaster... There, he never felt guilt. There, he could accomplish much without feeling something was lacking.

There, he was truly himself.

Everywhere else, he hadn't the faintest clue who he was.

Malcolm looked at Beth again, noticed how the sun seemed to highlight every pleasurable aspect of her from her golden hair to her perfectly sculpted cheekbones, and caught himself in a sigh, the sound jerking him from his reverie.

He didn't dare interpret that sigh, or what had prompted it. The answer might have been far too dangerous. He moved out to the terrace, setting his features and grinding his teeth, making up his mind on the spot about his situation.

Beth's eyes danced with a magical light as she continued with her recitation, more of an actress than he would have expected, and not yet noticing him.

" 'We few, we happy few, we band of brothers;' " she said, her voice taking on an emotional quality that stirred him. " 'For he to-day that sheds his blood with me shall be my brother; be he ne'er so vile, this day shall gentle his condition: and gentlemen in England now a-bed shall think themselves accursed they were not here...' "

Her voice rose, and she suddenly looked powerful, regal, and he could easily imagine her actually leading King Henry's men into battle like this.

" 'And hold their manhoods cheap,' " she continued, her right hand forming a fist, " 'whiles any speaks that fought with us upon

Saint Crispin's day.'"

No one spoke as her words hung in the air, and even Malcolm couldn't find it within himself to break the silence. He'd read the words so many times, listened to the speech given numerous ways by talented actors, and it never failed to stir him. But hearing the powerful words from Beth's lips… that had been something different entirely.

"What happened then?" Archer asked, breaking the still of the moment. "Did they charge off into battle?"

Malcolm looked at his oldest, now wide-eyed and staring at his stepmother without any of the shadows that had so recently troubled his young face.

If Beth were surprised by the sudden outburst, she gave no indication. She merely smiled rather slyly at him and transformed back into herself in an instant. "That is a revelation for another day, my Lord Talbot."

The other children laughed at the playful usage of Archer's title, which was rarely heard, given the formality of it all, and Archer scowled a little. "But I want to know what happened!"

Beth caught sight of Malcolm then, leaning against the wall where he was, and smiled. "Well, if you complete your lessons for the rest of the week and behave very well, I will tell you the rest at the end of it."

Samuel and Archer cheered while the girls clapped. Mrs. Franklin beamed at Beth as though she were a godsend and shooed the children up. "Shall we go for a walk, children?"

"Not too far," Malcolm broke in, stepping forward. "There is some flooding near the stream, so keep near the house."

They all nodded and started to move in that direction. Suddenly, six-year-old Jane darted over to him. "Papa," she whispered as best as she could, which was still rather audible for anyone in the vicinity.

He crouched down to her level and met her cornflower blue eyes seriously. "Yes, Jane?"

She glanced over her shoulder at Beth, who watched the interchange with interest but kept her distance. Jane looked back at him, confusion evident on her features.

"How do we address her?"

Malcolm reared back a little, ashamed that she'd had to ask the question, as it spoke to the poor manner in which he had handled the entire situation. Worst of all, he did not have an answer for her.

He could hardly tell his daughter to call her 'Mother', as Beth was not her mother, and 'Mama' was out of the question, as that title belonged to Caroline.

How had he never thought of this before?

Bewildered and lost, he looked to Beth, still watching them. She smiled and mouthed "Beth" with a nod.

He returned her nod and looked back to his daughter, rubbing her arms gently. "For now, you may call her Beth."

"Miss Beth?" she asked, tilting her head in question, her dark hair swishing against his hand.

"Just... Beth," he told her with what he hoped was a convincing smile.

Jane nodded and whirled out of his hold, looking up at Beth as she passed. "Thank you for the lesson, Beth."

Beth smiled and ran a hand along his daughter's hair. "You are most welcome, Jane. Hurry on with the others now, we can talk more later."

Off skipped his daughter to find her siblings and nanny, leaving the adults alone on the terrace.

Malcolm rose, clearing his throat awkwardly. "I am so sorry about that," he told her, edging hesitantly over to her. "I didn't think..."

"It's all right," Beth said with a shake of her head. "This is not an easy situation, and there is much to consider. The children may call me Beth for as long as they like, and we'll see if anything else sticks."

He gave her an assessing look, impressed despite his intention to keep his distance. "That is very good of you. Why are you so understanding?"

She quirked a brow at him and leaned against the balustrade near her. "Should I be difficult?"

He frowned a little. "Elizabeth, are you in the habit of being biddable and self-sacrificing?"

"Of course, I am," she scoffed, not taking any hint of offense at his words or his tone. "I am the youngest in a large family, and I learned from everyone else's mistakes. Do you know how much relief it brought my parents to have a child that did exactly as she was told without argument?"

He didn't doubt it and would be lying if he said he had not wished his own children would do exactly as she had said, but he didn't want her to be biddable and self-sacrificing.

What he did want was much less clear.

"Hmm." He shook his head, unwilling to further that conversation, fearing where it might go. He glanced around at the terrace. "They moved their lessons outside?"

Beth stood straight and nodded, smiling again. "It was such a fine day, I didn't have the heart to refuse them when they asked." Her tone was apologetic, even if her expression was not.

"I don't mind," he told her with a quick wave of his hand. "But… Shakespeare?"

She shrugged, tilting her head back and closing her eyes as the sun hit her face more fully. "Mrs. Franklin was trying to have a history lesson, and I thought I might help."

"But *Shakespeare?*" he asked again, looking away to avoid looking at her for far too long.

Beth gave a low chuckle which plucked a string deep within his tightly closed chest. "I couldn't think of another way to make history come alive, could you?"

No, he couldn't, but Shakespeare on the terrace for his children seemed… quite something.

"And this terrace was a perfect stage," she continued, lifting her head to look around. "I may have to do more lessons out here."

Malcolm turned to face her, setting his features firmly in his practiced careful consideration. "Well, you don't need to concern yourself with lessons, you know. A governess would do very well for them. You can take care of hiring one while I am gone."

Startled, Beth looked at him in surprise, her brow furrowing slightly. "Gone? Where are you going?"

"Back to London," he said stiffly, keeping his gaze fixed over her head. "I have duties to see to there. I really am gone quite a lot. Didn't I explain that?"

"Yes," Beth answered, the single word slow and drawn out. "But I didn't think... That is, it is rather..."

Malcolm let his gaze flick down to hers and waited, not sure if he wanted her to protest or not. All he knew was that her reaction would be important for some reason.

She stared back at him, her expression unreadable. Then she dipped her chin in a nod and swallowed hard. "I understand. Of course, you must go."

To his utter amazement, he felt disappointed by her answer, though it should have delighted him. A wife who let him have his way and would expect nothing of him? It was perfect for a man who wished to keep his distance.

But somehow, it wasn't.

"How long will you be gone?" Beth asked, smiling again, though the smile was different, forced.

He attempted a careless shrug. "A couple of weeks, probably. Perhaps a month."

Beth's dark eyes widened, and she clamped down on her lips.

Say it, he prodded in his mind. *Say anything.*

But Beth only nodded, her jaw relaxed, and she smiled again serenely. "Very well. When will you go?"

"Directly," he heard himself say.

Again, Beth nodded absently, as if unaware of it. "Well, the children will certainly miss you."

"They are used to it."

He would have given a great amount of money to know what thoughts were swirling in Beth's mind as she stared back at him, her eyes almost vacant, her smile fixed, and whatever had made Beth special was gone.

"Is there anything I need to do in your absence?" she asked, her tone bright but false.

The sooner Malcolm could end this conversation, the better. It was getting more awkward by the second, and the only escape for him would be to leave Knightsgate entirely. *Now.* As quickly as he could.

He shook his head and stepped back, speaking in clipped tones. "No, I don't think so. Mr. Russell will inform you if there is anything to do, but he will write me directly if he needs anything."

"And if *I* need anything?" she asked in a sharper tone than he'd ever heard from her, though it was still far too sweet.

Malcolm bowed carefully. "I am at your service, as always."

Beth looked amused and nodded slowly. "And I at yours, husband," she replied, sounding more natural, though the words did not settle well on him. She looked in the window towards her salon, then back to him. "If you will excuse me, Monty, I have some notes to finish for our wedding guests." She curtseyed, and then swept away without any hint of airs or superiority, leaving him rather speechless on the terrace.

Well, he supposed he could leave now, as no one seemed to need him here. And he would leave, just as he'd planned.

Just as soon as he figured out why he was upset.

Chapter Seven

"What the hell are you doing here, Cap?"

Malcolm looked up from his desk to see all three of his comrades staring at him with varying degrees of horror. It would have been comical, except that he noticed the severity in their gazes.

It was for this reason that he had avoided seeing any of them since his arrival last week. Given his seniority, he had more freedom to work where he pleased, and he had spent most of his time at his second house in London. It seemed excessive if he thought about it for too long, but when he was in London as Cap, not as Lord Montgomery, it proved quite useful. Fritz had been a frequent visitor, with orders from Tailor and Eagle on various topics, and his reports from the others in the League had been delivered as usual, having informed his regular contact of his presence.

Only having to alert one person that he was in London was rather convenient… until everyone else found out, and then things got messy.

He kept his expression composed as ever and raised a brow. "I'm doing what I come here to do, of course. Which is more than I can say for the three of you, if my reports are to be believed."

His words had almost no effect on them, and they continued to stare.

Malcolm sighed and sat back in his chair. "Rogue, what's this I hear about one of ours following you to monitor your activities? Are you questioning your own judgment now?"

Rogue's brow furrowed a little, but he did not react, which was surprising, as Rogue's temper was usually shorter than his hair.

"Fine representatives of the Crown's covert operatives you are," Malcolm muttered, going back to his work.

"You see that?" Rook said to the others, sounding mildly impressed. "Skillful misdirect."

"It serves him well," Rogue grunted. "Makes him a genius with interrogation."

"I'd like to see him interrogate," Rook commented, folding his arms nonchalantly. "I've heard tales."

"The real thing is much better than the stories," Gent said, leaning against the doorframe, not taking his dark eyes off Malcolm.

Malcolm snorted and pretended to shuffle papers. "I hate you all."

"That seems rather harsh," Gent remarked blandly to the others.

"Indeed," Rogue agreed. "Hardly polite."

"I'd wager he thinks those words often," Rook mused thoughtfully.

Gent hummed a little. "Yes, but to say them out loud?"

"I say them all the time." Rogue shrugged. "But then, I'm not Cap."

"There really are very important things you all could be doing," Malcolm informed them without looking up.

"At what stage do you think it would be important to point out to our fearless leader that he should be at home with his new wife?" Rook asked his colleagues. "Though no doubt with his skillful misdirection, he probably won't answer straightly anyway."

The mention of Beth made Malcolm stiffen slightly, and he focused with more determination on his reports.

"No, he would not," Rogue sighed, which was something Rogue never did unless he was taunting. "But he really should consider his new wife."

"He really should," Rook agreed mildly. "She is quite a beautiful woman."

"Mmm. Remarkably attractive."

Malcolm wondered what the Shopkeepers would think of him killing his own operatives. Surely his reasons would have been sound enough, and they were always encouraging him to consider younger candidates for positions.

"I told him," Gent said suddenly, throwing his hat into this ridiculous ring, "that if I were not already married and madly in love with my wife, I would have liked the new Lady Montgomery for myself."

"I am not married," Rook pointed out rather unnecessarily. "And I would have happily pursued her, and she would be Mrs. Pratt by now, and I would not be here if she were, loyalty to the Crown or not."

Malcolm gripped his pen tightly and paused a fraction of a second as he made notes. Other than that, he made absolutely no response to their banter. An incredulous scoffing sound met his ears, and he fought against the curiosity to look up at Rook.

"Did you see that, Rogue? He didn't even blink. He should be coming at me in a rage for saying anything of the sort about his wife, and he is simply sitting there."

"If you'd said anything like that about my wife," Gent told him in his usual offhand manner, "I would have my hands around your throat."

"I'd just gut you," Rogue grunted, which was Rogue's usual way, as well.

Rook hummed a little. "And you would be well within your rights there. I would expect no less. But this…?"

There was silence again, and this time Malcolm could not ignore the urge to look up.

Now his colleagues were not horrorstruck, they were speculative.

He could not do this. He would not discuss Beth or his marriage, he would not crack open what remained of his heart to let them see the chaos within, nor would he let them have a hint of that which absorbed his mind constantly these days.

He couldn't talk about Beth. He couldn't even pretend he could talk about Beth, because she was always swirling about in his thoughts. Where she was, what she was doing, how she was getting on at Knightsgate and with the children.

If she missed him…

He couldn't guarantee what would come out of his mouth if he spoke of her. He didn't know what he felt about her. He didn't know what to do about her. He didn't know anything at all. He was afraid to consider anything.

It was the only reason he could be composed during banter about his wife, something that really should have angered him, and might have done on a different day or in a month or in ten years. But right now, he couldn't even comprehend that Beth was his wife. She was simply the woman he had married. And in his heart, he still felt bound to Caroline, so most of the time, he couldn't even admit that he was married to Beth.

But he couldn't tell them that.

"Report in or go away," he barked at the others with a severe look. "Now."

One by one they gave him their reports, which were as he expected. Rogue was having someone tail him to make sure he wasn't being tailed. This added a measure of additional security, which was wise, considering the fear that he might be compromised. Things were only getting worse there, what with Mr. Herschel appearing to be everywhere Rogue was. Then finding ties between his personal assets and those of a known French sympathizer complicated things even more. Rogue was getting edgy, and Malcolm couldn't blame him, given what had happened to Trace.

Malcolm himself wasn't particularly comfortable with it.

They'd investigated all avenues related to Trace, every one they could possibly think of, and Malcolm was still personally investigating most of them again. He refused to accept that one of their operatives could have missed something significant enough to lead to his death, that they as a group could have been so ignorant where they ought to have been flawless. He'd never lost the weight of that guilt, and even Caroline, before she died, had not been able to talk him out of it or remove the burden.

They would need to keep a close watch on this before things got out of hand.

The smugglers he'd spent so much time with, on the other hand, were behaving just as they usually did; giving no information and acting as slippery as usual. Naturally, they denied all wrongdoing while hiding from anything resembling legitimacy. But the guns were still moving, and it was not clear where they were going, which was what Malcolm was looking into.

Gent's traitors were starting to act out again; more meetings in diverse places, and they were back to tracking finances, which made Gent irritable. But since no one was scheming to take his beloved wife for her money, he was manageable. There was no clear leader, but Gent was working on it, as well as looking into a way to get a clearer insight into their plans, which was proving complicated.

Rook flitted around London collecting details, then took up more time interacting with some tradesmen, and even he had some details to report. There had been whisperings about the current French state in the upper circles. The tradesmen, who had been oddly quick to take to Rook, had nothing suspicious to report, but Rook had a feeling all the same. Being a believer in instinct, Malcolm let him go with it.

Their reports finished, they left him in peace, and he worked through his information for several hours, including the reports from his informants on the groups involved and details surrounding the night Trace was killed. Then he read the most recent reports on a certain young woman in Cheshire, who had no idea that the London League kept a close watch on her and ensured she was well cared for.

If he didn't get all this straightened out, he would be taking on covert operations within the week, as well. He hadn't done that in years. Not since he became a father, come to think of it.

"You're worrying the 'children', Cap."

Malcolm jerked up at the words, panic taking hold of his heart. "I'm what?"

Fritz lifted a brow as he leaned against the wall inside Malcolm's office, somehow having entered without him knowing. "Do you normally react that way when I talk about your operatives?"

"My operatives?" he repeated, his heart still skipping in panic.

His friend looked confused for a second, then smiled as understanding dawned. "Yes, your operatives. That was a terrible reference. The actual children are fine."

Malcolm's heart settled, and he glared at Fritz. "You can't know that."

"Perhaps your children write to me. I am Archer's godfather, after all."

Malcolm snorted, shaking his head. "Archer would never write you without someone prodding him."

"Do you think it's possible that perhaps someone did?"

Malcolm paused, his incredulity fading into complete bafflement. "You… you *did* receive a letter?"

Fritz nodded, smiling a little. "I did. With a very kind postscript from your wife inviting Emily and me to Knightsgate, at our convenience, to better make our acquaintance."

Malcolm sat back hard in his chair, completely at a loss. "Archer would never do that willingly. He hates writing anybody, even me. But he also wouldn't do it unless someone he respected asked him." He looked up at his friend, his mind whirling rapidly. "Beth could get him to do this?"

"Beth *did*," Fritz pointed out. "Have you received letters?"

"I don't know," he admitted. "I didn't tell Clifton I was home, I've been staying at St. James. He usually holds correspondence for me."

"I think you'd better check." Fritz pushed into the room and sat down in the chair across from the desk. "So yes, I know the children are fine. But let's talk about your operatives."

Malcolm made a soft noise of amusement. "Yes, my operatives. Which one sent you a report of concern?" he asked, folding his hands and regarding his friend with steely eyes.

Fritz chuckled softly and tilted his head a little. "All of them."

Malcolm scowled and went back to his reports, though he had done all that he could there. "I knew I should have stayed away from here."

"I've avoided asking you all week," Fritz began slowly, "but really, Monty, what are you doing here? Nothing is happening that cannot be dealt with from Knightsgate. I would be happy to step in here."

"You can't do that," Malcolm told him in a low voice. "You're already exposed as a former operative, and you're a diplomat now. It's too much of a risk for you."

Fritz's features hardened and grew serious. "I've been a covert operative in more dangerous situations than even you know about, Monty, and in circumstances where I was also a very visible diplomat, and I am still standing here. I am the second-in-command to the spymaster of all England while still being a visible diplomat to several countries, including the one with rogue factions that concern us. I can handle your London band of merry men."

That was all true, and Malcolm felt like a heel for thinking that Fritz could not do the things that he had been trained to do, and had done, with such success. It was easy to assume that because Fritz was visible, he was somehow unfit for the covert world.

Nothing could have been further from the truth.

"Would you rather be here?" Fritz prodded without much care. "Is that it?"

Malcolm chewed on his lip for a second, weighing his options. Then he sighed. "Honestly, yes."

Fritz barked a surprised laugh. "Why? Beth is lovely, and you chose to marry her…"

"I married her for the children, not for me," Malcolm admitted, looking up at the ceiling. "If it had been up to me, I wouldn't have married for a number of years, if ever."

"Ah ha…" Fritz hummed a little, then exhaled noisily. "I can't say anything against your thoughts on that score. I imagine moving on from Caroline must be nigh impossible."

"There is no moving on." Malcolm shook his head firmly. "There is no moving on, there is no replacing her, and there is no way I can do this without feeling like I have betrayed the vows I took."

"To Caroline or to Beth?" Fritz softly asked.

Malcolm looked at him with a humorless smile. "You see my dilemma." He sighed and rubbed at his brow. "Two wives, two vows, and I am two very different men. I engage in my second marriage; do I betray the first? I live in and mourn my first marriage; do I harm the second?" He shook his head and looked back up. "Beth is good for the children, Fritz. But not for me."

Fritz watched him for a long time, then nodded slowly. "Very well. Tailor wants to meet with you tonight."

Malcolm snapped to attention instantly, his whole body on alert. "Where?"

"Covent Garden. Go as Lord Montgomery. You're going to love it."

Malcolm groaned, wishing he were brave enough to argue with

his superiors. He hated the theater, always had, and the only time he ever went to the theater was when he had to meet with his superiors in a public setting, or when Caroline had exerted her will in the matter. She'd done that quite frequently.

He prayed Beth wouldn't do the same.

"What farce must I endure this time?" he asked Fritz, not bothering to hide his displeasure.

Fritz considered the question and made a face, tugging at his simple cravat. "A bit of humiliation, too much introspection, awkward commentaries, and things that will make you want to pull your hair out."

Malcolm gave him a baleful look. "I meant the play."

Fritz grinned and repeated, "A bit of humiliation, too much introspection, awkward commentaries, and things that will make you want to pull your hair out."

Malcolm rolled his eyes but smiled a little. "What am I seeing?"

"I have no idea."

Malcolm nodded. "Of course, you don't. Thank you very much, Fritz."

"Happy to help."

Briefly stopping at his family residence to don formal evening wear, Malcolm officially established that Lord Montgomery was, in fact, in London, despite his recent marriage. In order to create a legitimate reason for him to be in London instead of in Hampshire with his new bride and children, there were several things he could do. He'd settled on setting up a meeting with his solicitor, which would occur in the morning. None of it had taken long, as the details never did for him. Arrangements completed, Malcolm headed off to Covent Garden for his meeting.

Now, it was time for the theater. Unfortunately.

The theater was crowded when he arrived, but finding Lord Cartwright wouldn't be hard. His wife was always quite a toast, though not as popular as Lady Raeburn or any of the Rivertons.

Wherever she was, he was, lurking and smirking. He never let her too far out of his sight. The residue of a life in covert operations, according to him, and he wasn't inclined to set aside so many years of surviving by his instincts.

A note had been sent to Malcolm an hour ago to come to the Cartwrights' box during the intermission, which unfortunately meant he could not leave before then. He braced himself to endure an entire first half of the accursed production.

What sort of man came to the theater alone? Particularly when those who knew him would already be wondering why he wasn't with his new wife?

No matter. Malcolm could spin any story he wanted and make it work. Perhaps he had business with his solicitor, and his wife wanted him to see this show and tell her about it. Perhaps his marriage was one of convenience only. Perhaps his business was unpleasant, and a night at the theater would relieve him of that burden for a time.

He couldn't imagine any night at any theater helping with that in any way, but the world didn't need to know that.

Malcolm settled himself in his solitary seat, taking a private box. He wouldn't have objected if any of his friends had asked to join, but he doubted any of his friends were in attendance tonight. Most of them agreed with him, but that was beside the point.

Thirty seconds later, a footman appeared beside him. "I beg your pardon, my lord," the young man said softly. The orchestra had thankfully ceased its infernal cacophony, signaling the start of the show. "A couple is asking if you will permit them to join you in the box."

He fought the urge to sigh. "Who is it?"

"Mr. Richard and Lady Lavinia Herschel, my lord."

Malcolm closed his eyes and exhaled slowly. He could not risk offending Mr. Herschel, for he was too powerful in Parliament. It would behoove him to keep the man close, given his recent suspicious activity. He would have to endure Lady Lavinia for the sake of her husband.

"Very well," he said with a curt nod.

The footman bowed and left quickly.

"Lord help me," Malcolm muttered, rising to his feet.

Lady Lavinia preceded her husband, her gown a brilliant red with a daring cut in the neckline that left very little to the imagination, and her dark hair provocatively styled with long, curling tendrils hanging over her bare shoulders.

"Monty," she purred, coming directly to him and sliding her hands along the lapels of his evening jacket, fluttering her kohl-lined eyelashes. "You are too gracious."

He stepped back and took one hand, bowing over it. "My lady." He stepped aside as Mr. Herschel entered and bowed to him. "Mr. Herschel."

"Montgomery," Mr. Herschel puffed, nodding repeatedly. "Rather sporting of you. My wife does so love the theater, and this box does have a better view than the one I reserved. I care nothing for the theater myself, far too much dramatics, but…" He tried to wink at his wife with a guffawing laugh. "Anything for the missus, am I right?"

Malcolm nodded in polite acknowledgement and gestured to the seats.

He waited until they were seated and then deliberately sat in the row behind them. He wouldn't mind sharing the box, so long as he could be separated from them.

The performances began, and he pretended at interest, nodding when the others did, smiling when others laughed, that sort of thing. It was mindless and boring, but he only had to get to the intermission.

Lady Lavinia rose a few minutes into the show and excused herself, making sure to brush against Malcolm as she exited, the heavy scent of her perfume nearly choking him with its potency. She must have heard he was in London, as he'd been told she only wore it when she was going to see him. He had known that sharing his box had been no coincidence, but he could hardly have expected her to maneuver so specifically for him.

When he felt her sit down next to him upon her return, he corrected himself. She *would* maneuver exactly that specifically for him.

"Why didn't you tell me you were in London, Monty?" she whispered with a pout. "I would have come to you."

Malcolm kept his gaze firmly fixed on the stage. "I am in town but a short time, my lady. I told no one I was coming."

"*I* should have been told."

"My lady, I have said before…"

She suddenly put a hand on his thigh and gripped hard. "How long will you deny the connection between us, Monty?" she hissed.

He pried her hand loose and returned it firmly to her lap. "My lady, I must protest! Such behavior is highly inappropriate."

"I could be more inappropriate," she purred, turning to press herself up against his arm. "I would be so very inappropriate for you, Monty."

Malcolm shuddered and angled his chair a little away. "My lady, please…"

"Say that again."

"Your husband is but three feet away!"

"The old fool can't hear us."

"People might see us!"

"I don't care."

"I insist that you behave with decorum, madam, and act in a manner befitting both our stations," Malcolm hissed fiercely. Confound her blasted husband, he thought. The man must be deaf as a post!

Lady Lavinia glared at him and turned her body, and her attention, back to the stage. She breathed more heavily than was necessary, attempting to draw more attention to certain personal assets she chose to display rather prominently. "I want you, Monty. And so help me, I will have you."

"I am married, madam."

"And I will make you want me more than that milksop wife of yours."

Monty clenched his teeth and purposely looked away, casting his eyes around to see if anyone was witnessing the woman's scandalous behavior. Thankfully, no one was. "Have a care when speaking of my wife, Lady Lavinia."

"Have I offended you, Monty? How delicious!" she purred. She reached over and slid her hand down his thigh, then drummed her fingers there before moving her hand back to her own lap.

Malcolm felt his skin crawl and shifted away from her as much as he could, given the limited space in the box. She sat silently beside him for the rest of the act, though she bore a smirk and continued to attempt to draw Malcolm's attention. Her husband sat in front of them, as ignorant of her behavior as ever.

The moment the act ended, Malcolm excused himself and fled for Lord Cartwright's box a short way down the gallery. He didn't wait to be announced as he brushed past the footman and snapped off a quick bow. "Please let me stay here with you for the second act, if I must remain, or let me leave altogether if you do not truly need me!"

Lord Cartwright turned and took in the younger man's distressed face with a benign smile. "Greetings, Monty." He looked at his wife. "Darling, what do you think?"

Lady Cartwright considered Malcolm with her clear eyes and smirked. "So long as Monty explains what in heaven's name he is doing in London so soon after his wedding, he may do as he pleases, I think." She glanced back at her husband and winked. "But you are his superior, my dear, so it is entirely up to you."

Cartwright nodded and observed Malcolm, the lines on his face belying the brilliant mind and limitless energy he still possessed. "Do as you please, Monty. We have business to attend to." He waved him into a seat.

Malcolm took it, greatly relieved, then tilted his head toward Lady Cartwright with surprise.

She waved her hand dismissively. "I am not listening, and I wouldn't understand even if I were."

He doubted that and suspected that Lady Cartwright had her own covert interests, but that was a discussion for another day. He turned to one of the most powerful men in England and inclined his head slightly.

"What can I do for you, my lord?"

Cartwright's mouth quirked a little. "First things first… What the hell are you doing in London right now?"

Chapter Eight

"*But* will I have wings if I become a fairy?" Greer wondered.

"Of course," Jane declared matter-of-factly. "A proper fairy must have wings."

"What color will they be?"

"What color would you like them to be?" Beth asked.

"Pink!"

"No, Greer, I want blue!"

Beth laid her head back on the grass, smiling up at the clouds. "Girls, you can choose the colors of your wings, I promise."

"Really, Bitsy?" Jane asked, lifting her head and looking rather suspicious. "Any color?"

Beth looked back at her stepdaughter, smiling at the nickname she had earned the other day through a rather entertaining game of make-believe. "Any color. Gold? Green? Gold and green?"

Jane shook her head. "No. Blue." She laid her head back down, the daisy crown sliding a little on her dark hair.

Greer, on the other hand, was lying on the grass with her eyes fiercely screwed up as she anticipated her fairy transition. Her flower crown was perfectly placed, and her dark golden curls were already tangling with the stems.

But they were out of the house, finished with the day's lessons, and the girls were playing with Beth. This was heaven!

The past two weeks without Malcolm had been surprisingly pleasant, despite the strain of her newfound responsibilities. Thanks to the diligence of the estate manager, Beth had managed to find the balance between duties of the countess and management of the house, as well as taking plenty of time for the children. Mrs. Rawlins had been her mentor in the house and staff, and it was easy to find her footing under such tutelage.

Mrs. Franklin had helped her to understand the natures of each of the children, and between the pair of them, they had coaxed Archer and Jane out of their solemn shells. Jane was now as talkative as Greer, and Archer had laughed more in the past three days than he had in the last three years, according to Mrs. Franklin.

Beth finally felt as though she had found her place in the family. They all called her Bitsy now, and she loved every utterance of it. The gleeful cry of 'Bitsy' was better than she had ever imagined 'Mama' sounding, and it made her heart swell.

This part of her life was perfect. If only her husband were around to see it... or to see her... or his children. Or to do anything at all!

She might as well have been the governess for all the interaction she had with him. If anyone had asked her how she enjoyed being married, she would have answered, "I really wouldn't know, but I've heard it's lovely."

But no one was asking. She was Lady Montgomery, but without Lord Montgomery, what did that actually mean? She could not introduce herself to the neighbors, even if it was proper enough to do so with the tenants. She didn't know her husband well enough to say anything about him. She knew that his children hung somewhere between fear and adoration of him, as evidenced by her attempts to get them to write him letters the week before. They'd done it, but it had been a struggle.

These children might not have a mother, according to Malcolm, but according to Beth, they also hadn't much of a father. But no one was asking that, either.

"Why is it that I find you sprawled on the grass becoming a fairy more often than not?"

Beth laughed and opened her eyes to look up at her friend, and now neighbor. "Because I am determined to become a fairy."

Lily grinned and held out a hand. "I want a walk. Come with me?"

Beth took it and rose, then turned to the girls. "You two keep working at it and listen to Mrs. Franklin. She's just over there."

"Yes, Bitsy," they both said, still focused on their transformation.

She nodded and linked arms with Lily, moving away from the transformation site.

"You seem to be getting on well with the girls," Lily told her with a smile.

Beth exhaled noisily. "Not for want of effort. Jane was so shy and formal with me. Greer was easy."

"Ah, but Greer turns four next month."

"Exactly."

Lily chuckled and turned a little to face her more fully. "What about the boys?"

"Well," Beth said on a sigh, "I must reenact the Battle of Agincourt with them later, for the fourth time in a week, if that tells you anything."

"On which side are you?" Lily asked, still laughing.

"Naturally, I'm the French," Beth assured her with a firm nod. "And I die quite a glorious death every time."

"I am sure you do." Lily rubbed her hand soothingly. "How is it going? Really."

Lily and her husband had returned to their home at Rainford Park shortly after Monty had left for London, and she had become Beth's chief confidante. She had seen Beth struggle to settle into her life during the past fortnight, trying to learn how to manage the children in their father's absence when she hardly knew them.

But there were things that Lily didn't know, things she hadn't seen, and questions Beth hadn't asked.

She didn't know if she wanted to ask them.

"The children are wonderful," Beth finally said, pulling off her flower crown to pick at it. "I adore them, and they are finally opening up to me. Well, Archer is confiding in me, and he is afraid to attend Eton. We'll address that later when Monty returns... if he returns."

"He'll return," Lily broke in. "Don't worry there."

Beth ignored that. "Then, there's Jane. She is wonderful with play time, she calls me Bitsy..."

"Bitsy?" Lily laughed in surprise. "Why?"

"I suggested it as my fairy name last week," Beth told her, rolling her eyes. "It was Michael's pet name for me as a child. Jane loved it and started using it all the time, and now the others do, too."

"That is absolutely adorable!"

Beth grinned and sighed, looking around at the grounds they walked, loving the beauty she so enjoyed. "It is. She is. But I'm a playmate for her, Lily. Not an older sister, not the woman her father married, not…"

"Her mother?" Lily prodded.

"I'm *not* her mother," Beth reminded her softly.

"No, but you are all she has." Lily sighed and folded her wrap around her more closely. "Jane was very close with her mother. She looks just like Caroline, you know, except for the eyes. Caroline's eyes were dark, like Greer's and Archer's."

Beth nodded. "I've seen the portrait. She was a beautiful woman."

Lily suddenly smiled a sad, but fond smile. "She was. She was also unfailingly kind, generous, full of wit, lively…"

"It's a good thing I'm not at all insecure about filling her place," Beth muttered dryly, tucking a strand of hair behind her ear.

"Oh, please." Lily snorted, tugging Beth against her side. "Caroline would scold you for even thinking that. She would want you to be your own person, not try to imitate her. I should know. I was her favorite cousin."

Beth looked at her speculatively. "What about your sisters?"

Lily made a face. "She liked Rosalind well enough. She could barely tolerate Emma and Eloise. I was her favorite, she told me repeatedly."

"I may consult with Rosalind about that," Beth teased, plucking at the petals on her crown.

"My sister has enough on her plate, dodging the attentions of Captain Riverton when she really ought to be accepting them with open arms." Lily shook her head, still smiling. "But that's not the point."

"Oh? Do enlighten me, Lily. What is the point?" Beth asked, tilting her head back to enjoy the sun.

"The point is… Caroline would have liked you."

Beth jerked in surprise and nearly tore a hole in her green muslin gown. "What did you say?"

Lily smiled, her dark eyes crinkling slightly. "She would have liked you a great deal. And I think, if she'd had a say in the matter, she would have wanted Monty to marry someone exactly like you."

Beth considered her friend's kind words but wasn't sure she believed them. What woman would contemplate whom her husband ought to marry next unless she knew that she was dying? From what Beth had been told, Caroline's death had been unexpected, so she had difficulty imagining her thinking about that.

"She would have wanted Monty to move on," Lily murmured, reading Beth's thoughts. "Caroline knew him so well. They had been planning to marry for years before they actually got around to it. Then Monty inherited, so they actually *could* marry... But they were friends before anything else. She was always very proud of that."

"She ought to have been." Really, Beth thought, it was a rare ideal for the world in which they lived. Monty and Caroline had enjoyed a marriage of romance and affection, the sort of match every young woman dreams of. To be friends first and to find love as well? It was a staggering thought, and one that Beth had not had for several years.

It was simply too far-fetched for an adult to truly comprehend.

And it made Beth feel even worse about her own marriage.

"Caroline once told me," Lily prattled on, "that it was the only way to truly have a marriage. To be friends first. To honestly and genuinely like the person that you marry, aside from all the love and romance and other details. Because if you don't, she said, 'when the fights come, and they will, how will you remember that you love him when you don't even like him?'" Lily shook her head and sighed. "I wish I had listened to her."

Beth put her arm around Lily and pulled her closer. "You didn't have a choice, Lily."

"But you did," Lily pointed out, smiling at Beth despite the shadows in her eyes.

"Please, don't question my marriage as my parents did at our wedding," Beth groaned. "It was the closest Monty has ever come to actually treating me like his wife."

"I wasn't going to." Lily pulled her friend to a stop and gave her a serious look. "I am relieved that you married him. I think you are exactly what he needs, and I think Caroline would think so, too."

"Well, we can't very well ask her, now, can we?" Beth snapped defensively, looking away and folding her arms in agitation.

Lily cocked her head, smiling mysteriously. "Actually..."

Before Beth could ask anything, Lily took her arm and pulled her away, fairly trotting towards the front of the house and the lane towards the Knightsgate chapel.

"I'm fairly certain I cannot pray to Caroline for insight," Beth told Lily, panting a little with their rapid pace.

Lily tossed a scolding look over her shoulder. "That wasn't what I had in mind."

The chapel was in sight now, and Beth smiled at it fondly. It was a quiet church with glorious stained-glass windows. All their tenants attended, as well as a few of their neighbors. The children were not particularly fond of church services, but their clergyman helpfully understood the value of brevity in his remarks, despite his relative youth and enthusiasm for deity.

Lily pulled Beth behind the chapel into the cemetery. "I wanted to bring you here," Lily told her rather unnecessarily.

Beth swallowed hard, not sure how she felt about this unusual introduction.

Sure enough, Lily led her straight to a large headstone engraved with the name "Caroline Rose Colerain, Lady Montgomery" with the respective dates. Below it read, "Beloved wife, mother, and friend."

"I'm not sure I should be here," Beth whispered, her eyes fixed on the etching. "It seems wrong." She started to back away, shaking her head.

Lily grabbed her hand and held her steady. "This is exactly where you should be. Who better for you to talk to than Caroline?"

"Do you think she can hear me?" Beth asked, looking at her friend.

"I think she would love to hear about her family," Lily assured her, smiling at the headstone as if it were Caroline herself. "Where better to do so than here?"

That was something to consider, Beth supposed. Here lay the woman who still owned her husband's heart. Caroline had brought into the world the four children that were coming to mean more to Beth than she had thought was possible. No one Beth had ever known closely had passed away, so she had no experience with finding comfort in cemeteries. Nor had she thought sincerely about what happens to one's soul after death. But this was a beautiful piece of land, and the idea of keeping Caroline abreast of their husband and her children was comforting.

"I can do that," Beth heard herself say as a smile crossed her face. "I'd like to think Caroline and I can become friends, in a way. At least, she may know that I am taking care of her children."

"And her husband," Lily added.

Beth turned and raised a brow at her friend. "*Our* husband. I am now married to him, too."

Lily grinned at her apologetically. "Yes, of course you are." She caught the crook of Beth's elbow and turned back towards the house. "Let's talk about that husband of yours."

Beth sighed, shaking her head. "I don't know what to do about him, Lily. He told me this wasn't a marriage of affection, but I didn't expect it would be a marriage of distance, as well."

Their walk back was much more leisurely. Lily exhaled, shaking her head. "Monty is a reserved man, you already know that much, but after Caroline died, it became more pronounced."

Beth listened closely, desperate for any insight into her husband.

"He is rarely at home anymore," Lily went on, "though I don't know what takes him away. He was away quite often even with Caroline, but it feels different now."

"His children need him, Lily," Beth insisted, a breeze catching her hair.

"I know they do." Lily looked over at her with a crooked smile. "I suspect he does, too, which is why he married you. Monty is an insightful man who is probably more aware of his shortcomings than we realize."

That made Beth snort, not because she doubted Lily, but because she didn't know her husband even well enough to be acquainted with his shortcomings.

What sort of wife was she?

"You are the sort of wife who has a marriage she doesn't

understand, yet," Lily replied.

Beth turned to her quickly, eyes wide. "Did I say that out loud?" She groaned and covered her eyes. "I don't know what I'm doing, Lily. I've been playing countess in this grand estate and playing stepmother to these children, and I don't know what I'm doing in any of this. I don't know what Monty wants me to do, or what he would do. I ask myself that every single day, and there are never any answers. I have written to him, obviously, but he has only sent a single missive. He hasn't even responded to the children's letters! Doesn't he realize I need his guidance, his instruction, his intuition? And they need their father! I cannot let anyone know how muddled I feel."

Lily gave a soft laugh and rubbed Beth's arm gently. "Oh, Beth. Nobody knows what they are doing at the beginning. Not a single one of us. You must learn as you go, as we all do."

"But this is different, Lily!" Beth protested. "You know it is."

"Tell me why," Lily insisted, turning them to walk again. "Explain it to me."

"He's my husband in name only." Beth shook her head, looking away. "I am Lady Montgomery, and the only thing that means is that I am married to Lord Montgomery, and I'm not even sure who he is. The man who met me in London and proposed to me is not the same man I married, nor the man who brought me to Knightsgate, nor the man who left me here. I have been given all the responsibilities of this position with no direction on how to properly execute them. Four young children have been left in my care who are in desperate need of a parent, and I am all they have."

"Don't sell yourself short, Elizabeth," Lily scolded in an uncharacteristically firm tone. "You are exactly who those children need right now. You are as warm as sunshine and as sweet as honey."

"As was my grandmother, Lily," Beth retorted, "and she was not thrown into my situation. Also, her husband actually liked her."

Her friend steered her towards the gardens of the house. "I am certain Monty likes you."

"Monty doesn't know anything about me, nor has he given me any indication of his preferences, for me or anything else."

"Well, then he can't really complain about how you do things, can he?" Lily shot back, raising her brows knowingly.

Beth stopped and folded her arms, incredulous. "Am I to understand that I must chart my own course?"

Lily shook her head slowly. "That is not exactly what I meant."

"Then what are you saying, Lily Granger?" she asked, curious despite her frustrations.

"I am telling you to be yourself. In every way. In everything." Lily stepped closer, her smile spreading. "Manage the household as *you* would like to do it. Those children need a parent, and they have you. Monty needed a wife, and he chose you. The tenants needed a countess, and they now have you. So instead of bewildering yourself trying to decide what you should be, or what Monty thinks you should be, or even what Caroline would think you should do or be, I think that you should be Elizabeth Colerain, Lady Montgomery. Whomever that happens to be."

Beth felt a mischievous grin form on her face. "So, I should stop waiting to be told what to do, and take charge of my life, as it were?"

"Yes."

"How very unladylike," Beth reminded her. "We are expected to do as we are told and to thank someone for the opportunity."

"Not so," Lily corrected. "As a countess, you have many responsibilities and do not need to wait for instructions on how to accomplish them."

Beth mused, "As I recall, Monty charged me with only one task."

"And that was?"

"He instructed me to hire a governess, and that Mr. Russell would tell me if there was anything else I was to do."

Lily nodded slowly. "There you are, then. With no directives, you may do as you choose. If he married you for his children, as he said, then you should do what you think is best for them."

"And my husband?" Beth queried, unable to stop smiling.

Lily shrugged, returning her smile. "Do what you think is best for him as well."

"Bitsy!" Archer called, suddenly, waving to her and running over with Samuel in tow. "I finished my lessons. May we play Agincourt now?"

Beth turned to him, still smiling. "Is there any chance I could win this time?"

Archer folded his arms and gave her a superior look that he no doubt learned from his father. "Did the French win that battle, Bitsy?"

Lily laughed outright, and Beth tried to stifle hers. "No," she admitted.

"Then neither will you."

Beth heaved a pained sigh and gestured towards the open grounds. "Very well, King Henry. Say your line and commence the battle."

Archer grinned up at her, then clasped a small hand over his chest. " 'Now, soldiers, march away: And how thou pleasest, God, dispose the day!' "

Chapter Nine

$\mathcal{D}$espite his assertion to Beth that his absence would only last a month, Malcolm was away for close to six weeks. Ignoring the opinions of both his operatives and his superiors, he remained in London for the entirety of it. There had been much to do and more developments, and he felt no trace of guilt for his actions.

At least, that's what he told himself. If he were truthful, he actually did feel an annoying sense of guilt undoubtedly eating away at various internal organs, if not his soul.

He could not deny that his home was a welcome sight, and he fervently wished to see his children again. He hadn't responded to their letters, however. He'd received a letter from each child every week, and in return, he'd sent a missive to Beth with comments for the children, as well as instructions for her based on Russell's remarks to him.

There was no saying how his arrival would be received by his wife and children. He imagined the children should at least be a bit pleased.

Beth, however...

He wished he had a better idea what she would think, how she would respond, what she felt... He wished he actually knew his wife a little, so he wouldn't live in this ignorance. If she were as maddeningly biddable as before, he knew he would be calmly and politely received. If she had somehow broken out of that shell, it could be very different.

Why that made him afraid, he couldn't say. He had faced far more dangerous situations in his lifetime as a spy, and certainly in battle years before, but the notion that his wife might act in a matter differently than he anticipated gave him the same uneasy crawling sensation in his stomach that he had before embarking in any battle or on any mission.

"Welcome home, my lord," Hudson, the stout butler, intoned as the footman took his things.

Malcolm nodded in greeting. "Thank you, Hudson. Did you receive word of my arrival?"

"We did, sir, and her ladyship had us prepare accordingly." He cleared his throat and stepped forward, his eyes fixed somewhere over Malcolm's shoulder. "She has directed that we prepare for a family dinner, the children included, and for the finer china to be set out."

Malcolm paused in the act of rolling back his cuffs, processing. "Did she seem happy when she gave these instructions?"

Hudson's high brow furrowed. "Happy, my lord?"

Malcolm shook his head quickly. "Never mind."

Hudson nodded once and followed Malcolm as he moved to his study. "Lady Montgomery also asked for a change of menu. We will now have pheasant, lamb cutlets, roasted potatoes, white soup, Yorkshire pudding…"

Malcolm eyed his butler as he rattled off the extensive menu, which included a selection of some of his favorite dishes. "Hudson."

"My lord?" Hudson replied, halting his recitation at once.

"What has prompted this excessive and particular choice of delicacies? Are we having guests?" He folded his arms and leaned against his desk.

Hudson smiled a little, which was a rare sight. "Lady Montgomery felt that, as you had been gone for some time, a celebration to greet you was in order. Mrs. Lyman was consulted as to the menu, my lord. She knows your preferences. I do believe the children, however, were consulted as to dessert."

Malcolm almost laughed at the thought of that. "Oh dear, I wonder what that means," he muttered with a smile.

"Indeed, my lord."

Malcolm exhaled slowly, giving his butler an assessing look. "Hudson, will you answer me something?"

"Yes, my lord."

"How has Lady Montgomery been handling her duties in my absence?" he asked, shifting his weight a little against the mahogany desk. "What have you seen?"

Hudson stared past him for a long moment, his discomfort growing.

"Speak candidly," Malcolm encouraged, gesturing a little.

The butler stood straighter and seemed a bit proud. "Her ladyship has been impressive, my lord. Everything has been handled with precision and efficiency, and her interest in the tenants rivals that of the late Lady Montgomery, if I might be so bold. Mr. Russell has expressed a similar sentiment and has commended her as well."

Malcolm could do nothing but blink and gape at his butler, who had known him for many years. For the first time, he wondered if the man might have gone a bit mad. There was no possible way that the woman he married, the one who had run about Lily's garden with several children, could be a capable and engaging countess so soon.

"Beth?" he managed to say, sounding just as stupefied as he felt. "Beth did that well?"

"Yes, my lord," Hudson said with a bow.

The confirmation of his words did not give Malcolm the satisfaction he had hoped. Nor did he feel a sense of pride that she had thrived, though he should have felt that. He was completely stunned by the words, and there was nothing he hated more than surprise.

She was doing it, by Jove! She was doing the job he'd wanted her to do. Had she even needed the instructions he had given her? Or had she laughed off the notion that she would need his help at all?

He didn't know his wife... He knew his first impressions, and those suddenly seemed far less certain. He shook his head and pushed off from his desk, heading for the door.

"Where might I find Lady Montgomery, Hudson?"

"I believe she is outside with the children, my lord."

Malcolm turned to face him quickly. "At this time of day?" He glanced at the clock on the mantel. "They ought to be in lessons with the governess."

Hudson's expression was perfectly blank. "There is no

governess, my lord."

Malcolm blinked, then blinked again. Then he turned from the room without another word, moving to the back of the house.

No governess? What in the world had she been doing the entire time he had been gone?

Surely, she hadn't been teaching them herself! She'd admitted to being a dismal prospect for the position, or something of the sort, and he was already feeling odd enough for marrying too soon and to someone so different from himself. He couldn't bear the added eccentricity of his lady wife also acting as governess to her stepchildren.

He stepped out onto the terrace and shaded his eyes, searching his view of the grounds. He more than half-expected to see frantically running children and hear squeals of delight. Nothing was drawing his attention, and he frowned, moving to the stairs and descending quietly. He was half-tempted to call for them, but that would disrupt whatever they were doing. Besides, his tone might have come out too aggressively, and then he would have to explain or apologize, and he wasn't willing to do either of those things.

Well, if they weren't roughhousing, what were they doing outside that could not be done inside?

"It's too hard!" he heard a child's voice whine.

He turned towards the sound, grunting in satisfaction. The garden, then. Why in the world would the children be in the garden? And what, precisely, was too hard?

Malcolm moved briskly past the ancient stone wall bordering the garden and turned down the path. He stopped when he saw all four of his children sitting on the ground, drawing on sheets of paper. Mrs. Franklin had Greer on her lap and was helping her, and Greer wore an expression of deep concentration on her very young face as she drew.

Beth crouched down between Samuel and Jane, speaking softly to both children, gesturing to the flowers before them. They each nodded, then returned their charcoal pencils to the paper, bringing a smile to Beth's face with whatever they had managed.

Archer was scowling at the rose in front of him as if it had personally insulted him, but he, too, was drawing without comment.

Malcolm watched the unusual sight before him with piqued interest, and then his gaze moved to his wife.

She was even more striking than he had remembered. Her hair was pulled back in a loose chignon, but several free strands curled gently against her cheeks. Her color was rosy and healthy, and she smiled with all the warmth he had seen in her that first day in London. She wore a simple blue-striped day dress and grey spencer, which only heightened her fair coloring, and the natural elegance of her figure seemed too perfect to be real.

Beth seemed completely at home here, and as she turned to speak with Mrs. Franklin, he noticed a measure of respect and deference from the older woman towards his wife. Whatever uncertainty he had seen in Beth before he'd left was gone now, and she moved with confidence and grace, a countess in more than name only.

Where had his wife gone, and who was this woman before him?

She was a mystery, but he suddenly very much wanted to know her.

Beth looked up and caught his eye, smiling a little. She glanced down at the children, still absorbed in their drawing, and stepped around them, moving in his direction.

Malcolm watched her approach, suddenly finding the thought of speaking with her a difficult one. She didn't look particularly pleased to see him, though he could not detect any disapproval either. For a man whose expertise lay in part with the interpretation of expression and discovering concealed truths, he was dumbfounded by his inability to accomplish either with his wife.

"Welcome back, Monty," Beth said with a curtsey when she reached him, her voice lower than he remembered.

Confused, he bowed, then reached for her hand and kissed it automatically. "Thank you, Beth."

She nodded and turned to face the children again, stepping back to stand beside him. "I trust your business in London went well?"

He stared at her unabashedly, wondering what exactly was different about her. "It did, yes."

She made no response, the same slight smile on her face as before, her gaze on the children.

"And how have things been here?" he prodded, clasping his hands behind his back. He was suddenly very tempted to reach out and touch his wife, just to see if she were real.

Her lips, somehow fuller than he recalled, quirked a little. "Very well, thank you. Mr. Russell and I have made great strides with some of the tenants, but you will have to see to the final details, as I am sure he has informed you. I've received two invitations from some neighbors, and Lily says I may accept."

"Which neighbors?" he asked absently, still studying her as if she were some exotic creature.

Her brow furrowed delicately in thought. "The Harrises and the Gardiners. I understand that Lord Kirkwood is still out of the country but may return soon. His wife doesn't like to invite callers while he is away."

Malcolm knew that. He knew all of that, and he knew that the Harrises and Gardiners were the sorts of people to invite his wife without a proper introduction. But many others ought to know his wife, and the thought occurred to him to do something about that, though the specific details were unclear.

He cleared his throat softly. "And the children?"

Beth gestured faintly. "They are as you see them. Archer has been struggling to complete his Latin lessons, but he is trying hard. Jane never speaks unless she plays, but her cold has resolved itself at last. Samuel scraped his knee when he tumbled down the stairs, which I told him was the consequence of trying to slide the banister improperly, and Greer has taken up the notion that *bonjour* sounds like a sneeze, so she combines the two for amusement."

It was as if he didn't know his own children, either. He had no idea that Jane had been unwell, or that Archer was learning Latin, let alone that Greer knew any French words or that Samuel…

Well, all right, he knew what sort of child Samuel was, so that was not a difficult thing to comprehend.

"Who is teaching Archer Latin?" Malcolm managed to ask once he had got over his shock.

Beth looked up at him with a hint of puzzlement, though her expression was still very much polite and composed. "Why, I am, of course."

He scowled without thinking. "I told you to hire a governess."

Beth shrugged, meeting his eyes steadily. "They aren't yet ready for a governess, my lord."

"What makes you...?" he started, his indignation rising.

"They've only just received a stepmother," she overrode, her eyes flashing slightly while her tone remained perfectly calm. "Let them adjust to one stranger at a time, or you will throw everything into upheaval."

Before he could say anything else, she turned towards the children. "Look who is here, children."

They turned and saw him, and each smiled in varying degrees. Greer shimmied down from Mrs. Franklin's lap and dashed over to him, clinging to his leg.

"*Bonjour,*" she mock-sneezed, grinning up at him. The sound was even more adorable than he'd thought it would be, and twice as amusing.

He lifted her up and kissed her nose. "*Bonjour, ma petit,*" he laughed.

Greer looked at Beth with a triumphant smile, and Beth shook her head. "It's not nearly as amusing the twelfth time, Greer."

"Papa thinks it's funny, Bitsy." Greer sniffed and turned to her father. "I need to finish drawing now."

Malcolm nodded and set her down, and she scampered to her nanny.

"Papa, I drew a bee!" Samuel called, waving the paper excitedly, though Malcolm couldn't see anything but scribbles.

"Make sure it doesn't sting your sister," he replied, wishing the words had sounded as light as he'd meant them.

Still, Samuel giggled and went back to it.

Jane waved at him but said nothing.

Malcolm found a little difficulty swallowing at that. "What are you drawing, Archer?"

His oldest gave him a long-suffering look. "A rose. I tried to tell her it wasn't something a boy draws, but she insisted."

Beth chuckled a little. "Why did I disagree, Archer?"

The boy rolled his eyes and heaved a sigh. "Because if you can draw a rose, you can draw lots of other things, and flowers teach you about details, and perhaps I will grow up to be an architect and need to draw buildings." He shook his head and turned back to his assignment. "This ridiculous flower doesn't look anything like a building, Bitsy."

"I promised him that if he would finish this without too much complaining," Beth murmured softly, "I would take him out to explore the grounds away from the house later. It was the only way to convince him. He really should learn to draw a little, don't you think?"

Malcolm looked at his children, then at his wife, and it was just too much for him. She was changed, they were too distant, and he was too confused by it all.

"You're teaching them," he said sharply, his chest starting to burn.

Beth raised a brow at him. "Mrs. Franklin and I are, yes."

No hint of apology or apprehension in her words or her expression. A firm acknowledgement and perhaps a little defiance, but nothing else. And this was his submissive wife? Hardly.

Malcolm ground his teeth a little. "If you wanted to be a governess, I would have just hired you and saved myself the trouble."

Beth did not react except to raise the other brow to match. "I didn't realize that marrying me had caused you any trouble. If I had become the governess, which is what I initially believed you wanted of me, and not the wife, exactly how would you benefit? You are the one who made me your wife, Monty, so you cannot shift your discontent to me." She gave him a knowing look and swept back towards the children, leaving him staring after her in a fuming sort of confusion.

How *would* he benefit? He couldn't actually say, and that angered him most of all.

Fists clenching, he turned out of the garden and back out to the grounds, thinking a long walk and some fresh air just might calm him. He was undoubtedly overwrought from his travels and needed some exercise and space to collect himself. His children were mindful of their work, not neglectful of him, and they would certainly receive him better when they were not so occupied. And his wife was a capable woman, just as he'd wished. He should be glad of her independence.

Except he wasn't. He was tempted to return to London already. "Monty?"

He glanced quickly over his shoulder and stopped at the sight of Lily walking towards him, the hem of her pale blue dress dirty from the walk. "Lily. Did you walk all the way from Rainford?"

She nodded, coming over to him. "Of course. It's only two miles, and quite pretty."

Malcolm shook his head as he kissed her cheek. "Still, you ought to come by carriage. What would Granger say?"

She sniffed and looped her arm through his. "Provided he cared? He would praise me for taking in a regimen of exercise so healthful as walking the countryside." She sighed and said, "Where are you bound?"

"Anywhere." He started strolling with her, letting his mind wander and whirl in silence with her beside him.

"What's wrong?" Lily asked gently.

"Must you be so intuitive?" he murmured, glancing over at her.

Lily chuckled softly, her dark eyes dancing. "Monty, you're not exactly hiding it. When did you get back?"

He looked out over his lands, strangely enough feeling lonelier for seeing them. "Just a few moments ago."

"Have you seen Beth and the children?"

He nodded without speaking. He had seen them. He had seen her manage the children with expert skill, he had heard of her conquests in his absence, he had witnessed the obedience his children paid her...

"Oh dear," Lily murmured beside him, shaking her head.

Malcolm gave her a look. "What?"

She returned his look with one of her own. "You're displeased with your wife."

"Don't be daft!" he scoffed, looking away.

"You don't have to lie to me because she is my friend. I know you." She tugged on his arm a little. "Monty, she is doing a splendid job of things."

"Yes, so I've heard," he snapped. Then he sighed and shook his head. "I'm sorry."

Lily said nothing and simply walked beside him, waiting.

"I'm not displeased with her," he told her, inhaling the fresh air and exhaling slowly. "How can I be? She's done everything I've wanted, surpassing all my expectations of her. If I weren't so blasted confused and torn up inside, I might actually be proud of her. I probably should be proud of her."

"Probably," Lily agreed with a smile.

Malcolm scoffed but returned the smile. "I don't know what I actually expected, Lily, but it wasn't this. She's so different from the woman I left, and I just…"

Lily suddenly laughed and turned her head, looking away from him over a small vista before them.

"What?" he asked, nudging her.

She turned back, smiling broadly. "She said the same thing to me not too long ago. She said you were changed, so different, and she didn't know what to do."

"I am not too difficult to understand," he protested moodily.

Lily tossed her head back on a laugh. "Please, Malcolm, there are passages in the Book of Isaiah more easily understood than you."

He threw her a frown. "So, you take her side against me?"

"I take nobody's side." Lily rolled her eyes and exhaled loudly. "I side with you both. I want your marriage to succeed, but for that to happen, your marriage has to take place in the same place." She shook his arm slightly. "You need to treat your wife as a wife, not as a caretaker."

Malcolm gaped a little. "I don't treat her as a caretaker!"

"What would you call it? You abandoned her at an estate she doesn't know, with children she's barely met, and a title to which she hasn't adjusted," Lily pointed out, tilting her head and smiling at him.

He frowned at her and removed his arm from her hold. "I think you must be needed at home now, Mrs. Granger."

She took his arm again and held more tightly. "You're not dismissing me that easily, Monty."

"Pity."

Lily sighed again, this time almost wearily. "Malcolm, you need to be here, at least for a little while. You'll never adjust to being married again if you aren't taking part in it. You need to get to know your wife. You need to show your children you approve of her. You need to show your neighbors and tenants you approve of her. For pity's sake, you haven't introduced her to anyone, or had a party or luncheon for her. How are the neighbors supposed to get to know her? You must show her off, use that perfect politeness you are so famous for, and take pride in your new wife."

"Should I be doing all that?" he inquired in a low tone, almost absently.

Lily looked surprised. "You're asking that question now? A bit late, don't you think?"

He wet his lips with embarrassment. "I don't really know her."

"Well," Lily replied after a moment's pause, "then perhaps we should have this party for you. Then you can get to know her, as well."

Malcolm nodded slowly, thoughtfully, but without answering her.

"I don't understand why you haven't already done something," Lily mused. "You're the one who asked to meet her. You thought she was perfect, and you're the one who wanted to marry her right away. What changed?"

He closed his eyes against the confession rising but couldn't contain it. "I think it was too soon." He swallowed harshly. "I'm afraid it was too soon. I wasn't ready." He shook his head and gazed vacantly out over the lands again. "She's not Caroline. She will never be Caroline."

"That's because she's Beth," Lily reminded him gently, "and if you'd give her a chance, you might find something to like in her, as well."

"I like her well enough," he assured Lily a little defensively.

She stiffened beside him, and he knew at once he had said the wrong thing. "Yes. My husband likes me well enough, and you see what sort of bliss that entails," she said bitterly.

He covered her hand with his and squeezed, apologizing with the simple gesture in place of the words he could not vocalize.

Lily took a moment to compose herself, then looked up at him once more. "Give it time, Monty. And give her your attention."

Malcolm felt his insides twisting, but beneath all that, he knew she was right. He was to blame for this situation, and he owed it to his family to try. He owed it to Beth, and to himself, if he were to be truthful. He had chosen Beth for some reason, and he could not believe that it had been all for the children.

"I'll have a dinner party later this week," he agreed softly. "Will you help with the invitations? And to get Beth prepared?"

"Of course," Lily replied easily. Then she smiled with a mischievous light. "Though I highly doubt she will need it."

Chapter Ten

"*H*elp me prepare? What exactly does he think I need help with?"

Lily grinned at her as she sipped her tea. "Well, you've never hosted anything before, and it is a party to introduce you to all of your closest neighbors properly…"

Beth stared at her without any of the amusement Lily seemed overburdened with. "You didn't tell him I've already met them all?"

Lily shrugged one shoulder in a surprisingly graceful motion. "He didn't ask. Besides, you didn't tell him, either."

That was true, and Beth didn't have a good reason for it. She could have told him that two weeks after he left her without anything to do, she had set about to meet all the tenants, and all the neighbors, on her own. Lily had assured her that none of them were so stiff as to keep to the London manners of refusing to receive a caller to whom they had not been formally introduced. Even Lady Kirkwood had come to call on her, once she'd received Beth's card, and that was apparently a small miracle.

Everyone had easily accepted that Lord Montgomery had wished to give his new countess time to adjust to new position and life with the children. They'd all understood her desire for acquaintances before being properly introduced.

Lily had informed her that there had been nothing but praises sung about the new Lady Montgomery, and while none of them had called on her more than once, she could safely say that she knew each of her neighbors well enough to not be intimidated by a roomful of them.

"Does he think he needs to hold my hand, so I don't cry?" Beth asked dryly.

Lily gave her a scolding look. "Be kind. He doesn't know what he's doing, but this is a start. Let him show you off a little. You said so yourself that the last few days have been better."

"Better than what?" Beth murmured, sipping her own tea. "Better than nothing? Perhaps."

It was true, Malcolm had been more present in the days following his return than he had before he'd left. He had taken an interest in Beth's doings; he had taken care to explain his part in their tenants' needs and had actually conferred with her on a few of them. He was still very polite and had yet to truly play with the children, but he had taken a moment to come out with them and watch Beth play with the children every day. He had smiled every time.

That smile was getting to her. Despite her irritation with him for his maddening aloofness with her and the children, his smile made her feel... *things*. She couldn't feel "things", not when she had to prove herself. She needed to be a strong woman, someone on whom he could depend, if he would let himself give up a little bit of control.

It was so much easier to be the woman she wanted to be when he was away. When he was here, before her face and in her thoughts, she became agitated and embarrassed and silly, wanting so desperately to please him that she turned into the biddable version of herself that he had married. But he had seemed almost disappointed with her easy agreement, and so, to please him in earnest, she would have to show her independence.

Daydreaming of running into his arms, or of kissing him while they watched a breathtaking sunset did not seem the best way to spend her time striving to be independent and capable. But it did help her to be more productive, as every time it happened, she would rush and scramble to accomplish things as a distraction.

If her husband didn't appeal to her so, despite his distance, she might have felt more settled. She rather liked his attractiveness, however. If only she knew how his lips would feel against her skin...

She jerked suddenly, spilling tea on her hand, but thankfully avoiding her skirt. "Ooh," she yelped, grateful it wasn't scalding, but it was still warm enough to irritate her skin.

Lily's eyes widened as she watched Beth blot the spill with a linen napkin. "What happened?"

"Probably a terrible feeling anyway," Beth grumbled under her breath as her face flamed.

"What is?" Lily prodded.

"Nothing." Beth sighed and shook her head. "I'm becoming cynical, aren't I?"

Lily grinned. "Yes, and it is entertaining to watch you change from sweet to cynical so quickly. I didn't think you had it in you."

"Neither did I." Beth leaned back against her chair and rubbed at her brow. "I don't mean to be. It's just... I was thinking of my..."

"Your what?"

Beth dropped her hand and gave her friend a very frank look. "My husband."

Lily's brow furrowed slightly. "Your husband?" Then her expression cleared, and her eyes grew round. "Oh..."

Beth smiled tightly and nodded. "Lady Montgomery is mightily attracted to her husband and is trying not to make a grand fool of herself." She groaned and covered her face again.

Lily laughed gently and set her teacup down. "Why would you make a fool of yourself? You are not a fool, and you never have been."

"Oh, yes, I am," Beth informed her, nodding very firmly. "I find myself attracted to a man who told me from the first that he did not love me and that I should not expect a marriage of affection. I should have known the infatuation would only get worse when I was actually his wife. And do you know what the worst thing is?"

"Enlighten me," Lily encouraged, sitting back herself with an amused smile.

Beth did not appreciate that her friend was ignoring the severity of the situation but chose to put that aside for a moment. "The worst thing is that I very much fear that if Monty ever opens up to me, I will find myself more attracted to the man within than I already am."

"And the trouble there is...?" Lily asked with that smile still fixed in place.

Beth heaved a sigh. "I will probably wind up trailing behind him and begging him to love me for the rest of my life, complete with flinging myself on him and stealing into his bedchamber at night. I shall become wholly ridiculous over the mere thought of his physical form, which my imagination is quite delighted to dwell upon, without his hidden qualities, which I have yet to discover. Then he shall cast me off for being so pathetic, and it will be my own fault because I was not sensible enough to marry an unattractive man."

Lily was laughing too hard to give any sort of answer, so Beth patiently waited for her friend to recover herself. It took quite a long while.

When Lily was sensible again, she smiled at Beth fondly. "That is the best thing I have heard in quite a long time."

Beth shot her a dry smile. "So happy I could oblige you."

"Attractive husbands are a trial, aren't they?" Lily offered, her smile fading a little.

There was nothing Beth could have replied to that. Lily had been secretly in love with Mr. Granger before their marriage, and then his fortunes had changed, and an agreement had been struck between him and her father for her hand strictly for her inheritance to rebuild what he had lost. There could not have been a crueler punishment for her tender heart, and Beth had often wondered if Lily's love for Mr. Granger had fallen by the wayside under his neglect and changed nature. He had been charming and agreeable before, yet he was dismissive and cold now.

What if Malcolm became the same way? Beth was not sure she was strong enough to endure that.

She grunted softly, shaking her head. "How am I supposed to manage when he makes me feel this way? We're not even friends, Lily, and I just want..." She put her head in her hands. "I don't even know what I want."

"You are just going to have to get over the fact that your husband is attractive, Beth," Lily told her without sympathy. "You ought to be friends with him, and you have it in you to be very friendly. You will find that you and your husband have much in common, and I think you will rather enjoy the process." She suddenly chuckled softly. "I'll have you know he finds you attractive, as well."

Beth jerked her head up and stared at Lily with wide eyes. "What? Are you certain? He said that?"

Her friend smirked a little. "He didn't have to. I've seen how he looks at you, and there is no hiding that."

"That doesn't make any sense," Beth stammered, shaking her head insistently. "I've seen the way he looks at me as well, and there wasn't anything there to make me believe anything of the sort."

Lily tilted her head, still smiling knowingly. "Do you know what it looks like when a man finds you attractive?"

A snort escaped Beth. "Apparently not."

"And how long are you staring at your husband to decide if the way he looks at you says something?"

Now Beth scowled at her. "If I look at him for longer than two seconds at a time without conversation, my knees forget their purpose, and my face begins to burn." She shook her head. "It's too embarrassing."

"To find your husband attractive?" Lily prodded, looking confused.

"I don't want him to know," Beth whispered, her cheeks flaming just as she'd said.

Lily frowned slightly. "He should know. You should have confidence in how you look at your husband and to your husband."

Beth grumbled, "This is not a marriage of affection, remember? I have to keep to the restrictions Monty set."

"What restrictions?" Lily demanded. "Why can't your marriage become something else? There are two people in this marriage, not one, and you have every right to make it whatever you like. It might not have started as a marriage of *affection*, but it can certainly be a marriage of *attraction*." Her expression softened, and she smiled at Beth gently. "Stop defending against him, Beth. Just be yourself, and Monty will be himself, and eventually, the two of you will find a way."

"As long as I can retain my sanity, that sounds lovely," Beth quipped, hiding the emotion swirling within her. She would've loved to have had her marriage become more than it was, for her husband to see her as more, and to be able to know him the way she felt a wife should. The dream of being comfortable when he was near, of seeing him look at her with desire and affection, all seemed nearly impossible. But she loved his children, and she had gained more in this marriage than she'd ever imagined she would.

110

Surely, she could manage to take an active role in this marriage rather than a submissive one. She'd been practicing independence and confidence while he'd been away, mostly for the sake of the children and the running of the estate. It should not be too difficult to apply it further now that he was here. She didn't want her attraction towards her husband to fade; she wanted to enhance it and see where it might lead.

What if she did come to know the man beneath the façade and her worries came to fruition? She was not as silly as she had described to Lily, which Lily knew full well, and she could certainly manage her own life and behavior.

Her husband, on the other hand… there was no managing him. Unfortunately.

"My lady," called the voice of Mrs. Franklin, sounding a little panicked.

Beth and Lily both turned towards the open door. "In here, Mrs. Franklin."

The older woman appeared in the doorway, her hair slightly unkempt, which should have given Beth enough cause for alarm, as Mrs. Franklin's hair was always pristine. Her dark eyes were wide, and the faint lines on her face were suddenly stark.

"My lady, I cannot find Master Archer," Mrs. Franklin panted.

Both ladies shot to their feet. "What?" they cried as one.

Tears were welling in Mrs. Franklin's eyes, and she sniffed loudly. "He said he needed to fetch a book and didn't come back. I've looked everywhere, and I cannot find him."

Beth came to her at once, steadying the nanny's trembling arms. "What has he been speaking of today? Anything in particular?"

She nodded frantically. "He's been talking of when you took him to explore the grounds. Nothing specific about it, just that he wished he could do so again."

Beth's heart leapt to her throat, and she bolted from the room. "Lily, get Monty! Tell him I've gone to the stables!"

She didn't wait to see if her friend listened as she raced out to the terrace, then around the side of the house for the stables, her legs pumping frantically beneath her skirts.

The stable hands were surprised by her sudden appearance but quickly heeded her barked orders to prepare a horse for her and one for the earl, as well as two for themselves. She didn't wait for one of them to help her as she smoothly mounted her own horse and gathered up the reigns for Malcolm's. She didn't get far out of the stables before Malcolm arrived on the run, and she tossed his reigns to him as he mounted.

"Where would he go?" he demanded.

"We stayed away from the water," she told him as she urged her horse to move. "He loved the rocks and the ravines, but we didn't get near the one to the south. We only went east. If he stays in familiar territory, I believe that's where he'll go." Beth shook her head as her emotions began to catch up with her. "Monty, I…"

"Not now," he ordered, his jaw set and his eyes cold. "Not now." He kicked his heels, and his horse took off, leaving Beth no course but to follow.

There was no sign of Archer as they galloped off towards their exploration area, and Malcolm said nothing as they rode on. He directed the two stable hands to go to the south, while the stable master, having chosen to follow despite orders, kept with Beth and Malcolm to the east. They called out for Archer repeatedly, but there was no response.

Beth could barely manage to breathe as she rode, fearing that her impulsive adventure with her oldest stepson might have been too much, trying too hard. Had she led her husband's son into danger? Was all this her fault? What if he…?

She couldn't let herself think that way. Archer was a smart lad, curious by nature, but hardly reckless. They had been very careful in their outing the other day, and he had been more mindful of her than she had of him. He would be well and whole, he was simply being an incorrigible, curious boy.

Beth veered off as they came near a series of rocks near a deep crevice in the ground, one she recognized from the day before and one that Archer had been particularly fascinated with. She dismounted and began climbing the rocks, crawling bare-handed over the rough surfaces.

"Elizabeth!" Malcolm roared, his voice ringing with fury.

Beth ignored him as she continued, wondering if Archer had

come back to the formations he'd found so enthralling before. She heard horse hooves nearing her.

"Elizabeth, do not injure yourself. Get back on your horse!" Malcolm ordered again, his voice much closer.

Perching herself atop her current boulder, she turned to glare over her shoulder. "Do not shout at me, my lord, when I'm searching for your son!" she bellowed, her voice matching his in irritation.

Malcolm's expression changed to one of shock, no doubt surprised that his wife would snap at him in such a way. His mouth twitched a little, and for a moment, Beth wondered if he might smile. But he did not, and only dipped his chin.

"Archer!" Beth called, scanning the rocks and peering down into the ravine for good measure. It wasn't too far down, thankfully, but it would still be enough to injure Archer if he had fallen.

"Bitsy?"

She whirled, nearly losing her balance and crouching to keep from falling. "Archer!" she called again, scanning the rocks.

"Bitsy, I'm over here!" his young voice called.

Beth scrambled from the rock towards a few others further down. "Monty!" she shouted over her shoulder. "He's here!" She raced forward, looking around every rock and outcropping. "Archer!"

He suddenly appeared as she rounded a granite boulder, sitting on the ground and holding his ankle. His face bore the stains of tears, but he smiled at her nervously.

"Don't be angry," he whimpered.

Tears obscured Beth's vision as she shook her head and moved to him. "I'll be angry much, much later," she managed, sinking to the ground and pulling him into her arms. "Right now, I am only relieved you are safe."

Archer sniffled and burrowed against her. "I wanted to come and see the rocks again. I was climbing and being careful like we talked about, and then my foot slipped, and I hurt my ankle. I think I can walk back, but it will hurt."

Beth exhaled slowly, willing her tears away even as two fell down her cheeks. She kissed Archer's hair and then pulled back to smile at him. "You don't need to walk back. Your father and I rode horses."

"Papa's here?" Archer said, his eyes widening. "He's going to be so upset."

Beth opened her mouth to protest when Monty appeared, looking more unkempt than Beth had ever seen him. He stared at his son with wide eyes, which darted over every feature. Beth saw his throat work on a swallow and bit her lip, praying he would act with the concern she could clearly see in him.

Archer pushed off from Beth gently and stood, shaking slightly before his father.

Malcolm exhaled a short breath and walked over to his son, pulling him roughly to his chest.

Beth closed her eyes on a silent sigh of relief, then opened them again to watch the interaction between worried father and frightened child.

"Are you all right, son?" Malcolm asked gruffly, still holding tight.

Archer nodded against him. "I'm sorry, Papa."

"You'll need to make your apologies to Mrs. Franklin. And to your stepmother. She would never have shown you this place if she knew you would have come back alone." Malcolm met Beth's eyes with a short nod.

Beth allowed herself a small smile and got to her feet, standing apart from them still.

"I'm sorry, Bitsy," Archer murmured, sounding teary again as he looked at her.

"You're forgiven, Archer," she replied, smiling more. "Shall we take you back home and call for the doctor about your ankle?"

Malcolm's brow furrowed with the question, but Beth shook her head slightly. He looked down at the boy and ran a hand over his hair. "Can you walk to the horse?"

"Yes, Papa," Archer said bravely, wiping at his nose.

Malcolm nodded, then steered Archer towards the horses. They had only gone a few steps when Malcolm noticed the way Archer limped. Lifting him up without a word, he glanced back at Beth. She watched them fondly despite the fear and worry they'd felt. He nodded at her again, his eyes showing a remarkable level of understanding. Whatever Malcolm's faults, whatever his aloofness, there was a depth of love and devotion to his children that was now plainly evident.

Seeing his response to Archer's disappearance, and to finding him once more, made Beth's heart lighten. Perhaps there was hope for him after all.

And if there was hope for him, there just might be hope for them.

But only time would tell.

Chapter Eleven

$\mathcal{B}$eth could not sleep. By all accounts, she ought to have been quite soundly asleep by now. She was certainly exhausted enough by the events of the day.

Their harrowing experience racing after Archer had been resolved. Dr. Durham had pronounced only a mild sprain and recommended bed rest and tarts, to his patient's delight. Beth and Malcolm had changed to prepare for their party and receive their guests. All of the invitations had been accepted, and it was destined to be quite the evening. Though she had suggested putting off the affair, given what they had endured, Malcolm would not hear of it. He'd claimed it was high time to show off his wife and let the neighborhood have the opportunity to meet her.

Beth smiled as she recalled the perplexed look Malcolm had worn when he'd escorted her about the great hall to meet everyone only to discover that she and the women were already acquainted. Each had asked after something particular that they could only have known had they spent time together.

After the fourth time, he'd steered her away and muttered, "Do you already know everyone in this room?"

She'd dimpled a mischievous smile at him and quipped, "Of course not, Monty. I only know the women."

Again, he'd seemed torn between laughter and irritation, but he'd not asked about it any further and had only taken her to the other side of the room.

Poor man. She really did not need him to lead her about so gently, as though she might break like a porcelain dish. She was quite capable enough to mind her own affairs, no matter how young or naïve she might appear.

Still, it had been delightful to be paraded on his arm most of the evening. They had not had dancing, much to Beth's disappointment, but the conversation had been enjoyable all the same. They were fortunate in their neighbors, and all seemed to like Malcolm a great deal. He was a bit harder to discern, but she did detect an underlying respect in return.

Her favorite moments of the evening, however, had been the first and the last. When she had descended the stairs to him before the guests had arrived, he had turned and bestowed a look of awe upon her in a manner she had never seen before. She had worn one of her new gowns as Lily had advised, as the colors heightened her looks considerably. The pale periwinkle silk with sheer sleeves and lace detailing made her feel elegant and graceful, and the sapphire necklace and earrings only added to the grace of her station, which she was coming to enjoy quite a great deal.

Malcolm had stared at her in an almost brazen fashion before recovering himself and complimenting her with the utmost politeness, but Beth had heard Lily's words echoing in her mind for hours into the evening. She kept wondering if it were entirely possible that her husband found her half as attractive as she found him. Oddly enough, instead of embarrassing her, the thought had been amusing. She had watched him the rest of the evening with interest, and the frequency with which he had looked at her had been something of particular fascination to her. He gazed at her she stared at him, and neither of them seemed to mind it.

What a delightful notion!

As the evening had drawn to a close, Malcolm had smiled at her with a measure of fondness, looking a little impressed, and had praised her for the manner with which she had received their guests and her perfection in playing hostess.

"You don't mind that I had already met the women?" she'd asked, smiling a little.

He had given her a searching look, the fondness retreating, and then replied, "No, I find I do not. In fact, I should not have been surprised. Next time, I will stand in a corner the entire evening and let you take charge of the whole affair. It seems I was not needed but for the expectation of the neighbors."

His words had the unsettling dual effect of both lifting her heart and yet chastising her. The praise she would treasure, but the rest…

Of course, he had been needed. He was always needed. But she had not had time to tell him that, as he had turned from her and gone up to his own rooms.

As she now lay in her bed, she wondered if perhaps that might be something she ought to inquire about. Did Malcolm feel that in replacing his late wife, he had also succeeded in replacing himself? Nothing could have been further from the truth, and if he would only open his eyes beyond his pain and grief, he might have been able to see that.

His children absolutely needed him. His tenants would be lost without him. And Beth… Well, she rather thought she needed him, too, though she could not have said to what extent. They had almost seemed a real married couple tonight. She would give a great deal for more opportunities to do the same.

Faintly, a noise reached her ears, and she propped herself up on her elbows, listening again.

"Mama!" a young voice screamed in terror, the words obviously choked with tears even to her ears.

Beth sprang from the bed, not even pausing for a wrap, and bolted out of her bedchamber and down the corridor. The nursery was not too far from her rooms, and if her instincts were correct, that scared voice belonged to her sweet and shy Jane.

"Mama!" the child cried again, her voice loud and heart-piercing in the empty corridor. "*MAMA!*"

Beth pushed herself faster, then felt her arm being grabbed from behind. Malcolm was suddenly there, his eyes wild, his hair in disarray, his nightshirt hastily shoved into trousers.

"She isn't calling for you!" he hissed, his grip on her arm tight.

Was he serious? Perhaps there was no hope for him after all. She gave him an utterly incredulous and disparaging look as Jane cried out again. "Do you hear her? She isn't calling for you, either!"

He seemed startled by her reprimand, a feeling which intensified when she wrenched herself out of his grasp and hurried on to the nursery.

The boys were awake on their side of the darkened room. Archer huddled close to Samuel as helplessly they watched their sister thrash and scream in bed. Greer sat bolt upright, wide-eyed and terrified in her own little bed, but Mrs. Franklin was quick to scoop her up once Beth entered the room.

"It's all right," Beth told the other children with a faint smile. "You can go back to sleep."

Whether they listened or not, she couldn't say, as she immediately crossed to Jane's bed, sitting on the mattress and reaching out to brush back Jane's hair.

"Jane, it's all right. It's all right. Wake up."

Jane whimpered and thrashed again but did not wake. "Mama," she moaned weakly.

"Janie," Beth said more firmly, moving her hands to cup the girl's face, her thumbs stroking over her tear-stained cheeks. "Wake up, sweetheart. Wake up."

A wrenching sob tore from the girl's throat as her eyes fluttered open, then darted around anxiously for her mother. "Mama?"

Beth felt tears sting her eyes as she shook her head. "No, darling. It's Bitsy."

Jane's lower lip quivered dangerously as her eyes met Beth's. "I dreamed my mama was still here, but I knew she was gone." Tears fell from the corners of her eyes and started their path down her cheeks. "I wanted her to stay, but she told me she couldn't. Why couldn't she stay, Bitsy? *I want my mama...*" She dissolved into tears that would have melted the coldest of hearts.

Beth moved to climb into bed beside the girl, shushing and soothing her as she pulled her into her arms and held her tightly. "I don't know, love," she whispered, closing her eyes and kissing Jane's hair. "I don't know, but I know she loved you so much, and she would have stayed if she could."

The little girl burrowed against her and cried softly, her tears dampening Beth's linen nightgown. "I miss her so much."

A faint creaking sound brought Beth's attention up to see Malcolm leaning against the doorframe, his gaze on them both, his expression as tortured as his daughter's words.

"I know you do, darling," Beth murmured, her eyes still on her husband, though he did not see it. "And it is only right that you should."

Jane sniffled and sighed, resting her cheek against Beth's chest. "Do you think she misses me, Bitsy?"

Malcolm closed his eyes in agony, and Beth dropped her gaze to the girl in her arms. "I'm sure of it, Jane." She exhaled softly and tucked Jane under her chin. "Do you know what I do every week?"

She felt Jane shake her head against her with a soft sniffle.

"I go to the cemetery," Beth told her quietly, running her fingers through Jane's dark hair. "I sit down by your mother's grave, and I talk to her."

She saw Malcolm jerk a little by the door, but she didn't look at him.

"Really?" Jane asked with innocent curiosity. "What do you talk about?"

Beth smiled and continued to stroke Jane's hair. "You. And Archer and Samuel and Greer." She lifted her gaze a little to Malcolm, who was watching her with an intensity that captivated her. "And your father, too."

She saw him swallow and looked away before she lost her focus.

"I tell her how you are doing," Beth went on, smiling softly. "I tell her amusing stories, I ask for her advice... She doesn't answer with words, but sometimes I think she answers in my heart. I feel better after talking to her, and I think she would feel better knowing I come to see her."

"You didn't know Mama," Jane reminded her, pulling back a little to look in her face. "Why do you go see her?"

Beth stroked Jane's cheek a little, still smiling. "Because she is still your mother, Jane. She will always be your mother. It is my responsibility to help you children to become the people your mother would have liked you to be, and I desperately need her help taking care of her family."

Jane seemed to mull it over and nestled against Beth again. "We're your family, too, Bitsy."

Tears welled up in Beth's eyes, and she hugged the girl closer. "Thank you, Janie."

"May I… may I come with you sometime?" Jane asked her in a suddenly timid voice. "To talk to Mama?"

Beth pulled back a little and brushed the hair out of Jane's face. "Of course, sweetheart. We can go tomorrow, if you like. And we can take flowers."

"Roses," Jane insisted. "Those were Mama's favorite. And never take lilies. She likes Cousin Lily, but not the flowers."

"Duly noted," Beth replied with a laugh.

Jane sniffed again and rested her head back down on her pillow. "I miss her, Bitsy."

Beth nodded and stroked her hair again. "I know. And that's quite all right. You go on missing your mother as long as you like. I'll be right here to hold you when you miss her, and we can talk about her anytime you want."

The smile Jane gave her then would warm Beth's heart for years to come, and she let Jane talk to her for several minutes while the little girl relaxed once more. Malcolm slipped out of the room without Beth noticing, and the other children had settled drowsily back into their beds. When Jane's eyelids began to droop, Beth kissed her brow, tucked her in, and slipped out of the room quietly, shutting the door behind her.

She sighed heavily as she leaned against it, smiling a little. Finally, a breakthrough with Jane! At last, she might be able to develop a sort of relationship with the girl beyond their simple playtime.

She made a noise of satisfaction and pushed away from the door, only to jump and screech a little in alarm. Her husband leaned against the wall in the shadows not far from the nursery, arms crossed, staring at her.

"Malcolm, what are you doing there?" she gasped, her hand sliding from her mouth to her chest, pressing her terrified heart into submission.

He straightened and tilted his head a little at her.

Beth realized she'd called him by his Christian name but couldn't find the words to apologize in the face of his haunted look. Even in the low light of the hall, his features were perfectly sculpted, and there was a heat in his eyes that rivaled any fire Beth had ever seen. She swallowed hard.

He slowly came towards her. "I've been blind," he murmured.

Some previously undiscovered strength filled Beth's frame, and she stayed rooted in place as he approached. "Have you?" she heard herself reply.

He nodded, stopping just in front of her. "So blind."

Suddenly, his hands were on her face, his lips on hers, grazing and nipping, then drinking deeply as if he could never get enough.

Beth almost cried out with relief as her desire fanned into flames in the face of his passion. She slid her hands into Malcolm's hair, desperate to pull herself closer, to give him all that she could of herself before he could change his mind. Fear licked at her. Fear that this was a mistake, that he wouldn't want her like this, that he would stop…

Malcolm's hands stroked her face, along her neck, moving down her arm, around her back, and his kisses grew tender, but somehow lost none of the passion.

She had craved his touch for so long, and she hadn't even known it. To be embraced in this way, to feel this sort of attention from him, and to feel this same excitement rising within her, filling her and spreading through her limbs. Had she ever felt this alive or aware of herself? She sighed against his mouth, arching up for more.

He broke off gently, one hand reaching up for her cheek again as he dusted kisses along her face and neck. "Oh, Caroline," he moaned, kissing along her jaw.

Beth stiffened even as she had felt herself rising up on her toes with his kisses. A sob welled up in her throat, but she forced it down with effort. Lowering back to the ground she pushed herself away from his chest gently.

Somehow, she looked up at him, and within his eyes, she saw desire, confusion, and anguish, all of which made her ache more than his misspoken words had. She brought a hand to his cheek and looked him squarely in the eye.

"If you're going to be with me," Beth murmured, her voice barely above a whisper, "you need to be with *me*. She can't be anywhere near us."

Malcolm covered her hand with his own, his breathing suddenly unsteady.

"It needs to be my name," she told him softly, trying to be firm. "Not hers."

His throat worked on a swallow while his eyes searched hers. He wet his lips and exhaled slowly. "I'm not ready," he admitted in a low rumble.

Beth knew that already. She could see that. She could feel that. But the pain of it still slashed across her with surprising sharpness. She nodded slowly, stroking his cheek once. Then she let her hand slide from his face, stepped out of his hold, and moved around him down the hall back to her rooms. She resisted the temptation to look back, to see if he watched her, and let her now quivering chin tremble fully, though she would not allow any of the welling tears fall.

How could he have done something so thoughtless? Malcolm berated himself. He'd known he was kissing Beth. Of course, he had! Logically, he had been fully aware of her. His mind had not left him entirely. But in his heart, things were less clear. With her in his arms, her lips against his, his heart only knew one cry, and everything seemed so right, so familiar, there had been no recourse but to say her name.

Except it had been the wrong name.

He had known it at once, but the awareness had not flooded him until Beth had touched his face. He hadn't slept after that. How could he? Beth deserved so much more than what he had been offering her, what he felt able to offer her. Her tenderness and understanding with Jane had taken his breath away, despite the pain he had felt, his utter helplessness in the face of his daughter's distress. And to remind Beth that she was not their mother? His own callousness had surprised him.

Of course Beth was not their mother. She had never once claimed to be. But she was standing in place of their mother and loved his children as a mother would. She was becoming a mother to them, even if she had not borne them herself.

And what was so wrong with that? In fact, it may have made him

123

feel more for her than he already did.

What exactly that meant was unclear to him, which was why he had eventually found his way into the gallery last night. Here he remained, staring helplessly up at Caroline's portrait, wondering what he could do, what he *should* do, and if he would ever be able to find his way without her.

Faint footsteps suddenly sounded, but he ignored them, assuming they belonged to a servant.

"Have you been in here all night, Monty?" Beth's voice asked, sounding surprised. Somehow, she seemed without any lingering pain from the interruption of their interlude the night before.

Malcolm nodded slowly and shuddered involuntarily, not looking at her.

"Why?"

"I don't know," he murmured with a shrug. "It makes no sense."

Beth came closer, and he could now see her in his peripheral vision. "It makes perfect sense. You miss her, and here she is."

A moment of silence passed as they both viewed the portrait.

It had been painted the year before Caroline's death, and it captured her strong spirit, her beauty, and her ability to captivate with only a look. Her dark hair and eyes perfectly reflected reality, and he remembered hovering behind the artist and attempting to smooth the subtle barbs Caroline had doled out during the process. She had never been one for portraits or standing still for extended periods. Despite the tranquility of the painting, the creation of it had brought out the worst in her.

"It's a fine portrait," Beth praised.

Malcolm snorted softly. "She hated it."

Surprised, Beth turned to look at him. "Why?"

Somehow, he managed a humorless smile. "She said it made her look stiff and severe."

Beth turned back to the painting, tilting her head and looking more closely. After a moment of analysis, she nodded once. "I can see that."

Malcolm dropped his head and laughed helplessly.

"But still," Beth went on, a smile in her voice, "it is a fine portrait."

Malcolm shook his still-lowered head, then looked up at his wife. "Did you seek me out intentionally, Beth?"

She smiled at him a little. "Naturally. I think it is time we had a talk."

"I agree." He slid over on the ottoman he occupied and patted the vacant spot.

She held out her hand, still smiling. "Not here. Come take a walk with me."

In his raw vulnerability, he didn't even hesitate, and it surprised him how easy it felt to hold her hand in his, to be led through the house and out of doors. Malcolm slowly walked the grounds of Knightsgate with her. Eventually, her hand slid out of his, and his fingers tingled slightly with the loss.

"Malcolm," Beth said gently, again using his Christian name, which he found somehow comforting and enticing, "I believe you are lost."

"I know I am," he replied without shame. "I have absolutely no idea what to do. It's been some time since her death, and I can't seem to manage being both father and mother to my children."

Beth's shoulder brushed against his as they walked, and she pushed a lock of her loosely bound hair behind her ear. "Which is why you decided to marry again."

He nodded once. "It was more an act of self-preservation than anything else. It didn't really occur to me that by marrying again, not only would my children have another female in their life, but I would as well. It was never supposed to be about me, aside from the roles that I could not fill." He slid a glance to Beth and smiled a little lopsidedly. "I didn't expect to find you."

She gave him a matching smile and quirked her head slightly. "I can imagine not. Whatever would you want me for? You wanted a simple, uncomplicated woman. Not simple-minded, for she would need to manage your affairs properly and comport herself with refinement." She moderated her tone to reflect the manners she was describing to a rather comedic effect, ticking off the list of many qualities on her fingers. "She must take care of your children and mold them appropriately, never act rashly, and be completely amenable to all of your wishes, requirements, and demands."

Malcolm snorted softly. "You're not far off."

Beth laughed a little, returning to her usual self. "So, what went wrong?"

He took the opportunity to look out over the grounds and sighed. "None of them were Caroline."

She made a soft noise of understanding, then clucked her tongue. "Malcolm... Neither am I."

"I know that all too well." He tossed a grin at her, then sobered. "With you, it was different. I couldn't remember any of the requirements I had in mind, but I knew that you would be perfect." He suddenly searched her features with a burning intensity he did not expect. "It didn't make sense until I came back and saw you with them. I lost myself in my business in London, as I usually do, and when I returned, I realized that I was no longer needed. It was you they needed, not me."

Beth shook her head, put her hands on her hips, and suddenly look disapproving. "There you go again."

He reared back a little. "What do you mean?"

"You said last night that you were not needed," she told him, her brow puckering, "and you've just said it again. Is that why you have been distancing yourself from your children since Caroline's death? Because I know all about your lengthy trips to London, which have only extended since then."

Well, that could not be entirely true. Beth couldn't know *all* about them, as no one knew their true purpose, but her instinct was spot-on. "It was easier than being here," he replied in a low voice. "They didn't want me, they wanted her. I have been useless! Hardly a father at all."

She slapped his arm with surprising sharpness, bringing him out of himself. "Of course, they wanted her, Malcolm, but that didn't mean they didn't want you!" She sighed and looped her arm through his, rubbing the spot she had hit. "I cannot imagine having to face them and this place without her, but you cannot avoid it all simply to save yourself the pain."

"I know," he rasped, his throat closing with emotion.

Beth leaned her head against him, and he found that oddly comforting.

"I like feeling needed," he eventually admitted. "The idea of a purpose, a conviction, something to drive me. I was jealous of you last night, handling everything so perfectly without any assistance from me. You didn't need me at all, and I didn't mean to marry someone so capable."

She chuckled and looked up at him. "I doubt you'll need to play the hero for me, Malcolm, but that does not render you useless by any stretch. Do you know who truly needs you? Your children. You keep telling me that I am not their mother, but at this moment, I am the closest thing to a parent they have. I realize that I am not Caroline, but I have a sense that she would agree with me about this."

Malcolm laughed humorlessly. "If she were here, she would have my head."

Beth grinned broadly. "There you have it. Both of your wives are telling you to be a father. Are you going to listen to us?"

He laughed again and gave her a look. "I don't suppose I have any other course, do I?"

"Not one I'd recommend," she quipped, a twinkle appearing in her dark eyes. She sobered only slightly, her expression softening. "Malcolm, I've been trying to be capable for you, to keep you from regretting your decision to marry me. I won't apologize if I have succeeded in my efforts, not even to salvage your pride."

"I would never ask you to," he broke in, his words rushed.

She smiled a bit further. "But that doesn't mean I don't need you, either."

The quiet admission stunned him. His wife had taken the life he had given her by the reins and steered it on a more perfect and precise course than he could have expected. She had mastered the intricacies and details with ease and given his children a chance to return to a childhood of joy. And she was claiming to need *him*? How? Where? His mind staggered at the implications, and he was suddenly eager to know just what she meant.

But Beth remained blissfully unaware of any of her husband's racing thoughts and only smiled. "It does, however," she went on, "mean that you do not get the pleasure of kissing me again until you want to kiss *me*."

"I agree wholeheartedly," he affirmed, his response more earnest

127

than he'd meant it to be. "You deserve nothing less."

Beth's dimple appeared briefly, and she gave him a playful, prim nod, then slid her arm from his and started back towards the house.

He watched her go for a moment with something stirring in his heart, forming the oddest desire to smile. He liked his wife. He liked her a great deal. The trial of a morning he had expected with her had, instead, been invigorating and freeing. It was the most meaningful conversation he'd had in months, if not years. He saw the promise of a fond friendship between them, if nothing else.

But if he were to be perfectly frank with himself, and perfectly aware of his current state, he would have to admit that there was very little chance that it would be nothing else.

"Beth?" he called softly.

She turned back to face him, her pale skirts twisting about her legs slightly in the grass.

He gave her a hint of a smile. "I don't think you'll have to wait very long."

Beth's eyes widened, and she blinked slowly. Then she tucked an invisible strand of hair behind her ear as her cheeks colored, her eyes darting about for something else to look at. She turned back around and continued up to the house, her pace quicker than before.

Malcolm's smile spread swiftly at that.

He rather liked seeing his wife's discomfiture when he flattered her. She was a beautiful woman to any set of eyes, but when she looked like that? He liked it rather a lot.

And he had half a mind to do it again.

Chapter Twelve

The next several days were markedly different for the pair of them, and Malcolm was growing more attached to his wife by the day. By the hour, if truth be told, but that was only today. At least, he hoped it was only today. He really could make no promises.

Somehow, between the breakfast meal and that of luncheon, he had sought her out three times, on perfectly legitimate matters. Each time, he'd found her doing rather menial tasks, though equally legitimate. She never seemed to mind, and somehow, she was lovelier each time he saw her. Whether she was going over the menu with Mrs. Rawlins or responding to a letter from her mother, she was pleased to see him either way and did not seem to mind the interruptions. Capably and perfectly, she'd answered each of his questions, all of which could easily have waited for a later time to be presented to her collectively.

He could not have said why he felt so compelled to seek her out, but reason seemed a trifling matter at the time.

Presently, he was seeking his wife once more, this time out of doors. She had taken the children from their studies for a bit of playtime, as the day was unseasonably warm. She tended to encourage time away from their classes in favor of activity. While he would have stopped it before had he known of it, now that he had seen the good it was doing his children, he did all he could to encourage it. His boys had invited him to join them in their army games, which he found more than slightly tempting, but first, he must find his wife.

The last thing he expected was to see her sprawled out on the grass with his daughters, their skirts spread out as if posing for a portrait from above, their hair nearly perfectly arranged and scattered with flowers. The little girls had their eyes squeezed tightly shut, while Beth lay as calm and serene as the day itself.

Malcolm took a moment to observe the sight, his throat suddenly constricting. It should not have stirred him so poignantly, but there was no denying that it did. He would never forget that sight as long as he lived.

But he could not stand here forever, and he rather wished his wife would spend time with him instead of with his daughters, selfish though the wish was.

"What have we here?" he asked, clearing his throat and stepping forward.

Beth cracked open an eye, her smile quick and easy. "Isn't it obvious, Monty?"

He fought the urge to smile back. "Not immediately, no."

She closed her eyes and smiled still. "Janie, will you tell your father what we are about?"

His dark-haired daughter lifted her head from the grass. "We're becoming fairies, Papa!"

"And Bitsy says this is how fairies get wings!" Greer added excitedly, her wild curls now tangled with flowers and grass.

Malcolm kept his face properly somber and glanced back at his wife, whose feet were now only inches from his. "Does she, now?" he mused.

Beth bit down on her lip, her eyes no longer closed.

"And how would Beth know?" he asked his daughters, still looking at his wife.

Beth suddenly nudged his ankle hard, her eyes mischievous as she fought to keep her smile contained.

"Bitsy, Papa!" Greer insisted.

He shifted his eyes back to his girls, unable to miss the correction. "Pardon?"

Jane pushed herself up to her elbows. "We call her Bitsy, Papa. She said we could. Especially when we're becoming fairies, we must call her by her fairy name, or it won't work."

Malcolm stared at his oldest girl, blinking slowly. "But you call her Bitsy all the time?"

Both girls nodded repeatedly. "It's a good enough name for all the time, don't you think?" Jane asked with a smile as she put her head back down on the grass.

Malcolm couldn't breathe for a moment. He'd heard the children call her Bitsy before, several times, but it never seemed to register in his mind that they were doing so. She'd found her name. She'd earned a name, a title, from his children! He'd remembered Janie's tear-filled voice telling Beth that they were her family, too, and that had struck him then, but now...

She was part of their family.

She was *his* family.

He moved his foot closer to hers, their eyes meeting as his ankle rubbed hers. She smiled a little, and he pressed more firmly against her, only to find her pressing back against him. Her smile turned softer, warmer, and it set his insides aflame, bringing the same sort of smile to his face. He suddenly could very much imagine kissing her and doing so quite thoroughly. He had no doubt he would enjoy the experience immensely.

But more than that, and somehow beyond, he felt the sudden desire to give in to the feelings stretching his heart. Something that told him to let Beth in, to open himself, and to forgo any semblance of pride.

There was too much swirling within him to manage sense, but staring at his wife gave him a remarkable sense of clarity. And the slight pressure against his ankle grounded him more than anything he could ever recall.

"Will you come with me?" he heard himself ask, keeping his gaze on her.

Beth tilted her head slightly in the grass, a twinkling light in her eye. "Where?"

He smirked a little, feeling as though she were intentionally toying with him, which was a bit of a rarity in his life. No one teased him about anything; no one would ever dare. Yet here was his young and impudent wife, lying in the grass and teasing him about his intentions towards *her*, of all things!

Did he really need another reason to want her?

"Anywhere," he replied in a low voice, letting his mouth curve into a smile.

Her smile flickered uncertainly, and her cheeks flushed a little, but then the playfulness returned, and she returned her head to its previous position, closing her eyes once more.

"I am still trying to become a fairy. I couldn't possibly go anywhere."

His daughters giggled, but Malcolm couldn't spare a glance for them. He felt his smile growing but kept it in check to contain his helpless amusement. He pressed his leg harder against hers. "I really must speak with you, Beth."

"And I really have promised the girls we could become fairies," she replied, her own smile quivering against her cheeks, her eyes still closed. "How am I to become the beautiful Fairy Princess Bitsy if I am up walking about with you?"

How, indeed?

"I have no doubt you would find a way," he murmured, letting his eyes rake over her. "You're already more than halfway there."

Beth's eyes sprang open, and she stared at him, her smile slowly shrinking to something that clenched his stomach and weakened his knees. Her gaze fixed on his, and somehow, amid the swirling sensations within him, he registered the fact that her breathing was growing unsteady. But then, so was his.

"Truly, Papa?" Jane cried in delight, sitting up from her position.

Malcolm smiled, still looking at Beth. "Of course. Can't you see the way she sparkles?"

Color rushed into Beth's cheeks, and she lowered her eyes, that soft and bewitching smile still distracting him.

Jane and Greer, who had also risen to see, giggled and nodded. "Yes!"

"And how the sun is making her hair and skin glow?" he added, ignoring the increasing pressure from her leg at his ankle.

"It's working!" Jane exclaimed, clapping her hands.

"And I think, if you wish hard enough," Malcolm continued, enjoying this far too much, "you may just find that our beautiful Bitsy fairy has been given wings..."

He saw Beth's breath catch, and his own may have stuttered at the sight, even as his girls scrambled over to check for her wings, disrupting the scene entirely.

Malcolm stepped back, exhaling slowly to settle his racing heart, and smiled fondly at the way his daughters so clearly adored his wife. Soon, she was tickling both girls, and all were laughing uproariously.

Flowers still scattered in her hair, she looked up at him and cleared her throat, the color high in her cheeks. "Perhaps now we might have that walk. Now that I am a fairy."

"I would never wish to burden a fairy with so unworthy a companion," he told her shaking his head and taking another step back. "Perhaps if you find yourself human once more, we may."

Beth tilted her head at him in confusion. "Monty?"

He stepped forward and offered her a hand at once, which she took, and he helped her rise.

"Malcolm," he corrected her in a low voice. "I insist."

Her lips parted in surprise, and he stepped away again from the temptation to kiss her senseless.

"Now, if you'll excuse me, Fairy Princess, I must go to battle with the boys." He bowed, and turned on his heel, striding back towards his sons.

As he'd half-hoped, he heard Beth following him quickly. "Malcolm."

He stopped, biting back a groan of satisfaction that surprised him. Swallowing, he turned to face her, forcing his expression to be playfully polite. "Yes, Beth?"

Her hair was coming nearly undone, which made her look more the magical creature she was pretending to be than the wife he knew, and yet he wanted her more for it. "You wanted to talk with me?"

Again, Malcolm shook his head, this time slowly and smiling. "No, Beth, I wanted to spend time with you. I didn't care what we talked about. I would have made up twelve different topics just to keep you longer."

Somehow, she blushed even more and fidgeted where she stood.

He gently reached out and stroked her cheek. "I love the way you blush," he whispered. "Especially when you blush for me."

"You have a way of bringing me to it," she replied, her voice barely audible, her eyes lowered once more.

He stroked her cheek again, then leaned forward to kiss it softly, letting his lips slide a little along her cheekbone. "I know," he breathed against her skin. Then, before he could help himself, he dusted his lips across hers, just a brief grazing of their fullness.

Beth's breath caught on a gasp, and Malcolm wrenched himself away, striding back towards the hill. "See you at dinner!" he called cheerily, even though he was coming apart at the seams.

Something was happening to his control and his sanity. Home was becoming quite the dangerous place. But if he were to be frank, it was also a remarkable amount of fun.

Beth's husband would be the death of her! One day he was flirtatious and charming and made her blush to the ends of her hair, and the next he was sweet and friendly and approachable. Just in the short weeks since that night outside the nursery, he had changed so much, and so had she.

He was never distant anymore, and sometimes it seemed he could see into her very soul, though she could sense secrets enough in him. Ever since that day on the lawn, he had made a point to spend a concentrated amount of time with her, and she had begun to crave it daily. They had walked the grounds together; they had gone out riding and seen the entire estate. They had even consulted over tenants' needs together, and that did not include the time they had spent together with the children. In all those times, they may not have been alone, but their bond grew somehow stronger.

But the hours spent with just the two of them...

Malcolm was an extraordinary man, if a bit confusing. Some days he held her hand as they walked; some days his look was more intimate than anything she could have imagined, and some days he exuded no romantic airs whatsoever. Through it all, he was becoming more than just the man she'd married. He was becoming a friend, and one that was growing dearer as the days went on.

Their conversations ranged from their pasts, to the children, to personal details that revealed more and more of themselves. Each was stimulating and engaging, as well as illuminating. Malcolm bore a depth of soul that she would never have anticipated, and he listened to her with the same intensity. Every word she spoke seemed important to him which emboldened her to share more of herself.

He told her stories from his life in London, and with such detail and ease that Beth felt she knew these people herself and had experienced these things. She had laughed so much her cheeks had ached, and she thrilled with the new insight into her husband. She had growled with disgust and irritation at his description of Lady Lavinia Herschel and her antics, and even now, the memory of it set her teeth on edge.

Malcolm had found her reaction amusing and endearing, he said, but Beth failed to see the humor in it. Oh, she knew it was utterly ridiculous, and if it had not been directed at her husband, she no doubt would have laughed. But as it was, she thought that she might scratch out the woman's eyes if she ever met her.

Malcolm's complete disinterest in Lady Lavinia's blatantly suggestive behavior settled Beth a little, but still, she wished she were bold enough to bind him to her side by her own wiles. She knew, however, that she would simply have to trust in his integrity, loyalty, and personal morality.

He had asked her to tell him more about the name that the children had given her, which seemed of peculiar interest to him, and never failed to bring a smile to both of their faces. Truth be told, it was a name her favorite brother, Michael had used for her as a child. Beth had been the youngest in her family and of a diminutive stature from the beginning. The moniker had faded from use as she had grown, and no one had called her Bitsy for ages. But on the day she had taught the girls how to become fairies, out of sheer desperation to interact with them, it had been the first fairy-like name to come to mind. She'd not enjoyed the name much when she'd been a child, but now it was perhaps the sweetest name she could imagine.

Malcolm had asked very few questions during her recounting, but his smile had kept her talking. Beth spoke of how Jane had been the first to call her Bitsy outside of the games. The others had taken it up themselves, one by one, until it was the name she craved to hear more than any other.

"You love my children," Malcolm had said softly.

Beth had nodded, swallowing with difficulty. "Very much," she had managed to squeak. "Though I know they are not, it feels as though they are mine, as well."

Malcolm had said nothing for a moment, which had given Beth a moment of panic. Would he once again remind her of the true nature of things? But instead, he had taken her hand in his, kissed the back of it, and then laced their fingers as they continued on their walk. She was not sure her heart had ever flown to such heights as then.

He had not kissed her since that day on the lawn either, other than polite kisses to her hand, and some that had been slightly less than polite. Beth admitted to herself that she was beginning to grow more uneasy about his amorous distance.

In every other respect, he was beyond reproach and kept her laughing and blushing on a regular basis. She was growing fonder of him, and more attracted to him, by the day. With every missed opportunity, a small but persistent itching sensation began to claw at her. But Malcolm needed to decide in which direction to take their relationship. It was he who was torn, and with perfectly good reason. Malcolm had to be the one to act, and Beth had to be the one to wait.

Unfortunately, she had never been very good at waiting. Today, she had chosen complete avoidance for a stratagem, feeling much safer outside the house than within it. The children would be in lessons for much of the morning, and her husband would be occupied with estate business, as he was meeting with the manager.

She prayed he would keep to his planned schedule. He was usually very dedicated to his commitments, but he was so changed of late that she could not pretend to anticipate what he would do. She needed space from him for a small moment. From his presence, from his essence, from anything that reminded her of him. But where could she go to accomplish that? In her present state, it would most likely require removing herself to a remote corner of Africa, she supposed.

Even the grounds reminded her of Malcolm, so often they had walked them together. Any glance towards the house had her scanning every window and balcony for a glimpse of him. The bleariness in her eyes told of a night's sleep lost thinking of him.

She ran her thumb absently over the ring he had given her only a few days ago. Its weight reminded her of the moment he had given it to her, sliding off the simple gold band from their wedding in favor of something a little grander. A little more appropriate, he'd suggested.

A little more heart-fluttering, perhaps.

Beth shook her head now, her heart skipping as she recalled the feather-light kiss he had given her fingers when the new ring had been placed. Any woman who had endured a true Season with courtship would undoubtedly have been immune to such actions. But Beth had not had a Season. She'd never had a courtship. She had never had any other man show such interest. Woefully ignorant, insecure, and downright terrified, how could she feel any other way? Everything was new and different, and she had no idea what to expect or what might follow.

These, however, were not the sort of thoughts to share with one's husband, as he was the one to blame for causing such turmoil. She could not even bring herself to truly confide in Lily about it, as she knew Malcolm all too well.

The only person she thought might be an appropriate confidante was someone who would not, could not, respond.

Caroline.

"I must be barking mad," Beth muttered to herself as she entered the cemetery, respectfully stepping around various late members of the Colerain family.

Imagine a woman going to speak to her husband's late wife about said husband in the hopes that the late wife might give some insight from her previous years of experience with the man. She must be truly desperate if she had come to this.

As she looked on Caroline's tombstone, she felt her stomach settle and her breathing slow, and an ironic smile lit her lips. Yes, she was desperate. But Caroline would understand.

Beth sank to the ground, as she usually did when she was here, and let her shawl fall around her. "Good morning, Caroline," she murmured, still smiling. "I am in need of your guidance. Again."

She paused as if she could hear the woman's warm and gentle laughter, almost rasping in its tone.

"I'm so confused," she confessed with a sigh. She reached out to touch the petals of the wilting flowers Jane had brought to her mother's grave a few days before. "I don't know what to say or what to do, I don't know what he is feeling, and I don't know if this change in him means that he is letting go of you or..."

She winced and clamped down on her lips in embarrassment.

"That was a terrible thing to say, please forgive me." Beth tilted her head back and let the sun warm and soothe her face. "It's just... Caroline, I want him to love me! I know it's a ridiculous thought, as I cannot even allow myself to say that I love him. I am afraid to hope that his recent attentions mean anything more than affectionate friendship."

She groaned and put her face in her hands. "That would have been more than ideal for me before. Why did he have to be more handsome and more wonderful than I thought? Why couldn't he have more flaws?"

At that moment, she would have sworn she heard Caroline snort with laughter, and she rolled her eyes as she grinned.

"Well, yes, I know very well he has flaws, thank you," she told the headstone. "They are not difficult to find. But... why couldn't any of them have been truly insurmountable?" She snapped off a small leaf from the flowers and made a face. "And why do some of those flaws make him even more attractive?"

She threw a derisive glare at the headstone. "You could have done something to improve him."

Again, she felt the imagined snort, followed by a blunt, "I did."

Beth smiled, shaking her head. Then she looked beyond the headstone, staring off into the distance. "I'm falling in love with him, Caroline. Or at least, I think I am. And he told me we would not have a marriage of affection. Am I a fool for desiring more?"

Sadly, this time there was no response from Caroline, but Beth should have known better. Caroline would have never answered a question like that, not even for the woman helping her husband to raise their children.

She decided to change the topic and give her usual report on the children when she heard footsteps in the distance behind her. She turned quickly, her eyes scanning the wooded area on the outskirts and the church beyond.

Malcolm was approaching, his head down. It seemed he hadn't

noticed Beth there, which she found difficult to believe. At least he was too far away to have heard the gist of her one-way conversation. She rose to her feet quickly, glanced back at Caroline's headstone with widened eyes, then faced her husband again.

He raised his eyes. When there was no hint of surprise there, she knew her instinct had been correct. He had seen her and had intentionally come this way.

"I did not mean to disturb you," he told her in a soft tone.

She shook her head quickly. "No, I was just finishing. I will leave you to your peace."

Malcolm glanced at the headstone and swallowed. "I did not come here for that. I came in search of you."

"You did?" Beth blurted out, forsaking all dignity.

He nodded once, averting his eyes from Caroline's grave. "Will you walk back to the house with me?"

Beth took his offered arm, wondering at his slight formality. He had not been formal in some time, and she did not want him to return to that version of himself. They walked out of the cemetery, then past the chapel, and only when they approached the house itself did he speak.

"I must return to London," he said, glancing over at her.

"Oh," she murmured, not bothering to hide her disappointment.

He surprised her by replying miserably, "I know."

It was strange how such small words could give her such comfort. "When must you go?"

"Straightaway. It's rather imperative, I'm afraid."

Beth nodded automatically, chewing the inside of her lip. Then she released it to ask, "And how long will you be gone this time?"

He sighed heavily and disconnected their arms only to take her hand and entwine their fingers. "Not long, I hope. Certainly not as long as last time."

She believed him absolutely, but there was an odd hesitation to his tone that gave her pause. But what could she do? "Very well, then," she responded, clinging to the warmth of his fingers between hers.

Malcolm stopped them both and turned to her, letting his fingers stroke hers. "Don't do that, I beg you. I can't bear to have you turn submissive and biddable as if I have ordered it. You are my wife, not a servant. Tell me what you truly feel."

Beth's heart swelled and ached as she looked at him. "How else can I respond, Malcolm? If you must go, then you must go. I don't wish to fight about it or say anything to keep you from your duties." She exhaled shortly and prayed for courage, then reached up with her free hand and touched his face, stroking his cheek with her thumb. "But I cannot pretend that I am not disappointed. Or that I will not miss you."

He closed his eyes, then took her palm and kissed it gently, turning it over to kiss the back of her hand twice, holding it tightly.

Suddenly fighting tears, Beth asked, "Will you say goodbye to the children?"

"I already have." He touched her cheek as well, his expression serious. "I won't be gone long."

"Do you promise?" she asked, trying for a teasing tone.

Malcolm only nodded, then stepped forward to kiss her brow and moved past her, heading for the stables.

Her mind in turmoil, Beth watched him go, just as confused as she was before, her emotions in disarray, her thoughts just as focused.

She was falling in love with her husband. Would that change while he was away?

Or would it only make things worse?

Chapter Thirteen

$\mathscr{I}$t was a good thing he had returned to London, Malcolm told himself.

It was.

Things were growing more complicated with their suspects, and he felt greater unease over Rogue. The reports he had received absorbed every waking thought. Well, every space in his mind that was not already occupied by thoughts of Beth, at any rate.

Mr. Herschel had been behaving even more erratically, according to Gent's street children who had been tailing him. Messages seemed to constantly go out while very few came back in, and the servants carrying them took great care to use stealth. Were it not for the fact that the Herschels' house was under constant watch, that detail might never have been caught, and they would never have discovered that particular avenue to investigate.

When it was discovered that the letters were going to known traitors and sympathizers, Malcolm had made the decision to come to London and take the reins.

The League had begun intercepting letters sent out from Herschel's residence, using a collection of thieves and pickpockets that could do so easily. They did the same with missives coming into the Herschels as well, though there were fewer of them. That was not surprising, even with Mr. Herschel's official parliamentary work. He was not a popular member, but he did have some influence.

Once they had the letters in their possession, the clerks furiously set to work copying their contents. Within an hour or two, the original documents had been slipped back into legitimate channels and on to their intended recipients. Back at the office, the contents were then analyzed. As yet, Malcolm hadn't heard whether anything had proven to be of any interest, but the others had not known he was here. Or, more likely, they had not let him know that they knew. It was only a matter of time.

But then, it had only been a couple of days. A miserable, tormented couple of days in which he had accomplished very little.

A growing feeling of dread nagged Malcolm over the League's current lack of progress. Without discovering the hidden objective of the traitors and their masters in the faction, there was not much for Malcolm to find satisfaction in.

"Please tell me I'm not seeing you right now."

Malcolm glanced up from his desk, which was uncharacteristically disorganized and cluttered, and met Gent's gaze rather mildly. "You are not seeing me right now."

Apparently, despite Gent's words, that was not what he wished to hear. "Cap…"

"What? Cap's here?"

"Is he out of his bleeding mind?"

Malcolm sat back with a grimace and waited for the other two to appear, knowing it was useless to do anything else.

Rogue's icy eyes were wide as he appeared, while Rook looked more like he would like to put his fist in Malcolm's face.

"How long have you been here?" Rogue growled in a low voice.

"Three days."

His jaw dropped. "Three days? How did we not know that? How did you come in without us knowing?"

Malcolm's brow rose in a hint of mocking surprise. "I'm a spy, Rogue."

Rook snorted, then covered it with several coughs to avoid being beaten by his colleague.

But Rogue was still absorbed in Malcolm's response, unaffected by the sarcasm. "We've been sending you reports. Nothing is happening. There is no reason for you to be here."

"I believe that decision lies with me," Malcolm snapped coldly, folding his arms. "And what do you mean 'nothing'? You call Herschel's sudden involvement 'nothing'?"

"It's a development," Rogue allowed, his expression never changing. "But there is no progress yet. You don't need to be here."

Malcolm scowled at him. "You think it's easy for me to be away while so much is unknown, and you could be in danger?"

"It ought to be easy," Rook muttered, snorting yet again.

Malcolm opened his mouth to reply when he saw Rogue nodding. "What? You agree with Rook, do you?"

"Of course, I agree. I'm always in danger, Cap. We are all in danger every moment of every day, including you." Rogue shrugged, finally looking less shocked and more like himself. "This is not the first time I have come close to being compromised. I would not risk entering the office if there were any real danger we could identify. You know I'd have gone underground and followed the proper procedures and protocols."

Gent was nodding as well now. "And do you know where Rogue learned all of that, Cap?"

Malcolm shifted uncomfortably in his seat. He knew full well that Rogue had learned that particular bit of insight and training from Cap. It was the same bit of insight and wisdom he passed on to the new trainees every time there was a new crop of them.

"I just felt that I was needed here," Malcolm said under his breath, averting his eyes. "You can't deny that there is work to be done."

They said nothing for a moment, which told him that there was truth to his words, and he felt a brief surge of satisfaction in that.

"There will always be work that needs doing," Gent finally conceded, drawing Malcolm's gaze with the smile in his tone. Gent's eyes twinkled a little as his smile grew. "But I suspect your reason for being here at this time has nothing to do with the country across the channel, faction or otherwise."

The other two looked at Gent quickly, then back at Malcolm with far more interest.

Malcolm bit back a growl and shook his head. "I don't particularly like what you are insinuating, Gent."

"So, you are not here to hide from your bride, then, eh, Cap?" Rook suggested without hesitation.

He ground his teeth together. "I don't see how that is relevant."

"I don't see how your being here is helping anyone," Rogue pointed out. "If you're too distracted by thoughts of your wife to focus on the work at hand, you're more of a hindrance than a help."

Malcolm's ire flared up, but it was quick to die down as he realized that Rogue was right. He exhaled slowly, which seemed to signal to the others that he would reveal something significant. Each made himself comfortable within Cap's office.

"I don't want to talk about it," he told them stubbornly, meeting the gaze of each.

"And yet..." Rook replied, gesturing for him to get on with it.

It was not in Malcolm's nature to confide in his men about personal matters. Or to confide in anyone at all. About anything. Yet he suddenly felt the urge to confess everything pressing against his chest and throat.

"I don't know what to do," he admitted with a groan. "Everything is shifting and changing so fast, and she is... She is..." The words did not seem to come to mind, and he struggled with how to describe just what he was experiencing. "She is lovely and charming and perfect for my children, and I find that I like her much more than I thought I would." He swallowed with difficulty as an echo of desire struck him. "A lot more. I don't know what to do."

"Well, Cap," Gent said slowly, his voice ringing with amusement, "you see, when a man and a woman find themselves attracted to each other..."

The other two snickered uncontrollably, and Malcolm tried to quell them with a look, but it proved useless.

"I *am* attracted to her," Malcolm heard himself confess, his voice hardly sounding like his own. "Far more than..." He shook his head quickly and forced his expression to clear. "At any rate, I decided it was best to stay away while I try to sort it all out."

No one said anything for a moment. No one moved. Then Rogue shook his head, his expression heavy with resignation. "Coward."

Malcolm stilled and felt his scalp tingle. "What did you say?" he inquired slowly.

Rook cleared his throat. "I believe my esteemed colleague called you a coward, sir. And I quite agree."

He was on his feet before he could even blink. His rage reached unknown heights, and he could already feel his fists pummeling them both into a bloody oblivion. But the stunned expressions on his men's faces reminded him who he was. His balled fists unclenched, slowly, and he pressed them hard into his desk.

"Perhaps I am," he murmured tightly. "I don't know anymore."

The others chuckled, though he could find nothing at all humorous in his statement.

"Poor Cap has a too-pretty wife," Rook announced with a nudge to Rogue's side.

"Woe is him," Rogue replied dryly with a mocking sigh.

Malcolm threw them a derisive glare, but both smiled at it sweetly.

Gent, who had been remarkably quiet by comparison, stepped forward and put a calming hand on Malcolm's shoulder. "Go home, Cap," he urged gently. "Go home and stay there."

He wanted to argue, he wanted to toss orders at them, to shout at them, to deny that anything they'd said had any effect on him! But he found that all he truly wanted was... *Beth*.

He wanted to go home.

He stared into the eyes of Gent, his most romantic colleague, and found a greater degree of understanding than he had anticipated. That alone convinced him, and he nodded once.

They left him alone after that, satisfied that he would do his duty. And as Malcolm had always been a man of his word, he had no choice but to do as he had agreed.

The moment he had turned his horse back towards Hampshire the next morning, he wanted nothing more than to be there. Gone were his reservations about his men, about their tasks, about anything in London at all. The only thing he cared about was getting home to his wife and children, and he rode like the devil to get there. He only stopped when he had to, resting his horse only when he had to, and probably not long enough. But the animal seemed possessed with the same drive that Malcolm felt rising within him, and the pair of them raced on towards Knightsgate, towards... home.

Hours later, sore and fatigued, he arrived, only grunting a word of greeting to the stable master. He made an impulsive decision to skirt the house in favor of a brief detour.

The cemetery was silent, as usual, and as he moved towards the one headstone he tended to frequent, he saw the evidence of recent visitors, some of whom were young, their bouquets far less refined, but no less beautiful.

Malcolm swallowed with some difficulty as he went to one knee before Caroline's headstone, wiping his hand across the smooth surface.

"I think you know why I've come," he murmured as his fingers traced the letters. "More than that, I think... I think you would give your consent. I think you would agree with me."

He paused as if waiting for an answer, though he knew none would come.

Still, he smiled. "I don't quite know what I feel for her yet, Caroline, but I think I could love her one day. I think she loves our children, and I think she might be the best decision I've made since..." His throat closed briefly, and he swallowed. "I will always love and treasure you, Caroline. You know that."

A rough exhale escaped him, and he patted the headstone gently. "I'm going to give myself to this marriage, Caroline. I am going to let Beth in and move forward."

His hair suddenly ruffled on a breeze, and he looked up at the sky, smiling with more warmth than he expected in this place. "I take it you think it's a good idea?"

He laughed as though she had given him her usual blatant look, though no such answer came. He rose from his knee and looked at the headstone once more. "It's time, Caroline. And I'm ready."

Again, the breeze came, and he closed his eyes for a moment, nodding.

Then he turned from the cemetery and moved back towards the house, and the grounds beyond, sensing that Beth would have allowed the children out of doors on so fine a day. He could barely sustain the mad pace his feet set, his strides long and brisk, but he could not bring himself to slow them even slightly.

His instincts were correct, as he saw them out behind the house. The children were rolling themselves down a small hill, laughing uproariously. His wife, though standing and watching, was rumpled enough that he knew she had done it once or twice herself.

He slowed, at last, watching the antics with a smile he could not contain.

Greer and Samuel wobbled and fell with obvious dizziness after their turns, laughing all the while as their older siblings attempted to aid them in their return to the top of the hill. He watched as Beth sank down to pick blades of grass from Greer's hair and kiss Samuel's brow as she smoothed his hair, her smile as warm as the day's sun. He watched as she turned to Archer and Jane, who were obviously begging to have another go. She beamed at them, nodding her consent.

Just as they were preparing to do so, Archer spotted him in the distance. "Papa!" he called, waving his arm.

Malcolm felt his heart lift as he waved back enthusiastically, then felt it soar when he saw the radiance on Beth's face as she recognized him.

He couldn't help it; he grinned at the lot of them.

The hill was forgotten as his children raced towards him, and he ran quickly to meet them. Archer reached him first, slamming into his side as his arms wrapped around his waist. Jane matched him on the other side, her exuberance less pronounced, as was her nature, but the joy in her eyes prompted him to kiss her cheeks repeatedly, making her giggle. He scooped up Samuel and Greer with a mock groan and let them hug his neck tightly despite the choking sensation that brought.

They jabbered rapidly at him about everything he'd missed, walking with him back towards the hill, and he tried his best to answer them, but his attention was distracted.

Beth had not run towards him, remaining on the hill, but she had taken a few steps in his direction, and now she stood there, smiling with warmth and, he hoped, relief. It was the sort of smile he would have crossed oceans for, the kind that set one's heart aflame. He suspected she would have been grinning wildly if she were not sensitive to his preferred restraint.

His *formerly* preferred restraint, he should say. At this moment, he wanted nothing more than to see that imagined wild grin, though he doubted it could eclipse the brilliance he was currently viewing.

"Malcolm," she greeted, her smile tugging at her cheeks.

He let Greer and Samuel slide from his hold as he ascended the hill to her. "Beth."

Only when he was directly before her could he see how she trembled, how her fingers clenched together, and that there was the faintest sheen of tears in her eyes.

He was a damned fool to ever have left.

He took her face in his hands, smoothed her cheeks, and whispered, "Sweet Beth." Then he closed his eyes and pressed his lips to hers, stunned with the ease with which her lips molded to his, with her enthusiastic response, and with how perfectly right it was to feel this way. His lips caressed hers over and over again, keeping things gentle, but also promising a future of much, much more.

He felt her rising response and broke off before they forgot themselves, smiling his amusement at her unsteady breathing and her faint moan of disappointment. He met her eyes and stroked her hair once, then tapped her cheek where a slight blush was forming. She rolled her eyes a little, smiling at his silent reminder, and then surprised him again by wrapping her arms around him.

"Welcome home," she murmured, laying her head against his chest.

Malcolm looked heavenward as his emotions skittered in five different directions, his arms encircling Beth tightly, holding her close, unable to respond.

"Papa!" Archer called, though he was not far off.

Malcolm turned to his son, keeping one arm around Beth. "Archer?"

His son, a perfect blend of his parents in appearance, gave him a singularly mischievous grin he could only have learned from his mother. Or his stepmother. "Will you roll the hill with us?"

The other children cheered their encouragement, and Malcolm made a thoughtful face, considering it.

"You would not refuse your son, would you, my lord?" Beth asked in a low voice.

He gave her a mock warning look. "You are the reason I am in this spot of trouble, and I suspect more lies in my future."

She shrugged one shoulder. "Perhaps. But for now, it is only a roll down the hill. The children and I have done it several times."

He exhaled heavily at the taunting words, then shook his head and kissed her quickly. "Troublemaker."

She grinned cheekily. "Always."

Malcolm turned to his children, then pulled off his jacket, eliciting cheers of delight. "Very well. How should I do it?"

Beth was not generally fond of athletic activity early in the morning, but her husband had suggested the night before that they enjoy a morning ride together. She had agreed so readily that she'd had no thought for what that would entail.

Even now, perched on horseback, she was confused by it. She was barely awake enough to blink without effort, how was she supposed to engage in conversation and flirtation with her husband while simultaneously riding a massive animal that could seriously injure her if she were not mindful?

All that she could say for herself was that she looked properly fetching, thanks to the attentions of two maids she had engaged for the endeavor. They, at least, had been alert enough to consider things properly. She did so love the deep green of her riding habit and hoped it might do for her complexion and figure everything that the girls had promised.

Malcolm, of course, looked utterly perfect. Perfectly dressed, perfectly poised, and perfectly tempting. He had changed somehow while he was London. He did not look as imposing as he once had to her, his hair a little less perfect than before, his cravat a little less formal. He looked more real, more human… more attainable. Even though Beth still felt half-asleep, she was very aware and appreciative of her husband this morning.

He had not said much to her yet, but it was early, and they had not eaten before they had embarked. He had posed the idea of a brisk ride together followed by sharing breakfast together, and she had thrilled at his offer, noting his repeated emphasis on the word together. His eager greeting with the children and subsequent play with them had been different, more relaxed and natural. He had surprised them all by suggesting they not return to lessons that day. He had raced the boys, twirled the girls, and had rolled the grassy hill a surprising five times.

His very warm greeting for her had shattered any restraint she may still have had with him. She had trembled with the anticipation of his return, keeping her feet planted where they were to avoid making a scene. Watching him with the children had brought tears to her eyes, and then to see the way he had looked up at her... It was as if his motions were half their speed as he approached her, her heart pounding twice its usual pace.

She could play out the entire kiss second by second, every touch and motion seared into her memory. More than half the night she had played it over and over, reliving the glorious experience of his lips on hers, his hands cradling her face gently, and she, helpless to resist and weakening further by the moment, could only tremble more in his hold and cling to the strength he provided.

And that had been a fairly gentle kiss, especially when compared with the one he had given her in the hallway that night.

But yesterday's kiss, and the small ones that had happened since, stirred her more than the passion she had felt from him before. Because this time, he was kissing *her*.

Her heart swelled, bringing a smile to her face, and she turned to look at her husband, riding wordlessly beside her.

As if he could sense her gaze, he tilted his head to look at her, smiling a soft, crooked smile at her notice.

"What is it, Malcolm?" she flirted coyly.

He shrugged a shoulder. "You make me smile."

She grinned cheekily in response, which made him laugh, which of course made her blush. "Stop!" she protested, lifting the back of a gloved hand to her face.

"You blush so delightfully," he teased, bringing his horse closer. "And apparently more easily in the morning. I shall have to remember that."

Beth sighed, shaking her head. "If only there were something in you I could exploit with such ease in return. It is most distressing to be so susceptible to your efforts."

Malcolm chuckled softly. "I have no doubt you will think of something, Beth. You are far too creative to let this lie for long."

"Truer words were never spoken," she chortled, sitting a little taller in her saddle. "Have a care, Lord Montgomery. I shall be watching you very closely."

Suddenly, she saw that bare hint of a smile that had once beguiled her, and she felt her chest tighten at the sight of it.

"I look forward to your keen observations, Lady Montgomery."

Good heavens, this was getting out of hand far too quickly, and she was swimming in far deeper waters than she could tolerate. Beth cleared her throat and quickly looked away. "Did you accomplish all you needed to in London?"

Malcolm's low chuckle told her he was not fooled by her rather weak attempt to divert attention. But he took pity on her and replied, "I did, which was rather convenient, as I had an intense desire to be elsewhere by the end of it."

She did not dare look at him for fear of what she might see in his expression. "Ah, so you went to visit your lover, Lady Lavinia Herschel?"

He coughed suddenly, and she glanced over, finding his face torn between horror and amusement. "Good lord, Beth..." he coughed again.

Beth found herself grinning at him. "What, surely she has not thrown you over? Not with how fervently she laid her claims to you!"

Malcolm clamped down on his lips, fighting laughter.

"I have half a mind to invite her here, you know," she said with a mock sigh. "It must be so inconvenient for her to be parted from you."

"I will have you know," he responded loudly, smiling in earnest now, "that I did not see her on this trip, nor do I intend to see her at any point in time if I can help it. Nothing, and I repeat, nothing she has ever said or done could possibly interest me. I intend to only extend the barest courtesy, and only when absolutely required."

Beth smiled at him with real fondness. "Poor Lady Lavinia."

Malcolm snorted softly. "I daresay she will rally." He tilted his head to look at her, his smile turning quizzical. "Did you know she was pursuing me even while I was married before?"

She gaped a little. "So, you being a lonely and troubled widower did not spark her attentions?"

He shook his head. "All that did was increase her fervor."

Beth shuddered and gave her husband a frank look. "If you ever succumb to her wiles, Malcolm, I will personally shoot you."

He returned her look with the utmost derision. "Really, Beth, I have no intention of being unfaithful in any way, let alone sinking myself into that particular pit."

She smiled at his sudden venom and nodded her acknowledgment of his vow before turning her gaze back to the hills and bluffs before her.

"You're far livelier than I expected you to be this early," he observed, still sounding amused. "What has you so invigorated?"

"Thoughts of returning to my bed for a bit more sleep," Beth muttered good-naturedly, trying for a sour look and failing.

Malcolm laughed softly, close enough now to nudge her. "Is that all?"

Steeling herself, she turned to give him a slow smile. "Well, I could also be invigorated by the prospect of a handsome and charming man riding beside me."

His eyes darkened as he looked at her, and back was the sort-of smile she adored. "And he might be invigorated by his beautiful and engaging wife."

Beth released a slow exhale to steady her skittering heart and attempt to quell her rising blush. "And she might be wondering what has her husband so changed in so short a time."

"And he might reply that he simply opened his eyes and found himself somewhere new."

His tone had turned warmer, softer, and it rippled like a wave over her arms and legs and all throughout her body. She could not find the strength to look away, her heart pounding ruthlessly in her ears. She could not speculate as to his meaning, not with the current state of her heart. All she could attempt was to not question his intentions or doubt his words. Though it was difficult for her to imagine such a man finding particular interest in her, she could not mistake what she saw.

Or what she felt.

Her horse suddenly snorted and trotted anxiously forward, breaking the rising tension of the moment.

Beth settled her, laughing uneasily as she fought to recover.

Malcolm came up alongside her, chuckling as well. "Your horse seems restless."

She patted the horse's neck gently. "She just wants to race this morning." Beth glanced at her husband with a teasing quirk of her brows. "What say you, my lord? Do you have a race in you?"

He looked a little offended she would ask and gave a brisk nod. "Certainly."

Beth straightened up, tightening her hold on the reins. "Good." She clicked her tongue and kicked her heels into the horse sharply, taking off without warning.

"Hyah!" Malcolm shouted to his steed. He soon closed the distance.

She did her best to flatten herself along the horse, forgoing the ladylike posture she ought to have maintained in the saddle. Malcolm would not care, and neither did she. Her horse moved with power and ease, striding long and hard, and she grinned at the rush of pleasure she felt at being able to ride so recklessly. She hadn't ridden all-out like this since she was a young girl, but as it had then, it still gave her a thrill.

But in those times, she did not have a fellow rider in pursuit, and one that was fast approaching. She could hear his horse's hooves pounding the ground just behind her, could hear his grunted words to it, and she urged her mount to race on.

Malcolm was a better rider, though, and was soon right at her side and then passing her, not even glancing at her as he did so.

Beth snarled under her breath, pressing the horse faster, harder, desperate to wring as much power out of her and the horse as she could. She had to win. She *had* to.

She glanced back and was unprepared when her horse suddenly jumped over a boulder. The change in motion and force sent her catapulting out of the saddle backwards. She seemed to fall in slow motion, end over end, tumbling through the air, the breath stolen from her lungs. She faintly registered the sound of a cry, unsure if it was her own or her husband's, and saw the ground fast approaching.

She couldn't move, couldn't do anything, couldn't prevent what was about to happen.

All she could do was wait, anticipating the shock of landing.

Then everything went black…

Chapter Fourteen

$\mathcal{M}$alcolm was usually a very controlled man. A man of restraint and reservation, not prone to emotional outbursts or open distress, and a steady head amidst any chaos. But as his wife lay unconscious and still in her bed with a physician examining her, he felt all his usual boundaries snap and his control shred. He provoked the doctor with questions, demanded that he rouse her, paced the room frantically, and went so far as to bellow at the servants for disturbing them, and then do so again when they could do nothing to help.

The only thing he did not do was come close enough to the bed to touch Beth. He couldn't.

She lay so still, so pale. He feared that if he touched her, he would find her as cold and lifeless as she looked, despite being assured that she was, indeed, alive.

He would never, as long as he lived, forget the sight of Beth lying on the ground, her horse standing expectantly a few paces away. She was not sprawled out grotesquely or injured in an obvious way, but she had not been moving. He had vaulted off his horse to race to her side, and only when he was there could he find that she was breathing, though it was faint. Although his whole world had just exploded, he had somehow managed the sense to gather up her limp body and bear her gently in his arms.

His single-minded focus had been on getting Beth to Knightsgate and sending for the doctor. It was not until she had been set down in the bed and the doctor sent for that he had begun to shake. He had trembled from head to foot as the servants removed

Beth's habit and bonnet, and he'd felt his heart sink to his toes at the blood they had discovered at the back of her head and into her fair hair. Malcolm could not recall the doctor's name, though he had seen Archer not many days before and had treated the Colerain family for years. He did not know the speed with which the old man had ridden to the estate at the desperate summons of Malcolm's groom. But he hadn't come soon enough for Malcolm in his frantic state.

He ought to thank him for that when all of this was over. Provided he remembered. Or felt gratitude.

He stared at the doctor now, waiting impatiently with his arms tightly folded. For what had to be the seventh time in as many minutes, the older man held Beth's wrist, watching her with interest.

Suddenly, everything about him irritated Malcolm, from his almost complete baldness and white sideburns to the pudgy girth constricted by his waistcoat. He hated the way the physician hummed without emotion as he examined Beth. He felt his teeth grind every time the man shifted his weight and made the floorboards creak.

And he utterly despised the way the doctor was not speaking.

When he had first arrived, he had been quick to assure Malcolm that Beth was alive, which Malcolm knew already, and that the cut on the back of her head was not severe, which had been small relief.

He had not said more than ten words since, and Malcolm was beginning to think very intently about employing some of his less-than-polite spy training.

"I think she is coming 'round, my lord," the doctor said in a hopeful tone.

Malcolm's aching eyes shot to Beth when at last she moved, and his knees buckled as the weakest of moans escaped her lips.

He was at her side in a heartbeat, still unable to reach out and take her hand. "Beth?"

She turned her head towards the sound of his voice, then winced with another moan. "Hurts…" she whispered, her words slurred and barely coherent.

Malcolm's throat closed, and he fought hard for a swallow. "What hurts?" he rasped, his eyes beginning to burn.

Beth swallowed, her brow still furrowed from pain. "Head."

"You had a fall," he explained weakly, his fingers rubbing

together as he stood awkwardly by. The doctor had warned him that she might not remember what had occurred, where she was, or even who he was. He hadn't dwelt on that thought overmuch, thinking it to be impossible, but now that she was awake and lying before him, it suddenly became his most predominant fear. "Do you remember?"

She rolled her head from side to side, eliciting a groan, and then she made a face, drawing in her pale cheeks slightly. "Perhaps. Were we… were we riding, Malcolm?"

He exhaled noisily as his emotions rose to the surface, nodding though her eyes were closed. "Yes, we were riding." He laughed in relief and put his hands on his hips, lowering his head. "We were racing."

Beth wet her cracked lips and hummed through her nose. "Did I win?"

He was tempted to lie, to say something charming and witty, something to make her smile. But he couldn't do it, couldn't tell her anything but the truth, though he found himself smiling at her. "No."

Her lips quirked just a little. "I demand a rematch."

Malcolm could have kissed her then and there, but he settled for a fond grin. "I'll see to it."

"How are you feeling, Lady Montgomery?" the doctor, Dr. Durham, Malcolm finally recalled, asked, looking her over.

Beth frowned and turned her head to him, her eyes still closed. "Dr. Durham?"

He nodded with a smile. "Yes, my lady."

She moved her head up and down slowly. "I feel… fuzzy. It's hard to think, and… what did you ask?"

Malcolm's eyes widened, and he looked at the doctor with some concern.

Dr. Durham held out a consoling hand, waving him down. "I asked how you are feeling, my lady. You hit your head earlier."

Beth nodded, screwing her eyes up as she did so. "My head is pounding. Which seems to follow, if I pounded it. You ought to advise against such things."

Dr. Durham chuckled and checked her pulse yet again. "I generally do, my lady. Anything else?"

He took her through a few commands, all of which she

completed beautifully, and with each success, Malcolm felt his tension and fear ebb away.

"Very good, my lady," Dr. Durham praised from the foot of the bed where he had been testing the sensation in her feet and her ability to move them. "If the light will not be too much to bear, could you open your eyes for me? I must examine them next."

Beth nodded and sat up gingerly as Malcolm rushed to prop up pillows behind her. She scrunched her forehead, blinking a few times before opening her eyes a little.

Malcolm wasn't sure when he knew that something was amiss, but the vacant expression in her eyes certainly gave him pause.

Beth smiled ruefully. "I seem to be having difficulty opening my eyes, Doctor."

Whatever breath had been in Malcolm's lungs froze, and he looked at the doctor in horror. Dr. Durham glanced at him, his expression not one of shock, but one of alert wariness.

Malcolm looked back at his wife, her hair matted but loose about her shoulders, and her dark eyes clearly open. "Beth…" he began slowly, his voice stiff but clear. "They are open."

She stilled completely, her eyes widening, but apparently not seeing. "They… They can't be." She blinked pointedly three times, and then she gasped a horrible, choking gasp, bolting upright, her eyes blinking and fluttering wildly. "I can't see!" she wheezed, her voice catching. "I can't… Malcolm, I can't see! I can't…" Her hands fluttered and flinched all about her, clutching at the bed covers, at her throat, and at her face. "I can't see!"

Malcolm moved to her at once, his own terror at her state fading into insignificance in the face of her anguish. "Beth…" he tried to soothe, his hands going to her arms.

But she would not be consoled, and her words faded into panicked and unintelligible screams as her hands flew to her eyes.

He quickly shifted to sit on the bed behind her, wrapping his arms firmly around her, pinning her arms to her sides and pulling her tight against his chest. "Beth," he murmured, settling his mouth right at her ear. "Shh, it's all right. Shh."

Her hands moved to his arms in a painful, clenching grip as her screams turned to sobs that wracked her frame. She lurched against his hold as if she would break it, tormented cries ripping from her throat. Her body rocked with the force of her screams, and he rocked with her, desperate to calm and comfort her, though what he could possibly do for her was beyond him. He whispered to her, unsure if she could even hear him but needing to say the words.

"It's all right, love," he told her, kissing her hair and holding her painfully close. "I'm here, it's all right. Shh."

Suddenly, her sobs became choked, and her expression turned almost vacant, her hands moving to cradle her head, alternating between pressing hard and holding limply. Her sightless eyes rolled a few times, the color draining from her face, and then her body convulsed, and she heaved. Dr. Durham was quick with a basin from the side of the bed, but nothing came forth as Beth heaved again and again.

"Why can't I see?" she whispered, her voice drowsy even as tears continued to fall, her chest hitching as she collapsed limply against Malcolm.

He had no words and pressed a feather-light kiss to her brow.

Her cries eventually faded into pained whimpers that may have hurt more than all the rest. Beth surprised him by pulling his arms somehow further around her, more tightly against her, now cradling her entirely as the tears rolled down her cheeks.

"Malcolm," she whispered, her voice cracking, causing his heart to splinter in agony. "I can't see."

Malcolm pressed his mouth to her hair, murmuring against her as his own eyes began to dampen. "I'm so sorry, love. I've got you now. It's all right."

As he felt her nod against him, he turned his eyes heavenward and offered a desperate silent prayer as she continued to cry in his arms.

"It may be permanent, but it may not be."

Malcolm glowered. "That isn't an answer, Doctor."

Dr. Durham sighed heavily. "I know, but unfortunately, it is all

I have."

Malcolm shook his head, then put it into his hands. They had moved down to the study once Dr. Durham had finished his examination of the now listless Beth, and Malcolm had held her all the while, unwilling to leave her for even a moment. She had clung to him but had not seemed aware of it or of him. She had asked the same questions of the doctor at least three times, and her reaction to the blindness had unmanned him every time, even if it was not as intense as the first. Distracted and unfocused, she had at first responded to the doctor's requests. As the examination had gone on, however, she seemed more fatigued and unstable.

"The room is spinning," she'd whispered to Malcolm as it ended, and he'd kissed her brow again, before glaring at the doctor and demanding that he give his wife something to help her rest.

After she'd begun to doze in a laudanum-infused sleep, the men had descended to Malcolm's study, and there, his legs had failed him, and he'd sunk into a chair, weary and heavy with his own grief and confusion. Dr. Durham had given him space in which to recover himself, though he had not done more than to exhale several shaking breaths.

Once Malcolm was able to vocalize, he began to ask questions, knowing Beth would have many when she woke. He needed to be prepared for that. At this moment, he was anything but.

Especially when the response to the first question, a rather simple one, was lacking. All he'd asked was when her sight would return. But the doctor had only shaken his head in response.

"Explain what you can, then," Malcolm demanded from behind his hands.

"Her pupils were dilated, my lord, but there was still a slight response to light, though slower and not similar on each side, and though she could not see it…"

The doctor continued to attempt an explanation, but the technical terms were unintelligible to Malcolm's current state of mind. He should have put together the examination he had seen the doctor do with Beth's vision, but he barely recalled a moment of it in the face of comforting her. What he could make out from the description was that time would be their best indicator. Either Beth would recover her vision, or they would need to accept a possibly permanent state.

He found himself nodding absently, as if he understood any of it, and dropped his hands. "What can we expect?"

Dr. Durham seemed relieved to move to a more comfortable topic, if such a thing were possible. "Well, she will have some raging headaches, and she will be quite unsteady until her balance returns. Her memory will be poor, as you saw just now, and she may forget I was here, so be patient with her. She may continue to react to the revelation of her blindness with the same behaviors for a while. She might be prone to being more emotional than usual, and changes in sleeping and eating habits would be quite normal. In fact, all of that aspect is perfectly normal, given the injury."

"Normal." Malcolm snorted softly, glancing up. "I doubt we can consider any of this normal, doctor."

The doctor looked down at him sympathetically, then indicated a vacant chair. "May I, my lord?"

Malcolm gave him a brusque nod.

He sat and leaned forward, rubbing his hands together a little. "You need to consider, my lord, how fortunate you are."

"Fortunate?" Malcolm's jaw tightened, as did his right fist.

The doctor nodded slowly. "Very, very fortunate. Do you have any idea, Lord Montgomery, how truly dangerous it can be to be thrown from a horse? How often the injured party could have fractured a limb or even a neck? Or have complete memory loss? Your wife was not unconscious for very long, all things considered, and she has no injuries that should prevent her from leading a fairly normal life, if her recovery goes well."

"But she can't *see*," Malcolm pointed out bitterly.

There was a long pause, and then, "You and I both know there are worse things."

Malcolm inhaled sharply and was unable to move for a long moment. Flashes of memory splashed across his mind of Caroline lying in their bed, her eyes closed in death, of his grief in those early weeks, of the empty house and empty rooms, the empties look in his children's faces...

There *were* worse things. But this certainly seemed bad enough.

Malcolm released his breath slowly, then grunted. "I may not see it as fortunate for a while, but I understand your point."

Dr. Durham smiled without humor. "Very well." He wiped his hands on his trousers and rose, nodding at Malcolm. "I will return in the morning to see to her. I shall give your housekeeper instructions as to her care until then. I doubt you would remember anything I told you at this moment."

Normally, Malcolm would have argued the point. He was a man who was used to cataloguing many details and pieces of information all at once while under the most stressful, and sometimes painful, situations. But this... this was different. And it was beyond him.

"Thank you," he said with real sincerity, beginning to rise.

Dr. Durham shook his head quickly. "No need, my lord. Take your rest while you can."

Malcolm nodded his gratitude and sat back in his chair as the doctor showed himself out.

The sudden silence in the room was deafening. More than that, it was eerie. After the frantic pace of the morning, combined with the heartbreaking cries of his wife, Malcolm couldn't bear the sound of his own heartbeat, unsteady and too loud in this room.

He had no notion of time, no conception of the day's schedule or the children's... He sucked in a harsh breath as that thought caught hold.

The children.

How was he going to explain this to them? Had they heard Beth's scream? The sound of them still rang in his ears and would for quite some time. As a grown man, he would be haunted by them. But if his children had heard... what impact would it have on them?

If this blindness was not temporary, they would need to aid him in helping Beth find her way. They would have to change everything. The way they played, the duties she undertook, the very layout of the house, all would have to adjust to this new challenge.

How would Beth adjust?

Before today, he would have said that Beth could handle any difficulty that she happened across with a smile and with ease. Then, he had witnessed her panic, heard Beth's screams, and felt the devilish power of both as he held her in his arms. Malcolm was not a typically demonstrative man, but it had been purely instinctive to take her in his arms, hold her with all his strength, and to reassure her that she was not alone.

But how accurate was that notion? She was quite literally alone in the dark, with no one to guide her through it. He could hold her hand, stay by her side, and wait upon her hand and foot, but he would not know the darkness she faced. He would have no idea how she felt, as it was not within her nature to show weakness, and he suspected she would hide all that she could from him.

His cheerful and warm Beth had screamed with the torment of the damned less than an hour ago.

He would have given his life to keep her from any such pain. Realizing the depth of his emotion for her was startling and humbling.

"Papa?"

Malcolm bit back a groan and slid his gaze to the door of his study, left ajar by the doctor's exit.

His two eldest children stood there, looking somehow both older and younger as they eyed him carefully. They were so alike in so many ways, each of them inheriting features from both parents, though none of the same ones. They approached life with the same solemnity, neither being prone to the giddiness their younger siblings exuded, but both being willing to smile more often than not. Beth had brought them both out of their natural reserve, and he had seen them blossom more under her tutelage than he had since Caroline had been alive.

Would their Bitsy now be able to continue to do so?

"Papa?" Archer asked again, taking a small step into the room.

Malcolm shook himself from his painful thoughts and gestured with his hand for them to come in.

They walked in hesitantly, then Archer looked at Jane. That caught Malcolm off-guard. Archer was the natural leader of the group, while Jane quietly followed or observed. It was not like her to be the one of the two to speak up.

"Papa, what is wrong with Bitsy?" Jane asked, her voice almost delicate in its tone, as if she already knew the severity of the answer.

His eyes darted between them. "Did you children hear anything this morning?"

Archer frowned, then shook his head. "No, Mrs. Franklin had us all go outside to race the garden path right after breakfast, and then we went to the stables to visit the horses. We've only just returned."

Malcolm closed his eyes in relief, reminding himself to thank the nanny repeatedly for her wisdom and foresight.

"Papa," Jane demanded again, her voice stronger. "What's wrong with Bitsy?"

He stared at her for a long moment, debating the wisdom of deflecting her question. Her somber blue eyes removed any alternative but offering the truth, though they were so young. Too young to have such trials in their lives, but there was nothing for it.

"Bitsy fell and hurt her head," Malcolm sighed, holding out his hand. Jane took it without hesitation. He fought hard for a swallow. "And her eyes."

"Her eyes?" Archer asked, frowning. "What's wrong with her eyes, Papa?"

Malcolm barely avoided closing his own eyes as his heart stuttered in pain. "She can't see, Archer."

Jane gasped softly but cut it off the moment it was audible. Her hold on Malcolm's hand tightened. "She's blind?"

He didn't think to ask how she knew the word and only nodded. "For the time being, yes."

His children shared a horrified look with each other. "Is she blind forever?" Jane asked in a much less steady voice.

"I don't know," Malcolm whispered. "But for a time, at least."

Jane suddenly put her arms around Malcolm's neck and hoisted herself onto his lap, laying her head on his shoulder. He wrapped an arm around her instantly, pulling her close. Archer laid his hand on his father's shoulder, trying for bravery, although his chin quivered.

"Can we... can we see for her?" Archer asked, his brow furrowed.

Malcolm put his arm around his son, unable to speak for a long moment as he touched his forehead to his son's. "It doesn't work that way, Archer," he eventually managed. "Bitsy is going to need to rest for a while, perhaps a very long time. She may not be herself for a time."

"We'll help her," Archer vowed. "I'll behave in lessons and draw anything she wants me to, even flowers."

"And we'll help with Greer and Samuel," Jane told him, surprisingly without tears. "We'll make sure Bitsy gets lots of rest."

Malcolm smiled at them both fondly. "That will be very helpful, children. I am sure she will appreciate your efforts."

"I bet she's scared," Jane suddenly whimpered, sounding distressed for the first time.

"She probably is," he murmured, nodding.

"Bitsy can't be scared," Archer said, shaking his head firmly, looking so fiercely stubborn Malcolm wondered if he might guard the door with a wooden sword. "I won't let her be, Papa."

Malcolm held these two children close and raised his damp eyes heavenward, unsure if he was tormented or grateful, but strongly suspecting it was both. "We'll manage something," he told them. "Somehow, we will find a way. Together."

The children accepted his words with fervent nods, but Malcolm was far less certain.

A sinking feeling told him that things would somehow get worse before they got better, and he did not even know what better would look like.

Chapter Fifteen

$\mathcal{M}$alcolm hated it when he was right and did not wish to be.

Most of the time, he quite enjoyed being right. There was a certain pride in being correct in one's statements and thinking, as well as predicting forthcoming events. It was a terribly satisfying feeling when it worked in his favor.

This was not one of those times.

Things did get worse... much, much worse. And as the days stretched into more than a week, he was utterly at a loss. He didn't know what to do or how to proceed. He did not know one single step to take.

Beth was not herself. She was the furthest thing from herself that he could have possibly imagined. He'd thought that when she had stopped forgetting so much, that all would improve. Nothing had improved. She was still listless, somehow more so than when she had discovered her blindness. The color had still not returned to her face, and she had no interest in having her hair dressed. She was completely uninterested in anything that anyone offered, whether it was tea or breakfast or flowers or fresh clothing. She mutely accepted the doctor's remedies and allowed him his examinations. She never questioned or complained about anything.

She did not speak at all.

Malcolm had tried, but his attempts at conversation had been somewhat limited, as he had no idea what to say to her. What did one say in the present situation? He wasn't particularly adept at talking for the sake of it under normal conditions, and this was quite beyond him. He'd never imagined his bright and vibrant Beth could be like this. She refused meals and visitors, hadn't asked after the children, didn't seem to notice when he spoke to her, and had not smiled in days. He hadn't realized how vital it had been to have her smiles in his life, but now it felt as though he had not seen the sun in years.

It wasn't until he had spoken with Lily, who had been equally unsuccessful with drawing Beth out, that a possible solution had come to him.

"How is she with the children?" Lily had asked him as they walked toward her home, her brow knit with worry.

Malcolm had drawn up short, realization dawning. "I haven't brought them to see her. I was waiting until she was feeling better, but…"

Lily had patted his arm, nodding firmly. "Bring them. Do it now. I will see myself home."

Normally, Malcolm would never allow such a thing, but as they could see the house from here, and he had a desperate need to see if this plan might be what they needed to bring up Beth's spirits, as well as their own, he agreed to it. He kissed her cheek and sent her on her way before dashing back to the house, rounding up the children, and leading them all up to Beth's bedchamber.

They knew how she fared, though perhaps not what to expect, but all he could tell them was that she needed some cheering up, and that seemed enough for them.

Holding his breath, he opened the door to her bedchamber. "Beth?" he called softly, grateful the maids still drew back the curtains, though Beth could not see the light and likely did not care.

He could barely see her form on the bed, and she did not stir besides tilting her head very slightly in the direction of the door.

"I have a few visitors who are quite desperate to see you." Before she could protest, he nodded at the children, who moved without hesitation to the bed.

Beth sat up, her eyes wide, but still unseeing. At first, Malcolm worried that he had gone too far, but then when Samuel leaped onto the bed near her, she laughed, the sound harsh and rough with lack of use. She fumbled for his hand and kissed it repeatedly as the boy moved into her hold. Archer and Jane helped Greer to climb on the mattress before they settled themselves there, as well.

The change in Beth was startling, if not downright breathtaking. Though still pale, weak, and gaunt, she was smiling and engaging, listening to every word they uttered with intensity. Her hands fluttered over their hair or their cheeks, squeezing their hands and kissing their faces. They loved every moment, and Jane was especially adept at describing recent events and scenes in great detail. Malcolm felt more than a little emotion as he observed it. His sweet girl was doing her utmost to help her stepmother in the only way she could at this moment, and he had a tiny sense of what it might mean to Beth to hear it.

Malcolm watched in silence until Beth began to look pale and weary once more, and then he stepped forward. "All right, children, Bitsy needs her rest now. You can come and visit her again tomorrow."

He saw the brief flash of relief on her face and felt it echo in his heart. Seeing any change in her expression was cause for celebration in his mind, and he wanted to ensure that she was never so vacant again.

Beth kissed each of the children repeatedly, running her fingers over their cheeks and hair repeatedly, her face tightening in a way that Malcolm did not like.

"May we come in before bed to kiss Bitsy good night?" Jane asked him, still holding onto Beth's hand.

Malcolm looked at Beth and saw her nodding.

"Yes," they said together, which made him smile and only seemed to heighten whatever distress was lying so near the surface with Beth.

He quickly shooed the children out, signaling to a servant in the hall to return them to the nursery. Once they were far enough away, he stepped back into Beth's room and closed the door.

Beth had curled into a ball beneath the comforter and was now trembling visibly. He couldn't hear any sound from her, but her fist was pressed to her mouth tightly, and he took a step in her direction, the floorboards creaking sharply beneath his feet.

She stopped her shaking, stilling herself with a muted squeak.

Malcolm couldn't bear this. "Beth…" he murmured as gently as he could.

She turned more fully away from him, trembling once more.

He shook his head and took another step. "What can I do?" he pleaded, willing to give anything, *do* anything, to make her smile the way his children had. He could not bear to be helpless to her, not when she clearly needed so much.

Beth didn't answer him, but her muffled cries were answer enough.

"I cannot bear to see you cry," Malcolm rasped, his fingers rubbing together anxiously by his sides.

"Then you sh-should probably l-leave," his wife stammered weakly, her voice hoarse from disuse and clogged with tears. "I'm afraid I will be crying for some time."

Somehow her words invigorated him, even as his eyes burned with unshed tears of his own. She was speaking to him, at long last, and showing some spirit, even if it was irritable and sharp. He could wait for the sunshine to return as long as there was life in her.

"Beth," he said again, approaching the bed very slowly, "I don't know what to do. I am... not usually a demonstrative man." He shook his head, though she wouldn't see it. "But... may I hold you? While you cry?"

Beth stiffened again, and Malcolm held his breath, watching her steadily, waiting...

Then his wife released a particularly loud cry, the sound choked and pained. She nodded and held a hand out to him. It was almost in his direction, but not quite.

The gesture struck him poignantly, and he was moving to her even as he swallowed back his own emotions. He rounded the bed and seized her hand, pulling her up to a seated position and drawing her up into his arms. She clung to him as fiercely as she had the day of her accident, burying her face in his shoulder, her fingers curling into his shirt tightly.

Malcolm sat on the bed, swinging his legs up and resting back against the headboard. He tugged the covers from under himself and draped them over Beth's legs as she sat across his lap, and then he held her, cradling her against his chest. He didn't say a word as she sobbed. He silently slipped one of her hands from his shirt and intertwined their fingers, drawing her hand to his lips and kissing it tenderly before pressing it against his heart. Dusting his lips across her brow, he held her close even as his shirt dampened with her tears.

"I want to see the children," Beth whimpered into his chest. "I want to *see* them!"

"I know, sweetheart," he murmured against her brow, kissing softly. "Is it too hard to have them visit you? I'll do whatever you want."

He felt her shake her head. Her fingers curled in his hold, gripping him tightly. "I do want to have them here. I want to hear about their days and touch their faces, and I want…" She broke off with another pained sound, and Malcolm tightened his hold on her, tucking her head beneath his chin.

"All right," he soothed, kissing her hair. "All right. Go ahead and cry, Beth. I'll hold you as long as you need."

He would hold her longer than that if she would allow it. But for now, this would suffice.

"Monty, what's happened? Monty!"

Malcolm looked up blearily, surprised at the tall and rather crisp-looking figure standing in the doorway of his study. He peered closely, feeling as though his brain was working in reverse. He had tried to sleep once Beth had settled herself, but it hadn't been possible. Sleep had been difficult since Beth's accident, as the horrors of it had continued to plague him, and so he had thrown himself into his work, both the duties of the estate and the reports from the London League.

He was doing a miserable job of both.

The man in the doorway entered, looking him over with wide eyes, concern etched in every line. "Good heavens, man. What's happened?"

The confusion swirling in his mind cleared, and recognition dawned. "Fritz."

His friend nodded slowly, a line of worry on his brow. "Did you forget my name?"

"I've forgotten far more important things of late," Malcolm admitted with chagrin. He sat back in his chair and waved him into another. "As you can probably tell."

Fritz gave a short laugh as he settled himself into the chair, still wearing his greatcoat. He set his hat on the table beside him and began stripping off his gloves. "Yes, I wondered about that. Your last missive about the reports was more cryptic than the reports themselves. I had to go to the League to figure out what you were saying."

Malcolm winced and shook his head, drumming his fingers absently on the armrests of his chair. "I apologize. I am... not myself."

"So I see." Fritz leaned forward and rested his elbows on his knees. "Monty, your letter had Emily and me in such a state that I left in the middle of a dinner party with three ambassadors while she made my excuses. But you didn't say what had happened or anything to indicate if things were well."

"I didn't mean to send for you." Malcolm looked up sharply, his fingers stilling. "Did I send for you in the letter?"

Fritz shook his head quickly. "No, but here I am all the same. Tell me what happened. Is Beth all right?"

Malcolm chewed on his lip for a moment, not particularly wanting to share the painful details of the past ten days, but also knowing that he was going to need his friend's support to manage everything he now faced. Malcolm shook his head, swallowing hard. "Things are not well. Not well at all."

He related the events of that awful day as best he could, sparing his friend the complicated details of his own personal torment, and sticking to the facts. He was a spy, after all, and extraneous details that did not help matters would be useless, not to mention unwarranted. He spoke of Beth's injuries, her emotional state, and the fear that she might never regain her former vibrancy.

Fritz had remained silent throughout the retelling, and now rose, pacing the room, his fingers playing near his mouth and chin. "And the doctor isn't concerned about this?"

"Of course, he's concerned," Malcolm snapped. "How often does a young woman of perfect health lose her vision?"

His friend paused mid-stride to give him a stern look.

Most people did not give Malcolm looks. Most of the time, he was the one doing that to others.

But now he was the one shifting uncomfortably in his seat. "Apologies, Fritz."

Fritz nodded in acknowledgement and then continued his pacing.

"Dr. Durham says it's too soon to lose hope," Malcolm told him, watching his friend pace, "but he says everything is perfectly normal, considering her injuries. He has been by every day to examine her, and each day he says that only time will tell if her sight will return." Malcolm rubbed a hand over his face and groaned. "I cannot bear to hear that phrase uttered one more time."

"And what does Beth think?" Fritz asked, folding his arms and stopping in front of him.

Malcolm sighed heavily, thinking back to the slight form of his wife that he had held in his arms only hours ago while she wept. That had been the most interaction he'd had with her in days, and the liveliest she had been since the accident.

"Beth seems to be mutely accepting everything she hears," he confessed, now rising himself and moving to the window, setting his arm against the frame. "She doesn't ask any questions, though I ask plenty for both of us. She says nothing at all. Not a word."

"And with you?"

He shook his head slightly. "Nothing, usually. She finally spoke today after I brought the children to see her, and she spoke with them here and there, but..."

His voice trailed off with a choked sound, and he pounded a fist against the wall.

Fritz suddenly gripped his shoulder. "What can I do?"

Malcolm took a moment to collect himself, then turned to look at his friend. "I need you to take over the League."

He could tell that Fritz wasn't expecting that answer, and the hand fell from his shoulder. "The League?" Fritz repeated with raised brows.

Malcolm nodded, exhaling slowly. "I need to be here," he explained. "I cannot be going back and forth to London when she is

172

in this state, and until we figure out how to manage her condition, I cannot devote as much of my energies to my work there."

Fritz snorted loudly and shook his head, grinning. "Of course, that all goes without saying. Your place is here with your wife. She needs you with her, and I think you personally need to be with her. That was never in question."

It had never occurred to Malcolm that he might need to remain at Knightsgate with Beth for his own sake, he only thought of how to help her and ensure that her transition into a sightless life was as painless as possible. He wanted to be here for her, with her, every single step of the way.

The traitors to the crown, the French faction working to shift the balance of power, and even Rogue's potential compromise were all going to have to wait. His place was here.

"Thank you," Malcolm murmured gruffly, looking away in the face of his sudden discovery.

"Did you really think I wouldn't agree?" Fritz asked with a light laugh. "I expected to assist you there, and knowing what I know now, I am ordering you to remain here."

The order drew a wry chuckle from Malcolm, and he leaned back against the wall. "You are ordering me?"

Fritz nodded, no longer smiling though his tone remained the same. "Absolutely and unequivocally. You were a good soldier, Monty, and you are an impeccable spy, all because you understand orders and obey them. Don't fail me now."

Malcolm laughed again, moving to the sideboard. "I have no intention of disobeying orders, Fritz," he assured him, pulling out the brandy decanter and two tumblers. "Believe it or not, I don't wish to be in London."

"I believe you," Fritz replied, all signs of teasing gone. "If I were in your situation, I would not hesitate."

"I'm not hesitating," Malcolm protested as he poured the drinks.

"Then why do I feel as though you are asking my permission?"

Malcolm paused, setting the decanter down. Was he asking permission? It seemed a ridiculous notion, as he knew that any of his superiors or associates would have said precisely the same thing that Fritz had said. They would have insisted that he take the time with his wife and family, taken up his duties and responsibilities, and managed everything perfectly until he had felt able to return. It did not make the asking any easier, as he currently felt a great deal of guilt knowing all that he was handing off.

He glanced towards Fritz, who was staring at him with a steady, knowing expression. "What if I can't help her?" he heard himself ask his oldest friend.

Fritz tilted his head and shifted his stance slightly. "How could you not?"

He turned, holding out a drink to his friend, and considered his words carefully. "Beth has drawn into herself, and I cannot blame her. I cannot imagine what this situation has been like for her, I can only know my own thoughts and feelings, and those are torment enough." He shook his head, slowly moving towards his chair once more, drink in hand. "What if my interference only draws out the worst in her? What if I am making her more miserable? She came alive for the children, Fritz, and I cannot seem to do that for her. I have held her while she cries, and seen to the best of her care, and that is all." He sank back into the chair and pinched the bridge of his nose. "If I cannot help her, I would be better served in London, despite this growing need to be with her."

Fritz crossed back to his own chair and sat, leaning forward earnestly. "Listen to me, Monty. As your friend. If it is a reaction that you are looking for, you would indeed be better served elsewhere. Your wife comes alive for the children because they bring her joy and remind her what she has in her life. But she also knows that the children must see the best. With you, she does not have to pretend that all is well. She can be as miserable as she feels, and as vulnerable. If you do not see the significance in that, then perhaps you should stay away in London and leave Beth to find her own way."

All the air rushed out of Malcolm's lungs at once, and he stared at the drink in his hand without seeing it. Fritz had always been honest with him, sometimes painfully so. This was no exception.

"Beth may not even know what she needs yet, Monty, but I can promise you that she needs you here," Fritz went on, sounding like the mentor he had been to so many. "She needs you to be ready for when she does know what she needs. And she certainly does not need you creating problems where none exist. You will worry yourself into a frenzy, and that will not help anyone. Set your own concerns and guilt aside and focus on her. Let her cry, let her rage, let her stew in silence if she needs to. When she is ready, she will know. And so will you."

Malcolm stared at Fritz for a long moment, processing the revelations heaped upon him. He was the sort to fix all the problems that arose in life, not to sit idly by and patiently wait for a solution to present itself. Patience had never really been his strong suit, but it appeared that patience was exactly what he needed.

He glowered in Fritz's direction, which earned him a cheeky grin. "When did you become so wise in the ways of women?" he grumbled.

Fritz saluted him with his tumbler, looking like the raffish man he once had been. "I've been married to Emily for twenty years. You start to learn a thing or two when you pay attention."

Malcolm frowned a little in amusement. "So, your wife had her penny's worth about what you should say before you came, did she?"

There was a brief moment of outrage on Fritz's face, and then he scowled playfully. "Yes, she did, and as she knows you almost as well as I, it happens that most of what she said was perfectly applicable." He sniffed dismissively. "Now, drink that beverage in your hand and tell me what else I can do to help."

Chapter Sixteen

*N*ights were the worst. No matter what Malcolm had accomplished during the day, nights were the time when all his doubts and worries plagued him more than ever. Any problem he had yet to solve revisited him with a vengeance then. Hours upon hours had been spent mulling over things, from the trivial to matters of national security, all at the expense of his sleep and peace of mind. Trying to figure out what he could do to help Beth, or what she might need, was occupying more of his nighttime hours than sleep.

Fritz's words the other day had given him pause, and he had focused his efforts on his wife's needs rather than satisfying some need of his own to be useful. She was still not particularly talkative, but it no longer felt as though she were shutting out the world. She responded to the doctor's questions when he examined her, though not in great detail, and she ate every day, though not much. The children continued to visit her during breaks in their lessons and before bed, and that was still the time when Beth seemed more herself. But the more Malcolm observed, the more he could see the strain it was on her.

Not that she was pretending at her delight with them, for there was real joy in her with every one of them, but there was an almost equal measure of pain. And she still had not recovered her strength, so she was weak and fatigued after each visit. It left very little time or energy for Malcolm to have any real opportunity to talk with her, and he could feel the tension of a distance forming.

He couldn't bear distance; not from her. They had grown so close before her accident, and now…

He couldn't go back… *they* could not go back.

A distressed cry raised him from the bed, and instantly he sat poised to move, waiting for a hint of who it might be. Jane hadn't had another bad dream in some time, but he knew her history with them. And any of the other children could have similar experiences at any time.

The cry came again, this time louder and more terrified. And it most definitely did not come from one of the children.

He was running for the hallway in an instant, grateful her room was not far as his feet practically pounded along the floors. The sconces in the hall were dimmed, having not yet burned out completely, and he was grateful for the added light.

Beth's door was ajar, which was odd, but he paid no attention as he pushed it open, her name on his lips. It remained there, unuttered, at the sight within Beth's room.

Jane was on Beth's bed, holding her stepmother's hands as she continued to writhe on the bed. "Bitsy!" his daughter said insistently. "Bitsy, wake up!"

"I *am* awake," Beth cried, whimpering loudly, thrashing a little. Then she slumped against the pillows, moaning pitifully.

Malcolm watched as his daughter brushed aside locks of Beth's hair that had fallen across her face. "Bitsy, it's all right," Jane soothed, still clinging to her hands.

Beth shook her head, crying helplessly, burying her face into her pillow as her cries escalated.

It was too much to witness, and far too much to bear. He needed to put a stop to this, protect Jane, soothe Beth, and find a way to dispel this darkness from the bright star that had been his wife. He entered the room further, moving towards the other side of the bed, when Jane settled herself under the covers with Beth and snuggled up against her, releasing her hands at last.

"Did you forget that you can't see?" Jane asked in a small voice, still managing to sound comforting.

Beth sniffled loudly and turned her face from the pillow, one of her hands tracing along Jane's arm to her hair, where her fingers slowly began running through it. "Yes… I did…" she sobbed, struggling to get the words out.

"That must be very scary." Jane looked up at Beth, whose eyes were unfocused but looking towards the wall. "Are you frightened?"

Beth nodded against her, still absently running her fingers through Jane's hair. "Yes, I am frightened. It's… very dark. All the time. And I miss the sun. I miss fires and candles and colors and faces…"

Malcolm's throat tightened as he listened to Beth talk about her fears, the things that she missed, all things he took for granted on a regular basis. The more Beth spoke, the more at ease he became, and the more relaxed she became. Jane listened to every word, asking questions on occasion that kept Beth talking, leaning against her more comfortably.

"I'm sorry, Bitsy," Jane said when Beth's voice trailed off. "It must be very hard."

"It is," Beth whispered with another sniffle. "But it helps when you children come to visit me, and when your father is with me."

Her words took Malcolm by surprise, and he stared at her, knowing she couldn't see him and using it to his advantage to be quite unabashed in his consideration of her.

"It helps to have my family here," Beth went on, her voice softening. "That makes everything a little less frightening."

Her family. *They* were her family!

Malcolm had difficulty swallowing for several moments after that and wanted nothing more than to cradle his wife in his arms. But he would remain here, and let his daughter tend to her stepmother as long as she was needed.

Jane hugged herself closer to Beth and sighed sleepily, closing her eyes. "Greer tried to turn Samuel into a fairy today," she said with a yawn.

Beth smiled and looked down at Jane, her eyes not quite reaching her face. "What happened?"

"Archer saved him before she could tell him about the wings." Jane shrugged against her. "Samuel would make a better troll than a fairy, anyway."

Malcolm stifled a laugh, as did Beth. "Perhaps he can become a fairy some other time," Beth offered, her smile so like her usual one it made Malcolm's breath catch.

Jane yawned noisily again and snuggled into Beth's side. "How did you learn so much about fairies, Bitsy?"

It was obvious from her sleepy voice that Jane would not be awake for much longer. Still, Beth told her about playing with her sisters and nieces, as well as with some other young girls of her acquaintance who had known far more about becoming fairies than she did. She talked about one girl she had known who had almost managed it and another who had the most beautiful dress ready for fairy transformation.

Jane was asleep rather quickly, lulled by Beth's tones, which were no longer emotional or tearful. Soon she was breathing deeply in the silence of the room.

Malcolm watched for a few moments more as Beth continued to stroke Jane's hair over and over, her expression thoughtful, if a bit wistful. It was the most at peace he had seen her since the accident, and he wanted to cling to it for as long as he could. Only when he heard Beth sigh did he move, trying to keep his steps light while still being audible to avoid startling her.

"She's the sweetest girl in the world," Beth said softly, her voice now tinged with tears again.

Malcolm paused, wondering how long she'd known he was there. "I think she must have learned sweetness from you," he replied, at last, continuing towards the bed. "She didn't learn it from me, I can assure you."

Beth kissed Jane's head softly, then sniffed back more tears.

"Here, let me take her back to bed." Malcolm moved towards his daughter, ready to scoop her up.

"She is in bed," Beth insisted, holding the girl closer to her. She kissed her brow again, then leaned her head back against the pillow, a pair of tears leaking from the corners of her eyes.

"Oh, Beth," Malcolm murmured, rounding the bed to the other side.

"Malcolm," she whimpered, holding out a hand on the mattress. "Help me."

He took it in both of his, and the strength of her grip on him weakened his knees. He brought her hand to his lips, kissing it repeatedly. "I'm here, love. I'm right here."

Her fingers brushed against his lips, then gripped his hand tightly again. She sighed deeply and nestled more securely into the mattress and pillows. Closing her eyes, her fingers entwined with his.

Malcolm watched Beth as she drifted off to sleep, holding her hand the entire time. Even when her grip slackened, his never did.

She had reached out for him again. She had called for him!

There would be no going backwards. He would move forward into this unknown future with his wife, and he would walk with her every step of the way, for as long as it took.

Under no circumstances would he leave her tonight. Careful not to jostle the bed, he settled himself next to her, remaining on top of the coverlet, and eased back against the pillows. He looked at her, so peaceful in her sleep, and smiled, her hand still in his grasp. Then he, too, allowed sleep to overtake him.

There had been a dent in the pillows the morning after the nightmares.

It had taken Beth some time to discover this in her blind state, but as she had little else to do but lay in her bed and recover, she had become quite familiar with her limited surroundings. She had sat up to have her breakfast, which the maids were still feeding to her, as she had yet to manage the thing. Her hand had felt the pillow beside her and found it had a discernible dent in it.

Malcolm had stayed the night.

She had mulled that over during her entire limited meal.

After the terrifying experience of a nightmare she could not wake from, she was frantic for some assurance, some comfort to bring her back from the brink of the darkness surrounding and filling her. She'd heard his pounding steps in the hall and had felt herself keening for him to deliver her, and then to feel a much smaller set of hands taking hers and a softer, sweeter voice soothing her…

It had humbled and shamed her. She was supposed to be dignified and composed, adapting to her situation with grace despite hardship, and her innocent Janie had come to her in a moment of raw vulnerability, in maternal imitation of her own rescue from nightmares.

Beth had resisted at first, but eventually let Jane gently draw her back from her torment with her soft questions and tenderhearted remarks. Once her panic had faded, Beth had allowed herself to confess more than she would have to one so young. But Jane had seen and experienced enough to deserve real answers, and with Malcolm standing somewhere in the vicinity, Beth allowed herself the luxury of a rare openness, giving them both a taste of what she was missing without her vision.

She would never be able to convey the true depth of the despair in which she lived, but it was not necessary for anyone to understand completely. It was enough that someone cared enough to come to her aid, to remind her of life beyond her sightlessness, and to hold her when the darkness was too much.

Jane had held her in her distress. And it appeared that Malcolm had held her for the rest of the night. He had been there, at any rate.

She would never forget the way he had taken her hand, which she had gripped as she might have a lifeline. She suspected he would have held her closely, as he had done more than once since her accident, had Jane not been asleep by her side. His hold on her hand, and the way he had kissed it, had been more than enough. She could not have felt safer or more soothed than she had at that moment.

And then he had stayed! He'd been gone when she'd woken that morning, as had Jane, but it was enough that she knew.

Beth had come to a very firm decision shortly after she finished her breakfast. She would no longer remain a helpless invalid. Blind she may be, but no longer helpless. She determined to find a way through this hardship and somehow live the best way she could. She would no longer be neither a wife, nor a mother, laid up in bed feeling sorry for herself. She needed to live her life, such as it was.

That day, she rose from her bed for the first time in over a week.

She'd not been able to do much more than that, as she was very weak, and the adjustment had made her head swim, but she'd managed it three more times that day and had even taken a few steps the final time.

It seemed that Malcolm had also made some firm decisions after that night, including moving Beth from her rooms to his. Despite her objections to being underfoot and fussed over, he insisted in the charming and superior way that was his, and she had no choice but to concede to his wishes.

"I just want to have you closer," he'd told her in a surprisingly gentle tone, running a hand over her hair. "The next time you wake from one nightmare to another, I want to be there for you."

He'd gone on to explain that he would sleep in the dressing room adjoining, and she would have all the privacy she wished for, but Beth didn't hear a single word of that explanation. She was clinging to the tender admission that he wanted to be near her.

Flashes of his tempting almost-smile came to mind, and her heart flickered within her.

Beth needed no other reason to improve than that.

She began learning her way around Malcolm's room slowly, feeling her way step by step. Her head soon adjusted to being upright and no longer perturbed her in her efforts. She was still not entirely steady, but her pace was slow enough that it was not a significant issue.

Her lack of sight, on the other hand...

She huffed a lock of hair out of her face now as she prepared to make another pass around the room. Three days of attempting the same path without incident, and she had yet to manage it. Her toes were bruised and swollen in places, she could tell, but she was determined to succeed. How could she manage to find her way around the vast expanse of the house if she could not manage to find her way around this room?

Still clad in her nightdress, as she always was these days, Beth began to edge around the room, her hand stretched out almost confidently for the wall directly across from her. Step by careful step she moved forward, remembering the corner of the large grandfather clock that had caught her by surprise a number of times. Just when she wondered if she had turned around and gone the wrong way, her fingers grazed the smooth wallpaper. She heaved a sigh of relief as she pressed her palm to the wall.

She would have to speak to Malcolm about the size of his quarters. There was entirely too much room in here, and it was quite terrifying. Faintly wondering about the pattern of his wallpaper, and unable to recall it, she turned, keeping her hand on the wall as a guide and began to walk again. Carefully maneuvering around the grandfather clock, she counted her steps, one hand returning to the wall while the other remained outstretched for the obstacles. The bureau ought to have been ten paces from the window, and she was only now feeling the cool glass panes.

It was a maddeningly slow process and one that she wished she could somehow avoid. She was as insecure in her steps as a child, and twice as vulnerable in the process. She could not protect herself if she fell, as she had no idea where she was falling or what was beneath her. Somehow walking without sight was far more difficult than it ever had been to walk with her eyes closed. How easily she became disoriented!

Her left hand found the bureau before her, and she grinned in relieved delight. She fumbled her way around it, and when she returned to the wall, she exhaled slowly. This was as far as she had come before, and she had no notion of what was next.

If her husband had had any sense, he would have listened to her when she asked to remain in her own room. But how could she confess to him that she was trying to explore her room and her abilities, when he would be more likely to tie her to the bed for venturing out?

Beth paused as she reached the corner of the wall. Right, she thought. She was still feeling strong and determined, so she would continue. There was no victory until she managed the entire room, and she could not pretend otherwise.

Turning, she began along the unknown wall once more. Five paces in, a chair met her feet and body and she, too accustomed to the ease of her way, was entirely unprepared for it. She gasped as she tumbled to the ground, turning herself to avoid falling face first into the floor. Her body landed with a loud crashing sound, and her head pounded furiously with the motion, though somehow, she avoided hitting it again.

Beth winced as her body began to ache in various places, and she felt her face burn with the shame of her failure. She'd never fallen to the ground in her attempts before, and if she hurt herself again, it would be some time before she could try again.

If she tried again.

Tears stung at her eyes, and she curled against the rug upon which she'd fallen, gripping it with her fingers. She could not even manage to walk around this room! How could she possibly manage to live any sort of normal life this way?

She heard a familiar set of footsteps pounding their way down the hall, and her tears intensified, knowing that her embarrassment would be discovered at any moment by the man she desperately wished to be whole for.

"Beth!" Malcolm called, nearer than she expected. "Beth!"

He ought not to sound so afraid. There was no reason for him to fear. It was only his invalid wife collapsed on the floor, but she was well enough. Blind, but otherwise whole.

The door to the room opened, and she heard his step pause only momentarily.

"Beth, are you hurt? What happened?" he asked, moving again, his arms suddenly scooping her up.

His voice was so tender, so familiar, that it soothed the aches in her body, though it only intensified the ache in her heart. They had grown so close before her accident, and their budding relationship had held such promise, and now her foolish accident stood in the way of their grand future. As he was an honorable man, he would see to her care all his days, tend to her every need. Instead of his wife, she would become his burden. It was all too much to bear!

Malcolm settled her back onto the bed, brushed back her hair and sat on the bed next to her. "Beth, what happened?"

She shook her head, forcing her tears back, though they refused to subside completely. "I was being foolish, please don't concern yourself."

He took her hand in his and pressed it gently. "I doubt that, and I do concern myself. With you."

Beth closed her eyes on her tears, though the darkness remained the same. "I was trying to walk the room. I've been trying to manage it for days, and I got as far as the corner. It's the furthest I've ever gone without injury to my toes. And then…"

"The chair," he finished, sounding as though he had turned to look elsewhere. He made an irritated humming sound. "I should have suspected you would do something like that. I should have removed the obstacles. I didn't even think about the complication it would raise for you in moving into my quarters. You don't even know this room. Of course, you would not know how to navigate it."

She stared where she imagined he was, trying desperately to recall every detail of his face and how it would look. "You're not angry?" she managed to ask, her voice breaking slightly.

A rustling sound told her he had turned back to her, and his hold on her hand tightened again. "Why would I be angry? You're a bold and independent woman, a fairy creature who needs room to fly. Why shouldn't you try to explore your new world and surroundings? I'm only upset that I didn't think to help you, that I didn't think of you with my actions, and that so many of your poor toes were injured in your efforts!"

She tried to laugh at his obvious attempt at teasing, but the slight laugh turned into a watery sob as the ache in her heart intensified tenfold.

"Oh, Beth," Malcolm murmured, wiping the tears from her face and taking her hands. "What is it?"

Beth hiccupped softly, squeezing his hands in return. "I miss you," she whispered as another sob escaped her.

Malcolm groaned a little, his hold on her hands growing tighter still. Then he brought her hands to his face. "I'm right here," he rasped, his breath tickling her fingers a little.

"I wish I could see you," Beth said through her tears as her fingers stroked against his skin.

He turned his face and pressed a warm kiss into one palm. "I'm right here, Beth," he told her again. "See with your hands. I am right here."

Her fingers wandered across his face, tracing the shape of his lips, the angle of his jaw, the line of his brows, the bridge of his nose... The bristle of whiskers scraped along her palms as she slid her hands back down his jaw, his breath was the slightest bit unsteady as her exploration went on.

Almost... She could almost picture him. And it almost was enough.

Beth shook her head, brushing her thumbs across his cheeks as she cupped his face, drawing him closer. He brought a hand to her face, and she leaned into it.

"I miss you," she whispered again as he touched his brow to hers.

Malcolm's hand moved to the back of her neck, and he lifted his head to gently kiss her nose.

Exhaling sharply, Beth tilted her face up and pulled him to her, pressing her lips to his, forgoing any hesitation. Malcolm responded gently, his hold on her neck increasing as he pulled her in, his free arm wrapping around her back. His lips slowly devoured her, churning something within her into a fervent fire. She slid her hands into his hair, threading her fingers through the locks, eliciting a moan of approval from Malcolm, who tugged her more fully into his grasp.

That night in the hallway was nothing compared to this heat building between them now. That had been sheer desire. This was something far more emotional, far more evocative, and far less simple.

And this was what she had always wanted.

"I miss you," she said against his lips, pulling at them again and again.

Malcolm captured her lips again, caressing them in an easy pattern. "I'm here, love. I'll always be here."

Beth sighed, her head beginning to swim in a pleasant way, and she rather thought she could get used to this particular sensation. The darkness might have terrified her, but so long as Malcolm was there to hold her, she could endure it. Particularly when he kissed her with such tenderness. She wrapped her arms around Malcolm's neck, collapsing against him, letting him hold her against him, scattering kisses and words against her hair and face.

"Don't leave me, Malcolm," she told him sleepily, nuzzling against his throat.

"Never," he vowed as he pulled her somehow closer, kissing her yet again.

Beth nodded against him, running her fingers through his hair absently. "I need you with me, Malcolm. I can't do this alone."

She felt Malcolm's breath catch and held hers until he tenderly kissed her brow.

"You're not alone." He dusted his lips over hers once, then took them with an almost fierce edge. "I'm right here, love. You're not alone."

Chapter Seventeen

$\mathcal{M}$alcolm stayed with her that night and every night since.

After their extraordinary kisses the other day, he'd been true to his word. Beth hadn't been alone for a moment, it seemed. Malcolm spent more time checking on Beth than with any of his duties, or with their children. She'd had to send him away multiple times just to get him to accomplish anything.

But she was also rather enjoying it, which Malcolm knew all too well.

He was more at ease and talkative than she had ever known him to be, and far more charming than he had a right to be. He would come in multiple times a day and give her a report of what he was doing, what the children were doing, and even though the children came in to talk to her and say goodnight, he would tell the stories again with such detail that she felt as though she had been there. He always took great care to be more descriptive with her to help her see things in her mind, and she would never be able to tell him how much that meant to her.

The children had picked up on that hint and were focusing on being more descriptive, as well, Jane and Archer especially. They made concentrated efforts to help the other two to describe things more clearly by prodding them with questions, which never failed to make Beth smile. They had ceased to be as gentle with her, bounding up onto the bed and crowding in around her, and she loved their energy and what it brought to her days. They had begun to help her navigate the room, first with their hand in hers, and then talking her through the endeavor. They were not perfect doing so, and neither was she, but at least now there was laughter when she met an obstacle instead of tears.

Malcolm always humored her with one more round of navigation before bed every night, and he was a far better guide than the children, though he laughed less. But he praised her every accomplishment with sincerity and enthusiasm. The night before, when she had made a circuit of the entire room, he had whooped in delight and picked her up, swinging her around and telling her how proud he was of her. They had shared enthusiastic kisses before he had tucked her into bed, joining her moments later and pulling her into his arms before falling asleep.

Every night, she had been held in his arms as they slept, cradled in his hold as though she were fragile and precious. As though she would break.

She didn't mind being treasured, but...

This morning, he had lingered in bed beside her, talking about rather trivial things, making her smile and even blush as he praised the way she looked in the mornings.

She was well aware that mornings were not a good look for her, but it was sweet that he pretended otherwise.

He had taken her hand and played with it a little, running his fingers over hers, through hers. He rubbed them gently, pressing his palm to hers, and anything else that was destined to drive her mad before finally speaking. "I find," he'd murmured in a low tone, "that I have very little desire to be anywhere else today." This, he followed with feather-light kisses to her fingers, and just when she thought the burning within her might rouse itself into flames, a servant knocked at the door to remind him of an appointment.

Beth had groaned in disappointment, and she hadn't been alone. Malcolm had been gone with a kiss to her brow, and she hadn't seen him since.

She sat contemplating in the bed now as Dr. Durham continued his examination of her. He praised her venturing out of bed and the progress she had made there, encouraging her to do even more, if she could bear it. She was making great strides in her recovery, and he was very pleased with that. Her sight, however, had not progressed at all.

189

"It might not return, my lady," he reminded her gently.

"I know," she sighed, plucking at the covers moodily. "I just wish we would know. I could move on if I knew for certain, but not knowing… It makes me hope, and hope is painful."

He made a conciliatory noise and patted her hand. "I understand. But Lady Montgomery, think of what is improving. Your headaches are much improved. You are no longer dizzy or forgetful. You are far more oriented to your place and situation. None of your activity seems to exacerbate any symptoms, and the only thing I could say you truly need to improve would be your appetite."

Beth scowled and looked where she thought he was. "You and my husband both," she muttered. "He is always telling me to eat more. And treating me with the utmost gentleness."

Too much gentleness, really.

Dr. Durham chuckled in his good-natured way. "Then I will not say anything more."

He patted her hand once more, then moved away, and she could hear him gathering his things together. "Doctor…" she began slowly.

She heard him still. "My lady?"

"When you say that I should do more by way of activity, what exactly do you have in mind?" She bit her lip and blushed, wondering if the thought was too bold. "For example, should I leave this room?"

"By all means," he replied at once, his voice booming slightly. "Get out of this room, get outside, get some fresh air."

"Run wild on the grounds?" she teased with a half-smile.

He laughed again. "Only with supervision, or I shall be treating a turned ankle for you. Do all that you can to return to normal activities, Lady Montgomery. You are strong enough now for that."

"So, you mean…?"

"*Any* normal activity," he emphasized clearly, and she thought she could hear a smile in his voice. "Except, perhaps, for riding a horse. I would avoid that for the foreseeable future."

Beth barked a laugh, leaning her head back against the pillow. "I can assure you, I have no desire to be on a horse again for a very long time."

"I am happy to hear it. Good day, my lady." His footsteps moved across the room, the door opened, and then they faded down the hall.

That was odd, she considered with a frown towards the door. Why would he not have closed it?

"And how did the good doctor find our patient today?"

She started slightly at the sound of Malcolm's voice, then scowled playfully. "He just left, as you know, why not ask him? If you run, you can catch him."

His footsteps moved into the room, and the door closed. "I could. But I want to hear it from you."

Beth sighed, ignoring the twinge in the pit of her stomach at the dip in his voice. "I am the picture of health," she replied in a voice dripping with cynicism. "Everything about me is absolutely perfect. Oh, except that I can't see."

"Yet," Malcolm replied firmly.

She rolled her useless eyes and ducked her chin, pretending she could see her fingers playing with each other. "There's no way to know if I will see again, Malcolm. Dr. Durham confirmed that for me. We just don't know."

"You might see again."

"I might not."

"But you might."

"And that doesn't help me!" she cried, slapping the bed. "I need to know, one way or the other. I can't sit around waiting for my eyesight to come back! I could adjust if I knew I would be blind forever, and I could bear it if I knew it would return, but not knowing? It's torment."

There was silence in the room, and Beth closed her eyes, not that it would help, wishing she hadn't let herself lash out. She needed to be positive and strong, not succumb to the discouragement that was pressing in on her.

"I'm sorry," Malcolm said quietly, sounding pained himself.

That didn't help, it only increased her guilt. She tried for a smile. "No, I'm sorry. I'm not the best version of myself right now. If you'd like to come back in a few minutes, I'll be much better."

"No, I think I'm all right," he replied easily. Then there was a jostling beside her as he climbed up onto the bed.

"What are you doing?" Beth cried, giggling.

"Spending quality time with my wife," he quipped, settling in beside her. He took her hand and laced his fingers with hers.

Beth laughed again, trying to tug her hand away half-heartedly. "In the middle of the day?"

He held her firmly. "Why not?"

"Malcolm!" She tried to push at him, but he wouldn't budge. "You have things to do!"

"Visiting my wife *is* a thing to do," Malcolm insisted. "Seeing after her welfare *is* a thing to do. Having a meaningful conversation and improving our relationship *is* a thing to do. I'm the earl, so I can decide what I do with my time. And I am spending the next little while lying here beside you because I can."

Beth shook her head, unable to keep from smiling. "Very well," she said with a dramatic sigh. "But don't blame me when you don't accomplish anything today."

"Everything else can wait."

It couldn't. She knew there were dozens of things to do, all of them important and requiring Malcolm's attention. There were always things to do, and they couldn't wait.

But if that's what he wanted, she would pretend they could wait.

She leaned her head against his shoulder, smiling when he immediately kissed her hair. "You're a terrible liar, you know."

He scoffed softly. "I beg your pardon, I am a very skilled liar."

"I may not be able to see your face," she said, poking his leg, "but I can hear it in your voice. You have a great deal to do."

"I always have a great deal to do." He kissed her hair again, lingering this time. "All of it stressful and important and pressing. None of it needs to be done at this moment, trust me. I need to be here with you. This is my haven. You are my haven."

Tears sprang into her eyes and she turned to kiss his shoulder. "And you are mine. I don't know how I would do this without you, Malcolm. You are my rock, the only thing I can cling to. All that I have."

He shifted suddenly and cupped her face, kissing her with a blend of tenderness and fierceness that robbed her of sense and thought. She tried in vain to match his fervor, but fell woefully short, gripping his arms as tightly as she dared.

Malcolm broke off and touched his brow and nose to hers. "You have no idea how incredible you are, Beth. I am humbled every day by what I see in you, and I find words singularly lacking to describe my feelings." He stroked her jaw gently, igniting a fire within her. "You were perfectly right. Everything about you is absolutely perfect."

"I'm nothing of the kind," she whispered, shaking her head against him. "I'm a perfectly ordinary girl from Abingdon, and that is all."

He kissed her again, with all the fierceness and far less of the tenderness. There was a wild edge to his kiss, and she felt it clawing at her, stirring up emotions and sensations she'd never expected. "Don't contradict me," Malcolm ordered roughly, once he'd managed a breath. "If I say you're perfect, the only thing I want to hear from you is 'Yes, Malcolm,' 'Thank you, Malcolm,' or 'If you say so, Malcolm.' Do you understand me?"

Beth slid her hands up her husband's arms and latched them around his neck, pulling him in for another kiss, this time thorough and lingering. There was no haste, no frenzy, and a deep, poignant edge that made her heart pound almost painfully.

"Yes, Malcolm," she whispered against his lips.

He sighed and ran his lips across her cheeks and down her jawline.

"Thank you, Malcolm," she managed as his mouth danced along her throat. "If you say so, Malcolm."

He chuckled against her skin, pressing a sound kiss where her pulse throbbed frantically at the base of her throat. "I do say so, sweetheart. I very much say so."

"Malcolm," Beth moaned weakly, her fingers gripping in his hair. "You should know…"

He pulled back and cupped her face once more. "What should I know, love?"

She offered him a brilliant smile. "I find you absolutely perfect, too."

She would have given a fortune to see his face at that moment, but she felt his breath catch, and then his lips were on hers again, somehow more passionate and almost desperate in their madness. He murmured against her lips and her skin, wordless praises that sank into her bones and set her aflame, stoking whatever fever was rising into an absolute inferno. She kissed him with an intensity she didn't know she possessed, with a single-minded determination to claim him as hers now and for always, no matter the cost or consequence.

Malcolm was hers, and she gave herself up to the knowledge that she was his, utterly and completely.

"I don't want to overwhelm you," Malcolm gasped, as Beth sank further onto the bed and he suddenly loomed over her. "Not in this state."

Beth shook her head, stroking his hair. "You won't." She pulled him down to kiss her again, and she felt his hesitation, almost resistance, though it was wavering.

"Tell me to stop," he whispered even as he continued to kiss her. "Tell me to stop and I will."

There was no way she would say anything of the kind, and she seized his lips hungrily to tell him so in the most convincing way she knew how.

Malcolm groaned as his lips molded to hers more fully, more perfectly. "Sweetheart," he rasped, their lips grazing, "tell me to stop. Tell me…"

"No," Beth whispered, cupping the back of his head and pulling him towards her.

Any and all resistance vanished between them, and no one said much of anything for quite some time.

Malcolm's days fell into a rather pleasant ritual after that. Mornings were devoted to work and the children, luncheon was spent reviewing letters and reports from the League, and afternoon hours were spent with Beth. In bed. Without disturbance.

He was as giddy and reckless as a young man, which was odd, as he had never been giddy and reckless even when was he was a young man, but Beth brought life and light and vigor to his soul. He counted down the seconds until he could be with her, even though their nights were filled with passion and tenderness, and he'd only left their bed scant hours before.

It wasn't enough.

How he was able to focus on anything at all was beyond him. He felt renewed and rejuvenated, and somehow it had little to do with their relations and more to do with the depth of feeling he was experiencing. There was nothing he loved so much as holding her in his arms late at night and talking of trivial things. Of laughing with her in their most intimate times, teasing her until her body shook with silent laughter, and bringing that engaging blush to her skin with praises and flirtation. He loved how playful she could be in the daytime, even with him, and yet how tender by night.

Though it would sound trite and contrived, he truly felt that Beth was everything. Absolutely everything. Everything he could want, everything he could ever need, and somehow everything he had never known he had wanted or needed. How could it be possible for one woman to be and possess so much?

Which only made his current frustrations more unbearable, as he went through his recent correspondence from Fritz. Things were far worse than Malcolm had thought, and for the first time in several weeks, he felt the familiar pangs of needing to be in London.

But while things with Beth were progressing in such monumental ways, he couldn't even think of it. He couldn't bear to miss a single moment with her.

The League was in good hands with Fritz at their helm, and the Eagle was in frequent contact via letter, but he was used to being there to see to matters in person. Caroline had been used to him riding off at any time with little warning and no real promise of when he would return. Beth did not know about this part of his life, and in her current state...

He couldn't leave.

He groaned and read over the most recent reports again, his recently lesser-used instincts coming to the forefront. Gent's band of informants had continued to steal letters from their suspects, rushing them to the office, waiting while the letters were transcribed, and then going back out to ensure their appropriate deliveries. The children were thrilled at the additional work they were receiving, particularly as it gave them additional coin, but also for the excitement of it all.

Apparently, young Daisy claimed that the only reason the older children had more was because she was smaller and couldn't keep up the same pace.

The contents of the letters, if taken at face value, held absolutely nothing of interest. They were poorly written, the grammar and word choices absolutely atrocious for anyone in the higher circles, and apparently the clerks were bored out of their minds with the tedium of transcription every other day.

That was well, as the operatives had chosen not to inform them of the true purpose for their task.

Rogue, for all his faults and maddening ways, had some skill as a decipherer, and Rook, for all his airs, had a keen mind that could detect patterns. The two of them went over the letters carefully, scouring their contents for any patterns and details of interest. Fritz joined them in this, having been involved in enough plots to encode his own messages with skill, and they had finally been able to discover the true messages within.

Thus far, the plans within were all based in London and spoke of nothing relating to France at all. Among them were names of certain docks, ships, meeting locations, and, as they feared, the name Lord Wharton.

Rogue's true identity had been compromised, it seemed, and as such, Lord Wharton had disappeared from London entirely. Most presumed he had returned to his country manor to tend to his wife, but in truth, he was just as active as ever in his lower realms where no one ever knew who he was. He could intervene as he needed with the docks and ships, and he dedicated his efforts to that front.

Impossibly, he had never been able to discover much of anything. Oh, the ships existed, and they were posted at the docks that correlated with the messages, but their shipments were perfectly legitimate and perfectly accountable. If something additional had been aboard or involved in any way, it was gone before Rogue and his dockside associates could discover it.

This was not typical. Something was afoot that seemed more involved than anything they had dealt with previously. Their enemies were several steps ahead of them, despite their skills and previous victories. A growing sense of uneasiness filled Malcolm as he sat at

Knightsgate, away from the action and the work.

Fritz did not seem concerned in his reports, but Fritz had seen and done so much that Malcolm wondered if he felt concerned regarding their work at all anymore. He had pulled operatives from other departments and teams to aid them in collecting intelligence. Nearly all their assets had been called in to help, and Rogue was always being followed for his own protection.

Rogue wasn't keen on that, but as the men tailing him stayed out of his sight and did not hinder him, he kept his complaints to himself. Mostly.

Eagle received the same reports as Malcolm, and the two of them corresponded over the contents, using only their trusted couriers to deliver the missives. It would follow that if Rogue had been compromised, there was a great risk of them all being compromised. If that were the case, the Shopkeepers would more than likely lean towards shutting down the League, giving their responsibilities to one of the other networks. They would all be reassigned, of course, but at what cost? Families would have to be uprooted, and identities changed, and while there was an entire department devoted to this very situation, though no one spoke of it, it would be an upheaval that would test the fabric of family in an unparalleled way.

Look at what it had cost Amelia and her mother, though that had been a peculiar situation in and of itself. For their safety, they had been relocated and had their names changed, and the record of such actions had been destroyed without the contents relayed to Eagle when he had been safely permitted to come out of hiding. There had been no warm reunion for them. Amelia had only met her father last year, though she had not been pleased to do so, having no understanding of the situation. Now all was mended, and Eagle was making up for the time lost with compounded interest, but was the pain then truly absolved by the joy now?

What had that disaster cost them?

The idea of moving his family, being parted from them for their safety, of his children forgetting him, of leaving Beth… It left him feeling chilled and desolate.

Malcolm hated not knowing what their enemies were about or what risks faced his men. That had only caused them pain and trouble in the past. Losing Trace the way they had still haunted them all, and until they had answers as to what happened there, the guilt would always weigh on him.

He couldn't lose another operative because of their inept work.

They hadn't known it was inept at the time, of course, but they should have. They knew it now, but could they actually do anything about it? He shook his head and went back to the letter from Fritz, noting the postscript this time. Apparently, Lady Lavinia had been inquiring about Malcolm and when he would be returning to London.

Fritz had quite a lot to say about that, which somewhat took away from the idea of a postscript, and his attempts at humor did not translate for Malcolm.

He groaned and folded the letter, putting it into his desk with the others. He had quite enough to worry and think about without adding the obsessive nature of Lady Lavinia into the mix!

Malcolm sat back, rubbing his hands over his face, trying to force back the unease the reports had given him. There was nothing he could do about it here. He had been ordered to remain while his wife needed him, and everything was being handled. Frankly, he had most likely only been informed out of consideration, not because they expected him to do anything or act upon the information.

It probably would have been better if he knew nothing at all. But then, being let out would have driven him mad. Fritz undoubtedly knew that.

"Malcolm?"

He turned in surprise to the doorway where Beth stood, her brow furrowed, her eyes distant. She wore a yellow day dress this afternoon, looking so like she had before the accident, except for the vacancy of her eyes, he would have forgotten all about it. She was the ray of sunshine he needed at this moment, and his chest constricted almost painfully at the sight of her.

"Did I fall asleep?" she asked wryly.

Malcolm chuckled and leaned against his desk. "You did. You always do."

Beth groaned, grinning ruefully. "I can't keep doing that."

"I don't see why not," he mused, reaching out an arm and taking her hand.

She gave him a look that almost made him think she could see him, aside from the fact that her eyes were attempting to focus on something just to his left instead of on him. "You don't see why not?"

He shook his head, knowing she couldn't see it. "No, I do not."

Beth's brow furrowed, and she tried to tug her hand out of his hold, but he only pulled her in, settling her squarely between his legs. "You must help me learn how to navigate this house without sight, Malcolm. Lying up there in bed is proving to be very dangerous for me."

"I find it very convenient," he replied in a low voice, leaning forward to press a soft kiss to her neck.

She gave a little half moan, and let her head fall back. "Do you want a wife or an invalid, my lord?"

"You don't seem very much like an invalid to me," he said, wrapping his arms around her tightly. "In fact, you seem quite robust."

Beth clamped down on her lips as her cheeks flamed red. "I'm assuming you can see this blush."

He stroked a flushed cheek with a laugh. "I can, and I find it quite charming."

She sighed in irritation and nudged him with an elbow. "Malcolm." Her legs shifted restlessly between his. "I'm serious. I love what we have, what... we've found, but I want to *do* things again!"

Until that moment, Malcolm wasn't entirely sure he had fully grasped this situation for what it was to Beth. He had been thinking of himself yet again, the convenience of having an obliging wife at hand to indulge in. He'd been tending to her as if she *was* an invalid. What woman would not wish to be waited on hand and foot by a man willing to think of nothing but her comfort and pleasure?

But Beth was hardly any other woman, and being laid up in bed without sight had to be an insufferable torment. Finding her way around the room shouldn't be an accomplishment for her. Eating a full meal without assistance ought to be her accomplishment. Beating the children at games, provided it was properly supervised and not particularly long, ought to be her accomplishment. Resuming her duties as Lady Montgomery ought to be her accomplishment. Not this. She was meant for so much more, whether she could see or not.

He shook his head and rose quickly. "Of course, you do, Beth, and you should. I'll help you in any way that I can." He tilted his head at her, looking her over as if suddenly realizing what it meant that she was before him. "How did you come down?"

She smiled at him now, or rather in his direction. "Mrs. Rawlins came to see to me. She brought Annie with her, and the two of them helped me change, and it was almost like before. It was so lovely, Malcolm, and they were so sweet. Then Mrs. Rawlins helped me down the stairs. She's quite good at it, actually. Did you know she has a niece that's blind? She lived with her niece for several years, so I think she could help me."

Malcolm stared at his wife in astonishment, thrilled to hear her say so much at once. She had lost her chattering nature since her accident, and only now did he realize that he had missed it. "I am sure she would be a valuable asset to you," he managed, smiling with more emotion than he meant to. He came to her, placing his hands on her arms, and kissed her brow. "I'm only sorry to have had my morning duties passed on to someone else. I love doing that."

Beth tilted her head up to give him a look. "You can't be there all the time, Malcolm. I won't be able to do everything I should if you are always about. You have things to do, and I have things to do, and we have servants to help us."

He rubbed her arms gently. "I know, love. I just didn't think... Well, you didn't want them involved before, what with..." He trailed off helplessly.

Comprehension dawned, and she smiled ruefully. "I can't afford pride in my circumstances, can I? Everybody in the house, and probably most of the people in the neighborhood, know of my situation." She ran a hand up his arm and felt for his face, laying her hand along his cheek. "I can't commandeer my husband for every little thing."

"I think you probably could," he murmured, turning to kiss her palm.

Beth rolled her eyes. "Well, yes, I *could*, but it doesn't follow that I should." She slid her hand around to the back of his neck and tugged, and he followed, kissing her gently, but thoroughly.

"I'll still commandeer you for other things," she whispered, grinning up at him.

He chuckled, touching his brow to hers. "I should hope so." The weight of his previous tasks suddenly returned, and he sighed heavily, pulling Beth into a tight embrace and burying his face into her shoulder.

"What's wrong, Malcolm?" Beth murmured as she wrapped her arms around him.

He shook his head against her. "I just need to hold you for a moment. Is that all right?"

Beth's hold on him increased, and she nuzzled against him. "Yes. Please. Thank you."

Malcolm laughed and kissed her shoulder lightly. "Impertinent."

"Probably," she agreed. "But I love when you hold me. I think I always will."

Her honesty struck him, and he had to fight for a swallow. For a man who was known for his reticence, he found himself completely unmanned by Beth's open nature. It prompted him to respond in kind, to be vulnerable with her, to reveal more of himself than he might otherwise have done.

"I can promise you this, Beth," he replied, grateful for once that she couldn't see his face. "I will always want to hold you. Be willing to hold you. Want to be near you. I'll never mind waiting on you hand and foot, because I will be with you. In truth, I am your servant. If you send for me, no matter the reason, I will come."

Beth sighed heavily and buried her face into his chest.

He ran a hand over her hair, smiling a little at the tremor he felt run through her.

She sniffled a little, then lifted her head. "I don't think you should talk like that, or you might make me fall in love with you, and you swore this was not to be a marriage of affection."

Malcolm paused at that. Could she be in love with him? Her words were teasing, but he heard the wavering tone. It was an intriguing thought, and his mind seized upon it.

Hang what he once had wanted, what he once had thought! He wanted Beth to love him. And if he could manage it, he wanted to love her, too.

He almost laughed at the sudden shift in his perspective, in his nature, and cupped her cheeks gently. "I don't know about you," he whispered, kissing her softly, "but I believe we may forget about that particular point." He leaned down to capture her lips again, slowly and with great tenderness. "I think we have gone far beyond it. I believe this is, in fact, a marriage of affection."

Beth's eyes were closed, but her throat worked on a swallow. "Oh dear," she murmured, her fingers latching onto the lapels of his coat. "My dear Lord Montgomery, whatever shall we do about that?"

He grazed his nose across hers, grinning to himself. "Don't worry, my lady. I'm sure I'll think of something."

She nodded, sighing a little. "I knew you would. But in the meantime…"

He understood her meaning and kissed her again.

Chapter Eighteen

There was a huge commotion with a great deal of screaming and shouting, and her husband was in the midst of it. Or perhaps he was causing it. Beth couldn't quite make it out.

When the day had dawned brilliant and bright, Malcolm had declared a holiday from classes and insisted that they all spend the day outside. Mrs. Rawlins had ordered a picnic for them, and Mrs. Franklin enjoyed a rare day to herself. The children had been beside themselves to have an entire day with Malcolm and Bitsy and had promised to behave with absolute perfection, as Archer and Jane proudly proclaimed. She could only imagine how earnest the younger two had looked.

It truly was astonishing that she could manage this at all, but the last few days had been amazing for her and for Malcolm. Especially with Malcolm.

They'd fallen into a pattern over the last several days, one where he would go down to the study and see to his duties, then come back up and help her dress, escort her downstairs, and the two of them would go from room to room while Beth found her bearings in each. Yesterday, the weather had been fine, so Malcolm had taken her outside for the first time, and it had absolutely delighted her.

In turn, it had delighted him and the children. They had been frantic to show her everything she had missed, forgetting briefly that she couldn't see, and then scrambling to describe things to her. Beth had taken it all in stride, and once the children had gone back to their lessons, she'd asked Malcolm to walk her around the garden.

He'd done it, slowly and carefully, describing how things looked now, seeming so pleased when she remembered something or when she instinctively turned on the path without his guidance. She was improving every day, everything was exciting and refreshing and new, and she was all smiles and determination.

Malcolm had showered her with praises, and she was convinced it was his strength that was carrying her through this trial.

Today, they'd begun with a long walk, which had felt heavenly to Beth. She'd been out walking every day, either with Malcolm or with Lily, and her strength was rapidly increasing. Mrs. Rawlins took time away from her busy schedule to familiarize Beth with the house in her current state, and she and Malcolm helped her daily to find accommodations.

It was strenuous and tedious, but absolutely necessary. She could not yet manage the stairs by herself, but she was close.

Being outdoors, however, was the closest thing to freedom she had felt in ages. Oh, she knew full well it was a hazardous thing for her, given the challenges with terrain and orientation, and she would never think of venturing out alone. But the sun on her face, the grass beneath her feet, the wind in her hair… It all felt incredibly perfect.

The children dashed about, wild in their unexpected independence, laughing and calling to each other. Beth and Malcolm strolled along behind them, with Malcolm calling out warnings and lighthearted scolding to the children. The girls began picking flowers for her, bringing them up and practically shoving them into her hands, telling her what color they were and where they had come from. The boys opted to race each other over and over, Archer only letting Samuel win twice.

By the time Beth had more flowers than she could easily carry, they had circled back to the house, and a few games broke out between her husband and the children. She had no idea what they were, but the laughter and screams had been enjoyable to hear.

The luncheon picnic baskets were brought out for them, and Malcolm called the children over. He spread out blankets and settled Beth on one while he unpacked the picnic. There had been much laughter and teasing from the children as they had begun to eat, and Beth smiled at the sounds.

Malcolm settled himself next to her, letting her lean on him as he handed her a plate of small items, discreetly telling her where everything was.

It was a grand thing to be able to eat without assistance, and that thought was odd to her. How peculiar things were for her now! The joy of navigating her way through her husband's rooms without assistance, of walking along the hall unescorted, of being able to know who was coming without hearing a voice... It was not ideal, of course, but those little victories meant the world.

Malcolm never made her feel as though she was anything less for her inability to see. He was always at hand if she needed him and gave her space for her independence when she asked for it. His attention to detail was nearly perfect, allowing her to picture everything with surprising clarity. He was doting without being overwhelming, helpful without being annoying, and praised every success without sounding patronizing.

And at night, he loved her with both tenderness and passion that left her breathless and hopeful.

Her heart had been his long ago, but she feared her soul was now his, as well.

Hope was a dangerous thing, as she knew full well. Try as she might, she could not stop herself from hoping that he would love her with the same single-mindedness with which she loved him. No more than she could stop herself from hoping she would see again. Her entire life seemed to be about waiting. Waiting for him to love her. Waiting for her vision to return. And yet, she could not wait anymore. She had to live her life as it was without focusing on something far distant, or something that might never be.

Things, as they were now, were not wholly bad, after all. She might not be able to see, but she had a husband she adored, a marriage overflowing with affection, if not love, and children who brightened every day. She did not want for joy or for blessings, that was for certain.

"You are quiet," Malcolm told her with a gentle nudge. "Are you all right?"

Beth turned to where she thought he was and smiled. "Yes. Perfectly so. I was only thinking how fortunate I am."

Malcolm made a sound of amusement and kissed the corner of

her mouth.

"You missed," she teased, wrinkling up her nose.

"You had a bit of sauce," he said, a smile in his voice. "I thought you might taste better with it."

Beth coughed a surprised laugh. "And did I?"

Malcolm kissed her full on the lips, then hummed a little in thought. "It was delectable, to be sure, but I believe I prefer you just as you are."

Oh, to be able to see his face when he said such things!

Her face flushed, and she shook her head, unable to keep from smiling. "There you go, making me blush again."

"One of my very favorite things to do."

Yes, so he was always saying. And him saying so only made her blush more, which seemed to make him laugh more. It was such a tormenting cycle that the only way out of it was to kiss him into silence. That was not an option here, so she could only hope for a distraction.

"Bitsy!" Jane called from the other side of the blankets. "Can we play becoming fairies? We haven't done that in ages!"

There was a very dramatic ring to her voice, and Beth chuckled. "Yes, darling, only don't stain your frock on the grass."

"We can take a blanket!" Jane cried cheerfully. She began urging her brothers off, and apparently, they obeyed.

Beth got to her feet, handing her plate to Malcolm.

"Shall I come with you?" he asked.

She shook her head at once. "Absolutely not. You would not be well suited to fairy life. Greer can walk me, can't you, Greer?"

"Yes!" Greer shouted, taking her hand.

Malcolm chuckled and kissed Beth's cheek. "All right. Don't be gone too long. I'll miss you."

Her heart danced a merry jig at his words as her youngest stepdaughter led her a short distance away, and she lay on the blanket laughing as the girls spread wildflowers around her, then around each other.

They lay in the sun for several minutes, and Beth could hear the slow, deep breathing of the girls, wondering if they had fallen asleep now that they were full and warm in the sun. She imagined Jane's brown hair strewn around her head like a chocolate halo, while Greer's almost copper curls would be more of a mess of tangles. Both would be absolutely adorable, precious beyond expression, and worthy of an artist's creative touch, could they manage to capture their essence. But she didn't know if that's how they looked, or whether they slept.

"Girls!" Malcolm suddenly called. "If you've finished your fairy transformation, your brothers want to play a game!"

The girls were up in a flash of squeals, and Jane, remembering Beth's condition, came to take her hand and walked her very carefully back. It made Beth smile, as she knew that the child would much rather run back to the house, but she would allow Jane to help in the way she deemed necessary.

"Very good, Jane," Malcolm praised as he looped Beth's hand through his arm. "That was very well done indeed."

"Mrs. Rawlins said we had to be careful," Jane chirped, bouncing next to Beth. "She had all of us practice with her. Archer was best, but I was the most careful. I was careful, wasn't I, Bitsy?"

She laughed and felt for her cheek. "Yes, darling. Now, go off with your brothers and sister, you must start your game!"

Malcolm kissed her cheek and started walking with her. "I need to get you settled, love, as I am playing the game, as well."

"Very well," she replied, smiling further. "You need to play with the children."

"I agree. We'll be playing blind man's bluff, I hope you don't take offense."

He actually sounded hesitant, and Beth laughed. "Of course not! It is a marvelous game, and I am quite jealous. How fun!"

Malcolm chuckled and settled her onto a divan on the lawn. "I wish you could watch us, love," he whispered with a kiss to her cheek.

Beth smiled and turned to kiss him properly. "I know. It's all right. Go play with the children."

He kissed the top of her head and then dashed over to them.

For a few moments, Beth sat there, imagining what was happening and leaning her head back in the warm sunlight. There were screams and laughs, calling out for Archer, who must have been in the center.

"Oh, he was so close to Monty that time," Lily's voice said suddenly from her left.

Beth jerked a little. "Lily! What are you doing here?"

"I just came by for a chat, and now I think I'll tell you what is happening in the game." She squeezed Beth's hand and then sat beside her.

Beth grinned and sat back to listen closely. Lily had been by as often as she could, and Beth would never be able to tell her just what that had meant to her.

"Monty is now the blind man," Lily reported, a smile in her tone. "He's got a dark cravat around his eyes, and the children are all behind him at the moment. Oh! He just whirled and caught Samuel, you can hear him squeal."

Beth could indeed, and she found herself laughing along with everyone else.

"Samuel has the cravat on now," Lily went on. "Oh, you should see it, they're all being intentionally slower. Except for Greer, she's trotting along in her usual way…"

Lily went on, describing the game for a while, also telling Beth what everyone wore and how they looked, as Beth didn't know any of those details. It was an entertaining combination; the more she could picture, the more real the scenario.

"And now, I think, we should let Bitsy have a turn," Malcolm called from where they were playing.

The children cheered, and Beth went wide-eyed on her divan. "I beg your pardon?" she squawked.

Malcolm was suddenly there, taking her hand and gently pulling her up, "Come on, sweetheart. It will be simple for you. Why shouldn't you participate?"

Beth laughed breathlessly and squeezed his hand. "I didn't think… I didn't…"

"Nor did I," he assured her. "But why shouldn't you? You might not be able to run from anyone else, but you can play this part perfectly."

"Bitsy! Bitsy!" all the children cheered, dancing around her.

"And for the sake of fairness…" Malcolm drawled, placing the cravat around her eyes.

Beth frowned. "Really, Malcolm?"

"We must be fair," he said close to her ear, making her shiver.

She chuckled and let him spin her once, and then she raced around trying to catch any of the children or her husband. Malcolm was right, it felt almost the same as it had when she had played this game in the past. She did not feel any sort of disadvantage for once, and she laughed merrily as she ran.

"Over here, Bitsy!" Archer called from her left, laughing.

She veered in that direction, and within moments, she had him in her grasp, to the jubilation of all, even Archer, who turned to hug her.

Malcolm, still laughing, came to her, his fingers working at the knot of the cravat. "Well done, Beth. How do you feel?"

"Alive," she sighed, grinning.

The cravat came off and Beth nearly gasped. The darkness was... different. It wasn't nearly so dark as it had been with the cravat, and it had that almost red shade that she recalled from closing her eyes in the sun before her accident. Everything had been the same sort of dark from the first day of her accident, and she'd never noticed a change.

But now...

Was this the start of an improvement? Or was this a new effect of sunlight?

"Are you all right?" Malcolm asked, sounding only mildly concerned.

She managed a smile, hoping it was convincing. "Yes, of course. I've never been better."

He rubbed her back gently and kissed her hair.

Beth kept the smile on her face as she returned to the divan, but her heart pounded furiously within her. She couldn't tell him. If her eyesight was changing, she needed to be sure. If it wasn't, there was no cause for concern.

But if it was...

She couldn't think about that. She would go on as she had been, as if nothing was different, and she was adjusting to life without sight.

She had to.

Chapter Nineteen

$\mathcal{B}$eth could barely breathe, and it had nothing to do with the snug fit of her corset and gown, though it did complicate matters.

A ball. Her husband was taking her to a ball.

Her. The blind Countess of Montgomery. The one that haunted the halls of Knightsgate. Not that anyone was calling her that to her knowledge, but they certainly could have done.

She gripped her hands together tightly, ignoring the way they slipped from the smooth gloves she wore. This was madness. Absolute and impossible madness.

She'd even argued with Malcolm about it and had insisted that she could not go.

There had been no hiding the amusement in his voice when he'd replied, "Why not?"

Beth had sputtered, waving her hand in front of her eyes dramatically. "Why not? Malcolm!"

He'd had the audacity to chuckle. "Yes?"

Her eyes had narrowed, and she planted both fists on her narrow hips, her cheeks flushing with indignation. "I suppose you find this amusing. I have to ask because I *cannot see*."

"I do, actually," he had replied easily. "I find it quite amusing that my intelligent, beautiful, remarkably capable wife thinks she cannot go anywhere because of the slight difficulty her blindness presents."

Then he had kissed her into submission and asked her to trust him.

Trust him…

She was more vulnerable than she had ever been in her entire life, but somehow, trusting him was the one thing she could do. Still, it was madness.

To say nothing of the fact that she had yet to tell her husband that there had been some improvements in her vision since that day they played on the lawn. She was getting better, she could not deny that now. Everything was still very dark, but she could tell the difference between light and dark and vague shapes were beginning to form. Every day was a little better, and she fully expected that colors would make themselves known before too long.

But Malcolm didn't know.

It wouldn't make any difference tonight. She still could not navigate any better than she had done before, so dancing would be impossible.

But in the morning, or the next day, or the next… It would make a difference.

She hadn't told him anything. Hadn't let on that she was beginning to actually see when someone walked in front of her, know when the fire was getting low, or used a candle to help her navigate better after the sun had set. He didn't know that shapes were beginning to make themselves known to her, and he definitely did not know that she no longer truly needed his arm if the light was decent. She hadn't let on any of that.

She couldn't.

Malcolm had been so kind and considerate with her these last few weeks. Any walls that had once been between them had completely vanished, and it was her lack of sight that had brought that about. If she didn't need him in the same way, would he treat her the same? Would he remain by her side and touch her with such tenderness and yearning? Would he leave her again?

She knew that he was fond of her, that he liked her, and certainly that he desired her, but she wanted more than all of that. She wanted him to love her. As much as she wished to see again, she would have given it all up if her husband would only love her as she loved him.

How pathetic did that make her?

Even now, riding in the carriage beside him, she was a bundle of nerves, fearing that her secret would come tumbling out in her agitation over the evening at hand. What if she made a fool of herself? What if this was a terrible idea, and all her hard work practicing had been for naught?

Malcolm suddenly took her hand and squeezed softly. "Don't be nervous," he murmured. "I've arranged everything."

Beth smiled to herself. Malcolm would have arranged something; he was always arranging things. Their marriage, his trips to London, the children's care, how Beth spent her days… Malcolm was a man of control and order, which made his marriage choice all the more astonishing. But he did it well, so Beth was content to let him.

"You aren't going to show me off, are you, Malcolm?" she asked, trying for a teasing tone. "It would not be an appropriate time to do so."

"It would *always* be an appropriate time to show you off, my dear," he scolded at once, his hold tightening. "But no, in this instance I am not."

She exhaled slowly, nodding to herself.

The carriage slowed, and Beth instinctively turned for the window, though it was too dark for her to make out the house. She could, however, barely see the candles alight in the windows. It seemed to be a great many, and she struggled in vain to remember what the house looked like. She'd only called on Mrs. Harris once, and the lack of sight at present seemed to affect her memory of sights previously seen.

At that exact moment, Malcolm leaned forward and whispered details of the house to her, and piece by piece, each stone fell into place in her mind until her limited sight was no hindrance at all. Her heart swelled with gratitude and love for the man beside her, knowing it was a simple thing he had done, and yet, it had meant the world to her. Whatever grand gesture might lie in wait for her here, it could hardly mean more to her than this.

Malcolm stepped out of the carriage and helped her down, then led her up the stairs, murmuring soft words of praise as she managed them without incident or hesitation. There were no other carriages that she could hear, and no other voices as they entered the house.

"Are you sure there is a ball here?" Beth muttered to her husband.

He chuckled, shushing her. "Yes, love. We are arriving fashionably late, and you will hear the music by and by."

"Lord Montgomery! Lady Montgomery, what a pleasure to see you!"

Beth perked up at the warm tones of Mrs. Harris and smiled with real delight. "Mrs. Harris, thank you so much for your invitation. I hope it didn't give you pause when my husband accepted."

"Not at all, my dear," she replied, taking Beth's hand. "I was thrilled by it."

"And even more by the promise of your late arrival," added the deeper tones of her husband's voice. "There is nothing my wife loves so much as an excuse not to dance."

Beth couldn't quite make his shape out, but there was a shadow to the right of where his wife stood. The light must have been bright in here indeed, for she could almost catch the shimmer of Mrs. Harris' silk in the candlelight.

"I will not allow Mrs. Harris to be kept from the dance for long," Malcolm said warmly. "If I might have the next with her?"

"The next?" Mrs. Harris laughed. "Should you not dance with your wife first, my lord?"

Beth forced a smile, slightly embarrassed. "I am not dancing tonight, I'm afraid. Unless you wish to create a scene, of course, and then I am at your service."

There was a round of uneasy laughter, and Beth tried to relax as much as she was able.

"A scene on our first event in the new house?" Mr. Harris sounded rather pleased by the idea. "I shall have to warn Gerrard, he thought he would have the honor of such a christening when he comes in a few weeks. Gracehill will be much the better for your fair hand pulling that string, rather than his scrawny ones."

Beth's aforementioned hand was raised to his lips, and she beamed at the kind-hearted Mr. Harris. "Only point the way, sir, and I shall begin the chaos."

"Alas, my dear," Malcolm said beside her, retrieving her hand and patting it, "the ballroom will not see your chaos, nor your grace. We have other plans for you."

"Do you?" she asked in surprise, looking around at them all, though she could not make out faces.

"You three need to get back into the ballroom!" chirped another voice, this one much bolder and ringing with a sort of amused authority, almost musical in its timbre. "And you, my sweet Lady Montgomery, are in my charge for a time."

Beth's arm was taken, and she was suddenly tugged away from her husband. "Monty?"

"It's Lady Raeburn, Beth," he assured her as his arm slid from her. "She was at our wedding, do you remember? I will be with you shortly, I promise."

There was nothing for it; Beth was hardly in a position to disagree or to run back to him. She'd already been pulled down a hallway, and while the music of the ballroom was now audible, she had the sense that they were not going to enter it.

"Up some stairs now, my lady," Lady Raeburn said, placing Beth's hand at her elbow. "Can you manage? If you need the balance, there is a wall to your left."

Beth nodded, feeling for it. Lady Raeburn might not have been well known to her, but she was rather well known to everybody else. She had bright red hair, a ridiculously large fortune, and wore the most outrageous ensembles, as she recalled, and instead of being reviled for such independence, she was adored for it.

"It's odd to hear you call me 'my lady', or for anyone else to," Beth confessed as they ascended the stairs. "Would you mind calling me Beth instead? I know we don't know each other well, but..."

"Oh, but I thrive upon bending the social formalities!" Lady Raeburn gushed. "I accept!"

Beth chuckled to herself and sighed as they reached the top of the stairs. "Very good. Would you be so good as to tell me, my lady, what I am wearing?"

"Tibby, my pet, call me Tibby. Everybody does unless there is a very good reason not to." She pulled Beth's hand back and looped it through her own. "And you are wearing a very fashionable shade of red, quite dark, almost the color of wine, and there is some exquisitely delicate black lace and beading around your bodice and sleeves." Her hand was suddenly squeezed. "You look stunning, Beth, and it is quite a shame we are not showing you off downstairs."

Beth's head spun with the details, and it was all she could do to follow. The gown was new, a gift from Malcolm, and the servants had been perfectly silent about its details, only praising how she looked in it. Until colors became clearer to her, she would always be in doubt about how she appeared and what she wore, and on a night such as this, with her husband having some sort of plan for her, she was more anxious than ever.

"Where are we going, Tibby?" she managed to ask, her heart in her throat for some inexplicable reason.

Tibby hummed a little. "I'd say 'you will see', but you won't, will you?"

Beth barked a surprised laugh, oddly refreshed by the bluntness of the statement.

"It's a lovely little room right off a balcony overlooking the ballroom," Tibby went on, the music suddenly growing in volume once more. "Geoffrey and Mary were quite wise to take a house with such a find, and I gave them my opinion decidedly on the subject. It's hidden away by a fine tapestry of Apollo and Daphne, which I find quite odd, as Daphne never gave three pence for him, but the artist apparently felt otherwise." She felt Tibby shrug as she pulled her into a room with a slight draft, but a warm fire was blazing off to her right. "Here, my dear, I've arranged a seat for you. The ballroom is just below, and the tapestry doesn't hide the room from our view, only the opposite. I can tell you anything you wish about what is happening until your husband joins us."

She helped Beth to a seat, and Beth felt herself unable to keep from smiling in disbelief. To be part of the ball, but not at all vulnerable to anyone. To be free to be herself as she was now without having to bear the pity of others. To be alone with her husband, when the time was right. It was all too perfect.

"Malcolm arranged all of this? For me?"

"No, for me, darling," Tibby scoffed. "Of *course*, it was for you. The man is entirely besotted with you, can't you tell?"

Beth clamped down on her lips hard, her emotions surging to the surface. "Tell me everything, Tibby. Everything you can."

Tibby, as it turned out, was an excellent resource with an eye for detail and a manner of speaking that made everything come to life.

215

Beth laughed and laughed at the stories Tibby spun for her, not feeling even once as though she was missing something by being up in the balcony and not down with the others. Tibby even encouraged her to dance about the room, though she had no partner, and Beth took her up on it, with Tibby teaching her whatever steps she didn't know from her own seat.

"Might I have this dance?"

Beth's heart skipped a beat as Malcolm's voice broke through the music from below and she whirled to a stop, facing the doorway he now stood in.

She couldn't make out Tibby's response over the sound of her pulse pounding in her ears, but she did hear the door close soundly, and she did hear the musicians below strike into a slow waltz. She heard the creaking of the floorboards as her husband moved towards her, and thanks in part to the fire, she did see her husband's form as it came into view.

And she would swear she could hear the shiver that raced up her arms and up her neck, raising gooseflesh on her skin when Malcolm reached out and took her hand. There would be no breath in her lungs when this was over.

"My lady," Malcolm murmured, his tone anything but formal, his words almost that of possession rather than politeness. "May I have this dance?"

"Yes," she whispered, unable to raise her voice any louder.

His hand slid around her waist, pulling her close, while the hand he held was suddenly raised into position.

"Malcolm," Beth said as momentary panic seized her, "I can't see."

Malcolm smiled, she could hear it, and his hold on her tightened a little. "That's all right, darling. I can. Follow my lead."

With that, he started into the waltz, and his steps were graceful and lithe, so smooth and easy that it was the most natural thing in the world for Beth to follow him. She had never been a particularly able dancer, only an enthusiastic one, and she'd thought that would all have to be given up without sight. But dancing with Malcolm did not require one to see, only to feel and to follow.

And oh, how she felt... And what delight from following!

216

Malcolm held her close, but said nothing, not that it made any difference. She knew he was holding her closer than was proper, and she loved that he was doing so. She loved the feeling of being in his arms while he quite literally swept her away. This was the sort of thing that every woman dreamed of, whatever she might admit to, and Beth was living in it.

Would wonders never cease?

"You waltz like an angel, Beth," Malcolm praised softly as it came to an end. "Or perhaps like a fairy?"

She smiled breathlessly up at him as he drew her hand to his lips. "I only dream to be a fairy, Malcolm, and I only follow where you lead."

"No, darling." He moved her hand to the back of his neck and traced his own back down her arm to draw her closer still. "I follow where you lead. Wherever you lead."

Beth couldn't breathe, her heart racing within her chest, and the need to kiss him rose with a fury.

But the moment passed as Malcolm chuckled to himself. "What do you think of my surprise, hmm? Will it do?"

She nodded, smiling in her delight. "It is wonderful. I feel as though I am down in the ballroom with all the fine ladies and gentlemen, without the fear of embarrassing myself or you. Tibby put me so at ease and made it all so delightful, but all I needed was you, Malcolm. And now here you are. It couldn't be more perfect."

Malcolm touched his brow to hers, his hands stroking at her back. "Sweetheart..." He shook his head against her. "I wanted to show you an evening of delights despite your condition. To remind you of what we can still have with whatever time we have if we don't waste a single moment."

There were hardly words for a response to such words, such sweetness, and though she had no idea what had come over her husband, she was delighted to let him continue. The music started up again, and Malcolm led her into another dance, and then another, and another. It made no difference that she did not know all the steps, as they were hardly following the proper patterns, and no other couples were present to witness it.

There were no walls between them now, no fear of any

vulnerabilities or embarrassment, and nothing Beth wanted to hide anymore. She would tell him about the improvements in her sight and let him celebrate the triumph with her. There would be no change in their relationship, not after this, and when her vision returned completely, they would be closer than ever before.

Beth parted from Malcolm as the song ended, out of breath and overheated. She moved towards the window where a cool breeze blew, and sighed heavily, reaching her gloved hands to her warm cheeks. "I haven't danced in ages. I don't even know what I look like right now."

"That's all right," Malcolm replied, his voice rough and his breath as unsteady as hers. "I do."

She laughed a little. "And that is supposed to make me feel better?"

"Doesn't it?" he asked as he came up behind her.

"Not at all."

"It should." His hands were suddenly on hers, gently tugging each glove from the fingertips, then pulling each completely off, the fabric gliding slowly down her forearms, leaving a tingling path on her skin in their wake. "Shall I tell you what you look like?"

Beth released a shaking breath and nodded, half afraid of what he might say, half afraid of what she might.

"You look like sunrise," Malcolm breathed, his lips grazing the rim of her ear as his hands traced along the exposed skin of her wrists and hands. "And yet, somehow, like sunset, as well. The most exquisite balance of colors in breathtaking shades."

She shivered and rubbed her arms instinctively, Malcolm's hands coming to her arms, continuing their sensuous torment as they traced down to her elbow, then back up.

"You look like the fairest rose in a garden of thorns," he continued as his fingers slid up to her neck, deftly untying the simple ribbon she wore as adornment, "though your skin is twice as soft. You are the definition of loveliness, the embodiment of spring, and the very shade of passion."

Beth's eyes fluttered at his touch, at his words, at the heated whispers in her ear. There was too much heat, too much emotion, too much everything, and she couldn't contain it. She was fraying at the edges, and Malcolm was only stoking the fire within her.

"You bring life to everything you touch, including me. You brought me back to life. You look like life itself, Beth."

His lips slid to her neck and kissed her softly, wringing a gasp from her. Her name had never come from his lips during their most intimate times, it had always been a sweet endearment, a soft word of praise, but never her name. He'd never called her anything else, and certainly never Caroline again, but never her name...

"Say it again," she whispered as his hands slid around her waist and pulled her flush against him.

Malcolm's mouth found its way to her ear once more. "Beth," he breathed.

With a soft mewl of distress, Beth whirled in his arms and dragged his mouth to hers, kissing him wildly, consumed by her need for him, her rising desire, and the thrill of his arms clenching her tightly. He responded with equal fervor, one of his hands digging into her hair and gripping tightly as he kissed her, deeply and without reservation or restraint.

"Take me home," Beth panted, her fingers latching in Malcolm's hair. "Malcolm..."

He kissed her again, and she could taste his hunger and need. "Yes, Beth. Yes."

Without a word, he lifted her into his arms and strode from the room, and once they were home, he loved her long into the night.

Chapter Twenty

*S*omething was amiss.

Fritz's writing had lost its playful, confident style, and Rogue was almost desperate in his reports. The others kept things fairly straightforward, but with all of them working on the leads from the traitors' correspondence, they were all of the same opinion.

Something was very wrong.

Twice in the last week, shipments had been incorrect. The associates tailing Rogue had reported someone else following him, but only when acting on the contents of the letters they were intercepting.

Fritz had pulled men from the Home Office to help, and Tailor had given them additional support from any of the other groups as needed. He'd given them leave to use anyone at all, and Milliner had offered her operatives and resources from the Convent as well.

Malcolm considered all of that, and Eagle had given him advice and directives, but they both felt the same way. There was no use in the additional manpower if the information was wrong.

They began using different methods to gain the contents of letters, including placing assets as servants in several houses. They kept the same pattern of interception in the streets, certain now that they were being watched somehow, but that was proving fruitless, as well. There were no changes in the letters, and everything they traced was wrong or late.

It occurred to Malcolm to wonder how anyone had managed to identify Lord Wharton as Rogue. Yes, there had been the etching in the newspaper nearly a year ago when Rogue had accidentally become a hero for the lower classes, but it had not been a perfect likeness. Certainly not enough for anyone to identify him, let alone know his real name. Yet the occasional mention of Rogue in their letters raised too many questions.

Thankfully, there had never been any mention of Amelia or Whitleigh, but they were all on edge as it was. No one in Society approached them, and there had been no reason to raise any sort of distraction in public again.

But all of them, every single one, had the sense that something was wrong. Not knowing what it was made everything worse.

Malcolm felt more and more drawn to go help in the investigation, to do as his instincts bade and find what had been missed, to go over everything with meticulous care, and to direct the actions of his colleagues.

But there was Beth…

Beth who was becoming everything. She was a vibrant woman, and not even her lack of sight could change that. Somehow, it only made her more incandescent, and when she was in the height of any emotion, she was a stirring sight, more alive than any woman he had ever known. Their last few days together had changed something within him, and he felt, for the first time in years, as though he were well and whole. The man he once was but changed in so many ways.

Beth had done that.

He needed time with her, endless moments and experiences, in an effort to show her what he wasn't sure he could say yet. He wasn't even sure he could admit it yet.

Malcolm was dangerously close to loving her, and he knew himself well enough to know that he was more than halfway there. Might have even been there, in truth, but while he lived in his denial, the words would remain unsaid. Once said, they could not be unsaid.

He wasn't ready.

This morning, he'd felt something different between them, though it had been days since their exquisite interlude after the ball. "Beth… Do you trust me?" he asked her gently as he'd changed for the day.

She had nodded once. "Of course, I do."

Of course, she did. It was the simplest answer he could have wished for, yet it had cut across his heart with a swiftness that stole his breath. She trusted him.

What a thought!

Malcolm had moved to the bed where she sat and pulled her into his chest, cradling her head gently. He smiled a little when her slender arms had wrapped themselves around his waist, tugging him closer still. "Do you trust me to be your eyes?"

She had smiled faintly. "Yes, of course."

"Do you trust me enough to believe I will always be here for you? Even if I'm not here in person?"

Beth had heaved a sigh, touching her brow to his. "Yes."

"Do you trust me enough to believe in me, even when I may not deserve it?"

She nodded against him, her fingers rubbing along the back of his neck and into his hair.

Her responses had slowly unmanned him one by one, and he could barely manage his next. "Do you trust me enough to be vulnerable with me?"

Beth had tugged at his neck in response, arching up to kiss him slowly, unraveling his already fading control. Her kiss was soft and sweet, and it had a familiar edge to it that he had come to know as uniquely hers. Beth kissed the way she did everything else; with all her energy and all that she was, her entire focus riveted on her subject.

At that moment, her subject had been him, and that kiss had been the end of life as he knew it.

Again.

He died a thousand deaths and was reborn nearly every time she kissed him, and he thrilled with the venture every time.

"Yes," she had whispered with a small, secret smile as she broke from him.

Yes? Yes, what?

He had stared at her for a long moment, not entirely comprehending.

Yes... Yes! "You do?" he had answered in an unsteady voice as he tried to recall what he had asked.

Her smile spread, and she chuckled throatily. "Yes, I do. I danced with you blind, didn't I?" She'd kissed him again, then sauntered out of the room without the aid of anyone at all.

He'd watched her go with reluctance and bewilderment, sighing to himself.

Beth was regaining her independence little by little, and the more she learned and grew, the more comfortable he became. And the guiltier he felt.

If he could prove to himself that she could navigate outside of the house without incident, he could leave for a few days. He'd have to come up with something to tell her, of course, and he would leave them with all the protection he could muster from the surrounding areas, as he had done in the past when leaving on an especially dangerous assignment. Not to mention that three of the footmen, two maids, all the stable hands, and his steward were all trained operatives, so there was quite a bit of protection at hand.

His family would always be safe, whether he was here or not.

But at what cost?

Leaving again, knowing how Beth depended on him, could be seen as a betrayal or some sign that he had tired of her, and he couldn't bear that thought. He didn't want Beth to think anything except that she was cherished and adored beyond all reason. He wouldn't leave her the way he had done before, to escape his own insecurities and avoid facing the truth. In fact, he had never been more inclined to remain at home and let the rest of the world fade into obscurity.

Alas, that was not his way or his nature. He had always been one who felt a keen sense of duty, thrived on loyalty and honor, and felt most himself when in the service of some cause greater than himself. The only thing that could force him from Beth's side was the safety and protection of his men, the kingdom, and his family.

This was beginning to feel more and more like one of those times.

But Beth had only just managed the stairs alone, and that had been with someone at the top and bottom of the stairs watching and waiting to help her. How could he possibly manage to claim, even to himself, that he would be leaving for the safety of the kingdom when his wife was not safe in her own home? No matter how capable his housekeeper or his children, she was *his* responsibility. If she suffered another accident and he was not here to see to her care, or worse…

No, he thought firmly with a rough shake of his head. There would be nothing worse. Beth was healthy and strong and capable, and surely anything else she suffered would be minor in comparison, if she must suffer at all. Surely, her condition and injuries were enough…

He couldn't bear the thought of anything else. She was still vulnerable, as much physically as emotionally. He could not leave until she was more sure of herself. He refused to abandon her, no matter how tormented he was.

Malcolm sighed heavily and returned to his desk, pulling out the barely-begun response to Fritz's recent report.

He had no idea where to begin. He was as lost as the rest and without the benefit of firsthand knowledge of the situation. He was damned if he did go, and damned if he did not. Time was running out, and he was trapped.

There was no way she could tell him now. Absolutely no possible way.

She would have to tell him eventually; he would know that she could see when it became clearer that she needed less and less help to get around, and she was not a talented enough actress to pretend blindness forever. The doctor would know fairly soon, if not the next time he came to check on her.

But after the ball at the Harrises, and the incomparable night that followed, something was different between her and Malcolm. He was incredibly demonstrative, even in front of the children and servants, not that she minded, and she was beginning to understand the depth of the man to whom she was married, and madly in love with. He continually surprised her, and she wondered if she would ever truly know the full measure of him.

She ought to have told him straightaway when her vision was returning. Perhaps a day or two would have been understandable, given the hesitation to admit that something she had hoped for endlessly may now be coming to pass. Now it was well on its way to fully being restored, with shapes and colors and light growing clearer daily. Details were still quite out of focus, and she had very limited abilities to see in the evening and nighttime. Nothing was perfect yet, and much was far from it.

But she could see... and Malcolm had no idea.

Something weighed heavily on his mind, something she had not noticed before due to preoccupation with her lack of sight, but now it was painfully obvious. He thought she could not see and so he did not hide his expressions. Now that she was beginning to see, she observed the somber look when he was silent, the furrowed brow that was becoming a fixture, and the way he tensed whenever the post arrived.

It had been just over a week since the ball, and he seemed more burdened than ever before. He hid it as best as he could, devoting every moment with her to pretending otherwise, but still, it was there.

If he had known she could see him, he would never have allowed his emotions to be displayed so openly. She knew that full well.

Two days ago, she had seen him in his study, though not particularly clearly, and he'd had his head in his hands, elbows propped on the large desk. She had been too far away to determine his exact expression, and even now she had to be very close to see it, but from that distance, she could tell enough. She'd seen him grip at his hair, his loose and disheveled clothing, and heard the sharp, though faint exhale of despair or frustration.

It had made her ache and given her pause.

"Malcolm?" she'd asked falteringly.

At once, he'd looked up, cleared his expression, and come to her. "Beth, I didn't hear you come down."

His tone had given absolutely nothing away, so neither had she. "That is well, isn't it? If you'd heard me, that would have meant I'd tumbled down the stairs, and that would hardly be fortunate."

Malcolm had laughed, surprisingly without sounding forced, and kissed her. "My impertinent wife is too clever for her own good."

Beth had run a hand over his cheek, wishing at the time that she could have seen him clearly, wondering if his eyes would have looked hollow or shuttered. "What's wrong, darling? I know something is."

225

He'd kissed her palm, sighed, and held her close. "Too clever, love. I'm only burdened with business, nothing to trouble yourself about."

"Is there trouble?"

"There's always trouble," he'd muttered in a surprisingly dark tone. "But I don't want to dwell on that."

Then, he'd changed the subject and taken her on a long walk while regaling her with stories from his youth, and while his mood had improved by the end, it had returned later in the day after he'd returned to his study.

She hadn't asked again, but it worried her. The only time he seemed himself was when he was either focused on her or playing with the children, and even then, the burdens seemed to weigh on him if he were not distracted.

Beth could not complain and would not. She had her husband's attention and affection, and both of those in excess, but not his confidence. She did not care if his troubles did not concern her, or if they were not something she would particularly understand. She wanted to share his cares and his sorrows, to help him find a way through them, and to be a source he could turn to for advice or to unburden his soul if nothing else.

But Malcolm suffered in silence, and obviously was not inclined to let Beth know what any of it was about.

She wanted to be his wife in truth, not just in name and in his bed, though she dearly loved both. Was it too much to wish for? She had already gained much more than she had anticipated in this marriage, and to ask for more than what she had seemed somehow wrong. A marriage of convenience had turned to one of friendship, and then to one of affection, and now enjoyed the privilege of something more, something less easily defined. She couldn't call it a marriage of love, though there was more than enough on her side, and Malcolm...

Malcolm...

At times, she would swear that he loved her as she did him. She thought she could feel it in his touch or in his kiss, in the way he held her at night. Yet other times, he seemed so far away that she wondered if he wished for the freedom he once had. Not that he would ever abandon her or treat her with any less affection and honor than he had done. He was a good man. One could not draw conclusions with such men.

He would always be the sort of man he was now, a devoted husband and father, a man who honored commitments and would not shirk duty, and one who valued loyalty and respect above all else.

With all of his current burdens, and considering how often he seemed to find relief in his wife and children, Malcolm would not take kindly to the revelation that his wife had kept something from him, especially something as significant as regaining her eyesight.

She feared his response more than she had feared anything in her life. She *would* tell him, but she needed the perfect moment to do so. Perhaps something with a hint of hesitation, and if she made it sound as though she had only just started regaining it... She had never had any talent for lying, and she doubted Malcolm, with all his keen skills in observation, would be any more fooled by her attempts than her parents had been.

She would have to have him sufficiently distracted to not make much of her sudden announcement, or the time to read into her lies.

Was Malcolm ever completely distracted, or even just enough for that? Beth doubted that very much. But she had to do something, and soon. Anything less could be perceived as a betrayal of sorts, and there was no telling how her husband might react when she was discovered.

"What in the world are you doing in this room?"

Beth turned with a quick jerk of surprise, her fingers skidding on the pianoforte which she had been aimlessly playing. "Malcolm!"

He strode into the room, looking almost relaxed for a change, his jacket off and his cravat loosened. "And why do you sound as if you are in trouble? I'm hardly going to scold you for venturing in here, I only wonder at it."

She swallowed and looked away, forcing a smile. "I did tell you once that I played."

"I recall that," he said, coming over to stand beside her, setting a hand at her back. "I also recall that you said you never played for yourself, only at the behest of others."

Beth shrugged, running her fingers over the keys again. "Perhaps

I've changed my mind and wished to explore the idea."

"An intriguing notion, considering…"

Her jaw tightened. "Why should I limit myself simply because of one small obstacle?"

"Steady on, love, that was not a criticism." He kissed her hair quickly and rubbed her shoulders a little. "On the contrary, I applaud your industry and efforts. What a bold and determined woman you are."

A flush of guilt lit her cheeks at his words, which he would undoubtedly mistake for modesty. "I can only play what little I remember," she admitted, which was true, as she could not make out the notes on the page yet, "and not very well…"

"I refuse to let you criticize yourself when taking on such an impressive task," he scolded, gripping her shoulders a little. "You'll find a way, Beth. You always do."

Oh, it was intolerable for him to speak so warmly of her when she had something so important weighing on her! The burden of her confession pressed down against her chest and made breathing difficult.

Thankfully, Malcolm didn't notice any of that as he gently turned her about on the stool. "Come outside with me, love. The children wish to play while the day is fine, and I don't want to leave you cooped up in here. Come and enjoy the sunshine and let me marvel at what it does for your already perfect complexion."

He stroked one cheek with the utmost gentleness, and Beth felt at once as though she had wings, and yet somehow further mired down. Stretched to her extremes, she was unable to move for the pressure building within her.

"Nothing about me is perfect," she whispered with more harshness than she intended, praying he would not notice.

She glimpsed a crooked smile in his face. "Surely we've argued on that subject more than enough. We don't need to do so again, do we?"

Now she blushed in earnest and rose to her feet, sliding her arms around Malcolm's waist and burying her face against him. His arms tightened around her, and he said nothing, no doubt accustomed to Beth's sudden bursts of affection. He'd never complained about them before, and he did not now.

She just needed to hold him while her heart pounded restlessly, afraid that this precious time together would end before long, and she would be powerless to stop it. She could not will her husband to remain with her, could not force his reaction to be one she wished for, and it would be her fault if all went awry.

He would be thrilled that her sight was returning, yet he would be livid that she had hidden it. Which of the two sentiments would win the day?

Beth held him closer still, sighing weakly against him.

"What's this, love?" Malcolm murmured fondly, running a hand over her hair. "Are you well?"

She nodded and forced herself to step back a little, ignoring the urge to look up at him with all the love in the world. He would see her eyes, and she couldn't risk the discovery. "Sometimes, I just need to be held," she admitted, ducking her chin a little.

Malcolm took her chin in hand, raising it gently and kissing her with the utmost softness. "You may always rely upon me to accommodate you there, Lady Montgomery. No matter the occasion or my occupation at the moment, there will always be time for me to hold you."

Beth cupped his cheeks and kissed him again, fearing words would betray her.

"Come on, love," Malcolm said as he broke away. "The children will be anxious, and you are too able a distraction for me." He took her hand and pulled her along behind him as they left the music room and moved to the back of the house.

Through the windows, Beth could see the small, shapeless forms of the children on the lawn. The day would be bright, almost blinding in the direct light of the sun compared to the relative darkness of the house. Only days ago, she might not have reacted at all to the change, being almost entirely unaware of it.

But now...

She closed her eyes as Malcolm led her, knowing it was the only way that she could avoid discovery.

"I've arranged a chair for you," Malcolm was saying, his hand warm in hers. "It is in the shade of the house, so you won't become overheated."

"Put it in the sun," Beth pleaded, forcing her eyes open a little. "The day is not so warm, and I want to feel the sun against my skin."

Truth be told, she only wanted the warmth of the sunshine to soothe the cold ache seeping into her bones. She wanted to be in the sun, now that she could see well enough to appreciate it, and everything was clearer to her under its influence.

"As you like." He adjusted the chair accordingly, then helped her to it.

"Papa!" Jane shouted, her hands fisted on her hips. "Bitsy is fine now, come and play with us!"

"Hurry, Papa!" Samuel echoed, slapping away Archer's hand as he tried to adjust his brother's collar.

Malcolm exhaled, shaking his head. "To be in such demand..."

Beth chuckled easily, not having to force the effort. "They do adore you." *As do I*, her heart added in a pained chorus.

As if he could hear the silent cry, Malcolm smiled softly and pressed a kiss to her cheek. "No matter what you may hear," he whispered, "I will be winning whatever it is I am induced to play."

She smiled back at him with a nod. "I have no doubt of it."

"Very accommodating, wife."

"I do try."

Malcolm strode away towards the children, surprising them all with a monstrous roar and scooping up Greer at once. The little girl squealed and giggled, flailing in his hold as Malcolm chased the others with her in his grasp. It was a merry game of chasing until the other children decided to form up against him and forced him to the ground to rescue their sister. Once she was freed, they all chased their father in turn.

The tides frequently turned in the game, and the energy only rose as it went on. At one point, Malcolm was a dragon, and the children were villagers bent on his destruction. Then the girls were princesses in a tower, and their father was the troll that had captured them while the boys attempted a rescue. Malcolm played as Beth had never seen him play before, with wild laughter and grand gestures, easy manners and completely lost in every game.

There was no proud earl here, and no reserve to be found. This was a devoted father stripped of pride and formality for the sake of his children. They would always come before anything else in his life, and he was not ashamed to have that known. How many men in the world, let alone one of rank and standing, would allow themselves to be so carefree with their children? How many of them romped and played more than just for show? How many children looked up at their fathers with the adoring looks these children bestowed upon Malcolm as he tossed them into the air or tickled them into hysterics?

It was a rare man that Beth Owens had secured for herself, and there was no course but to love him hopelessly and fiercely, with all that she was and more. She ought to tell him that. No matter if he could return the sentiment, he deserved to know that she loved him. Such a secret was too much to bear, and she was astonished to have kept it this long. But she feared telling him, knowing there would be no turning back once she admitted something so great.

She'd never thought of herself as being particularly afraid of anything, yet confessing her love was more terrifying than anything else. Except, perhaps, confessing the return of her sight.

And perhaps one other secret…

Greer suddenly ran at her father and Malcolm swept her up, tossing her into the air yet again, her red-gold curls dancing in the bright sunlight with a burst of delighted giggles to accompany them. Malcolm twisted her this way and that, tickling her sides and making her squirm precariously in his hold. He chuckled and drew her to his chest, kissing her soundly, and then setting her down to the ground, letting her dash off with her siblings.

Beth watched the scene with a soft smile, her heart full, and realizing just how much she had missed seeing the faces of those she loved most during her time of blindness.

She watched Greer run, then looked back at her husband, who had straightened up and was laughing to himself. He turned to look at her, his smile warm and open, and their eyes met.

His expression seemed to freeze, and then slowly the smile faded, and a furrow formed between his brows.

Her breath vanished in a swift motion, and her heart leapt to her throat.

He knew.

As if on cue, he marched towards her, stopping only two paces from. "You can see," he said in a cold, biting tone.

Beth averted her eyes, fixing them on Malcolm's boots, and she nodded once.

The children called for Malcolm again, and he exhaled in irritation. "You have five minutes to prepare a statement on the matter, and then you and I will go into the house where you will tell me absolutely everything. Am I understood?"

He had never spoken to her in such a manner, and it terrified her to hear it. "Yes, Malcolm," she responded meekly, wishing very faintly that he would just get it over with. Anticipation made the unknown so much worse.

Malcolm went back to the children, doing a passable job of hiding his fury and pretending that all was well. The children laughed as they had before, finding the same joy in their father they had only moments ago.

Beth sat as still as she could, though the temptation to writhe in her discomfort was gnawing at her. Her skin seemed to crawl, while deep inside, her bones seemed almost numb. She had never seen Malcolm truly angry, as he had always been perfectly controlled and composed, and she feared she was soon to discover what her husband was truly capable of.

Faintly, she heard Malcolm call a halt to the games and instruct the children to return to the nursery for lessons, still with no hint of distress in his tone. They complained a little but did as they were bid, each bidding her farewell as they returned to the house.

His hand was suddenly before her, and she let him tug her to her feet. "Come."

Beth nodded weakly and let him lead her along, noticing he no longer took any care to ensure her footing.

He no longer needed to treat her with such delicacy.

Malcolm marched her to his study and released her hand the moment they were in the room. He turned without a word and closed the door behind, pausing with his back still turned to her.

"Your sight has returned," he announced clearly, the words clipped.

Beth swallowed with difficulty. "Y-yes," she managed.

"How long have you been able to see?" he asked, his words deliberate.

"Not long."

His hands became fists at his side. "How… *long?*" he asked again, this time his words as clenched as his fists.

"Several days," Beth answered hesitantly. "Possibly more."

He dropped his head, and a faint tremor raced across his back. "Perfectly?"

"No." She shook her head even though he couldn't see it. "Never perfectly. Still not. Each day is slightly better than the one before."

"When did you know it was improving?" Malcolm's voice seemed far away, and she had the sense that he was drifting just as far from her.

Beth closed her eyes, wishing she might sink into the floor and escape. "I first noticed that day we played with the children. When you took the blindfold from my eyes, I could see a difference in the light. I didn't know for certain until two days following, and since then it has only been improving." She opened her eyes and reached for the desk behind her for balance. "Colors began to appear, and shapes took form, but it was blurry and disorienting, almost more than the darkness had been. I could still see almost nothing in the evening unless the fire or candles were bright."

"But you could see."

The short phrase might well have been a lash against her skin, and she gripped the desk. "Yes."

Malcolm slowly turned on the spot and folded his arms tightly. "Does Dr. Durham know?"

She shook her head quickly. "He has not been by since it's come back, and I haven't written for fear it would be temporary."

"And now?"

Beth bit her lip. "I don't believe it is."

"And how long have you had that conclusion?"

Her eyes burned, and her lashes fluttered at the sensation. "A week or so. Since after the ball."

Malcolm swore suddenly, a curse of a somewhat shocking nature, and he whirled back around, his hands flying to his head. "A week?" he cried hoarsely. "Why didn't you tell me? Why didn't you say anything?"

"I'm sorry," she whispered.

He turned back, hands still at his head. "Can you see my face?"

She nodded hastily. "But not well."

His hands dropped, and he came to her at once, his strides hard and purposeful. He took her chin in hand, gripping a little. "Can you see it well now?"

She clamped down on her lips as tears welled and fell, and barely managed a nod.

"Why didn't you tell me?" he rasped, his voice almost breaking, his eyes almost wild. "I have places I should be, important and critical things to do, people who need... I only stayed because I thought you needed me!" He shook her ever so slightly, his throat working. *"Why didn't you tell me?"*

Beth whimpered a little, her tears falling onto Malcolm's hand. "I was afraid," she admitted weakly. "I knew you felt bound to stay while I was in need..."

"So, you took *advantage* of that?" His voice rose with his indignation, and Beth felt her shame reach unmatched levels.

"You asked me to be vulnerable for you, and when I was blind, you were vulnerable as well!" Her voice cracked, and she shook her head. "I was afraid of the walls you would put up if I could see..."

Malcolm was also shaking his head but in disbelief. "If I was vulnerable, it was because you couldn't see!"

"You took advantage of my blindness to let your guard down?" Beth demanded, feeling outrage mingle with the guilt she felt pressing in on her.

"Don't turn this around. I am not the one who has been lying!" Malcolm insisted, holding up an accusatory finger.

Beth clamped her trembling lips together, then managed, "Lies can be told without words as well."

Malcolm stared at her, his eyes as cold as his features now.

"I didn't want you to go away again," she whispered, her indignation fading as the hurt rolled in.

He wrenched his hand away from her face as if stung, and stepped back a few paces, his expression changing from distress to a cold sort of sneer. "That is not up to you."

Unable to help herself, Beth reached for Malcolm's hand. "I am *so* sorry."

He stepped back even further, now almost perfectly composed. "That, I am afraid, is not enough." He gave her a clipped nod and turned away, banging open the door and letting it stand open as he stormed from the room.

"Malcolm!" she pleaded, though it only served to echo through the empty halls and vanish unanswered.

Beth covered her mouth and closed her cursed eyes, sagging against the desk. Her heart was breaking, crumbling into nothing, only to be blown away as dust with the slightest breeze. There would be no forgiveness for this. No returning to the joys she once had, the pleasures that had stirred her, or the comfort he had provided in her distress. He would be gone, within the hour, if she knew him at all, and Lord only knew when he would return.

If he returned.

Oh, he would come for the children. He adored them too much to abandon them, but she would never be held in the same regard after this. Nor should she be.

The sound of a horse's pounding hooves met her ears. Her knees gave way, sending her to the floor as though she had been trampled by the same horse who now carried away the man who held her heart.

He was gone, then. And without a farewell or instructions, without so much as a look.

The silent sobs that shook Beth's frame suddenly gained voice and volume, and with no one to hear or care, she let them come without restraint, gripping the rug beneath her as her heartbreak played out its bitter conclusion.

Chapter Twenty-One

$\mathcal{A}$ controlled man would have stayed until his head was clear, no matter what had infuriated him, particularly with regards to a wife he adored as he did. But Beth had done away with his control, and he could not stay.

She had hidden the truth from him! She, whom he had trusted with his heart and his children and his life, had intentionally kept him ignorant for her own ends! She'd been improving every day while he had worried about how to care for her in the future and how to provide a meaningful life to one in her condition.

While his men and associates struggled to discover the truth that could save them, and perhaps entire nations, he had been cozy and safe at Knightsgate tending a wife that did not need to be tended!

The fury that had crashed down on him had been swift and potent when he'd seen the truth, and it had been all he could do to remain playful for the children. They could not know how his darker feelings festered in the meantime, or ever suspect that he was at odds with his wife. When he had reached his limits, he'd sent them away, and only then did he feel able to deal with his wife's betrayal.

But he had been unable. He had been almost cruel, rather as if she had been a criminal he had discovered. His wife was no criminal, she was anything but. Yet in these uncertain times, with so much at stake, he could not differentiate enough to alter his treatment.

Malcolm did feel guilt at his behavior with Beth, and that only grew the further away from home he rode. There was nothing for it now, his course was set, and there was much to do. Until he could find the appropriate control over himself once more, he would not let guilt, shame, or remorse over his wife sway him.

He would apologize properly, probably by letter, as he could not guarantee he would be leaving London for some time. And they really ought to celebrate the return of her sight, so he would need to offer congratulations at some point, when he could feel the relief in it. And she would need to see the doctor to have it confirmed and to make sure all was well. He would remind her of that when he managed the sense and calm to write to her at all. All of that should suffice until he could apologize to her in person, should he still feel the need when he saw her again… *if* he saw her again.

There was really no way to tell what sort of danger he was riding towards, and his life was not certain in times such as this. He had not behaved at all well, but there was nothing for it now. If he died, he would die with regrets, just as other men did. In the meantime, he would do the one thing he knew he could do well. He would investigate, serve his King and countrymen, and offer his life for the good of all.

Whatever that might be worth now.

At this moment, he was filled with fury and guilt in equal measure, and the need to unleash somehow gnawed at him.

London was in his sights, and he headed directly for his club, knowing that he would really do better to find solitude, but he was disinclined to listen to his better nature at present.

Once within, he made no effort to be cordial or accommodating. He made his way to the fencing hall, stripping off his greatcoat and gloves as he went, practically throwing them at the astonished valet who trotted beside him.

Somehow, foils were available for him at a moment's notice, as well as an opponent. Malcolm looked up to see none other than Mr. Herschel standing at the end of the lane. A snarl curled Malcolm's lip, and he brought his foil up in a salute, then attacked.

Herschel was big, beefy, and stupid, and he moved as such, though the gleam in his eye gave Malcolm pause even as he began to strike. Foils clashed and clanged, and despite Herschel's girth, he was a capable swordsman.

It was a pity for him that swords had always been Malcolm's specialty.

Skill and agility came roaring back in abundance, and Malcolm's limbs, unused to this activity after so much time away, seemed filled with exhilaration at being now used in such a way. And on a traitor to the kingdom, no less!

It was too perfect a blend, and Malcolm was never one to let a perfect situation go unappreciated. Again and again, he attacked, lunging and striking with a rapidity that Herschel hadn't a hope of matching, and most of the blows were barely defendable. It was too fast, too fluid, and parrying properly was becoming less and less possible. It wasn't gentlemanly to fight with such aggression, nor to take advantage of a clearly weaker opponent, but Malcolm was beyond caring.

This man was to blame for so much of the strife that had reigned supreme in Malcolm's life in the last few months! *This* man had abused trust and created trouble for men that Malcolm cared about deeply! And while this particular man may not actually have been to blame for what had happened between him and Beth, at the moment he bore that sin, too.

He bore *every* sin.

Herschel's dark eyes were wide and terrified as Malcolm continued to attack, feinting and lunging at the large man without mercy. He could hear the cries of weak outrage from the few men that had gathered to watch, but Malcolm was beyond hearing them.

There was rage and indignation in every stroke Malcolm laid out, and every blink of Herschel's eyes only agitated him further. Traitorous, villainous, ridiculous man, whose wife was a constant thorn during Malcolm's London visits, and to have to endure this blubbering waste of parliament in his professional life as well?

To be parted from the woman he loved because this man felt that betrayal was a noble cause?

It was too much, far too much, and Malcolm intended to see him pay.

"Here!" a voice called. "Here, Monty! *En garde!*"

Malcolm turned around and saw Fritz there, eyes fixed and focused. He glanced back to see Herschel scurrying off with a scowl, though he looked more terrified than irritated.

"*En garde*, I say!"

Even Fritz's voice was too much to bear, and Malcolm growled darkly as he turned back, swinging his foil towards his oldest friend.

Fritz was a much worthier opponent, and he knew all of Malcolm's tricks. He matched him stroke for whirling stroke, parrying with ease and counter-attacking with brilliant stratagem.

"I haven't seen you like this in years," Fritz panted when he was close enough.

"In light of the fact that I have no enemy to run through," Malcolm gasped in response as perspiration gathered on his brow, "you'll have to do."

He shoved his friend away, and attacked hard, pressing and pressing even as his blade lashed out again and again, his agitation rising with every step he took, every inch of ground gained. Fritz's eyes narrowed, his foil barely keeping up with Malcolm's frantic attack.

Then suddenly, Malcolm roared and slashed his foil across Fritz's arm, and a sharp hiss and a wince brought him up short.

Chest heaving, sweat pouring off him, Malcolm watched as a faint red line appeared on Fritz's upper arm, and then was quickly covered by Fritz's other hand.

Fritz met Malcolm's eyes, and there wasn't a hint of recrimination or anger in his gaze. "Feel better?" he asked Malcolm with his usual light tone.

Malcolm grunted and handed his foil off to a terrified attendant. "Not even remotely. But I'm finished." He cleared his throat awkwardly. "Thank you for stepping in."

Fritz shrugged. "Not at all. You were getting carried away, and Herschel was going to cry." He looked down at his wound and hissed again. "Great. You can bind me up. And buy me a drink."

Malcolm nodded obediently and followed Fritz out of the hall, glancing around a little at the gawking spectators. "Think they'll be talking about that now?"

"Of course," Fritz told him with a snort. "That display was completely out of character for you. Probably going to give some credence to Lady Lavinia's claims about you, given it was her husband you lashed out on."

"Dammit." Malcolm most certainly did *not* need that added to his burdens.

"On the other hand," Fritz mused, stepping closer, "you should have seen Viskin's face as he watched. You might get recruited now."

Malcolm smiled without humor. "At a time like this, I would love a dangerous undercover mission."

"I'll have a solicitor check over your will and affairs before you leave, just to be safe," Fritz offered with a sage nod.

"Shut up."

"Gladly. Besides, I believe you're the one who needs to do the talking." Fritz hummed a laugh. "And based on what I just saw and the laceration I now bear, it will take a while. Better make it at least two drinks."

"I don't understand. He left?"

"Straightaway. I would not be surprised if Malcolm went straight from the study to the stables. He did not even have a single bag packed, and nothing has been sent for."

"All because you could see again."

Beth gave Lily a tight smile, which was the only sort of smile she had managed in the days following Malcolm's departure. She took a moment to sip her tea, though she barely tasted it, and examined the wallpaper in the front sitting room, which happened to match her pale green muslin nearly perfectly. A poignant thought, for she rather felt as useless and faded as wallpaper these days.

She'd been scolded by Mrs. Rawlins a number of times for her pallor, and several medicinal draughts had been made up by the kitchen staff, though she had refused to take them. She was not unwell, she'd insisted, only melancholy. There was no cure for that but time, and even that seemed lacking.

All that time had given her was regrets and remorse. But she couldn't tell Lily that, it was too great a burden to share. She had been unaware that Malcolm had left the neighborhood, and Beth had done nothing to spread that bit of information. She could barely admit it to herself every night when the bed was cold and empty beside her, and she still listened for his steps in the hall at every opportunity.

Still, Lily was wise and capable, and in her elegant lavender ensemble this morning, she looked far better than Beth did. She'd come to Knightsgate today with color in her cheeks and a warmer smile than Beth had seen her wear in months, and there was undoubtedly a story there.

Unfortunately, Malcolm and Beth were the chief topics of conversation, and it was no more pleasant to tell than it had been to endure.

"Not because I can see," Beth said, at last, bringing herself back to the conversation and out of her miserable reminiscence. "Because I did not *tell* him I could see."

Lily frowned slightly, her delicate brow furrowing. "Surely, he ought to have been only surprised, and afterwards he should have exuded joy at the recovery."

Beth shook her head, and her forced smile faded completely. "There was no joy, despite his evident surprise. None at all. I betrayed him, Lily! I've never seen him look the way he did then, and the manner in which he spoke… It was as if someone had stolen my husband completely and only a stranger remained."

Lily sat back in her chair, her tea untouched on the table, her gaze suddenly far away. "I know that feeling all too well," she murmured in a hollow tone. "It is painful and unsettling, to say the least. I would not wish it on anyone." She exhaled slowly, shook herself, and then turned back to Beth with a smile that almost reached her dark eyes. "I would say that he behaved badly, to be sure, though I think that you would disagree with me in this instance."

There was no simple way to answer her, particularly when she was absolutely correct. Oh, there had surely been a better way for Malcolm to have responded, but she knew full well that she had been the guiltier of the two parties. She had hidden the truth from him, knowing he would not like it. She knew him well, and his reaction had been only slightly worse than what she had anticipated.

And while it had hurt her exceptionally, she also felt that it was well deserved.

"You are correct," she murmured now, looking down at her fingers as they plucked at her skirts. "I would disagree. I should have told him the moment I knew I was improving instead of waiting until it was too late. I knew that he was burdened with matters, and suspected that he had a need to be in London, and I was afraid of being alone again, with or without sight."

"Understandably so," Lily soothed, reaching for her hand. "Monty is a complicated man, and exceptionally dedicated to whatever he sets his mind upon. He will never forget you, nor the children, but on occasion, he becomes so focused that he forgets himself."

"I know." Beth nodded slowly and sipped her cold and tasteless tea again. "I know. We had just gained so much with the loss of my sight, and having it return seemed almost a bad omen."

Lily tsked sharply. "Ridiculous," she snapped with a tight squeeze to her fingers. "I refuse to let you wallow in self-pity and blame when we ought to be celebrating your miraculous recovery! Monty might have been cross, but I doubt it had anything to do with you. If there was anything on his mind that made the revelation ill-timed, that is his own fault and nothing to do with you."

Beth looked at her friend in disbelief, and then, impossibly, felt a smile form, grow, and spread until her eyes crinkled. "You are an impossibly good friend, are you aware of that?"

"I have it on good authority that I am only impossible," Lily replied with a laugh, releasing her hand and taking up her tea. "But you are kind for saying so." She sipped her tea, and then made a wry face and set it down. "Good heavens, Beth, what in the world have you done to this tea?"

The unexpected outburst made Beth laugh, and she took another sip of hers, but without any sort of disgusted facial expression. "I apologize. I've had to temper my tea of late. If it is too strong, I become very ill, and I already wake up ill as it is."

There was absolute silence in the room for the space of three heartbeats. Beth counted each one. Then the teacup clattered against the saucer as it was set against the table and her hands were seized.

"Elizabeth Colerain, are you saying what I think you are saying?" Lily demanded without shame.

Beth closed her eyes on sudden tears and dipped her chin in a nod.

"A child?"

"Yes," she whispered, pained by the admission.

"That's wonderful!" Lily cried, obviously delighted by the news.

When Beth hesitated to reply, and the only sound in the room was the clock ticking on the mantel, Lily let her hands fall away.

"Is it?" Beth finally asked, raising her eyes just enough.

A frown graced Lily's fair face. "Why would you ask that? What did Malcolm say about it?"

Beth rose from her seat and went to the window, the panicked feeling this news always brought her rising yet again. "I never told him."

"Why not?" Lily remained in her seat, thankfully, but her tone indicated she would much rather fly at her. "Surely that is something he deserves to know!"

"Of course, it is." Beth sighed and stared out at the drive in front of the house, wishing for the thousandth time that a certain someone would appear on it. "And I had intended to tell him. But then he discovered my other secret, and it seemed ill-timed to announce such news in an attempt to keep him from leaving."

Lily made a soft noise that Beth could not interpret. "I suppose. How long have you known of it?"

"I suspected around the same time my sight started to return, but I was not sure until Dr. Durham came around last week." She swallowed with difficulty, the rise of tears impossible to stem. "He confirmed both that my sight was indeed returned, likely for good, and that I was with child, destined to make its appearance in the winter. And I have no husband to tell."

She hadn't said those words aloud before, but they had been haunting her thoughts since Dr. Durham had visited. Four times, she had sat down at her writing desk and begun a letter to Malcolm, expressing her apologies on her betrayal of his confidence, but she couldn't bring herself to call it such. It had been her sight that had vanished, and her sight that had returned.

He hadn't been involved at all. Which, naturally, caused her to regret the letter at all, and she either tore it to bits or crumpled it up.

She'd tried to write a letter as if she'd had nothing to apologize for, if only to tell him of her news, but she couldn't bear to do so. She had tried a cold, emotionless note of the bare facts, but that was not her nature, and she could not be less than herself. Not now, not ever.

She missed him fiercely, longed for his touch, for his words, even his presence in absolute silence. She would take the almost-distant man she'd married in a heartbeat, so long as he was here. She would go back to the comfortable arrangement of those days without a backwards glance.

But she couldn't say that in a letter either. She could not say anything she needed to in a letter. No husband about her and many things to say if only he were.

"Oh, Beth…" Lily said from somewhere behind her.

"I want to take joy in this, Lily," Beth confessed in hushed tones. "I want to be delighted that I can see once more and that I am no longer an invalid in any way. I want to be excited and relieved that I will bear his child. That I carry his child at this moment." Her voice broke, and her hand drifted to her midriff absently, as it tended to these days. "Part of me is delighted and exhilarated, humbled and touched, and utterly terrified." She managed a weak smile and cast a look back at Lily, who had risen. "But when I consider this child, Lily, all I can think about is Malcolm. He doesn't know, and I don't know how to tell him when we are at odds. How can we have this child like this?"

Beth bit her lip as the tears returned and turned back to the window.

Lily was quick to come to her, turning her from the window and taking her hands. "Beth, you cannot dwell on such things." She brushed away the tears on her cheeks and met her eyes steadily. "We have to focus on the good in any way. In every way. Monty will not stay angry forever, nor will he stay away forever."

Beth sniffled and gave her friend a despairing look. "How can I? My husband does not love me and will not love me now."

The look she received was severe and significant. "You think I don't understand the sentiment?"

That took Beth by surprise, and she reared back a little. "You love your husband?"

Lily smiled the saddest, faintest smile Beth had ever seen. "I have loved my husband since I was seventeen. Up until the day of our engagement, I had hope in it. But the day I married him was the day that hope ended, for the arrangement was one of business and not affection. I have a comfortable marriage, Beth. It is staid and proper and cordial, but very much separate and distant. I do not know, and cannot know, how my husband feels, but I know that the man I married was not the one I fell in love with. Yet somewhere inside him, that man still exists, and I hope one day to see him again."

It was worse than Beth had feared and far more than she had ever suspected. She had been aware of Lily's attachment to Thomas Granger in the early days, but she'd never heard of any arrangement between them until she'd heard of the wedding itself. She'd known that it wasn't under the usual circumstances, and that Lily had been monstrously wounded by the affair, but not why. To marry a man one loves only for the emotion to be lacking?

"I'm sorry," Beth said, hugging her friend for her situation, and for her attempt at comfort.

"I do not divulge this to earn your pity," Lily replied with surprising fierceness, pulling back. "I tell you this because I understand the loneliness that comes from this sort of thing, and I am telling you there is a way to cope without being utterly miserable."

What a startling thought.

Beth tilted her head curiously. "Is there? I've yet to discover anything but utter misery."

"Well, there will still be some misery," Lily admitted with a shrug. "We cannot avoid it altogether, especially being the idiotic women who've fallen in love with their husbands."

Beth laughed at that and found her tears completely gone, much to her surprise. She'd been on the edge of crying almost constantly since Malcolm had gone, and not even the brilliant lights of the children could put them off, though she had attempted to hide it. Laughter had certainly not been a part of her life of late.

"What fools we are," Beth said on a sigh.

"I have come to the conclusion," Lily announced, taking Beth's arm and walking her away from the window, "that it is the men who are the fools, and our souls are simply too good."

"There's a thought."

"A rather good one, I'm coming to find."

"Of your own discovery?"

Lily shook her elegantly curled hair. "No, I have several supporters of the idea."

Beth shook her head again, smiling at the inanity of the conversation. None of this would take away from her pain, but it would provide a distraction, if nothing else.

Lily rubbed her hand gently. "You'll find your way through. Just don't live in the darkness." She smiled at Beth in a sort of amusement. "I once described you as a woman that nothing dark could touch."

"Did you really?" Beth snorted a little at that and adjusted the shawl around her. "Why would you say something so plainly false as that?"

"Because it's true."

Beth nearly stumbled and turned to face her friend with a frown. "How can you say that? I am struggling to keep my wits about me, let alone put on a false smile for my stepchildren, so they will not think there is a true rift between their father and me. I quite literally lived in darkness for over a month, and there was nothing light about me in all of that. You know perfectly well that I am not immune to darkness."

Her friend did not look any less amused for her protests. "I never said you were immune to it. You are, after all, human."

"There's a fair point for you," Beth muttered, folding her arms about her.

"I said the darkness does not touch you. It does not linger." Lily shook her head, smiling further. "Your situation before your marriage was utterly dismal. You were planning to be a governess, though you are ill-suited for it, because there was no fortune for you, minimal support from your family, and no one to really care what you did with your life."

Beth frowned further still. She hadn't thought her life had been so very dismal, but when it was put that way...

"That does sound rather dreary," she allowed with a small smile.

"And you didn't even know it until I pointed it out," Lily said, taking her arms and shaking her a little. "A poor family with ten children and you the youngest? But you didn't care, and never paid much attention to the fact that you ought to have been panicked or distressed about your prospects."

Beth shrugged, slightly embarrassed. "I was concerned, but it hardly seemed like something to spread about."

"And you married Monty with all the optimism in the world," Lily went on, still smiling, "though that could hardly have been a fair prospect, aside from his looks."

There was a faint blush of embarrassment at that, considering the measure of truth there.

If Lily noticed, she said nothing about it. "You took on four children in need of a mother, with a distant father, and they have fallen completely in love with you. You lost your sight and learned how to make do without. You made an aloof, broken, emotionally crippled man come to life and fall in love with you…"

"Why would you say that?" Beth broke in suddenly, eyes wide. "He's never said anything of the sort."

A look rife with derision was flung at her. "If you couldn't see that, no matter what came out of his mouth, then you were blinder than I thought."

Beth swallowed hard and found no good response to that. Had she seen anything resembling love in him?

She must have done. Or had she only wished it there?

"Nothing dark can touch you, Elizabeth Colerain," Lily told her firmly. "And nothing dark will."

There was nothing she could say to that, so she cleared her throat and moved to the pianoforte, though she would be an absolute fool to attempt to play in Lily's presence. Lily was a gifted musician, and Beth was most certainly not.

"And to whom precisely did you give this false impression? I shall have to write them to let them know of their delusions." She ran her fingers over the keys soundlessly, smiling to herself.

"Your husband."

Beth pressed down two keys in her surprise, the dissonance in sound echoing that of her mind. "What?"

Lily clasped her hands before her, looking a perfect picture of an English lady, complete with the classic smirk that hid everything. "The first day he saw you, I told him that. And I stand by it."

An odd sort of calm settled over Beth's aching heart, and she exhaled slowly. It didn't solve anything, and it certainly didn't remove the wounds she felt, but she felt the burden lift ever so slightly.

And for now, that was enough.

She smiled a little at her sweet friend, who endured so much herself. "I can see, Lily."

Lily returned her smile. "Yes, you can."

Now Beth laughed. "And I'm with child."

Lily grinned outright. "Yes, you are!" She laughed merrily and came over to the pianoforte. "Slide over, I'm going to teach you a duet, and we are going to play and celebrate both!"

Chapter Twenty-Two

"Two weeks and no progress?" Malcolm grumbled, running his hand through his hair.

"Now you understand our frustrations," Fritz nodded.

"Technically, it's been four weeks and no progress. Only two since you arrived."

Malcolm glared at Rook, feeling the lack of sleep and increased stress eating away at him. "Was that input entirely necessary?"

Rook held up his hands in surrender, smirking a little. "Apologies, sir."

Fritz snorted softly from the desk they'd dragged into Malcolm's office, laying aside the papers he'd been examining. "Don't apologize to Cap, Rook, you were only stating the obvious."

Malcolm dropped his hand to his desk with an angry thump and shifted the glare to his friend. "I am no longer surprised that you sent Rook to be our replacement, Weaver. He is exactly your type, and I am tempted to ask if he is your offspring."

Rook looked at Fritz with new interest. "Lord, tell me there's a chance, Weaver. I'd be ever so grateful."

Fritz barked a laugh and waved a dismissive hand. "Back to work, Rook. You know exactly where you came from, and I am not old enough to have spawned you."

"You're old enough," Malcolm muttered, returning to the letters.

He'd been over each a dozen times at least, and he'd found exactly the same thing that Rogue had, and none of them had led to anything. There were other bits and pieces of the letters that did not make sense, such as stray grammatical errors and unusual punctuation. There was just an odd, disjointed feeling surrounding them, but he could not find any pattern. He was not accustomed to failure, and it was maddening.

"Hardly," Fritz replied. He rubbed at his eyes and sat back. "Rook, why aren't you more upset, like Cap?"

"I'm used to feeling lost," Rook said carelessly, propping his feet up on the edge on Malcolm's desk. "It's usually when my best ideas come."

Malcolm looked up at his newest associate, though it had been over a full year since he'd been brought in. "Then let's hear one, shall we?"

Rook gave him an appraising look. "I would, but you just said you were surprised that I was put in here, and I'm feeling disinclined to share."

Malcolm was beginning to understand why the others frequently asked to kill Rook, and he was giving the idea some serious consideration at this moment. "Your pride will survive the shock, I have no doubt."

Rook shrugged easily. "Most likely." His smirk faded, and his look became serious. "I'm not indifferent to this, Cap. Far from it. I simply don't have the attachments that the rest of you do, so at present, I do not feel the same sense of panic. I await further orders, and until then can only attempt to aid the rest of you in the tasks you have set for yourselves. Tell me what to do, Cap, and you'll find that I'll do it."

Malcolm stared at his youngest operative in a new light, surprised by Rook's maturity and depth, considering the air of mischief he'd always maintained. He glanced over at Fritz, who was trying in vain not to smile, no doubt feeling rather superior at this moment.

"That's why you brought him in, isn't it?" Malcolm asked him.

Fritz nodded and tapped his pen on the desk. "That's why."

And that was that, he supposed.

"Do you want a new task?" Malcolm asked Rook, straightening up. "Try to ascertain why someone is targeting Rogue if they aren't doing anything about it. I have no doubt Amelia would love to have her guard lessened before she gives birth, if we can manage it."

Rook whistled low and shook his head. "So long as I don't have to be the one telling her if we cannot. That woman terrifies me."

"That is one of the main reasons I married her," Rogue growled from the doorway. He and Gent entered, dropping themselves into the empty chairs, looking more fatigued than Malcolm had seen them in some time.

"No luck?" Malcolm asked, unable to manage any hint of hope.

Gent shook his head, groaning slightly as he leaned back in the chair. "Nothing yet, but I just sent more scouts out, and they'll report back soon."

"My assets will report after nightfall," Rogue sighed, shutting his eyes and stretching out his legs as if to sleep. "They're not half so respectable as Gent's, but they should be useful."

Malcolm stared at them both, then looked at Fritz and Rook as well. "So, we can only wait."

He received blank looks in return.

"We've been over the letters," Rogue reminded him.

"And interviewed everyone we know," Gent added.

"I've been to more parties than a debutante, and the traitors are boring," Rook said with a yawn.

Fritz shrugged and looked at him with a helpless expression. "We are doing everything, Cap. Even Tailor agrees."

Malcolm shook his head, unwilling to accept that. "It does not feel that way at all. There *has* to be something."

Gent sighed and reached for some of the papers that Rook was rifling through. "Then we go over it again."

Rook handed over a few, but his gaze remained fixed on Malcolm. "I'm surprised you came back up here, Cap, when there was nothing to tell, and not much happening since. Tired of the country, are you?"

Malcolm slowly looked up at him, a warning look brewing. "There is work to be done, and I am here to do it."

Rook pursed his lips a little, then gestured to his companions. "It is odd, though, isn't it?"

"I thought so," Gent murmured absently, pretending to look at papers, but glancing up at him.

"I remember someone telling him to go home to Beth and stay there," Rogue grunted, his eyes still closed, though apparently not asleep.

Fritz eyed Malcolm cautiously. "Don't pry, gentlemen," he warned.

At that, Rogue opened his eyes and regarded Fritz with raised brows. "I'm not a gentleman." He looked at the others. "Any gentlemen in here?"

Gent raised a hand reluctantly. "Guilty."

Rook snorted a laugh and looked back to Malcolm. "You haven't written Beth once since you've been here, have you? Unless you've done so at home."

"There's not been time to properly correspond with anyone," Malcolm grumbled, returning to his papers.

"I've written Amelia regularly, in spite of everything," Rogue replied with a raised finger. "And I'm not half as sentimental as you."

"I send notes to Margaret, particularly if I'm not coming home," Gent brought up.

Fritz stayed resolutely silent, but he did have a small smile that told Malcolm everything he needed to know.

Malcolm swung his gaze back to Rook. "And you?"

He shrugged. "I have no wife, but I did write my mother last week, for what that's worth." He tilted his head and looked almost thoughtful. "There's always time for that, unless we're undercover, which we are not. Surely your children…"

"Can we please get back to work?" Malcolm interrupted sharply. "Or at least pretend to respect the fact that I am your senior officer in this endeavor and give me the decency of privacy in my personal affairs?"

The outburst surprised them all, he knew, but he couldn't help it.

He missed his wife and children fiercely, and he was too ashamed to write any of them. To have his personal failings addressed while his professional world teetered on the brink of disaster was too much, and absolutely not to be borne when he had the authority to change the topic.

Rook dropped his feet to the ground and looked serious again. "This is no matter of disrespect, Cap. We have nothing but respect for you, and loyalty. You cannot blame us for being concerned, and your current madness is detracting from your ability to work this properly. Get your head on straight, Cap, or go back home and fix things."

That was the second surprise of the day where Rook was concerned, and Malcolm sat back in a sort of awe. Then he glowered and looked at Fritz, who was smirking by now. "And that is why as well?"

Fritz nodded slowly, his smirk growing. "That is why." Then he shrugged a little. "And I think it is quite good advice myself, as your own senior officer."

That sobered Malcolm, and he went back to the papers to hide the guilt he knew would be in his eyes. "Let's take a step back, shall we?" he announced with a sharp clearing of his throat. "What do we absolutely know for certain? Not suspect, but know."

There had never been a more maddening project in his entire life, and Malcolm had lived through quite a few things.

Six weeks he had been in London, and not a blasted thing to show for it.

More letters had been intercepted, and more messages discovered within, but every one of them had led to nothing. They had looked for a code within the code, wondering if Rogue was not referring to their colleague but to someone else entirely. Every word had been gone over at least twice, and all seemed very straightforward, but still, there was nothing. The operatives they'd pulled into their troubles from other offices were growing restless and bored, and he couldn't blame them.

He would have been bored if he were not so frantic.

None of his operatives, or their assets, were permitted to go anywhere alone, though in truth, it would have been simple enough for a determined group to do away with two instead of one, should they have wished it. But as yet, they had not seen any evidence of intent to harm. The street children had been pulled back to less treacherous tasks, which they were not pleased with, but with so much at stake and so much unknown, none of the League were willing to take any risks. Rook had abandoned his minding of traitors, giving it all back to Gent for the time being, and had proven surprisingly useful in assisting Rogue with the investigations in their less respectable realms.

But even that was not providing results.

Malcolm didn't know what else to do. The information they had was from the correct individuals but seemed to be a misdirection. Yet, the letters still came and went, and there had to be something of value to them. They had scoured every available possibility for correspondence between those they knew to be involved, and nothing except these letters passed.

Fritz had offered them to three different code breakers in their ranks, and all had come back with the same answers.

The sensation of running at full speed and not gaining any ground was becoming something of a normal state of late, and Malcolm hated it.

He'd kept to the most reserved schedule as possible in London, staying away from the family home in favor of his more secretive lodgings, and so far, it seemed to be working. No one seemed to know that Lord Montgomery was in London, and no invitations had been extended from any quarter. Not that he'd have been able to accept any invitations, nor did he want to, but he was at least settled in the notion that his presence had gone thus far unnoticed.

It was about the only thing that settled him.

No word had come from Beth. Not a single line. To be perfectly fair, he hadn't written her either, though he had written the children, and he wasn't sure what he'd expected. That apology he had meant to send off had proven impossible to formulate, given the sheer volume of things for which he needed to apologize, and the fact that all he really wanted to do was hold her in his arms and tell her that he loved her.

He really ought to have done that before leaving.

Perhaps not the day that he'd yelled at her for keeping the restoration of her sight from him, but sometime before that. She ought to have known that he loved her. That she consumed his thoughts... his dreams... his future.

She was the answer to every question, even the ones he had not known to ask. He needed her, far more than she could ever need him, no matter the circumstance. He needed her to survive this life he'd chosen to live, and the separation from her was only driving him further into darkness. She was the light that could make all this bearable, and he'd attempted to snuff it out.

He didn't deserve her, and never would, but it would not stop him from trying. If she could forgive him, there might be a chance that he had not lost the opportunity to make her love him in return. She was such a sweet, caring person, that she could undoubtedly love anybody if she put her mind to it.

He didn't want her to love him like anybody else. He was just selfish enough to want all her heart and all her love for him alone. And until he saw her again, there wasn't anything he could do about it. A letter would not be nearly good enough and seemed a complete waste of paper and time to attempt.

The best he could do under the circumstances was a weak "Give Bitsy plenty of love and affection," in his letter to Jane.

If Beth read it, perhaps she would understand…

But perhaps not.

"Cap, you look like you need a drink."

He looked up from his desk blearily, surprised at the sight of Hal in his office doorway in a proper, if plain, walking ensemble of a buttery tan that only enhanced her fair features. He wasn't used to seeing her in anything but her plain muslin dresses surrounded by books and sketches, spectacles precariously perched or slightly askew.

This was a rare sight altogether.

She was a peculiar woman; too young to be a spinster, yet determined to live as one. She was the most talented artist he had ever met and frequently was used for character sketches in their investigations. He didn't know the whole of her story, but she had been adopted by all branches of covert operations and was under more protection than anyone in England, saving only the royal family.

As far as he knew, however, she had only ventured to their offices a handful of times. And never recently.

He rose quickly, belatedly forgetting his manners. "Hal. This is a surprise."

She smirked a little, bobbing a slight curtsey. "I should think so. It's been ages since I've been here, and yet the dirt is still the same. Callie must not be particularly adept at her job."

Malcolm managed a smile, recalling that Hal had never managed to stave off her impertinence, which made her a favorite with his men. "She is busy at the moment, and I'd rather have her where she is than tending to us odious fellows who live and work in this squalor."

Hal grinned outright and sat herself down in a chair without invitation. "I always forget how well-spoken you are, Cap. I deal with Rogue and Gent more than you, but you are quite simply a cut above the rest."

He chuckled warmly and inclined his head. "You are too kind, Hal, which I know means you want something, and at this moment I am more than inclined to oblige you." He sat down and folded his hands atop his desk. "How may I be of assistance?"

He was surprised to see the calculating expression on her fair features, her eyes narrowed a little, but not at him.

"Hal?" Malcolm prodded gently, forgoing his amusement.

"I have something," she said slowly, still not meeting his gaze. "And I don't know if it will mean anything to any of you, but considering how frantic everyone has been these days, I wonder if I shouldn't have said something sooner."

It wasn't like Hal to be hesitant, and definitely not like her to hide anything, which meant the combination of the two set Malcolm's hair on end, all senses alert.

"What do you have, Hal?"

Her eyes raised to his, and he saw her hesitation. "I should have come sooner," she said again.

He gave her the most of a smile he could manage. "You didn't know. I relieve you of guilt or blame. Officially, if you like."

Hal's mouth curved gently, and she reached into her equally plain reticule and pulled out a letter. "I received this letter perhaps a week ago. Likely more. It is not dated, so I cannot say when it was written. You'll likely recognize the hand."

Malcolm took it and scanned the lines at once. He did recognize it. The hand was that of Hal's brother, widely believed by the public to be a reckless reprobate who only cared for his twin sister, and occasionally those he had served with during the army days of his youth.

Under Malcolm's command.

Now he operated under the name of Trick and was one of the most deeply-seated operatives in all of England, answerable to a very select few. He was one of the most brilliant minds Malcolm had ever known, and the most capable operative of his generation, including Malcolm's own men.

"Most of the letter is very droll," Hal was saying, coming over to him. "Just a bit of politeness and nonsense, as per usual. But this seemed out of place, even for him, and while it didn't strike me at first, I wondered…"

She pointed at the last few lines, and Malcolm's eyes obediently followed.

Thank you for tending my favorite scoundrel while I'm away. I know he can be a nuisance, but the poor dog must know that not everything is about him. You are too like our mother, you know. Perhaps you will meet a fine gentleman, or even a captain, who will see reason and find the hidden truths to save us from our lives of boredom. Who knows, perhaps we may all go to Egypt and see those great wonders everybody makes a fuss about.

Malcolm sat back a little, then peered up at Hal. "Tell me you're not actually tending a dog."

Hal's smile became tight. "I'm not actually tending a dog. And the only scoundrels I know come from this office."

Rogue. "It's not all about him…" Malcolm murmured, returning to the letter.

"He'll be so disappointed." Hal pointed out a word further down. "He knows how I feel about soldiers. This should be painfully obvious with that in mind."

Captain. And just before that, *gentleman.*

See reason. Find the hidden truths.

"Your mother?" Malcolm inquired, already getting to his feet.

"I look and act nothing like her, but…" Hal wrinkled up her nose in a hint of a wince. "She was French."

Malcolm swore and barked for one of the clerks to send for the others, wherever they might have been, and turned to apologize for his words, but Hal was already copying the paragraph from the letter onto fresh parchment.

"Save it," she barked, all business now. "I know where you're going, and if I know Trick, he already warned Sphinx."

Rogue appeared in a moment, looking startled. "I was just coming back, what is it?"

Malcolm showed him the letter, which Rogue quickly scoured. His brows rose in surprise, then he looked at Hal with blinding admiration. "Hal, if you were closer, I would kiss you."

She looked up from the desk with a grin. "Thank the Lord I am all the way over here, then." She straightened and exchanged her paper for the original. "Go on ahead. I'll tell Gent and Rook. Weaver already knows, I saw him on my way in."

Malcolm took Hal's hand and kissed it quickly. "We owe you greatly."

"Immensely," Rogue agreed.

Hal gave them a crooked smile that looked very much like her twin's. "I shall hold you to it once all of this is over." She nudged her head towards the door. "Off with you both, and don't forget whatever Sphinx needs. You know how he gets." She rolled her eyes dramatically.

That was odd, even for Hal. She wouldn't know Sphinx well enough to get a decent read on him, and he was far too reserved to have provoked her often. But there was no time to dwell on that. This was the first lead they'd had in months, and he was not about to waste it.

Rogue took up the pile of letters and shoved them into his satchel, then followed Malcolm out of the offices.

It was not far to Bow Street, where Sphinx operated as a Runner, as far as anybody knew. Fritz was already there, in his usual position as a highly respected diplomat, requesting the assistance of Mr. Pratt.

Malcolm and Rogue kept to the other side of the street until Fritz exited, and then they followed at a safe distance until they reached Fritz's residence. Using the servant's entrance, they found their way up to the study, where Fritz and Sphinx were already situated.

Sphinx appraised them with sober eyes, though there was a light of excitement in them. "I hear you have something for me. I wondered what Trick was talking about, but he's never led me astray before."

"Nor will he now," Malcolm assured him. He nodded at Rogue, who pulled the letters out and handed them to Sphinx.

He thumbed through them quickly, nodding carefully. "Clever. Very, very clever."

"What's clever?" Fritz asked, leaning forward and creasing his silk waistcoat.

"A double-coded message." Sphinx smiled a little, seeming impressed. "That explains why you couldn't break it."

"Not for want of trying," Rogue muttered.

Sphinx glanced at him, his grey eyes without rancor. "That's not a criticism, Rogue. I know your skills. And none of the others could, either. This is no easy task."

Rogue nodded his thanks. "The message from Trick said this was not about me," he went on, crossing his ankle over his knee. "Do you think that could be true?"

Sphinx nodded slowly, then looked at Fritz. "Rogue would be the easiest target. That news story and sketch some months ago, anyone could have drawn conclusions."

"I agree," Fritz told him. He looked at the missives once more. "But this might be beyond me."

"Not especially," Sphinx assured him, picking up a letter. "It only takes the eyes to see it. Give me a moment."

"If he does this in a moment," Rogue muttered out of the corner of his mouth, "I will quit right here and now and become a farmer."

Sphinx snorted softly. "You'd be a terrible farmer. And I won't solve it in a moment, simply…" He trailed off and tilted his head to one side. "Hmm. Very French of them. And to hide it beneath the obvious code…"

Rogue grumbled under his breath, earning himself a nudge from Malcolm. "What are you seeing?"

Sphinx looked up, suddenly surprised that someone was addressing him. "*Vigenère.*"

"Bless you," announced Rook, striding into the room without knocking, Gent on his heels.

His brother's gaze skewered him briefly. When this had no effect, he then returned to his explanation. "It's a complicated cipher, but it's been used for many, many years. Once you know how to break it, it's really quite simple."

Rook snorted and sank into a chair. "Everything is simple to you."

"Including you," Sphinx snapped, looking back at the letter in his hand. "Now, will you shut up and let me work?"

That earned him a grin from the entire room, and Rook held up his hands in surrender. "Have at, Sphinx, by all means."

They all sat in silence for the most part as Sphinx worked, muttering to himself and scratching ink to paper. Malcolm grew uneasy and impatient but hid it as best as he could. After all, there was nothing he could do but wait, now that they finally had decent clues. This seemed to be important. Perhaps he was only desperate for a break in the monotony of their investigation, but he would take what he could get.

"There it is," Sphinx suddenly murmured, smirking to himself and leaning back, tossing the pen on the desk for emphasis. "First letter after punctuation."

Malcolm perked up and snapped his fingers at the others, who were in various stages of drowsiness after long moments of waiting. "Yes?"

Sphinx nodded and handed letters out. "Yes. Ignore everything else. The first letters after every punctuation mark. Write them all down."

"What about the keyword?" Rook asked as he took his. "Do you have that?"

Sphinx shook his head. "Not yet. And with this cipher, the word most likely changes with each letter."

Rogue swore, holding the letter further away as he stared at it. "No wonder I couldn't see it."

"You saw exactly what they wanted you to see," Sphinx reminded him, his tone almost absent as he worked on his current letter. "They knew you would intercept them. That's how they could play the lot of you like chess pieces. You moved where they wanted you to move."

Malcolm looked at Rogue for a long moment, Trick's words playing over in his mind. "It wasn't about you at all," he said at last.

Rogue looked back at him, the same uneasiness brewing in his eyes. "I was the chess piece."

"A distraction?" Rook offered from his side of the room.

"But from what?" Gent asked, eyes wide with concern.

They all looked back at Sphinx, whose eyes raced frantically across the page, his lips moving wordlessly. "The keyword would have to be something here," he muttered to himself. "If it changes every time, it has to be here… The dates are correct, couldn't correspond to anything else, you would have found that…"

Malcolm returned to his own letter, identifying the code that Sphinx had directed and almost numbly recording the letters down. It was a scramble of letters, nothing making sense or forming anything at all. Page after page of randomness, enough to make Malcolm's eyes ache with the efforts of trying to see something he couldn't.

He would need Sphinx to come up with some answers soon, or he would give up on Trick's insight entirely. And he would have to tell Hal that unfortunate piece of news, and she wouldn't like that at all.

"Got it," Sphinx suddenly breathed, a true smile breaking over his stoic features and making him years younger in appearance. "I've got it!"

"What is it?" at least three of them demanded at once.

"In a moment, in a moment…" he rambled, going back and forth between manic scratchings and the letter itself. "It's in the salutation. In this one, the most recent, the word was 'greetings,' though I doubt they used it again. These must have taken ages to write, doubling the code and all…"

Gent gaped at Sphinx, then looked at Rook. "Does he always do so much at the same time? Explaining what he's doing and thinking while doing and thinking it and making us wonder what is wrong with our minds?"

"Every bleeding day," Rook replied at once with a shake of his head, though he bore a hint of a proud smile.

"I'm surprised you are both still alive," Rogue said, sounding remarkably relaxed now that they were so close to a victory of sorts.

Malcolm could not join in their bantering, nor could he feel relief. There was no reason, as yet, to be relieved about anything. Until they knew precisely what they were facing and had a plan in place to combat it, he wouldn't let himself enjoy any of this. Instead, he felt more on edge, his instincts ready to pounce on whatever was revealed.

The sooner they could end all this, the sooner he could return home.

To Beth.

"Why would anybody want to single out Rogue anyway?" Rook asked with a laugh, crossing his arms. "Of all the idiotic notions…"

"I will kill you, you know," Rogue offered, smirking slightly.

"It's not Rogue they're after."

All attention turned to Sphinx at his sudden declaration, hushed though it had been. There were no dramatics, but a deep severity that commanded them all.

"John?" Rook prodded, watching his brother with concern, foregoing any secrecy in names for a change.

There were deep furrows in Sphinx's brow, and he looked up at Fritz in confusion. "Do the words 'gate' and 'knight' mean anything to you?"

The room grew more silent than before. No one breathed.

Malcolm stared at the code breaker for a long moment, only able to blink as the words echoed in the suddenly vault-like expanses of his mind.

"Why?" Fritz asked carefully, his voice as tense as his frame.

Sphinx glanced around, the missive in his hand. "This letter, written yesterday, mentions going there, wherever it is. Seems rather significant."

Malcolm's heart stopped in his chest, and he lost all sensation to his frame. There were no emotions, no thoughts, no comprehension of what he had just heard for a heartbeat.

It wasn't Rogue they were after. It was *him*. They were going to his home where his wife and children slept. His family had no idea what he truly did or the danger they were in.

They were after his wife and children!

With another slow blink that was more painful than anything he had ever suffered in his entire life, Malcolm looked at his comrades, his brothers in arms, the men he trusted with everything important to him, and released the shortest, softest of exhales.

Then he was out of his seat, bolting for the door, with every man of them behind him.

Chapter Twenty-Three

They rode harder than they had ever ridden in their lives. The roads out of London passed quickly, pounded into submission by the hooves of the five horses in their group. They were soon joined by some others that had been sent for, per Fritz's orders, and the further away from London they rode, the more focused they seemed to become.

Malcolm had not paid attention to who had joined in the ride to Knightsgate, nor did he particularly care. He was not in command of this force, Fritz was, but for the first time in his life, Malcolm would be insubordinate if it came down to it. He regretted every harsh or critical word ever spoken to any of his men over something personal interfering with their missions. Malcolm now understood, perhaps for the first time, what they must have felt. His family had never been in danger, so he'd always been able to separate his work from his life at home.

Now they would be merging in the most horrifying manner possible. There was no control for this, none at all. He was only grateful that so many had rallied to his aid, riding with him to support the cause and the efforts to save his family.

Sphinx had stayed behind to decode the rest of the letters and give pertinent details to the operatives overseeing London in their absence, but nothing in them could possibly convey anything to alter this course of theirs. Even if the attack should be forthcoming and not present when they arrived, they would be strong enough to withstand it, and he would know his wife and children were safe. If it had already commenced...

He swallowed harshly and pushed his horse harder, unwilling to consider the possible ramifications.

His family ought to have been protected. There were measures in place to ensure that they would be. But with no warning and no idea of what they were facing, there was absolutely no guarantee that the measures would be sufficient. There were never any guarantees in times like these. Trace's death was proof of that.

If he lost any member of his family because of this…

There would be no recovering. That would be the end of him, of everything he was or wished to be. He wouldn't care about England or the state of affairs with France, or any uprising, traitors, or bonds of loyalty.

He wouldn't care about anything.

All he wanted at this moment was to get home and protect his family. He would rage and rail and beat the life out of whatever villain had done this to them, whether high ranking Member of Parliament or chimney sweep from Lancashire. The instinct to defend and protect had never roared with this much indignation within him, and he feared for his sanity if it was not to be avenged.

Fritz insisted that they stop to change horses, which Malcolm had resisted vehemently, hating the thought of slowing at all.

"We cannot keep this pace on these animals," Fritz had barked. "If you want to be able to get there and do anything about it, you will exchange horses now."

It chafed at his drive to push on, but he nodded firmly and followed him. Those that had joined in the ride later than the rest sped on, much to his disgruntlement, but minutes later, he had a fresh horse and was back to racing home.

No one said much of anything to him, but he knew they conversed with each other behind him. No doubt they were formulating some kind of plan; it was what he would have done in their situation.

He was not in the mindset to prepare anything. There was no plan for him. He needed to get to his home and scour every room in it until he knew his family was safe.

What would they think? Would they know to be afraid?

His mind conjured up images of a mob descending on his home, the dust from the horses' hooves billowing up behind them creating a more menacing impression. Would the children have seen them approach? Would Beth? Would his operatives in the area have acted, or would they be caught as completely unaware as he had?

Questions and fears preyed upon Malcolm as he rode on, his heart at least double the pace of his horse, his breath hitching nearly every inhale.

There was no telling what they would face, or whom. None of their usual suspects had strayed from their normal London lives and schedules, they would have been informed of that. Nothing in London had indicated a mass convergence anywhere.

Unless they had missed something significant. Unless the distraction of their recent endeavors had caused them to miss what was truly occurring.

It was a masterful plan, one worthy of the villains they were dealing with, and one he would have admired, had he been in a position to appreciate it. Their enemies had known they were being watched, and they had taken advantage of that knowledge. They had manipulated Malcolm and his men easily, twisting the League's attention where they wanted it to hide their true goals, whatever those might have been.

Why *his* house? Why *his* family? He almost never operated out of Knightsgate in matters such as these, which meant his identity had to have been compromised in some way. There were no ties between Cap and Knightsgate; none whatsoever. He had seen to that, and more than twenty years of working in this sort of position had given him plenty of time to hone his skills in secrecy and security.

Why now?

None of it made any sense, and the more he thought about it, the more muddled his thoughts became. They would find answers today, of that he was certain. There would be some clues found, either in London or at his home, and captures would be made. Interrogations would ensue, and confessions would spout forth. Real progress would be made, and they would not feel so lost in the field against this faction.

He took no comfort in any of these things, though he ought to have done. Comfort would not come until the end, whatever it was.

All their previous victories meant nothing to him at this moment. He did not care what they had once accomplished or what their abilities had been. He did not even care what they were capable of in a group of roughly fifteen.

He only needed this victory.

Just this one.

As the light of day began to fade, and the sun moved closer to the horizon, Malcolm felt his heart skip several beats.

Darkness would fall soon. In London, that would not be much of a hindrance, but out here in the Hampshire countryside...

"Go," he urged his borrowed horse. "Go, boy, go."

Whether his urging helped, he couldn't have said, but when the cold and too dark edifice of the house was rising before them, he felt a burst of exhilaration.

And then panic set in.

He vaulted from his horse and started towards the house, only to have his shoulder gripped tightly.

"Steady," Fritz urged, his voice tight. "I'm sending half the men to search the grounds, and our presence alerted your local connections, so they will stand guard. How do you want to do this?"

Malcolm glanced over his shoulder at his friend briefly. "Whatever will get me inside and end this in the fastest way."

Fritz nodded and dropped his hand. "I'll follow. The others will take the servants' entrance and secure the house."

Malcolm exhaled slowly, nodding, and then strode forward. They hadn't approached with stealth, so he saw no reason to proceed now with any. The most direct way into the house would be the main entrance, and he had no qualms about being predictable in this instance. It was his home, and if anyone thought to take him by surprise within it, they were sadly mistaken.

The large door creaked a little as they entered, and there was almost no light within but what the sunset allowed through the windows. He was suddenly grateful for the ride through the fading light, as it made adjusting to the dark of the house easier. He crept along, faintly surprised that there was no ambush waiting for him the moment they entered.

In fact, there didn't seem to be anyone about at all.

He glanced back at Fritz, whose widened eyes and furrowed brow told Malcolm that he was feeling something along the same lines.

Where was the contingent that had ridden for this house? Or were they forthcoming?

Light flickered from within one of the drawing rooms, the largest one, he recalled, and he could hear a wood fire crackling.

He moved forward, curious and cautious. No one would intentionally make themselves known in such a blatant way unless there was something to be gained by it, but there wasn't another option. He didn't know where Beth and the children were, or any of his servants, who knew their duty was to protect and defend the family at all costs.

If he was walking into a trap, so be it.

He approached the room slowly, unable to see anything from his current angle, knowing that whoever was within, if anyone, would have a far better vantage point than he did.

There was nothing for it, then. Malcolm straightened and entered the room calmly, as he might have done on any given day. The sight that greeted him could not have been more unexpected.

"Lady Lavinia."

How his tone managed to remain so mild, he would never know. He felt at once sickened and shocked, and he only prayed his expression was as contained as his voice.

Lady Lavinia? How in the world…?

Pieces slid quickly into place, one after the other, and the picture now unfolding was more terrifying and brilliant than anything he had imagined.

It was not the oblivious Mr. Herschel in the details and designs. Not the unpopular Mr. Herschel who had betrayed his country and his standing and his duties. Not the pompous Mr. Herschel who had plotted against Malcolm and his cohorts and sent them off on a mad dash here when the plot had finally been uncovered.

Not Mr. Herschel.

His wife.

And there would be no fighting that. Well, not with his fists or his sword, at any rate.

Lady Lavinia sat in a chair near the fire, though she faced the doorway. She sat with all the regal pride of a queen occupying on a throne. Her dark eyes were glinting in the firelight, fixed on him with the same mixture of interest and disdain that she had always displayed, wearing the same smirk he'd seen dozens of time in London. She looked far too refined for someone who had come on a traitorous mission, her gown a deep, wine-colored red with a daring cut of the neckline, even more so than her usual wardrobe.

"Lord Montgomery," she purred, eying him without shame, her gaze lingering where it would. "I so hoped that you would join us."

Thinking quickly, Malcolm took a further two steps into the room and bowed a little. "Had I known you would be here, my lady, I should have arrived in a more timely fashion. I had no idea you and your husband would be paying us a call. Have my servants left you in such darkness? I shall send for a footman right away."

Lady Lavinia laughed a deep, throaty laugh. "I am not here with my husband, you great fool. And you know better than to send for a servant. This is no social call."

"Is it not?" he clasped his hands behind his back and looked at her as if only a little curious.

Her painted lips pursed slightly. "Let me ask you this, my lord. Do you always come home to such abject darkness?"

Malcolm looked around a little. "Not particularly, but my son has been known to play a joke or two, and the servants tend to indulge him. I expect to be pounced upon the moment I get close enough to his hiding place."

"I think you will be looking for quite some time." She offered an utterly superior smile that set his teeth on edge.

"No doubt, no doubt," he agreed with a sage nod. "My oldest is quite adept at hiding. I have no idea where he learned such things."

"Probably from me," Fritz's voice answered in warm tones as he appeared in the room, all ease and friendliness. "I am his godfather, after all." He grinned at Lady Lavinia and gave her a low bow. "Lovely to see you, my lady."

Lady Lavinia considered Fritz with open admiration, and no small amount of derision. "Lord Rothchild. I hadn't thought to have you come in here along with Monty. Surely cowering in the hall is more like you."

Fritz shrugged. "Usually. But Monty's house is so blasted cold at the moment, I fancied being closer to the fire."

He and Malcolm shared a smile, as if this were all some very fine joke.

"Aren't you going to ask me?" she asked, sounding rather petulant.

"Ask you what, my lady?" Malcolm asked, tilting his head, his hands still clasped behind him.

Her thin brows knitted a little. "How I knew about your little spy game."

"Spy game?" Malcolm echoed with a frown. "I'm not aware of any spy game." He looked at Fritz, still frowning. "Did you start another game with Archer without telling me?"

Fritz shook his head, making a face. "Not one involving spies. He's always preferred military over covert. I did send him a letter spelling out the failures of the British army in the battle in the Americas, but other than that…"

"Don't toy with me!" Lady Lavinia snapped, rising from her chair. "I know that the pair of you are covert operatives working with the Crown! You have been intercepting letters for months to try to solve the puzzle my associates and I have laid out, and now you are here because somehow you broke the code!"

Malcolm blinked, keeping his emotions at bay, ignoring the rising tension within him. "Covert operatives?"

Fritz barked a hard laugh. "You think Monty is a spy? Oh, Lady Lavinia, that is a story worthy of the gossip sheets if I've ever heard one."

"How else would you know to come here?" she demanded with a sneer.

"It *is* my house," Malcolm reminded her. "I've been gone for a few days and was fortunate enough to be able to return early. Lord Rothchild was anxious to see the children and came back with me."

"Liar!" she half shrieked. "I know all about your little operations, your league of cohorts in London. All of it! My husband has access to all the most sensitive information, and he is too great an idiot to hide any of the evidence! I know what you all have suspected him of, and we have used that greatly to our advantage! Why do you think he has suddenly become so important as to warrant your attention? Who has been making it easy to examine his dealings and his activities? *I* hold all the cards, gentlemen, and I have been playing a beautiful hand."

Fritz tsked slightly, shaking his head. "Dear Lady Lavinia, have you been abusing your husband's position of power? For shame, that is badly done indeed. I have no authority in the government, to be sure, as I am only a dignitary now, but if I did, your confession just now would land you into a great deal of trouble. But how could you think that Monty would be party to such operations, should they exist?"

"He is!" she insisted. "You know he is! Get in here!" she suddenly barked, looking behind them.

Four very large men dressed in dark clothing entered, and three came to stand behind them while one stood by the door.

"See here," Malcolm protested, oddly not feeling in any way pressured by them and still maintaining his proper demeanor. "You are all entering my house without permission. That is trespassing and is a punishable offense. I am a magistrate, and I will be obliged to act."

"You are a bloody spy!" Lady Lavinia spat. "You came riding up just now with a party of men in response to the letters you intercepted!"

Malcolm shook his head slowly. "Lady Lavinia," he sighed sadly, giving her a pitying look, "has my spurning of your repeated offers to be my lover, and all the physical attentions you've attempted, truly driven you to this?"

He hit a mark, he could see it in the slight flicker across her furious features. The men behind him shifted restlessly, darting confused glances at each other.

"Intercepting letters?" He made a disapproving noise. "That is also a punishable offense, and I would never do anything so intolerably rude. The men I rode in with are fine members of the local militia. They had just finished their monthly drills and saw fit to escort me home, as I am their superior officer when in residence. I thought my children would find the spectacle amusing."

Now the men were muttering to each other and eying Lady Lavinia with suspicion.

"You should have taken me when you had the chance!" she half shrieked. "I would have given you everything and kept your every secret!"

"I have no secrets," he assured her, trying for a smile. "None at all. I am the most boring Englishman I have ever met, and I have no doubt you would have discovered that yourself."

"I'll vouch for that," Fritz chuckled. He glanced back at the men behind him. "He followed every single rule as a captain in the army. I've never met anyone so tiresome."

That drew a small chuckle from one of them.

"Where are his mouse of a wife and the little brats?" Lady Lavinia demanded. "*Where?*"

"We never found them, my lady," the guard by the door replied, his tone indicating he was not altogether sure about her. "Nor any sensitive documents. Nothing in the study or any of the rooms. We've searched."

His servants had done the job correctly, then. He was never so careless as to leave anything lying around, but there were caches about in case of emergency. Either they had been hidden enough to avoid discovery or they had been emptied, as they ought to have been.

"My house was searched, as well?" Malcolm asked with all the imperiousness he could muster. "Without my consent or permission? By what authority?"

The men behind him looked slightly ashamed. "She said..." one of them offered, trailing off uncertainly. "Well, you see..."

"Monty," Fritz broke in firmly, "I do believe you must take action. Clearly, there have been crimes committed against you and your home, and if you will permit me to call for your fine militiamen, I shall see these men apprehended until the truth will out. And," he leveled an utterly superior look at Lady Lavinia, "Lady Lavinia will be escorted back to London, and held under guard at Bow Street until the proper measures may be taken."

The men all nodded in agreement, obviously not entirely convinced that the woman who had led them here had done so for the right reasons. What part they had played in the scheme would remain to be seen, but playing on their doubts was only too easy.

"I agree, Fritz," Malcolm answered easily, staring down his nemesis. "Perhaps these fine men might be able to shed some light on how Lady Lavinia managed to persuade them into such lawlessness."

Fritz gave a short whistle and some of their men appeared, dressed in the garb of Malcolm's stable hands. "Will you fellows kindly escort these men and this... *lady*... out to the front until the militia comes? And one of you ride to inform them, eh? We'll need a carriage for the lady."

Two of the men came in to escort out a sputtering Lady Lavinia, while her men traipsed outside obediently. They had either been trained enough to avoid unnecessary trouble, such as causing a stir at an earl's home, or they truly had no idea of the true nature of their assignment. They would know soon enough, however. Once taken to Bow Street, they would know indeed.

"You just try to imprison me!" Lady Lavinia shrieked, her face contorting. "I won't say anything, not a single word! You'll see! *J'ai vecu!*"

J'ai vecu. I lived. That phrase alone would have given him cause to have her incarcerated and questioned. It was a phrase they knew to be used by the traitors and sympathizers of the faction, as well as members of the faction itself. He doubted that Sieyès had intended his memorable line from the inquest into the French Revolution to take hold with such force, but this group had made it their battle cry, it seemed, and Lady Lavinia Herschel could now be counted among those ranks.

Malcolm did not wait to see the woman carried out, as she undoubtedly would need to be, given her squawking in indignation. He didn't care. He strode from the room with a brief nod at her, and turned down the hall, Fritz hot on his heels.

"Where are they?" he hissed to Fritz.

"No idea," he replied. "The house has been searched. We'll go out to the grounds."

Malcolm nodded, allowing himself to feel the panic that had been welling. Lady Lavinia didn't have his family, but that did not mean they were safe. He had no idea how many men she had brought;

there could be more on the grounds, and those had not been persuaded that Lady Lavinia was a jilted lover with a taste for vengeance.

"I didn't see that coming," Fritz muttered behind him. "This is not going to go over well up the ranks."

No, it most definitely was not. Mr. Herschel would be investigated thoroughly for any part in his wife's treachery, and likely be forced to give up his position in Parliament. The fallout could be immense.

He would think about all that later... if he remembered to.

Gent, Rogue, and Rook were waiting for him just outside the house, having rounded up some of his servants.

"Beth and the children left the house some time ago," Rook reported just as Malcolm opened his mouth. "Your footmen saw them safely escorted into the woods. Two more are still in hiding somewhere around, we haven't attempted to reach them yet."

Malcolm stared at the woods intently, as if he could somehow penetrate them and find his family.

Rogue stepped forward with a nod. "The rest of the enemy has been rounded up, we believe, and Gaines is leading a group back to the city with them in custody. We still have four of your local contacts scouring the grounds."

Malcolm nodded almost frantically, his emotions growing harder and harder to control.

"Hudson, Mrs. Rawlins, and Mrs. Franklin had the maids with them in the gamekeeper's cottage," Gent told him. He smiled a little. "Hudson apparently shot two men and is quite pleased."

"I expect so," Malcolm managed.

Fritz clapped a hand on his shoulder. "To the woods, then, Cap. The sun will be gone soon, and your children will be getting cold."

Malcolm was already moving before his friend had finished, his gaze having never left the trees. He was all-out running before he knew what he was about. "Beth!" he bellowed as he neared them. "Beth, can you hear me? Beth!"

They spread out, each of them calling for the children and for Beth, and no answers were coming. He happened upon one of his footmen, who seemed relieved to see him and returned to the house on his orders, after pointing him in the direction his family had gone.

The sun dipped beyond the horizon, and with it his vision. One of the others had had the foresight to bring a lantern. It was close enough to allow him to see a bit further into the gloom, though he was beginning to think they would need to light torches and roust the entire village to find them.

"Beth!" he called again, his voice almost breaking as he looked around him.

Just then, there was a rustling in the brush to his left. He stopped, holding his hand out to halt the others.

A lean figure appeared through the leaves, dressed in oversized trousers, boots, and a coat, her fair hair braided and littered with twigs. A pistol trembled in one hand and her eyes were wide and terrified, almost eerie in the faint light of the lantern as she stared at him in disbelief, her jaw tightly clenched.

Malcolm couldn't breathe, couldn't move, all his abilities suddenly consumed by a choking sensation in his throat and chest.

Beth wet her lips a little. "Well," she managed to announce in a shaking voice, "you can come out now, children. The… the surprise I promised is here."

On that cue, four smaller figures pushed through the brush with squeals of delight, which only grew when they caught sight of Malcolm.

"Papa!" they all shrieked, running at him and slamming their little bodies against his legs.

Malcolm dropped to his knees, hugging and kissing each one of them repeatedly, fighting the tears that were rising within him.

"Bitsy played such a fun game with us!" Archer was saying, pounding Malcolm on the shoulder. "We were so quiet, and we heard all kinds of things!"

"I was the quietest!" Jane told him proudly.

"Were not!" Archer argued.

"I found a flower!" Greer told him, ignoring the other two and showing it to him.

"The ground was cold, but I liked it," Samuel said.

Malcolm smiled and laughed and tried to say something to each, but his eyes kept travelling to Beth. She stood there watching him, not smiling, but fixed on him with an intensity that struck him to the core.

The pistol shook more tremulously in Beth's hand and Rook, thinking quickly, moved to her at once and pried it gently from her hold. She shook herself and looked up at him, finally managing a wan smile.

"What about hugs for us?" Gent demanded, putting his hands on his hips. "How long has it been since Uncle Rafe received a hug?"

"Or me?" Fritz countered.

The children giggled and ran to each of them, and even Rogue swept one of them up with a whoop of delight, and Rook watched it all with a wide grin. "I need an introduction to these brave children!" he demanded. "I want to be an uncle, too!"

Malcolm ignored all of them, still kneeling on the ground, staring in agony at his wife.

Beth stared back, her jaw quivering slightly, her eyes filling with tears.

"Introductions back at the house, I think!" Fritz announced too quickly, eying the pair of them. "Mrs. Rawlins will be ordering a fine dinner, and we can eat dessert first, if you run fast enough."

They all left with remarkable haste, leaving Malcolm and Beth alone, their voices fading in the distance.

Slowly, painfully, Malcolm got to his feet. Beth watched him, her breathing growing more unsteady. He stared at her in wonder. She had been alerted to the danger and dressed in his clothing to make her venture easier and had turned the whole thing into a game for the children. Somehow, she had avoided showing any hint of fear while lying hidden in the forest with a loaded pistol she likely had no idea how to fire. She had been prepared to give her life for his children.

He had thought his wife an incredible woman before, but now...

She was nothing short of magnificent.

"Malcolm?" she whispered as one tear rolled down her cheek.

He was to her in the space of a heartbeat, sweeping her into his arms and pulling her trembling frame against him.

"Oh, my love," he rasped as he shuddered with relief and pain. "Oh, Beth, I'm so sorry."

Her arms clenched a tight grip around him and she gave way to her tears in full. "Malcolm, you're here…"

He kissed her head quickly, pulling back to rain kisses across her cheeks and nose, her hair, her brow, anything he could reach. "I'm here, love. I'm here. I'm so sorry, I had no idea…"

Beth shook suddenly and fisted his shirt in her hand as a sob broke free. "I missed you so much, and I was so afraid…"

Malcolm groaned and took her face in his hands, kissing her hard as a tear or two fell from his own eyes. "I love you," he told her with all the fervor and intensity he could manage. "I love you, Beth. I swear to you, I'll never leave you alone again, never… I'm so sorry."

She silenced his rambling with a fierce kiss that stirred his soul and humbled him beyond measure. "You love me?" she whispered against his lips, her disbelief making him ache.

He winced and forced her to look at him. "I love you," he said slowly, emphasizing every word. "I would have loved you had you never seen again. I would have loved you if you had never lost your sight. I would have loved you no matter what, I know that now. Loving you was the easiest thing I have ever done, and it was inevitable. I was always going to love you. I should have seen that from the start." He smiled and ran a hand over her hair, then stroked her cheek. "I love you with a depth that terrifies and exhilarates me. I didn't think I would ever love again, but here I am, weak at the knees and on the verge of tears for loving you. And if you can forgive me, if you can take pity on me, I will prove my love to you every day for the rest of our lives."

Beth beamed at him, then slid a hand up to cup the back of his head as she dragged his lips to hers again for a slow, maddening, breathtaking kiss.

"I love you, too," she whispered.

He touched his brow to hers, sighing. "Do you forgive me?"

She nodded at once. "Absolutely. Do you forgive me for lying to you?"

He kissed her nose softly. "I forgave you even as I was riding away, I was just too proud to turn around." He exhaled in a rough noise. "But I should have. What happened tonight is my fault, too, and if I had been here, it might not have…" He shook his head and pulled back a little. "I'm a spy for the Crown, Beth. I have been for years."

Her brows rose in surprise, and her mouth curved in a smile. "Well, I didn't quite expect that, but I can't say I'm entirely surprised." She laughed a little and linked both hands around his neck. "You're probably one of the best, aren't you?"

"You're not upset?" he asked, his chest tightening in anticipation even as his confusion and amazement grew.

She shook her head, still smiling. "Why should I be? I am well, the children are well, you are well, the house is well, and now I understand how you are friends with such an odd group of men." She leaned back in his hold a little. "I find the idea absolutely splendid, so long as you never leave after a fight again."

Malcolm kissed her smiling lips at once, hungrily and without hesitation. "Never," he vowed. "And no matter how many times I must leave you, Beth, I will always come back to you. Always." He kissed her again, much softer. "It's not an easy life, my love, but I promise to protect you at all times. And to honor you, cherish you, love you until the very end of time."

She covered his lips with her hand, smiling breathlessly. "No need to recite all the vows again," she teased. She sobered a little. "Was that why you stayed away so long? Your work?"

He nodded, then shrugged a shoulder. "Some. It was a convenient excuse. I couldn't bear the shame of coming home." He held her closely and exhaled. "I didn't think you'd need me anymore, if you could see. What use is a man like me to a woman like you?"

That seemed to surprise her, and she went up on her toes to touch her brow to his. "I need you," she whispered. "I'll always need you, sight or no sight. Because I love you. With all my heart and soul, I am yours. And now I need you more than ever."

"Why?"

Beth giggled softly and nudged her nose against his. "Because later this year, we will find ourselves with another child to love."

Malcolm pulled back in shock, staring at her. "What?"

She grinned and touched his chin with a finger. "I'm expecting. We are."

"That's what I thought," he managed. He stared at her, shaking his head. "Are you sure?"

Beth nodded. "Yes, I am quite sure. Dr. Durham confirmed it shortly after you left. I am three months along, perhaps four."

It was incredible. It was unexpected and madness and the absolute most wonderful news he could have ever received. He grinned wildly and kissed his wife with heat and passion, then drew her close for a tight embrace, his heart pounding in near-perfect time with hers.

"I cannot tell you how pleased I am, sweetheart," he murmured in her hair. "I had only thought about getting to you in time, apologizing, and starting again. I never considered..."

He felt her shake her head against him. "I know. It was agony to know about our child and not know how you felt. Where we stood. Knowing now that you love me... Malcolm, I'll never need anything else."

Malcolm pressed a kiss into his wife's hair, then pulled back, cupping her face in his hands again. "I vow here and now, Elizabeth Anne, that I am yours. Your husband, your companion, your humble and willing servant... Yours in every respect, in any way that you need. Yours, my love. No matter what happens, never doubt that."

Beth smiled and brushed his hair back from his brow tenderly. "And I vow to love you with all of my heart and all that I am. To trust you implicitly, and to be by your side through any and all troubles."

Something stirred in Malcolm's heart, something he couldn't explain and couldn't put a name to, but it centered, began, and ended with the woman before him. He pressed a soft kiss to her lips and smiled when she sighed.

"Shall we go home, then, Lady Montgomery?" he whispered, stroking her hair.

She smiled dreamily at him and nodded. "Please, Lord Montgomery. Walk me home."

Malcolm laced his fingers between his wife's, then drew the back of her hand up for a kiss. Her fingers rubbed against his gently, infusing the skin with heat and sensation that seemed to ripple through him with a slow but fervent intensity.

There would be time to explore that later.

There would be time for everything later.

But for now, in this moment, all was absolutely perfect.

"Was that Mr. Pratt and Lord Wharton I saw with you in the woods?" Beth asked with blatant amusement. "I take it they've put their differences aside."

Malcolm chuckled, which then turned into full-blown guffaws as the stress, worry, and desperation of the night finally released. "Oh, Beth. You're not going to believe half of what I have to tell you. It's going to take ages to properly explain."

"I don't mind," she murmured with a smile, her fingers rubbing against his once more. "I have all the time in the world."

Malcolm smiled at his beloved and kissed her hand once more as they slowly walked back to the house. "So do I, my love. So do I."

Epilogue

The house was full of people, and there was absolutely no excuse for it. Nobody really cared about the Grangers all that much, and they never had, but ever since they had let it be known that they were anticipating the birth of a child, they were all anybody could talk about.

Now, the long-awaited child had arrived, and only this morning been christened, and it was as if the whole of London had come out for the event. There was nothing that London loved so much as a good tale, and this one was especially grand.

A rather unfortunate match to begin with, but rather typical, with each of the parties involved not being particularly fond of the other. Yet they had seemed more miserable than usual, and more downcast. There had been rumors of Mr. Granger's fortune being rather depleted after a badly laid scheme had gone awry, but his marriage had sustained them sufficiently. Now they were predominantly wealthy, happy, and this child had been born, after more years of marriage than anybody had expected.

And *that* was what people were curious about.

What had changed between them? Why were they suddenly happy and far too affectionate for the stoic and respectable members of London that had thought them one of their own? Those with suspicions were being remarkably observant at this gathering, and it was an amusing spectacle.

Beth watched her oldest friend fondly as she continued to be swarmed by various members of Society, some of whom truly wished to have a look at young Ross Arden Granger, currently dozing contentedly, while others seemed to be peering at his mother's glowing face as she spoke of him.

Those with Beth's vantage point had the opportunity to see just how often Lily Granger looked at her husband, and just how often Thomas Granger looked at his wife.

It really was shocking.

"There's a story there," the woman beside Beth murmured as she sipped her cordial, "and I am determined to sniff it out."

Beth turned to the elaborately dressed woman in yellow silk with a raised brow. "You think you can, Tibby? Lily and Granger are not particularly forthcoming."

Tibby's bright eyes flashed with mock indignation. "Of course, I can! I figured your marriage out, did I not?"

"It's hardly the same thing!" Beth laughed. "Monty and I were fond enough of each other to begin with."

Now Tibby snorted and rolled her eyes. "Please, darling, the pair of you were practically strangers. He was desperate for a wife; you were desperate for a solution. The fact that you are utterly charming is the only thing that saved you from the most boring marriage on the planet. Aside from your having gained a remarkably handsome husband, of course."

Beth smiled softly as she looked across the room where her husband stood, conversing with several members of high Society, all of whom were rapt with attention. He had that effect on people. He'd hardly aged at all in the four years of their marriage, and had somehow grown only more handsome. He saw her looking at him, and the corner of his mouth lifted as he dipped his chin in acknowledgment, never once altering his speech.

"I didn't know you found him handsome," Beth commented as she slid her glance back to her companion, who seemed to be smirking.

Tibby gave her a knowing look. "Elizabeth, there isn't a warm-blooded woman alive on this earth who doesn't hate you just a little for having that man in your bed."

Beth coughed in surprise, laughing when she was able to. "Tibby!"

Her companion shrugged. "I only speak the truth, darling.

Always do." She eyed Beth carefully, her brow creasing. "Should you even be here? In your condition, child…"

There was another warm smile as Beth cradled her swollen abdomen gently, though it was barely visible with the voluminous skirts fashion had chosen to dote upon of late.

"I am very well, Tibby, and a full month from delivering. Dr. Durham swears by it, and you know I was late with my other two."

Tibby's nostrils flared a little as she hummed. "Yes, well, with your boys, darling, I wouldn't put any stock into timelines or patterns. I've never met a pair of lads more intent on doing whatever they wished whenever they wished. They will either be the most roguish highwaymen that ever lived, or some reckless secret operatives for the government."

Beth had to bite her cheek to keep from laughing at that all-too-perfect description. Michael and Francis were still very young, only three and one, but they would be prime candidates to follow in their father's footsteps and serve the Crown in such a way. They seemed to have inherited the same tendency towards mischief from their half-brothers, though both had the sweetest temperament their parents had ever seen, which Malcolm assured Beth was entirely from her side.

Beth knew better.

Her boys worshipped their father with a fierceness that amused her to no end, and she hoped they always would. He took special care with them, always treating each with his undivided attention, as was his way. Malcolm still travelled quite a bit for his work in the covert operations, but he had now assumed command over the London League, as his predecessor had gone into retirement. He was not in the same sort of danger anymore, but now bore the stresses of management rather than in practice himself.

For the most part…

He never told Beth the details, and she didn't want to know. But she could tell when he returned by the way he held her or how he doted on the children if it had been a trying mission. He always worried about her when he left, lingering longer and longer when departure was at hand. His returns were always sweet, sometimes breathtakingly so, and she craved his return from the moment he left her side.

Malcolm had told her once that he felt the same way, and that was her chief comfort in this mad and unpredictable life.

That and the joy of their children.

No matter what weighed upon him, or how exhausted he was from his travels, he always had time for them, especially his youngest. He never wanted them to have cause to doubt his love for them, and they never did.

Their older siblings never failed to include and mind the littlest boys, somehow their guardians and their tutors all in one. If either of them ever injured themselves, their sisters would have the heads of the elder brothers, who would undoubtedly be to blame.

This little one within her, however, seemed quite different. She'd had a far more peaceful time of it all, and while she was growing more uncomfortable by the day, she was also growing more filled with anticipation. She hadn't admitted this to Malcolm, but she was fairly convinced she would give birth to a daughter, which was what her husband had wanted all along.

"I love my sons," he'd assured her only this morning as they lounged in bed together. "I think they shall grow to be very fine men. But a girl…" He'd felt for the baby to kick, which had come as if instructed, and he'd smiled with all the love in the world. "There is something very special about being a father to a little girl."

How she ached to give him such an experience again! She'd been quite unable to contain her emotions after that, particularly when he had kissed her stomach and spoken sweetly to their unborn child.

She'd given him several kisses as a reward and been sufficiently distracted from telling him her thoughts on the matter.

He'd know soon enough as it was.

"They are their father's sons," Beth finally replied to Tibby's claim.

"And young Master Granger over there?" Tibby inclined her head towards the infant, who was now in his father's hold and being shown off to the room. "Is he his father's son as well?"

"That's hard to say," Beth sighed, following her gaze. "He has the coloring of both parents, and with both having more reserved demeanors, it would be difficult to distinguish one from the other in him."

"If he is musical, he takes after his mother," Tibby stated firmly. "If he is a perfect gentleman, his father."

Beth smiled at that and at Lily, who was now watching them with a curious expression. "If he is slightly interfering but endearing, he takes after his mother. If he is content to let people be, his father."

"If he has the patience of a saint, he is Lily's. If he wishes to suffer in absolute silence, he is Granger's."

Beth chortled a laugh. "And if he happens to fall in love passionately and never say a word about it?"

"Both!"

They snickered together, and Beth sighed, shaking her head. "Oh, Tibby, I didn't think they would ever be happy. And look at them now!"

"I always knew they would be happy," she insisted adamantly. "The question would be how happy and if the other were the cause of such happiness." She shrugged a little. "They were destined to be happy. As were you."

"Was I?" Beth murmured, looking over at her husband once more, who only had Lord Marlowe for company now, and both looked very bored.

Malcolm stared back at her, his expression only barely changing, but his eyes now entirely alive and warming her.

"Naturally. Your marriage was enviable even in its early days, and now that you are both utterly besotted, even more so." Tibby offered a sigh that was somehow mournful and satisfied at once. "It's a wonder the pair of you don't run away to the continent and set all Europe talking. You could have quite the time of it in London together and make quite an impressive splash with all the events and social gatherings, you know. Think of all the merriment there!"

"I wouldn't know," Beth murmured as she smiled shyly at her husband, at whom she was still staring quite fixedly. "I never had much experience in London before my marriage. And I have spent more of my marriage being with child than not."

That seemed to amuse Tibby a little, even as she huffed with what was supposed to be proper indignation. "Perhaps you ought to speak to your husband about his attentions. He really ought to have a care for you."

Beth wrenched her gaze away from her stirring and very attractive husband to give the woman an utterly incredulous look. "Why in the world would I want to do that?"

Tibby clamped down on her lips, and her eyes widened with muffled laughter.

Beth looked back at Malcolm with a knowing smile, which he returned, and her breath caught almost audibly at his wink.

"I can assure you, madam," she managed with a steadying exhale, "the feelings are entirely mutual."

Author's Note

$\mathcal{W}$ hat Beth goes through after her head injury is a real condition called transient cortical blindness, caused by a traumatic brain injury, or TBI. The impact to the back of her head caused an area of bleeding and swelling, which put pressure on the back of her brain, called the occipital lobe.

As the bleeding and swelling resolved, her vision slowly returned. Some who suffer from this condition have symptoms that resolve in a matter of minutes or hours, and others develop a lengthier cortical blindness that can linger for weeks or months. For the purposes of this story, Beth's injury took longer to heal, but she makes a full recovery, though it is possible her vision would never be as sharp as it was before the injury.

Coming Soon

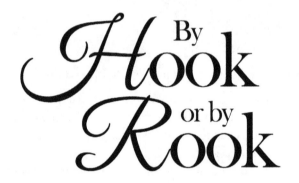

The London League
Book Four

"A rook of all trades..."

by

Rebecca Connolly